KU-766-123

THE DOOMSDAY SHOW

Also by Mark Alpert

Final Theory series

FINAL THEORY
THE OMEGA THEORY

Six series

THE SIX
THE SIEGE
THE SILENCE

Novels

EXTINCTION
THE FURIES
THE ORION PLAN
THE COMING STORM
SAINT JOAN OF NEW YORK

THE DOOMSDAY SHOW

Mark Alpert

First world edition published in Great Britain and the USA in 2022
by Severn House, an imprint of Canongate Books Ltd,
14 High Street, Edinburgh EH1 1TE.

Trade paperback edition first published in Great Britain and the USA in 2023
by Severn House, an imprint of Canongate Books Ltd.

severnhouse.com

Copyright © Mark Alpert, 2022

All rights reserved including the right of
reproduction in whole or in part in any form.
The right of Mark Alpert to be identified
as the author of this work has been asserted
in accordance with the Copyright,
Designs & Patents Act 1988.

British Library Cataloguing-in-Publication Data
A CIP catalogue record for this title is available from the British Library.

ISBN-13: 978-1-4483-0926-9 (cased)
ISBN-13: 978-1-4483-0966-5 (trade paper)
ISBN-13: 978-1-4483-0959-7 (e-book)

This is a work of fiction. Names, characters, places and incidents
are either the product of the author's imagination or are used fictitiously.
Except where actual historical events and characters are being described
for the storyline of this novel, all situations in this publication are
fictitious and any resemblance to actual persons, living or dead,
business establishments, events or locales is purely coincidental.

All Severn House titles are printed on acid-free paper.

Typeset by Palimpsest Book Production Ltd.,
Falkirk, Stirlingshire, Scotland.
Printed and bound in Great Britain by
TJ Books, Padstow, Cornwall.

For Lisa

ONE

The enemy was handsome. Which was unfortunate, Max thought. He preferred ugly enemies, vicious and scowling, their faces as twisted as their hearts. It made things simpler, from a theatrical point of view.

But this guy, this Hollister Tarkington, just look at him. Dressed in a beautiful gray suit, he stepped out of his limo and flashed a perfectly white smile at the seething crowd in front of his corporate headquarters in midtown Manhattan. Thousands of protesters – they were mostly young people, Max observed, college age and a bit older – had come to New York for Climate Emergency Week, and they had every reason to hate Tarkington, who was the CEO of Stygian Energy, America's biggest coal-mining company. And yet the protesters lowered their volume once they saw their enemy in the flesh, as if his good looks were enough to make them reconsider. Their shouts faded as Tarkington strode past the security guards standing shoulder to shoulder on the sidewalk, holding back the hordes that packed West 57th Street. He actually waved at the crowd, grinning like an Oscar winner, stunning everyone into silence with his colossal self-regard. Then he marched toward the glass doors of the Stygian Energy building, followed by a pair of corporate underlings and a TV reporter with a video camera on his shoulder.

Max Mirsky, lurking behind the security guards, wasn't impressed. *Keep grinning, asshole. It's show time.* He was already in his costume: a long blue cloak, an old-fashioned bicorne hat, and a bushy white mustache glued to his upper lip. He was supposed to look like a character from a Dickens novel, a ruddy Englishman from the grim nineteenth century, but his slapdash cosplay hadn't been completely successful. In truth, he looked more like Cap'n Crunch.

Max pressed a button on the remote control in his palm, and music suddenly blared from the powerful loudspeakers that Janet had set up half an hour ago beside the building's entrance. The brassy notes of a Broadway orchestra boomed over the street, so deafeningly loud that several of the security guards turned around, cringing and glaring. A gap opened between two of the startled guards, just as Max had hoped.

He dove through it, his blue cloak flapping and flouncing behind him.

He charged into the narrow lane of cleared sidewalk, right in front of Hollister Tarkington. Standing tall and straight and stern, Max put an exaggerated frown on his face and pointed accusingly at the CEO. At the same moment, the first lyrics of Max's song blasted out of the loudspeakers and over the crowd:

Hack him! Sack him!
Tax him! Ax him!
Close his coal mines,
Make him pay for his crimes!

Max sang along with the recording, belting out the lyrics he'd written, although the music booming from the speakers was much louder than his voice. It was a parody of a song from the musical *Oliver!*, the opening number that kicks off in the orphans' workhouse after Oliver Twist holds up his empty bowl and pitifully whispers, 'Please, sir, I want some more.' Max was playing the role of Mr Bumble, the stern boss of the workhouse, but instead of castigating a hungry Oliver Twist he now poured his lyrical scorn over the greedy Hollister Tarkington, who stood there on the sidewalk, thoroughly confused.

Prune him! Moon him!
Smack his dirty punim*!*
Bonk him, bait him,
This planet really hates him!

If Stygian Energy's security guards had been on the ball they would've pounced on Max, but his absurd performance discombobulated them. Although he was blocking Tarkington's path, he clearly wasn't a threat. No, he was harmless, just an amateur actor who also happened to be an activist. Max was a widower in his fifties who'd suffered a midlife crisis and started an unlikely new career – in street theater, of all things – which he had to admit wasn't going so well, judging by the latest evidence. This awkward attempt at musical parody and political messaging was baffling everyone at the climate-change protest, including Tarkington's security detail. The guards vacillated, turning their heads this way and that, taking a moment to confer with one another. They were trying to figure out how to handle this nutcase.

And Max was grateful for the moment of vacillation. It gave his co-stars their chance to join the show.

The first to step forward was Janet Page, Max's on-and-off girlfriend, who'd helped him start the Doomsday Theater Company two years ago. Now she leapt through another gap in the line of guards and took her place by his side, flushed and eager. She was playing the role of Mrs Bumble, in a severe black frock and a drab white mobcap, which Max had found for her in a vintage-fashion shop downtown. Janet had a nice voice, and she lustily contributed to the musical excoriation of Hollister Tarkington, singing Max's parody lyrics as she pointed at the befuddled CEO. A moment later, three more Doomsday Company members – Larry, Adele, and Eileen – jumped into the performance, all of them barefoot and dressed in rags, a chorus of workhouse orphans. The TV reporter aimed his camera at them, recording their wild dance across the sidewalk.

Hollister, Hollister!
Never before has a man burned up SO MUCH COAL!
Hollister, Hollister!
He's scalding the world from pole to pole!

Last but not least, Nathan Carver – Max's best friend and, in his opinion, the most underappreciated comic actor in New York – slipped past the guards and strutted over to Tarkington. Nathan was about the same height as the CEO and wore a similarly stylish suit, but Nathan's jacket was festooned with dollar bills that had been scotch-taped to the sleeves and lapels and collar. Although Nathan wasn't nearly as handsome as Tarkington, his face was wonderfully elastic, so it was a simple matter for him to imitate the CEO's bewildered expression. While Max and Janet and the rest of the Doomsday troupe sang the parody song,

Nathan stood right next to Tarkington and hilariously mirrored the man's movements.

There's a hot, smoky future where the greenhouse gases swell,
That's the place where Hollister's taking us, his private Climate Hell.

The crowd was warming to the show, Max noticed. No longer baffled, the protesters had realized that this performance was a protest too, a political statement with Broadway flair and Dickensian references. So they laughed and cheered and pushed forward, trying to get a better look, and the security guards automatically pushed them back. The rent-a-cops were too preoccupied with crowd control to make any attempt to stop the show, and they couldn't get rough with the actors anyway because the TV cameraman was filming the scene. Max felt a giddy rush of delight, and he gleefully shouted his song's next verse.

Hollister, Hollister!
He's screwing our planet 'cause he likes his money more!
Hollister, Hollister!
Let's give him a push and kick his fat tush!

Now Tarkington frowned. Clearly, he'd had enough. The CEO reached inside his jacket and clamped his hand over his stomach, as if the performance had given him a bad case of indigestion. Then he stepped to the side and tried to move around Max and Janet, his eyes fixed on the glass doors of his headquarters. But Nathan stepped right alongside him, mimicking him mercilessly. Contorting his face into an agonized grimace, Nathan clutched his belly and pretended to writhe in pain, while the dollar bills fluttered all over his jacket.

'Oh heavens! Oh dear me!' Nathan shouted at the top of his lungs, so the crowd could hear him over the music. 'I'm feeling the heat! I need to pass some greenhouse gas!'

The protesters roared. The TV reporter trained his camera on Nathan and Tarkington, trying to get both of them in the same shot, which would've made a very funny clip for the evening news. But Tarkington shoved the cameraman aside and lunged toward the building's entrance. He and his underlings wrenched open the glass doors and dashed for the safety of the Stygian Energy reception desk, swiftly followed by the retreating security guards. Meanwhile, Nathan pretended to faint on the sidewalk, and Janet and Larry blew raspberries at the fleeing guards' backsides.

Max watched the CEO's escape, amazed that a man with so much money and power could be undone by a measly bit of satire. He used his remote control to turn off the music, and the loudspeakers stopped blaring the parody of *Oliver!* Then Max faced the crowd and flashed his own grin, which was a lot more sincere than Tarkington's.

'Did you see those assholes run?' he whooped. 'Did you see how scared they were?'

The protesters cheered. Encouraged, Max took off his old-fashioned hat and swept it in a big circle, a gesture meant to include everyone in earshot. 'They're scared of *us*! And you know what? They *should* be scared! We're gonna shut down Stygian Energy! And all the other corporations that are destroying our planet!'

The crowd roared again. Max threw his hat in the air and deftly caught it. For a moment he felt pretty damn good about himself.

But then he glanced over his shoulder at the corporate headquarters, where Hollister Tarkington and his associates were probably rocketing to the top floor in a high-speed elevator. They were on their way to their next meeting, planning their next fossil-fuel venture, their next crime against the Earth. Max's parody had definitely annoyed them, but it hadn't changed anything. Carbon emissions were still rising and the planet was still warming. Max thought of his daughter Sonya, a climate activist herself, organizing her classmates at New York University and leading her own protests, but despite all their efforts the world was still hurtling toward apocalypse. In fifty years, the whole East Coast would be under water.

The protesters on 57th Street must've sensed the futility too, because soon they turned their backs on Max and drifted away. There were other demonstrations planned for that afternoon, dozens of rallies and sit-ins across the city, organized by the various nonprofits that had joined forces for Climate Emergency Week. The Natural Resources Defense Council was leading a march to the United Nations, and the Sierra Club was parading outside the offices of ExxonMobil. There were also spontaneous protests erupting everywhere, mostly incited by activists in guerilla attire, their faces hidden behind masks and bandannas. They would publicize their skirmishes online, urging their followers to converge on Wall Street or Times Square or some other iconic capitalist site, and within minutes the chosen location would be jammed with black-clad demonstrators, all of them blocking traffic and raising hell.

Max watched the young people turn away from the Stygian Energy building. They took out their phones and swiped the screens, figuring out where to go next, choosing from the long menu of disruptions. And believe it or not, seeing this gave Max some hope. Maybe, just maybe, the next protest would be a game-changer. Maybe it would open a few eyes and sway a few hearts. It was probably ludicrous to entertain such hopes, Max thought, given the long history of indifference and inaction. Still, he felt a little better now. A little less impotent.

The TV reporter had tried to follow Tarkington into the headquarters, but the security guards had kicked him out, and now he was wandering outside the entrance, looking for someone to interview. Nathan Carver rose from the sidewalk and demanded some camera time, continuing to imitate an outraged Hollister Tarkington as the reporter asked him questions. Although Nathan had a day job at a small advertising firm, he was a natural-born comedian, a leading man at the West Side Community Theater and a regular at open-mic night at Stand Up NY. He loved attention of any kind, and sometimes his need for constant laughter annoyed the hell out of Max, but it also made him perfect for the Doomsday troupe. Their mission was to grab attention by any means necessary.

Max observed the interview from a distance, leaning against the façade of the headquarters and chuckling now and then at Nathan's inanities. Janet picked up the loudspeakers and loaded them into her foldable shopping cart, getting ready to haul the things to the Doomsday Company's next gig. Larry and Adele and Eileen sat on the sidewalk nearby, slapping the dirt from the soles of their feet and then slipping on their socks and sneakers. They were all wonderful actors, Max thought, and they put their hearts into their work even though he paid them nothing for performing. He'd assembled a first-rate group of volunteers, idealists who still believed that theater could change the world. So he told himself to stop the self-pity. They were fighting the good fight. What more could you want?

Max smiled at the thought. He peeled off his fake mustache and slipped it into the pocket of his cloak, keeping it safe for future performances. Then, while he was still feeling optimistic, a masked woman approached him.

'Hello?' Her voice was low, almost a whisper. 'Are you Max Mirsky?'

She stepped close to him, too close, less than a foot away. The woman was almost as tall as Max, so her mask loomed right in front of him, one of those creepy Guy Fawkes masks with a black goatee on a smiling white face. She wore a tight-fitting black T-shirt that showed off her lean figure, and Max assumed at first that she was a skinny young protester, a college-age activist. But then he noticed her long gray hair, braided into an intricate ponytail that dangled down to her butt.

Curious, Max tried to peer through the mask's eyeholes. 'Can I help you?'

'Are you Max Mirsky from the *Journal of Climatology*?'

This was a surprise. Max was indeed an occasional contributor to *Climatology*, and he'd once been the journal's managing editor, in charge of a staff of four science reporters and two fact-checkers. But he'd stepped down from the top job at the journal when he started the Doomsday Company. Very few people outside his circle of friends knew about his weird career switch from journalism to acting, so he wondered how this masked woman had found him. 'Uh, yeah, that's me. And who are—'

'We sent you an email several months ago? Asking a question about the worst climate crimes?'

'I'm sorry, I don't—'

'And you sent us a reply. A list of the five people who were doing the most damage to the environment, in your opinion.'

After a moment, Max remembered. Someone claiming to be

a college student had asked him for a free copy of an article titled 'The Worst Climate Criminals,' which he'd written for *Climatology* last winter. Usually you had to subscribe to the journal to get access to the full story, but Max had been willing to send a free copy to this student because she said she was taking a course on the subject.

He caught a glimpse of the woman's eyes through the holes in her mask. They were bloodshot, filmy, gleaming between dark pouches and wrinkled lids. She was clearly a lot older than a typical college student. 'Well, I hope the article was useful to you.'

She nodded. The creepy mask moved up and down. 'Oh yes, it was useful. We just got number five. Now we're going after the other four.'

Max stared at her. He couldn't see her eyes now, only the smiling white face on her mask. 'Number five?'

'Yeah, Tarkington, the guy who was just here. He was the fifth criminal on your list, remember?'

He remembered. Hollister Tarkington was one of the corporate polluters he'd mentioned in the *Climatology* article. 'I don't understand. What do you mean, you got him?'

She kept nodding. 'Did you notice how he grabbed his belly? That's the first sign, a sharp pain in the abdomen.'

'The first sign? What are you talking about?'

'You'll see in a minute. They're going to do an autopsy, and they'll figure out what we did. So I came here to warn you.'

The woman stepped backward. She was ending the conversation, getting ready to leave. But Max was alarmed now. 'Whoa, hold on! What do you—'

'Don't wait. Delete that email we sent you.'

She took two more steps backward, still eyeing him through the holes in her mask. A siren screamed in the distance, several blocks away. The woman turned her head toward the noise, and the Guy Fawkes visage looked even creepier as it gazed down 57th Street. Another siren wailed, louder than the first one. It came from the same direction, from Fifth Avenue.

The woman turned in the opposite direction and broke into a run.

Max lurched forward, off balance. He was confused and

distressed, and for a moment he wondered if he should run after her. But he hesitated too long, and within a few seconds she was already halfway down the block. Her long gray ponytail tossed back and forth as she jogged down the sidewalk.

Then the sirens grew painfully loud, and two ambulances screeched to a halt in front of the Stygian Energy building. Half a dozen men in blue uniforms jumped out of the ambulances and pulled a gurney out the back of one of the vehicles. At the same time, a security guard opened the building's doors and waved frantically at the paramedics. 'COME ON! HURRY UP!'

Max watched them rush into the building with the gurney. And then race across the lobby toward the high-speed elevators.

He thought of Tarkington. The handsome enemy clutching his stomach and grimacing.

Shit. What the hell's going on?

TWO

Angela Nova looked down at Manhattan from an unfinished apartment twelve hundred feet above the sidewalk. This luxury skyscraper was still under construction, its walls unpainted sheetrock, its floors bare concrete. But floor-to-ceiling windows had been installed on all four sides of the penthouse residence, giving Angela a sweeping view of the entire island.

The streets of Midtown, directly below, swarmed with protesters and gridlocked traffic. The crowd noise and car honking were loud enough to ascend a quarter-mile and penetrate the penthouse's double-paned windows. To the north, Central Park was dotted with colorful tents and banners, the encampments of the college students and miscellaneous drifters who'd descended on the city for the weeklong protest. And to the south, the sloops and catamarans of the Greenpeace armada cruised in the gray water lapping Battery Park, their rainbow sails barely visible in the distance. The sun hung over the harbor, edging toward New Jersey, and the Manhattan skyline gleamed in the mid-September light.

It was beautiful. It really was. As beautiful as anything Angela had ever seen. As beautiful as any city could be.

And yet the sight of it agitated her. She plunged her hands into the pockets of her jumpsuit and toyed with her key chain, which clinked against the other items she'd stuffed down there. It was a nervous habit, and it always got worse when she wore this jumpsuit, which was loose-fitting and olive-green and had very deep pockets.

No, it's not beautiful, she thought. *This city is a lie. Everything you see now, all the buildings and boats and banners, they're all fucking lies. The only things you can trust are your revelations. Your truths.*

She was trembling. She needed to calm down.

Take a deep breath. Get your head together.

Angela took her hands out of her pockets and raised them to

her temples and rubbed her forehead in slow circles. She closed her eyes and withdrew from the world, ignoring all the lies. She cleared her mind of everything but the truth.

Then she saw it again. A different New York. The city she'd glimpsed in her first revelation.

The image appeared with awful clarity on the dark screen of her closed eyelids. In this landscape, the skyscrapers were vacant hulks. Each building was dark and pocked with broken windows. Every office was closed, every apartment abandoned, every streetlight extinguished. Seawater swirled around the buildings' ground floors and rushed in brown torrents down the avenues. The flood poured into Manhattan from both the East River and the Hudson, streaming through the streets of Chinatown and Chelsea, inundating the parks and playgrounds. The filthy water submerged the sidewalks and rose above the parking meters. All kinds of garbage bobbed in the waves.

The worst thing, though, was the silence. There were no cars honking, no people shouting. Nothing.

When Angela had seen this vision for the first time, this picture of the dead city, she'd had no idea where the revelation had come from. Or why she, of all people, had been chosen to receive it. But now she knew beyond a doubt what the message was, what the vision was telling her. She could hear it even in the silence.

Nothing but green!

She opened her eyes. Someone had just knocked on the apartment's unpainted door. A moment later she heard his deep voice reverberate through the wall. 'Angie? You got a visitor.'

It was Carl's voice. Her bodyguard was a giant bald man with oversized hands, gruff and uncouth, but absolutely loyal. He was the head of security for Prophecy, the organization Angela had started a year ago after her rich-as-fuck father killed himself and left her eight hundred million dollars. Carl had some friends in the construction crews who were building this skyscraper, and in exchange for a small payoff they'd allowed Angela and her followers to occupy the unfinished penthouse. But it was only a temporary headquarters. They were executing a tricky operation against powerful foes, so it was important to keep moving.

Angela turned away from the window. She'd been expecting

this visitor, who was here to deliver an update on the operation. 'Send her in.'

Carl opened the door, and a masked woman in a black shirt slinked past him. The giant bodyguard frowned, clearly disapproving. He saw the problem immediately, just as Angela did, but he said nothing. He just closed the door, leaving the two of them alone.

The woman's name was Lauren. She'd joined Prophecy six months ago and quickly moved up in the ranks by volunteering for several civil-disobedience operations. She was a retired veterinarian, enraged by the global extermination of wildlife, especially the millions of animals incinerated in the Australian bushfires. She boasted that she'd be perfect for the more aggressive protests, the ones that involved trespassing into power plants or throwing pies at the faces of climate-change deniers. She was an innocent-looking, gray-haired seventy-five-year-old, and how could any police officer put a pair of handcuffs on such a sweet old lady?

Angela saw the value of this strategy. And she wanted Prophecy to include people of all ages, not just hundreds of college students. But she'd always been a little wary of Lauren, who seemed to have more conviction than intelligence. The older zealots could be just as careless and stupid as the young ones.

Lauren stopped in the middle of the room and lifted her Guy Fawkes mask until it rested horizontally on top of her head, smiling upward at the apartment's unfinished ceiling. Her unmasked face was smiling too, her forehead and cheeks creased with delight, her watery eyes glistening. 'It's done. We eliminated the first target.'

Angela took a step toward her. The two women were about the same height, but Lauren was so thin, almost skeletal. Angie outweighed her by at least twenty pounds, not to mention the fact that she was twenty years younger. She cocked her head and narrowed her eyes at Lauren. 'What about the next one?'

'Everything's ready.' The older woman nodded enthusiastically. Her mask jiggled on her head, and her long gray ponytail swayed behind her back. 'We're making an example of those criminals. All the other bastards will think twice now, right?'

Senile idiot, Angela thought. But her manner stayed calm and professional. She took another step forward. 'Tell me about the last thing you did. Right before you came here.'

Lauren nodded some more, practically bouncing with excitement. 'I listened to the police scanner and heard the dispatcher send ambulances to One-thirty-nine West Fifty-seventh. Then I made contact with Mirsky and told him to delete the emails.'

'And you took precautions? Against surveillance? Like I asked you to?' Angela stepped closer to her. Now she stood just an arm's length away. 'That stretch of Fifty-seventh Street has plenty of security cameras. More than just about anywhere else in the city.'

'I never took off my mask.' She raised her hand to the top of her head and tapped the ugly thing. 'Afterwards I ran to Columbus Circle and went down to the subway. There was a big crowd in the station, at least a hundred protesters, and I joined the group. We all looked the same, all dressed in black, all wearing the same mask. So I blended in with the crowd before I came here, just like you instructed. Nobody could've tracked me.'

Lauren smiled again. She was so goddamn proud of herself. And Angela smiled back at her, pretending to be satisfied. At the same time, though, she pointed at Lauren's ponytail. 'But what about *this*?'

The stupid bitch stared at Angela's finger. Blank-faced. She still didn't get it. 'What?'

Angela reached out and, with some reluctance, gently grasped the woman's braid. It felt dense and greasy in her hand, like a dead snake. 'Did anyone else in the subway station have hair like this?'

After a few seconds Lauren finally understood. She let out a cry, a breathy 'Aiieee' full of surprise and embarrassment. 'Oh no! *Oh my God!*'

'Yes, it was a mistake. A very serious one.' Angela put a look of sober disappointment on her face. It was a struggle to keep herself from strangling the bitch, but she managed it. 'You actually made it easy for the police to track you. The very first detective who looks at the security-camera footage from Fifty-seventh Street is going to notice the masked woman with the gray ponytail. He'll see you talk to Mirsky and go into the subway station. Then he'll see you walk out of the station and come here.

He might even be able to identify you from other footage they have. You were at the sit-in we did in Brooklyn two months ago, and the police surveilled that operation too.'

Lauren started to weep. 'Oh, Jesus!' She shook her head, and her mask dropped to the floor. 'I'm sorry! I'm so sorry!' Tears leaked from the corners of her eyes and seeped into the wrinkles in her cheeks.

Which only made Angela angrier. And more agitated. While she held Lauren's ponytail with her left hand, she thrust her right hand into the pocket of her jumpsuit. 'I told you to be careful, didn't I? All you had to do was pin your hair up and put a cap over it. Tell me, Lauren, what was so hard about that?'

'I don't know, *I don't know*! But it won't happen again! I promise!'

More tears dribbled down her face, more stupid fucking tears. It was too much, it was un-fucking-believable. Angela tightened her grip on the ponytail and pulled Lauren's head back. At the same time, she dug her hand deeper into her pocket, fingers scrabbling, until she found what she needed.

She pulled out the switchblade and flicked it open.

'You're right. It won't happen again.'

Then she slashed Lauren's throat.

Angela held the bitch's hair while her blood sprayed out. It splattered across the room and splashed on the concrete floor. Amazingly, though, none of it got on Angela's jumpsuit. Which was a minor miracle.

After a couple of minutes Lauren stopped twitching. Angela let go of the corpse's hair, and its head thunked the concrete.

What a fucking mess.

But it had to be done. She couldn't let some careless idiot fuck up their plans. Better to make Lauren disappear than give the cops a chance to identify and interrogate her. It was for the good of humanity, the future of billions of people. The greatest good for the greatest number.

Angela wiped her knife on the bitch's shirt before putting it back in her pocket. She had to clean up this mess fast and get the hell out of there.

'Carl!' she yelled. 'Come here! I need some help!'

THREE

Max stared at the glass doors of the Stygian Energy headquarters. At any moment he expected to see the paramedics rush back outside with Hollister Tarkington strapped to their gurney.

The other actors in the Doomsday Company changed out of their *Oliver Twist* costumes. Janet took off her Mrs Bumble mobcap, and Nathan removed his Tarkington-lookalike jacket, the one with the dollar bills fluttering from its sleeves. Larry, Adele, and Eileen peeled off their workhouse-orphan rags and wiped the charcoal powder from their cheeks and foreheads.

But Max didn't move. He stood there on the sidewalk, in his long nineteenth-century cloak and bicorne hat, alone in his anxiety. He hadn't told his friends what the masked woman had said. He was afraid to.

The minutes passed, but there was no sign of the paramedics. In fact, no one at all exited the Stygian Energy building, which seemed unusual. Janet got a call on her cell phone and began a rather loud conversation with the people at the venue of the Doomsday Company's next gig.

And Max just stood there, focusing all his attention on the building's glass doors. He wanted to know what was going on inside the headquarters, and he didn't want to know. His chest tightened.

After several more minutes Janet got off the phone and came toward him, probably to tell him the details of their next performance. But then another vehicle sped down 57th Street and stopped outside the headquarters. It was a white van with the words 'NYC Medical Examiner' written on its side.

Now Max's throat tightened too. 'That's from the coroner's office.' He pointed at the van. 'Tarkington's dead. The paramedics couldn't save him.'

Nathan looked at the van for a second, then put a comically sad expression on his face. 'Poor Hollister.' With elaborate formality, he made the sign of the cross. 'He couldn't take a joke.'

Janet seemed confused. She stared at Max. 'Why do you think they're here because of Tarkington? It could be anyone in that building.'

Max turned away from her and looked again at the coroner's van. Two men came out of the vehicle, both wearing dark blue polo shirts and light blue latex gloves. He watched them step into the headquarters, somber and slow. They could take their time, there was no need to hurry. Because Tarkington was dead. Max was certain of it.

He was horrified. He turned back to Janet, but he couldn't say a word.

Luckily, Nathan filled the silence. 'You're right, Janet. It's wishful thinking, I guess. But Hollister *did* look a little sick during our performance. For a second I thought he was going to throw up on me.'

'That's no surprise. You have that effect on people.' Janet frowned, curling her eyebrows, which were reddish like her hair but slightly darker. Then she pointed at Larry, Adele, and Eileen. 'What do you guys think? Did Tarkington look sick to you?'

Larry shrugged. Adele tilted her head to the side, pondering the question. But before either of them could say anything, Eileen let out a booming '*HA*! Sick? Hell, no! That guy is smoking *hot*!' She leaned against a mailbox, her back arched, her chin raised, as if she were surveying the upper floors of the Stygian Energy building, hoping for another glimpse of the company's CEO. Eileen was a libidinous fifty-year-old blonde who looked a lot like Dolly Parton. She was fond of tight jeans, low-cut blouses, and obscene banter. 'If he wasn't a climate killer, I'd do him. Anytime, anywhere.'

Nathan sidled up to her, leaning on the other side of the mailbox. He enjoyed egging her on. 'Even in one of his coal mines?'

'Well, if he promised to shut down his mines, why not?' Eileen lifted one of her legs and pointed her sneaker at the glass doors of the headquarters. 'I'd give him another place to dig.'

'Miners *are* proud of their shafts.' Nathan edged closer to her. 'But is Tarkington a hard-coal man? Or soft?'

Janet let out an impatient grunt. 'OK, enough. We have a four o'clock slot at the Great Lawn main stage. So we better get over there.' She grabbed the handle of her foldable shopping cart, which held their loudspeakers and various stage props. 'Max, you should get out of that costume. And don't forget the makeup kit.'

Moving mechanically, Max took off the old-fashioned cloak and hat. His heart thudded against his sternum, but he kept a neutral, professional look on his face. He had no reason to panic, because he'd done nothing wrong. All he did was write a piece of journalism that condemned Hollister Tarkington – justifiably – and a piece of street theater that made fun of him. Which wasn't a crime. Max wasn't responsible for anything else that had happened to the man.

Nevertheless, his pulse raced. He felt like an accomplice. He'd directed the murderers to their target.

He folded his cloak into a compact bundle, then stuffed it in his backpack along with the hat and the makeup kit. 'Uh, Janet?' He managed to keep his voice steady. 'I gotta make a phone call. You go ahead, and I'll catch up with you.'

Janet nodded, already pushing her cart down 57th Street. Nathan and Eileen fell into step beside her, still exchanging vulgar puns, while Larry and Adele followed close behind. Max waited until they reached Sixth Avenue and turned the corner, heading north toward Central Park.

Then he pulled out his iPhone and opened his Gmail account. Holding the phone close to his chest to make sure no one else could see the screen, he rapidly scrolled through his emails, most of which were spam. They blurred under his index finger: Groupon, Chowhound, StubHub, Teleflora. Shit, why did he hang on to all these messages, all this crap streaming into his inbox? He kept swiping the phone's screen until he reached the emails from last February, and then he slowed down and looked more carefully at the subject lines. Finally, he found it: a message with the headline 'CLIMATE CRIMINALS,' sent by someone named Mary Smith (in retrospect, clearly a pseudonym).

Max was so anxious he could barely read it. The email was seemingly innocent, a simple request from Mary – a student at Columbia, she claimed – for the article he'd written about the world's worst polluters. There was nothing suspicious about it, nothing to raise any alarms. No, the problem was what Max had written in his reply email, to accompany the copy of the article he'd graciously attached to the message: 'I hope this list of environmental hoodlums helps your research project. To keep my journalistic objectivity, I refrained from stating my opinions so boldly in this article, but I believe that future historians will rank these five scoundrels as the worst mass murderers of the 21st century. Unless we do something about it. Soon.'

There were two more emails, and they were even worse. Mary Smith wrote a brief thank-you message: 'Don't worry, we'll do something. I'm a dedicated environmentalist who believes we need to take more serious action, and all my friends feel the same way. Nothing but green! We intend to stop all those traitors to the Earth, and your list will be very helpful. Can I contact you again if I need anything else?' And Max's even briefer reply: 'Sure, anytime. I will heartily support any effort to nail those planet-killing bastards.'

His heart started thudding again. Max looked over his shoulder at the ambulances in front of the Stygian Energy headquarters, and the coroner's van parked behind them. Blood pounded in his ears and sweat trickled down his neck. He stared at the flashing lights of the emergency vehicles and thought about all the wrong impressions someone could get from reading those emails.

And at just that moment, the building's glass doors opened. The two men in polo shirts and latex gloves pushed a gurney outside. Lying on it was a black-plastic body bag, zipped closed around its occupant.

Max faced forward and walked away. *Not too fast, not too fast!* He wanted to run, he wanted to tear down 57th Street, but he tamped down his terror and limited himself to a brisk walk, trying his best to act casual. *No, no, I'm not running away! Nothing unusual is going on here! I'm just an ordinary New Yorker hurrying to his next appointment!*

He turned left at Sixth Avenue and quick-stepped north. Halfway to 58th Street he saw a narrow alcove between a Starbucks and a CVS, and he ducked into it. Facing a gray, urine-stained wall, he bent over his iPhone and trashed all four emails from his account, the two messages from 'Mary Smith' and his two replies. Then he permanently deleted them from the trash folder.

As soon as he resumed walking uptown, though, he regretted what he'd done. *Fuck! That was stupid! What the hell was I thinking?*

He clenched his fists so hard, his nails dug into his palms. He should've gone to the cops and showed them the emails. He could've told them he had no idea who that masked woman was and explained what he really meant when he wrote 'do something about it' in his message. *Believe me, officer, it was an innocent statement! I was simply advocating a practical solution to the climate crisis. Like carbon taxes, that kind of thing. I certainly wasn't encouraging anyone to kill the bastards!*

But it was too late for that now. In his panic, he'd acted like a criminal and covered up the evidence. And that made his situation a hundred times worse.

Max bit the inside of his cheek, punishing himself. He was a brainless schmuck, there was no other explanation. Now his best option was to go to the Port Authority bus station and get on a Greyhound heading for Mexico. Which of course was another thing a criminal would do.

Or he could go back to his friends and pretend that nothing bad had happened. And pray that the whole thing was just something he'd imagined, some paranoid nightmare he'd concocted from a weird encounter with a masked lunatic and a random medical emergency at the Stygian Energy headquarters.

So he crossed 59th Street and hurried into Central Park, trying to catch up to the Doomsday Company.

As Max walked through the park, he couldn't help but think of Woodstock. The *original* Woodstock of 1969, the concert with Jimi Hendrix and Janis Joplin, the legendary Three Days of Peace and Music. Max had been there, believe it or not, when he was only two years old, a toddler brought to the music festival by his long-haired, tie-dyed, blissed-out parents. He remembered none of it, of course, but over the years he'd tried to fill in the blanks by watching the *Woodstock* concert movie on his TV. Every time he watched it, he hoped to see himself in the teeming crowd of hippies, a little naked boy dancing in the mud with his Flower Girl mother and Guru Poet father.

Now he thought of that movie again as he stared at all the protesters. Hundreds of thousands of them had gathered on Central Park's lawns. Every square yard of the Sheep Meadow, that great expanse of lush grass, was packed with shirtless tattooed kids and their tents and banners. Some of them clustered in drum circles and chanted protest songs, while others waved their signs and flags at the TV news helicopters hovering overhead. The Climate Emergency Week was their Woodstock. Maybe they would save the world, and maybe they wouldn't, but at least they would have a good time trying.

Max walked fast. He was in good shape – he'd run three marathons over the past two years – and in a few minutes he reached the promenade next to the Sheep Meadow. It was a beautiful September day, with temperatures in the low seventies, which was ideal for the comfort of the protesters but not so great for their cause. It would've been much more dramatic to shout their climate-change warnings on melting streets under a blazing sun. And their opponents – the stubbornly moronic climate-change deniers – loved to gloat whenever temperatures dropped. It didn't matter how many times you told them that weather and climate are two different things, and that even in a warming world you would still have beautiful cool days every so often. No, the deniers preferred to ignore the facts and claim that every momentary dip in the temperature was irrefutable proof that global warming was a hoax.

And look at this, Max thought. One of those ignorant morons was right there on the promenade, just thirty feet ahead. A reporter from the True America Network was pontificating into his microphone while his cameraman focused on the crowd of activists. The moron's hair was perfectly combed, and his voice was jokey and loathsome. 'The police estimate that half a million protesters have come to New York, most of them in their teens and twenties. Are they naïve? Misguided? Or are they simply here for the party? It's hard to tell. All we know for sure is that they're enjoying the good weather.'

Max couldn't stop himself. He rushed over to the reporter and stood between him and the camera. 'Today's weather doesn't matter, you idiot! What matters is the average global temperature, and that's shooting up to record highs *every year*!'

The asshole just smirked. He'd already finished his on-air monologue, and now he nodded at his cameraman, a big bearded guy with impressive forearms. This *shtarker* lowered his camera and stepped forward, coming to his partner's aid.

Max was no slouch himself, but he was more of a runner than a fighter. So he darted sideways and took off, racing for the Naumburg Bandshell. After a few seconds he looked over his shoulder and saw that neither of the True America minions was running after him. And when he realized he was safely out of their reach, he couldn't stop himself from shouting at them again. Max had once been a full-time science journalist, and he hated to see those assholes degrade his profession.

'You're a disgrace, you know that? Your network is a fucking tool of the fossil-fuel industry!'

He gave them the finger, then kept running. For the briefest of moments he felt triumphant.

But all that shouting was really a mistake, another dumbass move. Less than half an hour after his confrontation with Hollister Tarkington, he'd put himself in front of a news camera and acted like a crackpot. If anyone saw that footage, they would have no trouble believing he was a climate-change maniac, eminently capable of murder. He was going out of his way to create more evidence against himself.

Oh God. What's wrong with me?

He had poor impulse control. That was his problem. He ran faster, passing the bandshell and hundreds of milling protesters.

Soon he vaulted into the plaza surrounding the Bethesda Fountain, and that was where he caught up with the Doomsday Company. He spied the back of Nathan's head, tilted toward Eileen's, and Janet to their left, doggedly pushing her shopping cart past the fountain's splashing basin. Max was especially glad to see Janet. He wanted to take her aside and tell her everything, starting with the email he'd received from 'Mary Smith.' He and Janet were currently on the outs – they'd had a bad argument last month, over his gym membership of all things, and now they were 'taking a break' from their relationship – but she was a great listener and a levelheaded thinker. She had a knack for giving him good advice.

Instead, though, he headed straight for Nathan. At the advertising firm where Nathan had his day job, he was the IT guy, in charge of all the firm's hardware and software. Max had an urgent computer-related question for him. A question about emails and what exactly happened when you deleted them.

But before he could get there, someone grabbed Max's arm. He froze, nauseous, the plaza swirling around him. *It's the cops. They found me.*

It was Adele. She was a small woman, barely five feet tall, but she had an incredibly strong grip, probably because she used to be a dancer. She'd hoofed in Broadway musicals until she turned forty, at which point she switched to teaching dance and performing with Doomsday. She was the only member of the company with serious professional experience, and sometimes she got a little arrogant about it. She would scrunch her tiny face into a look of disgusted disapproval, like the look she was giving Max right now. She let go of his arm and pointed at his chest.

'I have some notes for you. I think we can improve the *Oliver Twist* sketch.'

He waited a second before responding. Adele was touchy, so he had to be careful around her. 'Could we, uh, do this later? I don't—'

'Max, you promised you would listen to my concerns.' She tilted her head back so she could look him in the eye. 'Remember the meeting we had? The big talk?'

'I know, but—'

'Just hear me out, OK? Your song parody isn't working. You need to rewrite the lyrics.'

At that moment Larry approached them. He was a dancer too, tall and thin and pale, although he'd dropped out of Juilliard's dance program a long time ago and now worked as a financial analyst. More important, he was Adele's boyfriend, and a very loyal one at that. He always backed her up, even when her arguments were ludicrous. As he stepped toward Max, he reached into his pants pocket and pulled out a folded sheet of paper.

'Hey, man, don't get us wrong.' He smiled apologetically as he unfolded the paper, which was covered with scribbles. 'Your concept was great. Mashing up Oliver Twist and Hollister Tarkington, that was genius. But some of the artistic details are a little off, you know? So we jotted down a few suggestions.'

Polite and tentative, Larry held up the piece of paper. He was the Good Cop in this interaction, trying to deliver the criticism in the kindest way possible, and Adele was definitely the Bad Cop. She snatched the paper out of Larry's hand and began reading from it.

'In the second stanza of your song, you used the word "punim." Most people have no idea what that word means. I know you grew up with a Yiddish-speaking grandmother, but you can't expect everyone in the audience to understand the language.' She raised her head to give Max a pointed look. 'And in the same stanza, you wrote, "Bonk him, bait him." What is "bait" supposed to mean in this context? Wouldn't "berate him" be better?'

Max nodded, suppressing his instinct to defend himself. First of all, it was a protest piece, so the 'artistic details' didn't really matter. Second, it was strictly a one-time performance, intended to mock Tarkington as he walked into his headquarters. Max had no plans to polish the number and open it on Broadway. So what was the point of even thinking about revising it?

Third, and most important: if Tarkington was dead, as Max suspected – no, he *knew* it – the parody was yet another piece of evidence, a rhyming proof that he hated the Stygian Energy CEO with a murderous passion. So now he just wanted it to go away. He wanted to forget he'd ever written that stupid, stupid song.

Adele waited for Max to say something, but he kept his mouth shut. Unfortunately, she took his silence as encouragement to continue her critique. 'And there are other problematic lyrics. Such as "Let's give him a push and kick his fat tush." That's juvenile, Max. You can do better than that.'

He nodded again, still silent. He was so worried he could barely think, much less respond to Adele's comments.

Then he remembered where he was and looked up at the familiar statue on top of the Bethesda Fountain. She was the Angel of the Waters, the bronze embodiment of miraculous healing, holding a bunch of lilies in one hand and blessing the fountain with the other. Max had admired that statue ever since he was a kid growing up on West 77th Street, half a mile from here, and for forty years he'd swung by her fountain whenever he went jogging or biking in the park. He'd come to her for consolation at the worst moments in his life – when he had his breakdown in college, when he lost his wife to cancer, when he realized he was wasting his life writing journalism that made no difference whatsoever. So maybe it wasn't a coincidence, coming to this place right now. Maybe he was here to ask the Angel for some help.

Miraculously, as soon as this thought occurred to him, his prayer was answered. Janet and her shopping cart came to a halt, and she looked over her shoulder at Max, Adele, and Larry. She had an annoyed grimace on her face, but Max thought she was beautiful no matter how much she scowled. In fact, he realized for the first time, Janet sort of resembled the Angel. Her hair – dark red, the color of autumn – was cut short and parted in the middle, and it curled above her forehead like the ripples in the fountain's basin. She had the statue's long straight nose, the sad half-lidded eyes, the adorable round chin. And even Janet's long black dress, which she'd worn to play the role of Mrs Bumble, looked a bit like the Angel's gown, its creased fabric revealing only the slightest hint of the hips and legs underneath.

Fortunately for Max, Janet directed her scowl at Adele. More specifically, at the scribbled paper in Adele's hands. 'What are you doing? Giving notes again?'

Larry heroically stepped to his girlfriend's defense. 'Just a few suggestions. To improve the *Oliver Twist* piece. It—'

'We don't have time for that now. We're supposed to be onstage in forty-five minutes.' Janet stretched her arm to the north, toward the Great Lawn's main stage, several hundred yards away. 'And we still have to change into our costumes and do a quick run-through. So let's keep moving, all right?'

Adele wanted to argue, you could see it in her eyes. But after a couple of seconds she marched ahead, following the path that Nathan and Eileen had taken. Larry hurried to her side.

Max was impressed once again with Janet's leadership abilities. Although he was the one who'd conceived the Doomsday Company and who wrote most of their sketches, Janet was the director. She set the schedules, led the rehearsals, and kept the troupe together. Now she fixed her commanding gaze on Max and positioned the shopping cart in front of him. ‘It’s your turn to push.’ Her face softened a little, and she patted his back. ‘Come on, use those muscles you’ve been building up at the gym. *Mush!*’

He grabbed the cart’s handle and heaved it forward. They took the path that ran past Central Park Lake and curved uphill toward the Great Lawn.

Janet glanced at him, narrowing her eyes, clearly sensing that something was amiss. It was hard for Max to keep a secret from her; they’d known each other for decades, long before they started their theater company. Janet had been best friends with Cheryl, Max’s late wife. Both women had been political science majors at Columbia, and after graduation they started a nonprofit that served the homeless. Then, four years ago, Cheryl got cancer, and for the next ten months Janet sat with Max in the cheerless waiting rooms of Sloan Kettering. She helped him with the appointments and prescriptions and insurance, and at the end she went with him to the funeral home. But he was most grateful for how Janet consoled his daughter. Sonya had been only sixteen when her mother died.

Janet had consoled Max too. They started dating a year after Cheryl’s death, about the same time Max became disillusioned with journalism. He’d finally recognized the limited impact of his endless reporting on environmental catastrophe, and he was desperate to find a better way, as he told Janet, to ‘sound the fucking alarm.’ He had the financial wherewithal to try something new – he’d done very well in the stock market, mostly investing in renewable energy companies. So he resigned the editorship of *The Journal of Climatology* and Janet quit her job at the nonprofit, and they opened the auditions for Doomsday.

They’d had plenty of ups and downs in the two years since then, breaking up and reconciling every few months, but they’d learned how to gauge each other’s moods. And now, as they walked side by side through the park, Max wasn’t surprised to see Janet eyeing him. She obviously recognized his distress, but she said nothing. She was waiting for him to start explaining.

Strangely enough, though, he couldn’t do it. Only a minute ago he’d wanted to tell her the whole story, but now he just looked straight ahead. He needed to think things through. Telling Janet about the masked woman would certainly help *him* – simply talking about his fears would be a relief – but was it the right thing to do for *her*? If this matter was as serious as Max suspected, wouldn't it be better for Janet to know nothing about it? But at the same time, he had to say *something*. She was looking at him too carefully. She wouldn't rest until she got to the bottom of it.

So, he came up with a plan. He would distract Janet from his biggest problem by talking about his second-biggest problem, the one that had seemed like the worst thing in the world until half an hour ago.

'I'm worried about Sonya.' Max tightened his grip on the shopping-cart handle. Even his second-biggest problem was still pretty big. 'The crazy right-wingers are going after her on Twitter.'

'Shit.' Janet stepped closer. 'What are they saying?'

He remembered all too well what he'd seen on his laptop that morning. The screenshot from the Twitter page was burned into his brain. 'The internet trolls are mouthing off about the Climate Summit. Saying it's ridiculous that the UN invited Sonya to speak there. Saying she's a brainwashed college kid who got famous for nothing, and now she should shut the hell up.' He could barely bring himself to say the horrible words out loud. They were insulting *his daughter*. 'They called her an elitist bitch. And worse.'

'Fucking assholes.' Janet's voice rose. She had a low opinion of men in general and an even lower opinion of conservative Republican misogynists. 'Is there gonna be enough security for her at the Summit? She's getting support from that group at her college, right?'

'Yeah, I called NYU this morning after I saw the shit on Twitter. They put me in touch with some kid named Jason, a sophomore who said he was running Sonya's "protection squad." Which is essentially a bunch of undergrads who'll go with Sonya to the UN building tomorrow.' Max shook his head. 'They're not real security. I guess they could step between Sonya and anyone who tries to hassle her, but they'd be useless against a serious nutcase with a knife or a gun.'

'Well, that's unacceptable. They should hire some real guards.'

'That's what I told them. But this Jason idiot said they couldn't afford it. So I offered to pay for it myself, and he said he'd get back to me. Then five minutes later Sonya calls me, and she is royally *pissed*.'

'Uh oh.' Janet was familiar with Sonya's temper. 'Did she rip you a new one?'

'Oh, more than one. She said I'd humiliated her by calling the college. She said everything was under control and I was treating her like a preschooler. Then she hung up on me.'

'Where is she now?'

'I don't know. Before she hung up, I mentioned that Doomsday was going to perform in Central Park, but now I'm not sure if she'll come. You know how she gets.'

Janet reached out and clasped Max's shoulder as they trudged along the path. She had a college-age kid too, a son from a marriage that fell apart ten years ago, but he never made any trouble, not like Max's daughter. Sonya was an attention-grabber from birth, a child who charmed and infuriated people wherever she went, and her true power became apparent when she arrived at NYU and organized her climate-change protests. Campus newspapers across the country wrote about her carbon-neutral crusades to Washington and the sit-ins at the Capitol. She became a celebrity for Generation Z, or at least the left-leaning kids. So it was only natural for the leaders of the UN Climate Summit to invite Sonya to speak at their conference, as a Voice of Youth and a New Symbol of the Movement. Unfortunately, she also became a target for the movement's critics.

And Max, of course, was partly responsible. When Sonya was a senior in high school she'd performed with the Doomsday Company, appearing in some of the shows they'd staged on the weekends at Riverside Church. She had a beautiful voice, and she'd loved singing Max's improvised lyrics about greenhouse gases and ocean acidification. That sparked her interest in climate activism, and soon she was holding fund drives for the Sierra Club and urging her classmates to protest outside her high school every Friday. Max was proud of her, sure, and he encouraged all of it. But now he was worried. Although he was willing to sacrifice a lot of things for the cause, his daughter's safety wasn't one of them.

In a few minutes he and Janet reached the Great Lawn. The

event staffers had erected a fence around the huge grassy oval and were directing people toward the appropriate entrances. The general public filed into the southern half of the lawn, while the northern half was reserved for the VIP donors who were paying for Climate Emergency Week. The main stage had been set up at the oval's northernmost end, where there was a separate entrance for 'Event Staffers, Speakers, and Performers.' A man in a Hawaiian shirt stood onstage, delivering a long, boring speech to the crowd, which responded with tepid applause. They were in dire need of some entertainment, Max thought. The Doomsday Company had arrived just in time.

He and the other Doomsdayers showed their passes at the performers' entrance, then headed for a fenced-off lawn behind the stage. This area served as an outdoor green room and rehearsal space; there was a table loaded with snacks and bottled water, as well as several portable booths for costume changes. Janet huddled with one of the event staffers, a young guy in a bright green T-shirt. Then she came back to the rest of the troupe.

'I got some good news. Lucky for us, the guy onstage now is the head of Greenpeace, and he's a big talker.' Janet raised her right hand and made the blah-blah-blah gesture. 'The program is running way behind schedule, and we have plenty of time to do a run-through before we go onstage. So let's get into costume, folks!' She bent over the shopping cart and zipped open a duffel bag.

Everyone else lined up for their costumes. Max, standing behind Nathan, now had the chance to ask him the all-important question about email deletion. Nathan was still chatting with Eileen, so Max tapped his best friend's shoulder to get his attention.

'Uh, Nate? Can I talk to you for a sec?'

'Certainly, Mr Mirsky! Always a pleasure, sir!' His eyes darted back and forth between Max and Eileen. 'Did you know that our esteemed colleague Eileen Donovan worked as a carnival barker in Ohio when she was a teenager? She just revealed this fascinating tidbit of personal history in an *intimate* conversation with me.'

Nathan seemed to be hinting that he wanted to keep talking with Eileen, but Max couldn't wait. He grabbed Nathan's arm. 'Really, it'll only take a second.'

They moved a few steps away from the others. Nathan frowned

and lowered his voice. 'Your timing is dismal as always. Miss Donovan was warming to my witticisms. For the first time in six months she actually laughed at one of my jokes.'

Max frowned too. 'Sorry, but this is important. I have a question about emails.'

'Would you like to know if the world would be better off without them? The answer is yes.'

'When you delete an email from your phone, is it erased *everywhere*? Or is there another copy that lingers somewhere else?'

'Max, my man, are you trying to hide something?' He lowered his voice still further. 'Are you having an affair, perhaps? A dalliance you wish to conceal from our lovely director? What's the current situation between you and Janet anyway?'

Max took a deep breath. 'Look, right now I really need your computer-world expertise, OK? So please just answer the question.'

Nathan finally got it. His ever-contorting face turned serious. 'OK. What kind of email service is on your phone?'

'It's a Gmail account.'

'Ah, that means all your messages are in the sticky hands of Google. The company stores backup copies of your emails on its servers, just in case there are system-wide failures.' Nathan spoke slowly, enunciating every syllable. Much of his day job consisted of educating the less tech-savvy employees at his advertising firm, and now he treated Max as if he were the least savvy of the lot. 'Google's stated policy is to erase all those backup emails no more than sixty days after you permanently delete the originals. But does the company actually abide by this policy? Your guess is as good as mine.'

Max's stomach churned. '*Sixty* days? That's insane. Does it really take that long to press the delete key on their servers?'

'What are you worried about? You think Janet will call Google and ask to see your salacious messages? Well, she can't do it, unless she has your password. And even then, it's not so simple.'

But a cop could do it, Max thought. *Or an FBI agent.* They might not even need a warrant.

Nathan leaned closer and studied him carefully. Although empathy wasn't one of Nathan's strong points, he seemed to be on the verge of asking Max if something was wrong. But before he could do so, Janet came toward them carrying two bundles of clothing. She thrust one of them at Nathan and the other at Max.

'Stop lollygagging and get changed.' Janet pointed at the row of costume-change booths, which were plain metal-frame things with black drapes hanging from the top like shower curtains. 'We need to start the run-through.'

Max looked down at the bundle in his arms. He held a pair of tattered jeans, a plain white T-shirt, and a black-leather vest jacket, like something a motorcyclist or gang member would wear. On the back of the jacket were four big white letters, spelling out the word 'JETS.'

His stomach churned again, more violently than before. 'Wait a second. We're doing the *West Side Story* number?'

Janet nodded. 'It's the best choice, I think. We've performed it more than any of the other sketches, so everyone knows their lines. And it always gets a big laugh at the end.'

Max knew the piece well. He'd written it just three months ago, and Doomsday had staged it at least a dozen times since then, at Riverside Church and the Goddard Community Center and last month's Brooklyn Climate Action Festival. It was a parody of 'Gee, Officer Krupke,' the hilarious number sung by the members of the Jets street gang in *West Side Story*. Max had rewritten the lyrics to turn the song into a comic indictment of Jonathan Humphrey, the chief executive of Texxonoco Oil & Gas. It was a good fit because the lyrical scanning of 'Jonathan Humphrey' exactly matched that of 'Officer Krupke.' The number of syllables in each name was the same, and so was the placement of the stresses.

Janet, noticing that Max hadn't moved an inch, placed her hand on the small of his back. 'Get going. You're the star of this sketch, remember?' She nudged him toward the changing booths. 'There's something else you should know: Jonathan Humphrey is back in the news today. Just an hour ago, he announced that Texxonoco discovered a giant oil deposit in Alaska. I saw a news alert about it on my phone.'

Max shook his head. He'd been too anxious to look at his news alerts. 'I didn't see it.'

'Well, you're in the minority. The protesters are already yelling and screaming about it. So they're gonna love this number.'

A moment later Max was inside the changing booth, the black curtain closed around him. He stood there, paralyzed, clutching the Jets costume to his chest. He'd focused his parody on Humphrey because the man had done vast damage to the environment. As a journalist, Max had written scathing denunciations of Humphrey; in fact, he'd mentioned the Texxonoco CEO in his 'Worst Climate Criminals' article, which had listed Hollister Tarkington as the number five offender.

Jonathan Humphrey was number four.

FOUR

Jonathan Humphrey stood at the head of the immense conference table in his company's boardroom. The mahogany tabletop had been polished to a high shine, and at its center was a big silver bucket holding half a dozen bottles of Dom Pérignon. Jonathan was alone in the room for now, but in a few minutes the celebration would begin, and he wanted to make sure that everything was perfect.

Six plush armchairs were positioned on either side of the table, one for each of the twelve board members of Texxonoco Oil & Gas. At each place setting was an ounce of beluga caviar, surrounded by toast points, arranged prettily on a thousand-dollar Sèvres plate. The caviar spoons were mother-of-pearl, and the champagne flutes had gold-plated stems. The champagne itself was Dom Pérignon's Plénitude Brut, priced at two thousand dollars a bottle.

Jonathan was a numbers man, good at summing profits and losses, and he instantly calculated that this small party would cost at least thirty thousand dollars. But in the grand scheme of things, that was nothing. The discovery he'd announced an hour ago was the biggest windfall for Texxonoco since 1967. His experts estimated that the deposit near Kaktovik, Alaska, held 200 billion barrels of recoverable oil and 500 trillion cubic feet of natural gas. The ultimate profit was impossible to predict, but Jonathan knew one thing for sure: it would pay for a shitload of champagne.

He turned to the flat-screen TV mounted on the wall, which was tuned to True America Business News and playing without sound. Jonathan's announcement had run live on the 'MoneyWorld' show, and the share price of Texxonoco's common stock instantly jumped a satisfying 25 percent. Unfortunately, though, the show had devoted only a few minutes to the Alaska news before switching to coverage of the Climate Emergency protests. Now the wall-mounted screen displayed panoramic views of the thousands of raggedy-ass protesters in Central Park. And even without any sound from the TV, Jonathan could still hear their asinine chants, because his New York offices were on East 56th Street, just a few hundred yards away. Although the boardroom was on the building's top floor, the crowd noise came through the picture windows as a deep rhythmic rumble.

He went to the room's thermostat and turned up the fan, trying to drown out the noise. Then he pointed the remote control at the TV and changed channels, but CNN was showing videos of the same damn protests. The only useful news was in the chyron scrolling along the bottom of the screen: a layoff at General Motors, a small rise in bond yields, a big drop in the share price of Stygian Energy.

He looked more closely at this last piece of news. According to the chyron, the stock plunged half an hour ago after Stygian Energy CEO Hollister Tarkington collapsed and died at his headquarters.

Jonathan let out a grunt, but he wasn't really surprised. He'd never liked Tarkington. The man was too damn impressed with himself. He was a playboy and a know-it-all and a smug, conceited bastard, and he drank like a fish at energy industry conferences. Probably his liver gave out, the stupid fucking asshole.

Jonathan changed channels again, trying CNBC this time, but the protesters were there too, banging on their drums and waving their idiotic signs. He wanted to throw the remote at the screen, but instead he switched off the TV with a savage click. He wasn't going to let those fuckers spoil his big day. He'd worked too hard for this.

A moment later Charles Roche stepped into the boardroom, and Jonathan's mood immediately improved. Charles was a distinguished silver-haired legend of the oil business, a robust seventy-five-year-old who wielded an onyx-handled cane even though he didn't need it. His eyes lit up when he saw the champagne and caviar on the conference table, and his pale, patrician face broke into a smile.

'Wonderful! Marvelous! A very fitting festivity!' His voice had a self-assured, old-money resonance. He came across the room in long strides and grabbed Jonathan's hand. 'I'm proud of you, my boy. Savor the moment!'

Jonathan definitely wasn't the sentimental type. He had many business acquaintances but few friends, and he'd thoroughly alienated his two ex-wives and five ungrateful children. And yet he felt a pang deep inside his chest as Charles shook his hand. The emotion was so sudden and sharp, he could barely speak. 'I . . . I need to thank you . . . you've been so . . .'

'Nonsense. It was all your doing. You've earned this.'

Charles kept pumping his hand and smiling. In truth, the old man had contributed a lot to Jonathan's success. The company he owned, Roche Industries, built the drilling rigs, refineries, offshore platforms, and pipelines that Texxonoco put to good use across the globe. More important, Charles was a mentor and confidant. He'd befriended Jonathan twenty years ago and helped him fight his way to the top of Texxonoco's corporate hierarchy. And after Jonathan became chief executive and chairman of Texxonoco's board, he made Charles the vice chairman and relied even more heavily on his advice. The old man was particularly helpful in dealing with the government. He'd donated boatloads of money to both political parties, and he had friends galore in Congress.

After several seconds Charles finally let go of his hand. Jonathan had mostly recovered from his unexpected burst of emotion, but he still felt the need to change the subject. 'You're right, it's a great day. It would've been perfect if it weren't for the protests.'

'Ah yes, Climate Emergency Week.' Charles tilted his head toward the window and the protesters outside. 'I saw some of it from the backseat of my limo on the way over here. It's quite a party.'

'Did you have trouble getting here? On the news they said the agitators were blocking the streets.'

'No, no, it wasn't so bad. It's just a temporary inconvenience.' He smiled again and gave his cane a twirl. 'My philosophy is, let the kids have their say. Let them have their demonstrations and make as much noise as they want. And then next week they'll go back to what they really enjoy doing, which is getting high and fucking each other's brains out. And for the rest of us, life will go back to normal.'

Jonathan disagreed. He had no patience for ignorant extremists. These people had no idea how the global economy worked, how each energy source had its most effective uses, and how governmental interventions could devastate the oil business. The problems they kept crying about – wildfires, floods, droughts, whatever – were all things that had been happening since the dawn of time, and they would surely go on happening no matter the rate of carbon emissions. It was astonishing, the number of people who'd been fooled by this climate claptrap.

'Well, Charles, you're more tolerant than me. If I were the police commissioner, I'd put a stop to it.'

He looked askance at Jonathan. 'What would you do? Order mass arrests? Send thousands of screaming youngsters to jail?'

'It wouldn't need to be thousands. Just make an example. Put half a dozen of them in a cell with the usual rapists and murderers. Then wait for the bad news to get back to the other protesters. Believe me, within minutes they'd fold up their tents and run home to their mamas.'

Charles laughed. 'An interesting idea. Very efficient. But as your friend, I'll advise you to stick to what you know best. Just focus on turning this new oil from Alaska into cash. I'll take care of the political issues.' He stepped toward the conference table and lifted a champagne bottle from the silver bucket. 'So where's the rest of the board? Are they going to be late for our revelries?'

But before Jonathan could respond, the other board members started filing into the room. Most of them were pretty useless, to be honest. They were over-the-hill corporate types from other industries – the former chairman of IBM, the former president of Pepsi – who enjoyed hobnobbing with one another and pretending to be important. Jonathan had appointed them to Texxonoco's board because they were unfailingly compliant and could be trusted to rubberstamp every proposal he made. Naturally, he had nothing but contempt for them, but now he disguised his disdain and shook their hands warmly as they congratulated him.

Coming into the boardroom at the same time were four lovely young women in caterer uniforms – identical aprons, tuxedo shirts, and bow ties. They reached for the champagne bottles, expertly popped the corks, and poured the Dom Pérignon into the twelve gold-plated glasses. A fifth woman, even lovelier than the others, entered the room holding a silver tray, at the center of which was a thirteenth glass, already filled with bubbly. She headed straight for Jonathan, smiling at him steadily, her blond hair bunched in a tight, glossy bun, her blue eyes shining like spotlights. She gave him a mischievous look as she came near, and for a moment he imagined that they were lovers in secret. As soon as this board meeting was over, he would whisk her to his penthouse on Park Avenue and slowly extract the black studs from her tuxedo shirt.

But no. That was just a fantasy. Although Jonathan did share a secret with this woman, it was of a different sort. When he'd hired the catering firm, he'd instructed them to fill his glass with ginger ale instead of champagne.

He grasped the glass from her tray. 'Thank you, darling.' Feeling reckless, he leaned toward her, bringing his lips close to her beautifully curved earlobe. 'I appreciate your discretion.'

She nodded, still smiling. She had a tattoo on the back of her neck, a green-and-blue mandala that looked like a flower with a hundred petals. 'It's no trouble at all, Mr Humphrey.'

'Please, call me Jonathan.' He pulled back a bit. Trying to look suave, he took a sip of his ginger ale. 'I'd like to give you a full explanation, you know. In case you were wondering about the reasons for my teetotaling.'

'No worries, sir. You don't need to explain a thing.'

'It's an interesting story, though. Perhaps we could meet sometime for a chat? Maybe after this meeting?'

He wasn't sure if this tease would be enough to intrigue her. His secret wasn't really that interesting; he'd had a drinking problem in college, and he'd squelched it by vowing never to touch alcohol again. No one at Texxonoco knew this about him, not even Charles Roche, but the whole thing had happened decades ago, so it wasn't a very dangerous secret. If it got out, it wouldn't torpedo his career, and it probably wouldn't shock or excite this sexy caterer either. He took a bigger sip of ginger ale as he waited for her reply.

She started to turn away, then looked over her shoulder at him. 'I'd love to talk afterwards.' She had a faint trace of an accent, probably Irish. 'If you're still willing and able.'

She punctuated this remark with a sly wink, an unmistakable

invitation, before she stepped away. Several of the board members ogled her as she carried the empty tray out of the room, and Charles Roche seemed particularly impressed. He turned to Jonathan and gave him a broad smile of approval.

Jonathan took a third sip from his gold-plated glass. It was a day of triumphs for him, both large and small. Almost dizzy with exuberance, he bent over the conference table and rapped his knuckles soundly against the mahogany.

'Gentlemen! May I have your attention please?'

The room quieted. The board members flanked the table, each holding his champagne flute at the ready. Charles stood just a yard to Jonathan's left, his wizened face full of pride and satisfaction. The four caterers lined up at the far end of the room, their arms clasped behind their backs like soldiers standing at ease. The fifth woman, the one with the mandala, hadn't returned to the boardroom yet, but Jonathan hoped she'd come back before the end of his speech.

He raised his glass high. 'Gentlemen, this is a momentous occasion. And not just for Texxonoco Oil & Gas. This is a great day for America. The Kaktovik Field in Alaska is one of the biggest fossil-fuel deposits *ever* discovered. That's right, my friends. If our estimates are correct, it'll be even bigger than the Ghawar Field in Saudi Arabia. Once the oil and gas start flowing from Kaktovik, they'll power America's economy for many years to come!'

His voice rose on the last word and echoed against the boardroom's walls. Although Jonathan had fully expected the big discovery in Alaska – he was in close contact with Texxonoco's exploration unit, which had informed him of the oilfield's potential several months ago – now the enormity of it struck him anew. This was going to be his legacy, his crowning achievement. He felt dizzy again, overwhelmed by his good fortune. With his left hand he gripped the edge of the conference table to steady himself.

'Just think of it! Every time someone flips a light switch, they'll have *us* to thank for the electricity. Our natural gas will heat millions of homes across America, for decades on end. And our petroleum will fuel *billions* of cars and trucks and motorcycles. Not to mention all the airplanes and buses. And outboard motors, and lawnmowers too. And whoa, let's not forget *the entire US military*! Just think of all those jet fighters and tanks and whatever. *Just think of it!*'

Jonathan paused, trying to remember the next thing he was supposed to say. He'd practiced this speech yesterday until he had it all memorized, but for some reason he was losing his train of thought now. Something was distracting him, some irritating rhythmic noise, and after a moment he realized it was the sound of the protesters outside. Now that the boardroom was quiet, he could hear them so clearly, their chants and drumbeats coming right through the fucking windows. The noise pounded in his ears. It was nauseating.

The board members stared at him. Charles lowered his glass, his brow creased with concern. Feeling panicky, Jonathan decided to improvise the rest of his speech. He tightened his grip on the table.

'And let me tell you something else. This job wasn't easy. From day one, the environmentalist maniacs tried to stop us. You know what I'm talking about, all that bitching and moaning about the animals on the Arctic plains, all those delicate, darling creatures of the tundra. "Oh no! You're gonna kill all the caribou in the wildlife refuge! And all the polar bears in the fucking Arctic Ocean!" Which was total bullshit. I mean, that refuge is enormous, twenty million acres. Even if there's a spill, you think the oil's gonna spread over the whole motherfucking continent? Seriously, does anyone really think that?'

Jonathan paused again, waiting for an answer, but no one said a word. They just stood there like idiots, with their mouths wide open, gawking at him. He wanted to shout in their ears and wake them the fuck up, but he was short of breath and trembling all over.

'OK, fine . . . let me ask you another question. Let's assume . . . let's assume the worst, all right? Let's say we kill a million caribou . . . and a billion cocksucking polar bears. Does anyone . . . truly give a shit? Who the fuck . . . is ever gonna give up . . . *their fucking SUV* . . . for the sake . . . of a filthy . . .'

The air in the room suddenly felt very hot. Jonathan wished he could open one of the windows, but that would just let in more of that fucking crowd noise, which was already making him want to vomit.

He gagged, choking. His throat tightened and closed. He let go of his glass and lost his grip on the table.

Jesus Christ! I can't breathe!

Then he lay on the floor, looking up at all their faces. Charles knelt beside him, prodding his neck, trying to feel his pulse. The old man screamed something, but Jonathan couldn't understand him. Mercifully, all the sounds in the room were fading, including the noise of the protesters.

Fuck. I'm dying.

His last thought was a good one, though. He remembered the lovely face of the blue-eyed caterer, the Irish blonde who'd brought him his last drink.

And who'd never returned to the boardroom.

FIVE

West Side Story was Max's favorite musical. Maybe it wasn't as funny as *Fiddler on the Roof*, or as clever as *Cabaret*, or as heartwarming as *South Pacific*, but Max loved it just the same.

A big part of its appeal was the fact that the West Side was Max's home. He grew up on the same Manhattan streets where the musical was set, the mythic slum where gangs of juvenile delinquents once roamed. Much of the neighborhood had been bulldozed in the late Fifties, a decade before Max was born, and since then it had been gentrified beyond recognition, but sometimes when he strolled down Amsterdam Avenue he imagined seeing the musical's characters congregating on the street corners. He pictured the lanky white boys in the Jets storming into a Starbucks, and the Puerto Rican kids in the Sharks dancing outside the Duane Reade.

But the main reason why Max loved *West Side Story* was that it had shaped his life. The first time he saw it – the film version, that is, which ran on Channel Eleven's *Movie of the Week* show in 1976 – he was a nine-year-old living in his grandmother's apartment on West 77th Street. Five years before, his hippie parents had split up and flown off to find their separate nirvanas, one in an ashram in Northern California, the other in a fishing village in Sri Lanka. Max was left in the care of his Grandma Sadie, a cheerful widow fond of brisket and canasta, and he became a lonely, quiet kid who spent most of his time reading comics and watching TV. So *West Side Story* was a revelation for him, a glimpse of a wilder, livelier future. Although he knew he would never become a gangster or a street brawler, for the rest of his life he saw himself as a rebel.

Most of all, the musical shaped Max's ideas about love. The scene that really mesmerized him was the big dance at the school gym, where Tony and Maria meet for the first time. Years later, during his first semester at Columbia, Max thought of that scene when he met Cheryl Barnes, the brilliant student from Barbados who would become his own true love. He wooed her by writing romantic poems that were blatant imitations of 'Maria' and the other songs in his favorite musical. Unfortunately, his poems failed to impress Cheryl, who was more interested in campus activism, so he turned to journalism instead, writing stories for *The Columbia Spectator* about the student protests of the Reagan–Bush era. He demonstrated beyond a doubt that he shared her passion for social justice, and they started dating. They broke up when Max had to leave college for a semester, but after he finally graduated he became a crusading journalist and Cheryl became his wife.

And though he was in his fifties now, a widower and an anxious father just a decade from retirement, Max was still obsessed with *West Side Story*. Which was why he'd chosen 'Gee, Officer Krupke' as the starting point for one of his Doomsday sketches. He liked the fact that it was a comic song about a serious topic, but in Max's parody version he changed the topic to global warming and replaced the original song's target – Sergeant Krupke, the blowhard cop who hassles the Jets and Sharks – with an appropriate corporate villain, selected from his top-five list of climate criminals. And, in Max's humble opinion, he did a good job. In fact, he considered it one of his best efforts.

But Max didn't feel quite so good about the song now as he sweated in his Jets costume. He stood in the outdoor rehearsal space behind the Great Lawn's main stage, surrounded by the other members of his troupe. Nathan stood beside him on the close-cropped lawn, dressed in a blue short-sleeved jumpsuit. It looked like something a gas-station attendant might wear, and it had the words 'Texxonoco Oil & Gas' stenciled on the back. To make the identity of his character even more obvious, Nathan held an old rusty gas-pump nozzle, which Janet had found in a junkyard in New Jersey. As a final touch, the name 'Jonny Humphrey' was stitched on the front of his jumpsuit, just above Nathan's heart.

Max winced at the sight of it and closed his eyes. He wished they were performing any sketch but this one. He couldn't help but think of the masked woman with the long gray braid. Her words came back to him, perfectly recalled: *We just got number five. Now we're going after the other four.*

'Max! Are you paying attention?'

It was Janet. He opened his eyes to see her irritated face, adorned with bright red lipstick and blue eye shadow. She wore a slinky orange dress, very similar to the one worn by the character of Graziella in *West Side Story*. Graziella was the girlfriend of Riff, the leader of the Jets, which was Max's role. He and Janet were playing a couple again, but now she looked a lot more attractive than she did when she was Mrs Bumble. Underneath his panic, Max felt a pang of desire.

'Whoa, nice makeup job. You look hot.'

This failed to appease her. She was directing this sketch as well as acting in it, and she always got frazzled when she had to do both jobs at once. 'Look, we have some time to rehearse, but not an unlimited amount. As soon as that Greenpeace dude is finished talking, they're gonna call us onstage.'

Because they were about a hundred feet behind the main stage, Max couldn't see the dude who was addressing the crowd on the Great Lawn, but he could hear his amplified voice droning on and on. 'I don't think we have to rush. He's taking his time.'

Nathan nodded in agreement. 'Yes, nothing in the world is more loquacious than a do-gooder preaching to the choir.'

Janet frowned. 'Whatever. Let's just get started, OK?' She turned to Larry, Adele, and Eileen, who were all dressed like Fifties gang kids, standing behind Max in their ripped jeans and leather jackets. 'Everyone ready? For this run-through we'll have to sing the song without the recorded background music.' She pointed at Nathan. 'You have the first line, Mr Humphrey. Take it from the top.'

Nathan got into character. He jutted his chin and bunched his shoulders in a menacing fashion. Then he pointed his gas-pump nozzle at Max. '*Hey, you!*'

This simple cue had a remarkable effect. Although Max's stomach was still sour with anxiety, he forced it down. As far as acting went, he was no De Niro, but he had the essential skill required of all performers, the ability to drop *everything* and focus on his lines.

He put an innocent look on his face. Now he was Riff, the charming juvenile delinquent. 'Who, me? What do you want, Chief Executive Officer Jonathan Humphrey? I'm just a concerned citizen who wishes Texxonoco Oil & Gas would stop destroying our planet.'

'You want to talk about destruction?' Nathan stepped closer and shook the nozzle above Max's head. 'Give me one good reason why I shouldn't douse you with petroleum and set you on fire, you protesting *punk*!'

Max dropped to his knees in front of Nathan and clasped his hands in supplication. Then he began to sing.

Deeeeeeaaaarrrr wily Jonny Humphrey,
How can we make you see?
The world's like Humpty Dumpty,
You can't fix a rising sea.
The carbon you're releasing
Will make the planet boil.
Holy shit, stop drilling for that oil!

While Nathan glared at him, unmoved, Max jumped to his feet. Larry and Adele rushed to either side of him and slipped their arms around his waist in street-gang solidarity. Then the three of them sang the next verse together.

Hey, Jonathan Humphrey, we're very afraid.
We won't have any future in this world that you've made.
It's not like we're asking for something too strange,
We only want a little change!

The trio dispersed in a flurry of comic choreography, with Max striding toward Janet, and Larry rushing toward Eileen. The two couples hooked arms and twirled in rapid circles, while Adele stepped forward and sang the refrain – 'We want change!' – in her mezzo-soprano voice, which was actually quite nice. Then Nathan approached Max, yanked him away from Janet, and threatened him with the gas-pump nozzle again, holding it like a gun to his forehead. 'Well, well. That sounds like a reasonable request.'

Max grinned, pretending to be elated. 'So your company is gonna cut back on fossil-fuel production and switch to renewable energy sources?'

Nathan grinned back at him. '*No fucking way!* Go talk to the judge.'

He pointed his nozzle at Eileen, who quickly took off her gang jacket and put it on backwards. Because the black leather totally covered her from neck to waist, it sort of looked like a judge's robe. To complete the picture, she removed a prop from one of the jacket's pockets, a toy gavel made of brown plastic. Max stood beside her and, just before he started singing, raised his right hand as if he were taking an oath.

Deeeeeeaaaarrrr wise Supreme Court justice,
You gotta stop this man.
He thinks the laws are bupkes
And won't halt his evil plan.
A strong restraining order
Would maybe slow him down.
Jesus Christ, if you do nothing we'll all drown!

While Max sang, Nathan stood on the other side of Eileen and began stuffing Monopoly money into the pockets of her backwards jacket. Soon the orange, yellow, and blue bills overflowed from her pockets, so Nathan began stuffing them down Eileen's collar. She gave him a lascivious look, licking her lips and completely ignoring Max. Then she tapped Nathan on the head with her plastic gavel and started crooning to him.

Jonathan Humphrey, you're such a bad boy,
If you weren't so damn wealthy, I'd get really annoyed.
I'm dying to spank you on your moneyed backside,
But unfortunately my hands are tied.

Nathan gave her a grateful bow, then bent over in the opposite direction, allowing Eileen to tap her gavel against his butt. Then she put a serious expression on her face. 'Hear ye, hear ye! In the opinion of the Supreme Court, the corporate rights of Texxonoco Oil & Gas are more important than any worries about a climate apocalypse.'

Nathan stood up straight and nodded in agreement. 'Corporations have rights just like people do. And they have feelings too.'

Max threw his hands up in the air, dramatically exasperated. 'All our laws favor the oil companies! We have to change them!'

Eileen grabbed a fistful of Monopoly money from her pocket and tenderly sifted through the colored bills. Then she turned back to Max and gave him a dismissive look. 'You came to the wrong place, dummy. If you want to change the laws, go talk to Congress.'

She pointed at Janet, who'd slipped an expensive-looking white jacket over her slinky orange dress. Larry and Adele pushed Max toward her while Nathan crept off to the side. Janet eagerly shook hands with all the other performers, acting like a politician greeting her constituents. When it came time for her to shake hands with Max, he held on tight and serenaded her.

Deeeeeeaaaarrrr canny Madam Speaker,
You gotta help us out.
The laws are getting weaker
And they sure could use some clout.
We need some serious taxes
Slapped on their oil and gas.
Motherfuck, let's kick Texxonoco's ass!

Max let go of Janet's hand and got ready for the next comic maneuver, which involved Nathan bonking him on the head with the gas-pump nozzle and pouring an entire bag of Monopoly money over Janet. But before any of that could happen, someone behind them yelled, 'Cut!'

It was a woman's voice, but it didn't belong to their director. Janet looked over Max's shoulder and scanned the rehearsal area, searching for the interloper who'd usurped her directorial powers. Max, though, already knew who it was. No matter the situation, and no matter how bad his hearing got, he could always recognize his daughter's voice.

'Sonya!' He turned around and rushed toward her. He was happy beyond words. 'You came! You're here!'

Max wanted to hug her, but something in her face made him stop short. Her eyes were wide, her mouth half-open. Sonya was a slender, beautiful nineteen-year-old with smooth dark skin and long black hair dangling in beaded cornrows, but right now her expression was that of a frightened five-year-old. She looked at her father the same way she used to look at him when a barking dog or a thunderclap had scared her. 'Dad, what are you *doing*?'

He instantly imagined the worst. Those right-wing idiots who'd trolled her on Twitter, had they confronted her in person? Had any of those sick bastards tried to carry out their threats? 'What happened? Are you OK?'

'I'm *fine*. The problem isn't me, it's *you*!' Her fear swiftly gave way to anger, which was another familiar trait. 'I came here to show you some support, but this is freakin' *horrific*. You're actually rehearsing the Jonathan Humphrey sketch?'

Max was relieved, but confused. He nodded uncertainly. 'Sure, the *West Side Story* parody. You've seen it. We're going onstage as soon as that Greenpeace guy stops talking.'

By this point Janet and Nathan had approached. Sonya knew both of them well, although she liked Janet a whole lot better than Nathan. He was always trying too hard to make Sonya laugh, and now he waggled the gas-pump nozzle to get her attention. 'I'm quite perturbed by your behavior, young lady. You interrupted our run-through before we got to the funniest line.' He went back into character and conked himself in the head with the nozzle. 'Hey, Jonathan Humphrey, HUMP YOU!'

Sonya glowered. Her eyebrows lanced downward like accent marks, and Max was stunned once again by how much she resembled her late mother. In addition to inheriting Cheryl's Caribbean beauty, Sonya had the same fierce temper. She ignored Nathan and aimed her fury at Max. 'Didn't you see the news? You can't perform that sketch! Do you want to make the whole climate-change movement look like a bunch of heartless assholes?'

Nathan cocked his head, clearly trying to think of a clever retort, but Janet elbowed him in the ribs. She realized that something serious was going on. And so did Max.

He leaned closer to his daughter. His throat was so tight, he could barely get the words out. 'Did something happen to Jonathan Humphrey?'

Sonya pulled her iPhone out of her jeans pocket. 'They announced his death twenty minutes ago.' She tapped the phone's screen and held it up for everyone to see. 'He dropped dead in his company's boardroom. And the TV networks are saying it looks suspicious.'

Max took a step backward. He skin went cold. His knees almost buckled.

Janet shook her head, uncomprehending. 'Why do they think it's suspicious?'

'Look at this.' Sonya held the phone right under their noses. 'Another CEO, Hollister Tarkington of Stygian Energy, collapsed at his office building less than an hour before. At first they thought it was a stroke or a heart attack, but after Humphrey died there was a news bulletin on CNN. Someone sent the network an anonymous message saying they were gonna kill all the climate criminals.'

Janet and Nathan turned to Max, their heads swiveling in sync. They were probably remembering what had happened after their musical encounter with Tarkington, how Max had stared so anxiously at the glass doors of the Stygian Energy building. And how, after the coroner's van arrived, he'd announced with absolute certainty, 'Tarkington's dead.'

In that same moment, there was a commotion at the other end of the backstage area. The Climate Emergency volunteers in the bright green T-shirts were running behind the stage and shouting. Then the source of the disturbance came into view, a pair of tall men wearing sunglasses and dark gray suits. Barging past the volunteers, they strode across the lawn toward the rehearsal space, with half a dozen New York City cops trailing behind.

The men in suits halted ten feet from the Doomsday Company. One of the men pulled an ID badge from the pocket of his suit jacket, while the other stood there with his arms at his sides, ready to draw his gun if anyone made the wrong move.

'FBI,' said the man with the badge. 'We're looking for Max Mirsky.'

SIX

Erin O'Malley frowned at the protesters outside City Hall. They were a pack of impostors. Trying to look oh-so-badass in their black T-shirts and stupid Guy Fawkes masks. Pretending to be guerillas or anarchists or whatever.

She wanted to tell them, *You have no fucking idea what you're doing. Come with me to County Armagh and I'll show you some real-life terrorists.*

Dozens of NYPD officers stood behind the crowd-control barriers surrounding City Hall Park. The protesters jammed the sidewalk outside the park and spilled into the street, blocking the traffic lanes on Broadway. The cars and trucks and buses couldn't move at all, and their drivers leaned on their horns. The honking was so bloody loud, it drowned out whatever shite the protesters were shouting.

Erin shook her head, disgusted, as she maneuvered around the crowd. If they thought this asinine jamboree would do any good, they were out of their fucking minds.

She headed for the subway entrance, the City Hall stop for the R and W trains. Erin had come to New York three weeks ago, and to say she was disappointed would be a massive understatement. The subways reeked of piss. The streets were a goddamn nightmare, loaded with garbage and perverts and filthy drunks on every corner. But the dumb gobshites in Manhattan thought the place was a paradise. They paid thousands of dollars every month for the holy privilege of living there. It was madness.

Frankly, she couldn't wait to go home. The minute she finished this job, she planned to jump on the next Aer Lingus flight back to Belfast. Her hometown had plenty of drunks and garbage too, but at least it wasn't a fucking circus. In Belfast, the battle lines were clear: Catholics versus Protestants, as simple as a catechism. And when the boyos put on their black shirts and masks, you knew damn well they weren't playing any games.

Cool and casual, she went down the steps to the subway station and swiped her way through the turnstiles. Then she strolled to the far end of the platform, where the piss stench was strongest and nobody was lingering. There was another descending stairway here, with a sign that said 'Authorized Personnel Only' and a locked gate at the top of the stairs. But the gate was only a meter high, and after a quick look-around Erin climbed over it. Luckily, she'd changed out of that ridiculous caterer's uniform – the apron, bow tie, and tuxedo shirt – and put on jeans and sneakers, making it easy for her to maneuver. At the bottom of the stairs was a more formidable obstacle, a barred door. Erin supposed it was usually locked tight, but now the door hung ajar.

How considerate. They unlocked it for me.

She swung the door open and peered down the length of another subway platform, a vacant station directly below the City Hall stop. The transit authority obviously used this lower level as a storage facility for out-of-service trains. The track on the right side of the platform was occupied by a stationary R train that had been shunted off its regular route. Stepping more stealthily now, she headed for the subway car at the train's front end.

Unlike the rest of the train, the front car had its lights on and its doors open. And though Erin heard no voices coming from that direction, she could tell there were at least two people inside. It was a sixth sense she had, a special feel. She'd inherited it from her father, who'd fought the good fight in Belfast for many years, long after his mates in the Provos put down their guns. He'd taught her everything, all his tricks and tactics, but she'd also learned from his mistakes. Unlike him, Erin wasn't a diehard for Irish unification or any other lofty ideal. She used her skills strictly for her own benefit. And she never took a job unless it offered a brilliant payout.

When she reached the front car, she put a smile on her face and stepped inside, very nonchalant, as if this were her usual end-of-the-day commute. It was important to show confidence in the face of your enemies – that was another lesson her father had taught her. The two people waiting for her in the subway car weren't exactly her enemies, but that situation could change if her meeting with them didn't go well.

Angela Nova sat in one of the car's rear-facing seats. Erin had met her once before, three days ago, when they'd negotiated the price for this job, and now Angela wore the same thing she'd worn for their previous meeting, an olive-green jumpsuit. It was an odd fashion choice for anyone who wasn't a petrol-station attendant. She was similarly careless about her hair, which was dark and straggly and hadn't been washed in a while. She certainly didn't look like she was worth eight hundred million dollars, but it was true; Erin had done a thorough background check. According to her research, Angela had put a substantial fraction of her assets into an organization called Prophecy. The money was held in a Swiss bank account, from which it could be wired to independent contractors. But Erin, like any good businesswoman, always insisted on payment in cash.

Standing beside Angela was Carl Hauser, her bodyguard. For twenty years he'd worked for Angela's father, Sam Novacek, who'd run one of the biggest construction companies in America until he offed himself a year ago. Erin had looked into this incident – it raised her suspicions since the construction business was rife with mobsters – but she hadn't found any evidence of foul play. The old man left his company and fortune to his only child, and Angela also inherited Carl, an ugly bald bruiser who looked a lot like Mr Clean. Now he stepped forward, moving past Angela's seat, his eyes fixed on Erin. His weapon of choice, she'd learned, was a Glock semi-automatic, which he was surely carrying in a shoulder holster under his blue blazer.

Erin stopped two meters in front of them, within reach of one of the subway car's vertical poles. She ignored Carl and aimed her smile at Angela. 'I guess you've seen the news, eh?'

Angela nodded. Her face was pale and puffy, and she looked a bit dazed, as if she'd just woken from a nap. 'Yes, I saw it. Although it only confirmed the inevitable.' She closed her eyes for a long moment, her lids quivering. 'I knew you'd succeed. There was no doubt in my mind.'

Ordinarily, Erin would've been pleased by the compliment, but Angela was a strange one. She didn't fall into any of the usual categories. For the great majority of Erin's clients, the motivation was revenge, so her typical victims were cheating spouses and backstabbing business partners. Angela, though, had grander ambitions. Her targets were the big shots, the VIPs. It was a campaign of assassination, designed to strike fear in the hearts of all plutocrats. Which Erin admired, she truly did. But she also knew it couldn't last. Very soon the Feds would put a stop to it, and Erin didn't want to be there when that happened. So she'd decided to turn down any further assignments, even if Angela offered more money.

But Erin was going to be polite about it. Polite and cautious. She was dealing with an unpredictable person. 'Well, you were right about Jonathan Humphrey. He was a bit of a wanker. Dressed like a billionaire but drank his ginger ale like a wee boyo. It was downright comical.'

Angela didn't smile back at her. 'And Tarkington? Everything went according to plan?'

Erin nodded. 'That was dead easy. I broke into his garage last night and slipped a few grams of the strong stuff into his Stolichnaya.'

'So the rumors about him were correct?'

'Yeah, the man was a tippler. He kept a bottle of vodka in the backseat of his limo, and he always took a few nips on his way to work. So he was chock-full of poison by the time he got to his headquarters today.' She stepped forward, keeping one eye on Carl but focusing on Angela. 'In between the two jobs, I made contact with your friend Lauren. You know, the skinny hag? With the awful ponytail?'

Angela shifted in her seat, as if she'd just felt something sharp under her bum. 'Yes, Lauren relayed your message. But unfortunately she compromised the security of our headquarters, which is why I had to change the location of this meeting.' She tilted her head toward her bodyguard. 'Carl knows some people in the transit workers' union, and they were kind enough to provide this temporary refuge.'

'Ah, sure, it's grand.' Erin pretended to admire the piss-reeking subway car. Then she casually grasped the shiny steel pole beside her. 'So look, I think it's time we concluded our business. I've completed the tasks you contracted me for, and now you need to make the final payment. Eighty thousand in hundred-dollar bills, just like we agreed.'

This was the crucial moment. Erin would know in half a second whether there was going to be trouble or not. Either Angela would hand over the money or she'd start making excuses. But the strange bitch did neither. She just stared straight ahead, as if she'd forgotten what they were talking about.

'No. We're not done yet.' Angela shook her head. 'We're going to keep working together.'

'I'm afraid not, love.' Erin's voice softened but her body tensed. Trouble was coming, and she was getting ready for it. From the corner of her eye she monitored Carl, who stood less than a meter away now. 'I'm a big fan of risk analysis, understand? And the risks involved in working for you have gotten too high.'

Angela closed her eyes again. 'Nevertheless, you'll agree to do it. I can see the future, Erin, and this part is very clear. You'll change your mind in the next few minutes.'

Erin tightened her grip on the pole. 'Do you have my money or what?'

'We'll give you forty thousand now' – she opened her eyes and slipped her right hand into the pocket of her jumpsuit – 'and another two hundred thousand when you complete your next assignment. It's a generous offer.'

Without waiting for a reply, Angela glanced at Carl and gave him a nod. He reached into his jacket and pulled out a stack of cash, about five centimeters thick.

In that same instant, Erin leapt forward and kicked him in the ball sack. Gripping the pole for balance, she drove the toe of her sneaker deep into Carl's crotch, and when he doubled over she slammed her forearm into his face. As he collapsed, Angela jumped from her seat and pulled a switchblade out of her pocket, but Erin had expected something like that. She pivoted around the pole and launched a back kick into the bitch's stomach, sending her flying. Then Erin bent over Carl and removed the Glock from his shoulder holster. She also grabbed the cash and the knife Angela had dropped, then retreated a few steps, pointing the gun at both of them.

That's all it took. Game over.

Erin closed the knife and stuffed it in her pants pocket. Then she inspected the stack of bills. It was indeed forty thousand dollars, only half of what they owed her. She stuffed the money into her pocket too, then turned back to Carl and Angela, who were squirming on the floor of the subway car. 'You OK down there? Still breathing? Sorry about the dustup, but a girl has the right to protect herself. So I took a little preemptive action, so I did.'

Carl lifted his head for a second, blood streaming from both nostrils, before it clonked back to the floor. But Angela didn't look up. She clutched her belly and climbed back to her seat, averting her eyes all the while. She seemed shaken up, but not surprised or angry. She actually looked kind of sheepish, as if she felt she'd deserved that kick to her stomach.

Erin had no remorse. Anyone who tried to cheat her *did* deserve some punishment. 'You see, I got suspicious when you changed the place for this meeting. It seemed a bit sudden. So before I came here, I went to the original location, that bare penthouse in the half-built skyscraper, and I saw a big stain on the floor, kind of dark and reddish. Soaked deep into the concrete, so it couldn't be washed away. Care to explain?'

Angela kept her head down. 'I already told you. Lauren compromised our security. I did what I had to do.'

'Ah, grand. That's what I thought.' She cocked the pistol, loud and deliberate. 'Anyway, let's move onward. You still owe me forty thousand, in cash, and you're not gonna wriggle out of it by sticking that knife in my guts. I sincerely hope, for your own sake, that you have a plan for paying me.'

After a second, Angela finally raised her head. And nodded. 'We can adjust the payment schedule. I can get you another forty thousand in a couple of hours. And one hundred and sixty thousand after you complete your next assignment.'

'Excuse me? Haven't I made myself clear?' Frowning, Erin pointed the gun at Angela's forehead. 'Our contract is done. Finished, terminated. I have a strict policy against working with high-risk customers.'

'You'll make an exception for me. Once you realize how much I know.' Angela ignored the gun and looked at her steadily. 'For instance, I know that Jonathan Humphrey tried to seduce you today. After you delivered his ginger ale, didn't he whisper in your ear and make a lewd proposal?'

This struck Erin as the ultimate non sequitur. 'As a matter of fact, he did. But what does that have to do with—'

'Aren't you curious about how I came to know this fact?'

Angela's eyes gleamed. Her face, so pale and puffy before, now seemed to glow under the subway car's fluorescent lights. It occurred to Erin that something was seriously wrong with this bitch. 'No, I'm not curious. I don't give a fuck.'

'I can assure you that I didn't have any other spies in the boardroom. If you don't believe me, you can check with all the caterers who were there, and all the—'

'Enough!' Erin curled her lip. She wouldn't stand being toyed with, not when she was the one holding the pistol. 'What are you trying to do? Distract me?' With her free hand, she pointed at Angela's half-conscious bodyguard, who was groaning and rolling his head from side to side. 'If you're hoping your man Carl will come to your rescue, you're in for a disappointment. He's gonna be useless for hours. So stop fucking around and tell me how you're gonna get my money.'

'Don't worry, you'll get it. But first I want to prove something to you.' Angela rose from her seat. 'Many years from now, after we change the course of history, you'll be a hero, Erin. You'll tell the whole world what you did today, how you struck the first blows in the battle to save our planet. That's how I know what Jonathan Humphrey said to you in the boardroom, and all the other details of what happened there. Because I can see the future.'

Erin was so furious, the gun shook in her hand. Most of all, she was angry at herself, at her own blindness and stupidity. *Jesus, Mary, and Joseph! I'm doing business with a lunatic!* 'You know what? I don't even care about the money anymore. I'll get more pleasure from blowing your brains out.'

'Just do one thing for me first. Check your phone and look up the share price of Texxonoco Oil & Gas.' Angela raised her right arm and looked at her watch. 'It's two minutes after four, which means the stock market just closed. And even though I've been busy talking to you for the past ten minutes, I can tell you the exact closing price for Texxonoco, which was reported only two minutes ago. It's ninety-six dollars and thirty-three cents.'

'I'm not going to—'

'You've been watching me closely ever since you came down here, correct? And I never once looked at my phone to check the markets, did I? But because I can see the future, I knew the closing price hours ago, right down to the penny. That's proof of my clairvoyance, indisputable evidence. If I didn't have this ability, how could I predict such a thing?'

Erin was *this* close to pulling the trigger. Seriously, she was ready to shoot the crazy bitch and the useless bodyguard too, just to put all this nonsense behind her. But Erin prided herself on her professionalism, and it wouldn't be very professional to leave two bodies on the floor of that subway car, would it? So she lowered the gun and reached for her phone. Her only desire now was to shut the bitch up.

The wireless signal in the station was weak, but after a few seconds she got Google on the phone's screen and looked up the closing price of Texxonoco Oil & Gas.

It was ninety-six dollars and thirty-three cents.

Angela took a step forward. 'I know you're Catholic, Erin. And so am I. We've both been taught that God works in mysterious ways.'

It was a trick. It had to be. Erin raised the gun again. 'Don't come any closer.'

Nodding, Angela raised both hands in surrender. 'God has called on us to save His world. We are merely the instruments of His will.'

'Bullshit. You're insane.'

'Is it insane to want a livable future? All the so-called sane people are just letting the crimes happen, letting the corporations befoul our planet until it becomes uninhabitable. Which will come to pass in a few decades if we keep following the "sane" path.' She looked Erin in the eye. 'I've seen all the possibilities, all the branching paths of human action, and only one choice will save us. We have to be as steadfast as Moses, as firm as Saint Paul. We must strike down our enemies. *Nothing but green!*'

Angela was breathing hard now, her chest rising and falling inside her jumpsuit. Her hands quivered as she held them in the air, and a bead of sweat rolled down the side of her neck. She certainly looked like a lunatic, but for Erin this was a familiar kind of lunacy. She'd seen it before, in the faces of her former comrades in the Real IRA and the New IRA and the Continuity IRA, all the fanatics who'd refused to stop killing and dying, even a quarter-century after the peace talks and the Good Friday Agreement. It was a madness of belief, intense and unswerving.

It made Erin wince. She didn't want to be reminded. 'Stop saying "we." This is *your* fight, not mine.'

Angela shook her head. 'No, you're in it. I've seen you so many times in my visions. Like I said, you'll be a hero, famous across the world, the Irishwoman who fought back, the brave rebel who took down the genocidal billionaires. And the reward will be much greater than a few stacks of money.'

'What do you mean?' Erin stepped right up to her and pressed the barrel of the gun against her stomach. '*What are you talking about?*'

'I've seen it. They'll grant you a pardon for all your crimes.' Angela lowered her hands, unhurried and unafraid. 'And they'll release Derek O'Malley from prison.'

It was absurd. Ludicrous. The wild fantasy of a madwoman. Erin should've shot the bitch for even mentioning her father's name. And she almost did it too, almost ripped open Angela's guts with one of her bodyguard's bullets.

But instead Erin pulled back. She retreated to the aisle of the subway car, her jaw clenched, shaking with rage. *How did this happen? For fuck's sake, what's going on?*

She'd worked hard to forget. After her father's arrest, she'd realized the futility of his struggles, his bloody quest for redemption. With a great effort of will, she'd discarded that dream and focused on strictly rational priorities. It would be a terrible thing to undo all that hard work, all those years of methodical renunciation.

And yet . . .

Erin took another step backward. She kept the gun pointed at Angela, but she moved her finger away from the trigger.

'Let's consider a hypothetical situation. Let's say I agreed to do another job for you.' Erin winced again. She couldn't believe she was saying this. 'Who would be the target this time?'

Angela smiled. 'That's the easy part. You've already met him.'

SEVEN

Long before Max Mirsky became a political performance artist, he'd been an environmental journalist who sometimes broke the rules. When he'd worked on stories that were especially important – for instance, his exposé of toxic waste dumps in the Everglades, or his investigation of the fossil-fuel industry's political bribery – he hadn't been averse to seeking out whistleblowers and persuading them to steal incriminating corporate documents. So, he'd always imagined that he might get arrested someday.

But *this*? A pair of FBI agents handcuffing him in front of the whole Doomsday Company? On suspicion of involvement in *terrorism*?

Somehow, Max managed to hold his head high as the two men in gray suits hustled him out of Central Park and shoved him into the backseat of an unmarked car. But his composure didn't last. By the time the car barreled into the garage of the Federal Building downtown, he was shaking.

The agents dragged him into a windowless sub-basement room that had a gray table and two steel chairs bolted to the linoleum floor. They dropped Max into one of the steel chairs and restrained him by running the chain between his handcuffs through an eye bolt jutting from the table's edge. As they secured his hands, he caught a glimpse of a third agent entering the room, and that was the moment of maximum panic, the awful climax of this fascist nightmare.

But it turned into a moment of wonder. Max stared at a petite fortyish woman with dazzling auburn hair brushing the shoulders of her blue FBI windbreaker. Her skin was tawny, her lips slightly parted, her eyebrows curved like tildes above her brown eyes. Max had expected a huge brutish interrogator with a face like ruddy granite, but the agent standing on the other side of the table had an aura of calm and empathy. Even more surprising, her face seemed familiar, like a framed portrait that had been hanging inside Max's skull for decades.

After a second he figured it out. She looked like Maria from *West Side Story*. And there he was, still wearing his costume from the Jonathan Humphrey sketch, the black-leather vest with the word 'JETS' on the back.

The agent didn't smile at him, but she didn't frown either. She tilted her head and gazed at him pensively, like Maria gazing at Tony on the fire escape outside her tenement apartment, pondering the trouble she was getting herself into by falling in love with such a dopey, earnest white guy. Max knew of course that this FBI interrogator was gauging him as a suspect rather than a sweetheart, but he couldn't help but feel hopeful. This woman would surely understand his situation. She would listen to him and forgive any mistakes he might've made.

She sat down in the chair opposite Max's and gave a hand signal to the other two agents, who quickly exited the room. As the door closed behind them, she placed a manila folder on the table and looked Max in the eye. Then she did frown at him, and though her face was still ineffably beautiful, it seemed much less empathetic now.

'I'm Special Agent Aleida Reyes. We need to talk, Mr Mirsky. As you may be aware from the news reports, an anonymous group is claiming responsibility for the deaths of Hollister Tarkington and Jonathan Humphrey. And we believe you've been in contact with one or more individuals who may be part of this dangerous group.'

Max knew what a clever suspect was supposed to do under these circumstances: lawyer up. Only a fool would cooperate with the Feds. He was furious at them for arresting him in front of his daughter and his friends, and then throwing him into the FBI's downtown dungeon. But at that moment he was even angrier at the bastards who'd made him look like a conspirator, the stupid zealots who'd taken advantage of his trust and used his climate criminals story as a blueprint for their idiocy. He was particularly enraged at the old woman in the Guy Fawkes mask, the one who'd called herself Mary Smith in her emails. Agent Reyes was right, these fanatics were dangerous. They thought they were advancing the cause, but instead they were doing irreparable damage to it.

He leaned across the table toward Reyes until he felt the tug from his handcuffs. 'I'm not part of any conspiracy, OK? I didn't know that woman with the mask.'

'Are you referring to—'

'She came over to me in front of the Stygian Energy building and started talking crazy, saying they were going to kill Tarkington and all the others on my climate criminals list, and I didn't—'

'This woman admitted to participating in the murders?'

'Yes, but I thought she was nuts. What else was I supposed to think? I didn't believe any of it until I heard that Tarkington was dead, and then—'

'Slow down, Mr Mirsky. I need to check something with you.' Agent Reyes opened the manila folder and pulled out a glossy color photograph. 'Because of the UN conference this week, we have teams of agents inspecting the traffic in and out of Manhattan. They found this inside a garbage truck headed for New Jersey a little while ago.'

She handed the photo to Max. It showed a skinny nude figure lying facedown on a bed of heavy-duty black garbage bags. The wrinkled skin on her back and legs and arms made it clear that she was an older woman, but otherwise it could've been anyone. Max stared at the corpse, looking for anything distinctive about it, and that was when he noticed that the woman's arms ended in rough brown stumps.

Agent Reyes kept her eyes on him. 'I have some more photos of the victim but there's no point in showing them to you.' She held her hand over the photo and tapped a polished fingernail on it. 'Whoever hacked off that woman's hands also mutilated her face. To destroy any dental evidence and make it impossible to do a quick ID.'

Max kept staring at the body. He was a stranger to this dark side of human affairs and therefore unable to process what he was seeing. As he looked at the photo, he couldn't get past thinking, *Is that real? Those stumps? Is that how it's really done?* He couldn't look away. He was repelled and riveted at the same time.

After a few seconds Reyes took back the photo and gave Max another one from her folder. 'Once our agents found the body, they did a thorough search of the garbage bags in that truck. They didn't find anything of interest in them, but then they checked the bags in another garbage truck owned by the same company, and they discovered these two pieces of evidence.'

The photo showed the items against a blank white background. The first was a Guy Fawkes mask, splotched with grime. The second was a severed ponytail, long and gray and braided.

'Mr Mirsky?' Reyes raised her voice. 'We have surveillance video of you and the masked woman on West 57th Street. It was recorded by a security camera across the street, shortly after Hollister Tarkington entered the Stygian Energy headquarters.' She tapped the evidence photo. 'Given what you see here, do you think the body we found might be the same woman?'

Max nodded but said nothing. He was afraid to open his mouth.

Reyes picked up the photo and mercifully returned it to her folder. 'In your conversation with this woman, did she reveal the names of any accomplices? Or any other details of their plans?'

'It . . . it was a short conversation.' Max swallowed hard. He tried to recall exactly what the masked woman had said, but it was difficult. 'She didn't say anything about accomplices. First she mentioned an email she sent me a few months ago, asking for a copy of my article about the climate criminals. Then she said something about Tarkington clutching at his stomach, and how an autopsy would show what they'd done to him. And right before she ran off, she told me to delete all the emails we exchanged.'

'Yes, we know about those emails.' Reyes reached into her folder again and pulled out a sheaf of papers. 'Because the murders of Hollister Tarkington and Jonathan Humphrey appear to be politically motivated, this case has national security implications, so the FBI is authorized to search the electronic records of anyone involved. After we identified you in the surveillance videos, we checked your email accounts and found the messages to and from the suspicious Gmail address linked to a "Mary Smith."'

She placed the papers on the table in front of him, transcripts of the emails about his climate criminals list. As Max had feared, deleting the messages from his phone hadn't put them out of the government's reach. Now he had to convince this intimidating

FBI agent that what he'd written was very different from what he'd meant to say.

'OK, there's a simple explanation.' He tried to make a conciliatory gesture, but the handcuffs inhibited him. 'Whoever sent me that first email said she was a college student. And I get a little overdramatic when I'm talking to young people, see?'

'And that's why you wrote, "I will heartily support any effort to nail those planet-killing bastards"?'

'Exactly!' He nodded again, more vigorously this time. 'By "nail," I meant hurting them in a strictly non-physical way. Like holding them up to public scorn, or bringing down their companies' stock prices. That seems obvious once you consider the context of the messages, right?'

Agent Reyes scowled. She wasn't buying it. 'You physically confronted Tarkington this afternoon. Just ten minutes before he died. We have surveillance video of that too.'

'What? I never touched the guy! It was street theater!'

'On the video, it looks like you were blocking Tarkington's path. Were you trying to delay his entrance into his company's headquarters for some reason?'

'This is ridiculous! Do you seriously think I'd sign up to be an assassin?' Max gritted his teeth. He felt an uncontrollable surge of self-righteousness. 'Killing fossil-fuel tycoons won't help the climate-change movement. It's an idiotic strategy and totally self-destructive. It'll make all of us look like terrorists, and that's not a good look!'

'But didn't your piece of "street theater" encourage violence against Hollister Tarkington? Weren't you urging your audience to kick and smack him?'

'For Christ's sake, it was satire!' He shook his hands in frustration, rattling his cuffs. 'I was exercising my First Amendment rights in a peaceful protest! I have nothing to hide!'

'Then why did you delete the emails?'

Reyes narrowed her eyes. Max leaned back in his chair, out of breath and off balance. He struggled to remember the defense he'd prepared in case he was asked this question. 'Look, I freaked out after that woman ran off. I had no idea what was going on, but I was scared, OK? It's not a crime to get scared, is it?'

'No, it's not. But you showed some terrible judgment. You

should've alerted the authorities.' She shook her head. 'You know very well whose name sits at the top of your climate criminals list. Any threat to his safety is an extremely serious matter.'

Max's throat tightened. Agent Reyes was right, and the stern look on her face was crushing. He thought once more of *West Side Story*, specifically the scene where Maria and Anita sing 'A Boy Like That' in Maria's bedroom after Tony has just left. Such a beautiful song about love and betrayal, and at the end Maria shakes her head and cries, 'You should know better!' Her expression at that moment was just like the FBI agent's, although Maria's anger was more surprising, because she'd been so cheery and hopeful until that point in the story. But wasn't *West Side Story* all about Maria's journey from innocence to experience? And how could a journey like that be complete without a dose of fury?

All these irrelevant thoughts flew in and out of Max's head while Agent Reyes glared at him. He needed to pull himself together. 'OK, I agree, I made a mistake. But now I'm ready to fix it. I'll do anything I can to help you stop those lunatics.'

'Really?' She tilted her head, unconvinced. 'How can you help us if you won't tell us everything you know?'

'I just did! I told you everything!'

'What about your phone conversation this morning with Jason Torricelli?'

Max stared at her. The name rang no bells whatsoever. 'Who's he?'

Reyes extracted yet another paper from her folder. 'According to Verizon's records, you called Mr Torricelli from your cell phone at nine fifty-nine a.m. and the conversation went on for seven minutes. We don't have a recording of the call, though, because we had no surveillance warrant at that time. What did you talk about, Mr Mirsky?'

Max bit his lip, trying to remember the call. Then it hit him. 'Yeah, OK, that was the NYU student. The guy in charge of the group that's supposed to protect Sonya.'

'You mean at your daughter's speech tomorrow? At the UN?'

He didn't like the way Reyes had said this, so quick and knowing. It sounded like the FBI agent was thoroughly familiar with Sonya and her much-publicized campaign of environmental protest. Although Max was proud of his daughter's fame, it also worried the hell out of him. 'That's right, and she's been getting threats from right-wing troglodytes. Did you know about that? Is that in your files too? Because it should be.'

'I know she's scheduled to speak at the UN General Assembly. Mr Torricelli has organized a group of bodyguards for her?'

Max grimaced. 'No, they're all undergrads. A bunch of NYU kids. Not exactly the best candidates for a security job, right? I told Jason I'd hire some real guards, but then he ratted me out to Sonya, and she went ballistic.'

'And that was the full extent of your conversation with Mr Torricelli?'

Now Max felt a tingle of fear in his guts. 'Why are you asking me this? What does this have to do with your investigation?'

'Answer my question first, Mr Mirsky. Did you talk about anything else with—'

'No, we only talked about Sonya!' Max tried to stand, but the chain linking his handcuffs to the table went taut. 'What do you know about this Jason guy? Why are you so interested in him?'

Reyes opened her mouth but stopped herself. Her forehead wrinkled and for the first time Max saw a look of true concern on her face. This wasn't something he remembered from *West Side Story*, some emotion of Maria's that he was projecting onto the FBI agent. No, this was genuine, and it scared Max shitless.

'Please,' he whispered, bent over the table, edging as close to her as his handcuffs would allow. 'Please tell me.'

She said nothing for several seconds. Then she nodded. 'Jason Torricelli's father runs the Torricelli Demolition Company. Which owns the garbage truck in that photograph I showed you.'

'What? What are you saying?' Max's guts were roiling now. 'Is Jason part of it? The conspiracy?'

'We don't know for sure yet.' Her voice was calm and infuriatingly professional. 'It could be a coincidence.'

'But what if it's not?' Max felt his skin go cold. 'That bastard might be working with the lunatics! And Sonya might be with him right this minute!'

Max's knees buckled. He sank back into the steel chair and doubled over. At the same time, Agent Reyes turned her head toward the wall and lifted her eyes toward a security camera mounted up high. 'Wilson, Martinez!' she shouted. 'Get back in here and take his cuffs off.'

The two agents who'd arrested Max re-entered the interrogation room. The big blond one – that must be Wilson, Max thought – unlocked his handcuffs while the other one stood nearby, ready to jump into action if anything went wrong. But the agents had nothing to worry about, because Max was paralyzed with terror. After his hands were freed he just stared at the floor, studying the cracks in the linoleum, dazed and appalled. He didn't care anymore whether the FBI believed him or not, whether the agents thought he was a criminal or a kook, whether they would let him go free or throw him into prison. All he cared about was Sonya.

After a moment Max raised his head and stared hard at Reyes. 'I need to call her.' He pointed a trembling finger at Agent Wilson, who'd confiscated his iPhone when they'd arrested him. 'Give me back my phone.'

Wilson glanced at Reyes, who nodded. The big agent removed the iPhone from his pocket and handed it to Max, who immediately dialed Sonya's number.

He pressed the phone to his ear. In the silence of the interrogation room, he heard it ring.

And ring.

EIGHT

Jamaica Bay seemed lovely, Erin thought, at least if you ignored the shit-stench wafting over the brackish water.

She crouched in the bow of an inflatable rubber dinghy, peering at the marshes and mudflats in this godforsaken corner of New York City, while Carl Hauser sat in the stern, steering the boat's outboard motor. Angela couldn't be there – she'd said she had another matter to attend to – so she'd ordered her bodyguard to introduce Erin to Prophecy's equipment specialist, a secretive man who'd insisted on rendezvousing in the remotest part of this urban cesspool.

Carl's left cheek was bruised and swollen from the forearm slam Erin had inflicted on him an hour ago, but he obediently escorted her through the maritime twilight toward a small sandy island called Ruffle Bar. Overhead, a 747 ascended from JFK Airport, and Erin felt a sting of regret as she watched it bank to the east, headed for Europe. She could've been flying on that jet right now, sipping whiskey in the first-class cabin, instead of bouncing across the choppy bay with a silent bald goon who surely wanted to strangle her. She'd made a rash choice, senselessly risky, maybe even suicidal. But Erin had a reckless hunger in her – what Irishwoman didn't? – and she'd glimpsed something similar in Angela. The mad queen of Prophecy had promised to satisfy Erin's most hopeless desire, and maybe that was worth a try, yes?

Soon they reached the shoreline of Ruffle Bar, which was littered with all the fetid crap that spilled from New York's sewers into the bay. Carl raised the outboard's propeller and beached the dinghy on a stretch of tarry sand, next to the rusty skeleton of a refrigerator. Erin kept one eye on him as they stepped out of the boat, because this deserted islet of sand and marsh grass would be the perfect place for Carl to exact his revenge and dump her body. But he merely scanned the horizon and pointed at a grove of low, scrubby trees about a hundred meters away.

'Stroman said he'd meet us there.' Carl scowled at the rendezvous point, then started walking in that direction. 'Tom's a paranoid asshole. Always does things the hard way.'

Erin followed him across the filthy beach and a hummocky weed-choked field that squelched under her sneakers. As they approached the clump of trees, she spotted a yellow kayak hidden under a green tarp, very nicely camouflaged. A few seconds later she saw the kayak's owner sitting under one of the trees, with his back against the trunk. He was a skinny fellow in his late thirties or early forties, wearing a ratty brown T-shirt and cutoff denim shorts. He looked like an aging surfer or a tropical castaway except for his extraordinary paleness, which suggested that this island adventure wasn't a typical activity for him. Another anomaly was the bulky black suitcase beside him. Carrying that thing in a kayak must've been a real bitch.

Tom Stroman stood up when he saw them coming. He waved them forward. 'Hurry! Get under the trees!'

Carl reluctantly quickened his pace while Erin bounded into the shade. Close up, she gave Stroman a more careful inspection, noticing his bad haircut, his unfashionable glasses, and the dandruff sprinkled on his T-shirt. She found it disturbing that Prophecy would have anything to do with this man. He looked entirely unprofessional.

'You're the equipment specialist, are you?' Frowning, she circled him. 'The local expert on the technical paraphernalia of homicide?'

He frowned too and turned to Carl. 'You're late. The park rangers always send a patrol boat to this side of the bay at seven o'clock, so we have to finish our business quickly.' He squinted behind the thick lenses of his glasses. 'What happened to your face?'

Carl ignored the question and removed a small package, tightly wrapped in black plastic, from the inside pocket of his blazer. It was a stack of bills, Erin guessed, probably twenty thousand dollars in hundreds; she was good at estimating the size of cash payments. Carl held the package in the air but pulled it back just as Stroman reached for it. 'Not yet. First let's see what's in that suitcase.'

Stroman didn't move. 'Where's Angela? She was supposed to be here.'

The two men glared at each other. Erin waited a few seconds, then sighed in irritation. *Men and their pissing contests.* She got Stroman's attention by snapping her fingers in front of his nose.

'Excuse me, Tommy boy? You don't need Angela now. You have me instead.' She edged closer and pointed at his suitcase. 'I'm the one who's going to use the equipment you're providing, see? So, I should be the one to inspect it.'

He studied her for a moment, his eyes wandering up and down, probably imagining her in the act of committing various types of assassination. He didn't seem overly surprised, for which Erin was grateful; she hated men who assumed she was biologically incapable of doing her job. But he had a condescending smirk that was almost as annoying. 'Look, whoever you are? This is complicated stuff, very advanced hardware. Angela has a background in research, so it's easier to explain these things to her.'

'Sorry to make your life difficult, love. But why don't you give it your best shot?'

Stroman hesitated. He pursed his chapped lips and wiped the sweat from his forehead. Then he knelt on the sandy soil beside the suitcase. 'Do you know anything about control algorithms? For swarm communication?'

'Now, now. I'm not planning to write a doctoral thesis about this.' Erin wagged her finger. 'I just need to know which buttons to push.'

'Without knowledge we're doomed. That's one of the things Angela taught me.' Stroman unlocked the suitcase. It opened like a clamshell, displaying a dozen shiny silver devices, each resting snugly in its own compartment. 'This is the drone swarm.'

Erin bent down low. The devices were the same size and shape as lipstick tubes, but when she looked closer she saw tiny ports and sensors at the tip of each tube, and metal flaps folded against the sides. 'Drones? These things can fly?'

Stroman picked up one of the tubes and tapped its flaps. 'It has retractable wings and propellers. They extend from the drone's fuselage after you launch it.' He pointed at a bigger device in the case, a cylinder about five centimeters wide and sixty centimeters long. 'That's the launch tube. You load the drones into it like bullets and fire away.'

'Well, Christ on a bike. Look at that.' Erin grinned wide. She didn't have a lot of experience with high-tech weaponry – an old-fashioned pistol with a silencer was usually sufficient for her needs, thank you very much – but she still appreciated the genius of the thing. 'And after you launch the drones, you pilot them with a remote control? I saw that on TV once.'

'No, that wouldn't be optimal for your kind of work.' Stroman gave her that condescending look again. 'If your target is in a dynamic environment – like a man in a crowd, surrounded by bodyguards – a remote operator could never guide the swarm effectively. Human reaction times are *way* too slow for that.'

Erin decided not to get insulted by his tone. Better to fawn and flatter and keep him talking. 'So how do you steer your swarm?'

'The navigation is autonomous. Once the sensors in the drones identify the target, they plot their own paths around the obstacles.' Stroman removed another drone from the display case and held it next to the first one. 'The drones also sense each other and adjust their trajectories accordingly. Each flies on a different route, guaranteeing that at least one of them will hit home.'

'But if they're autonomous, how do they recognize the target? Do you download a photo of the guy into the drones' software, so they'll know which person to go after?'

The question seemed to make Stroman uneasy. He bit his lip, looking sheepish now. 'Visual identification would be ideal, but that kind of software isn't quite up to snuff yet. The targeted person might try to obscure his face with a hat or sunglasses. There's too much chance of error.' He put the drones back in the case and removed a glass vial, about the size of a pill bottle. Inside the vial was a small mound of gray metallic specks. 'That's why this operation requires someone like you. If you dip your index finger into this pile of micro-transmitters, at least half a dozen will stick to your fingertip. Each is less than a millimeter wide, so they won't set off any alarms on an X-ray machine or body scanner.'

Erin smiled again. 'Let me guess the next step. I shake hands with the target? No, wait . . . I pat him on the back, right?'

Stroman nodded. 'You clandestinely place the transmitters near one of his vital organs. On his head, neck, back, or chest. Then you retreat from the target and one of your partners sends a radio signal that activates the microchips, which start broadcasting a beacon signal. Then your partner launches the drones, which home in on the beacon. You can launch them from as far as a mile away and they'll still detect the signal.'

'And the final step? Do the drones have explosive charges?' Erin pictured it, still smiling. Her face warmed and her belly tingled. Her excitement was sharp and sweet, almost sexual. 'It would make a grand fireworks show, so it would.'

'But then you'd have collateral damage. To anyone standing nearby.' Stroman reached once again for the display case and removed a slender spike, about ten centimeters long. 'Instead, you attach these things to the noses of the drones. That turns it into a surgical strike. And I mean "surgical" in the most literal sense. The drones will be diving in so fast they'll tear right through skin and bone.'

The tingling in her belly intensified, spreading up and down. Her muscles tensed and her mouth watered. She noticed Stroman staring at her with renewed interest, and he no longer seemed so annoying. Sure, the boyo was as ugly as a bucket of snots, but Erin had to admire anyone who could dream up such a clever killing machine. 'So, you invented this thing on your own, did you? In your private little workshop?'

Stroman shrugged. 'Some of the hardware came from my contact at the Naval Research Lab. The Navy has a low-cost drone program called LOCUST.' His voice bubbled with false modesty. 'But yeah, I modified the weaponry for the new purpose. That's my specialty.'

'Ah, brilliant. A tinkerer. Were you in the Navy yourself once upon a time?'

Before Stroman could answer, Carl cleared his throat, making an unpleasant phlegmy grunt. 'Shouldn't we wrap this up? Didn't you say that a patrol boat was coming around soon?'

Stroman looked at his watch. 'Uh, yeah. But we still have forty minutes.'

Erin gave Carl her most withering stare. 'Why don't you stand lookout until we finish talking? You can do that, right?'

Carl curled his upper lip but didn't say anything. Erin took Stroman's arm, gripping it gently above the elbow, and moved a few steps away. She needed more information from him, and she didn't want Carl to overhear. 'Sorry about that. He's a right gobdaw, isn't he?'

Stroman nodded and smiled. 'Yeah, sure, whatever that means. Anyway, to answer your question, I never served in the Navy, but I used to work for Boeing's defense and security division. Before that, I was a physics post-doc at Columbia.'

Erin raised her eyebrows, pretending to be impressed. 'And how did you become acquainted with Angela? She used to work at Boeing too?'

'No, no, I met her at Columbia. Angela was a field zoologist in the bio department.'

'A zoologist? Well, that makes sense, I suppose. She fell in love with the little creatures of the field and forest? And she got upset when she saw them all dying off?'

Stroman stopped smiling. He seemed offended on Angela's behalf. 'You shouldn't make fun of her. Angela is the most remarkable person I know. She's the only one brave enough to take the necessary steps.'

'Oh, I agree. She's remarkable, all right.' For a moment Erin thought of the meeting in the subway car and the unnerving look on Angela's face when she proved she knew everything about Erin's father. It was disturbing and distracting and confusing as hell, and so Erin pushed the memory away. 'How did Angela recruit you? I get the feeling you're not just doing this for the money?'

'That's right. I'm doing it for the future.' Stroman swept his arm in a circle, gesturing at the marshes around them. 'Angela can see what's going to happen here. If we don't put a stop to carbon emissions *right now*, every bay and harbor on every seacoast will be inundated. Angela can see it all, the islands and beaches submerged, the millions of people drowned or homeless or starving.' He looked Erin in the eye. 'She sees it, she knows it *for a fact*. All those people will die if we stay on the same course. And if you're absolutely certain of that, wouldn't you do *anything* to stop it?'

He furrowed his pale brow, and his eyes narrowed behind his glasses. He gave her the firm, fierce gaze of a true believer, a look that Erin was all too familiar with. She stared back at him, frowning, suspicious of his certainty. 'You said you studied physics, correct? And you still believe Angela can see the future?'

His gaze didn't waver. 'I studied quantum physics. And the main principle behind the theory is that different versions of reality can exist simultaneously. What we call the universe is just the most probable distribution of those realities.' He raised his hand and tapped his forehead. 'Physicists also theorize that brain cells use sub-atomic quantum interactions to generate thoughts and create a sense of consciousness, a mind. And out of all the billions of human minds on the planet, it's inevitable that at least one of them will be especially well-tuned to the fundamental interactions. So, the thoughts generated by that mind will align with the probabilities of the universe, allowing that person to recognize our most likely futures.'

Erin didn't understand him. She couldn't make heads or tails of it. He'd gone deep into the weeds of esoteric science, and Erin's inclination was simply to dismiss whatever shite the guy was spouting. But that wasn't so easy to do. Stroman clearly knew his physics, and he didn't strike her as a bullshit artist. In short, Erin was unsettled. She didn't like the fact that a scientific explanation for Angela's prophecies was possible.

She was about to probe a little deeper, maybe ask Stroman what the hell a quantum interaction was, when Carl cleared his motherfucking throat again. The bald goon stomped toward them. 'Time to go. I think I heard a boat engine.'

Erin cocked her head and listened. Utter silence. But she was cautious by nature – what assassin wasn't? – so she took Carl's warning seriously. She stooped over Stroman's suitcase and closed it. Then she pointed at the plastic-wrapped stack of cash that Carl still held in his right hand. 'Go ahead and pay the man. I have what I need.'

As Erin hefted the suitcase, Carl tossed the cash to Stroman, who clumsily caught it. The boyo seemed a bit flustered now, a bit disappointed maybe. It occurred to Erin that the poor fellow had taken a shine to her. She flashed him a smile as a parting gift. 'It was a pleasure doing business with you, Tommy. Let's hope your little contraptions perform as well as advertised.'

'Oh, they will.' He nodded reassuringly. 'The operation will be successful. Angela saw that, too.'

Erin turned away from him. She was far from reassured.

NINE

Sonya Mirsky hated to admit that her father was right about anything, but this time he definitely was. She should never have trusted Jason Torricelli.

The irrefutable evidence of her mistake was the silver baling wire that bound her hands behind her back and trussed her ankles. Also, the grease-stained rag tied around her face to gag her. The most painful thing, though, was the sight of Janet Page, her dad's sometime girlfriend, sitting on the floor near her and restrained in the same brutal way.

They were in a solitary-confinement cell in an honest-to-God prison. Sonya sat with her back against the cinderblock wall, next to the cell's steel toilet, while Janet sat close to the heavy gray door with the sliding panel for delivering prison meals. And Sonya knew exactly which prison it was: the Arthur Kill Correctional Facility on Staten Island. New York State had closed down the penitentiary long ago and sold it to a film-production company that occasionally used it as a set for movies and TV shows, which was how Sonya had identified the place. When Jason and his buddies had hauled her out of their van and into the building, she'd immediately recognized the cellblocks from the final two seasons of *Orange Is the New Black*.

Sonya fumed. The situation was fucked. She had no idea who Jason was working for, but they were obviously people who knew what they were doing. An abandoned prison was an ingenious place for kidnappers to stow their captives. Except for the infrequent periods when it was used as a movie set, it was empty and secure. Sonya doubted that the cops would *ever* come looking for her there.

Worst of all, she'd been so damn naïve! She'd met Jason for the first time only a week ago, at a meeting of the student activist club she'd started, NYU for Climate Action. During the meeting she mentioned the anonymous online threats she was getting in advance of her planned speech at the UN, and Jason offered to organize a group to protect her. He was a big guy, with plenty of tattoos on his arms, and although she'd heard some disquieting rumors from her friends – Jason was failing all his classes, they said, and his father owned an eco-unfriendly garbage-hauling company – Sonya took him up on his offer. The vile slurs from the right-wing trolls on Twitter and Reddit had truly scared her. In retrospect, she wondered if Jason himself had posted some of them.

And there were more warning signs. When Jason introduced her to his 'protection squad' just a few hours ago, she didn't recognize any of his three brawny friends, even though they all claimed to be NYU students. They were quiet and cagey as they accompanied her to Central Park, and they stayed in the background when Sonya confronted her father and when the FBI agents came to arrest him. But as soon as the men in suits marched off with her dad, Jason told Sonya they should get in his van and follow the agents' unmarked car, and he urged Janet to come too. There were so many goddamn questions Sonya should've asked then – for instance, why was his van parked so conveniently nearby? – but at that point she couldn't think straight, she was too worried about her father. She didn't grasp the danger until she and Janet were already in the back of the van and Jason brought out the baling wire.

Her self-disgust grew with each passing minute in the cramped cell. In all likelihood, her kidnappers were alt-right militants who'd decided to shut her up. In their perverse quest to deny the reality of global warming, they'd found a way to stop her from shouting the truth at the UN's General Assembly. Gullible and oblivious, she'd fallen right into their trap, and she'd dragged poor Janet down with her. And what would happen next? Would the fanatics be content simply to frighten her? Would they wait until the UN conference was over and then release her and Janet? Or would they want to make an example of them?

Sonya cursed her stupidity, mouthing obscenities behind her gag. Then she started banging the back of her head against the wall, harder and harder. Janet's eyes widened in alarm above her own gag, but Sonya wouldn't stop. She looked up at the security camera on the ceiling, glowering at its lens, silently daring her kidnappers to return to the cell and intervene.

But when the heavy door finally slid open, neither Jason nor any of his friends stepped inside. Instead, a tall middle-aged woman in an olive-green jumpsuit peered into the cell. She seemed disheveled and unglamorous, her face blanched and devoid of makeup, her black hair tangled and curling in all directions. It looked like she hadn't slept in days, but at the same time she projected a serene confidence, like an astronaut who'd just steered her crippled spaceship back to Earth. Her eyes were darkest blue, the color of deep space, and the intensity of her gaze made Sonya sit up straight and stop hurting herself.

'My name is Angela. Sorry to keep you waiting, Ms Mirsky.' Her voice, clipped and impersonal, echoed against the cell's walls. 'I've been busy today. I know everyone says this when they're running late, but in my case it's true.'

At first Sonya was too stunned to move. *Who the hell is this woman? Why does she talk like a robot and dress like a car mechanic?* It was such a strange combination that Sonya didn't know how to respond. *If she takes off my gag, what should I do? Plead for mercy? Scream like a banshee?* Neither strategy seemed too promising.

After a moment, though, Sonya decided to scream, and she didn't wait for the gag to come off. Staring at Angela, she shrieked as loudly as she could, high-pitched and wordless. It seared her throat, screaming like that, and very little of the sound made it through the thick rag, just a low, desperate whine. But Sonya kept it up, stopping for only an instant between shrieks to take a breath. She did it partly to express her outrage and partly in the hope that someone else would hear her.

Angela's reaction was underwhelming. The screaming didn't seem to bother her or make her curious. She stepped forward, neither frowning nor smiling, and then she lowered her gaze and examined Janet, who'd backed into the corner of the cell. Angela held out her hands and patted the air, a gesture apparently intended to be calming. 'It's all right, Ms Page. I owe you an apology too. This experience must be upsetting.'

Janet cringed on the floor, pulling her knees to her chest. Angela stared at her for a few more seconds, then turned back to Sonya and waited for her to stop screaming. The woman folded her arms across her chest and stood there like a statue, patient and blank.

About a minute passed before Sonya concluded she was getting nowhere. She quieted down, and in response Angela stepped forward again. The woman sat on the edge of the cell's shelflike bed and leaned toward Sonya until their faces were just inches apart.

'I'll remove your gag if you promise not to scream anymore. I have sensitive ears. And you've probably realized by now that there's no one in the building except my associates.' She reached for the back of Sonya's head, where the corners of the rag were knotted together. 'Please nod if you agree to those terms.'

Sonya grimaced, but after a few seconds she nodded. She took a deep breath as Angela untied the foul cloth and set it aside. Then, struggling to stay calm, Sonya jutted her chin in Janet's direction. 'Now take off *her* gag.'

Angela shook her head. 'You're my primary concern right now, Ms Mirsky. Once we finish talking, I'll move on to Ms Page.'

The conversation was already going badly. Sonya needed to assert control, or at least make it clear that Angela couldn't bully her. 'OK, let's do this fast. What do you want from me?'

'First, I'd like to say I have nothing personal against you. In fact, I think your story is inspiring.' Angela leaned back, settling into a more comfortable position on the bed. Her nonchalance was disturbing. 'Over the past year you've reinvigorated the climate-change movement. You've reinvented it for a new generation and greatly increased its appeal to young people like yourself. You seem especially adept at drawing media attention to your clever protests and carbon-neutral strategies.'

Sonya couldn't believe it. This woman didn't sound like an alt-right militant. She was talking more like an interviewer for *People* magazine. She had the same flattering tone and used the same insincere verbiage. 'I'm sorry, I don't understand. What the hell are you trying to say?'

'I've thought a great deal about why you've received so much publicity. I believe the reason is the contrast between the huge importance of your planet-saving message and your slight, inoffensive appearance. People find it interesting to watch a pretty young woman confront the powerful fossil-fuel interests. It's like the story of David and Goliath, the silly myth that has entertained and heartened people for thousands of years.'

'Excuse me? I still don't—'

'Please, let me finish. My point is that your strategy is temporarily appealing but ultimately ineffective. People enjoy rooting for you when you're speaking out at shareholder meetings and testifying before congressional committees, but that admiration isn't enough to force the corporations and politicians to change their ways. Did you hear what the senior senator from West Virginia said after your last protest in Washington?'

Sonya stared at her. The woman was insanely single-minded. Or maybe plain insane. 'Look, you—'

'The senator said, "I deeply respect Ms Mirsky's passion and intelligence. I believe this young woman will someday accomplish great things. But the Green New Deal policies she's advocating would devastate West Virginia." You see what he did? He essentially joined your fan club while opposing everything you stand for.'

'Angela? Can I get a word in?' Sonya looked her in the eye. 'Please tell me why you kidnapped us. If you don't, I'm gonna start screaming again.'

'All right, I'll tell you. I want you to consider switching to a more effective method of climate activism. Specifically, the method *I'm* pursuing.' Angela pointed at herself, at the lumpy front of her jumpsuit. 'Inspirational stories won't stop the capitalists and plutocrats from slow-roasting the planet. Rational discussion won't sway them either, because they love their short-term profits and pleasures much more than they care about future generations. No, the only effective strategy is deterrence. We have to make the capitalists afraid for their lives. If they know we'll kill them for destroying the Earth, they'll stop doing it.'

For the first time since Sonya laid eyes on her, Angela displayed a smidgen of emotion, a barely perceptible smile. She seemed pleased by her own rhetoric, by the unassailable logic of her argument. But Sonya noticed something else in her expression, a twitch of righteous triumph, and she realized then that this woman wasn't just pontificating.

Angela nodded. 'Yes, I think you understand. I ordered the

killing of Hollister Tarkington and Jonathan Humphrey. For the sake of a better future. Nothing but green!'

Sonya's stomach clenched. She felt nauseous and horrified. She looked across the jail cell and saw that Janet's reaction was similar – her eyes widened and the rag over her mouth shuddered rapidly, in time with her hyperventilating breath. It was bad enough to be bound and gagged and thrown into a jail cell, but it was much worse to share that cell with a murderer, especially one who seemed so proud of her crimes.

Angela turned her head, examining both of her captives, clearly waiting for them to absorb her piece of news. After a long while, she broke the silence.

'We're in this fight together, my friends, and much more work needs to be done. We have to make it clear that every corporate chieftain in the world is vulnerable, no matter how many precautions they take.' She focused on Sonya, leaning forward from the edge of the prison bed, training those deep-space eyes on her. 'Our next targets are the three men at the very top of the list your father drew up. I've allowed them some time to realize they've been targeted, and now they're doing everything they can to protect themselves. They've already demanded that the FBI give this case the highest priority, and I'm sure they're hiring squads of new bodyguards. But it won't do them any good.'

Sonya tried to squirm away, but she was already backed up against the base of the wall. She pressed her spine against the concrete, her bound hands going numb behind the small of her back.

Angela reached toward her. She placed a cold hand on Sonya's cheek. 'Don't worry. We're allies. You're going to help me prepare for the battle.' She moved her hand slightly, caressing Sonya's face. Her fingertips felt like sandpaper. 'All three of our remaining targets are in New York City right now, since they're participating in the United Nations conference. And they're so arrogantly confident in their security measures, all of them will stay in New York despite the danger. I can say this with perfect certainty, Sonya, because I know exactly what will happen to those men. I've already seen their final moments.'

Sonya shrank from her touch. She would've screamed again, but she could hardly breathe.

Angela moved her hand to Sonya's hair and adjusted one of her dangling cornrows, tucking it behind her ear. 'Here's what I want from you. I need to stir up trouble on the city's streets, riots and looting near the UN building, a heightened level of chaos. It'll divert the New York police force and allow my assassin to operate more freely. And you can help me do that with just a few words, Sonya. I'll give you a script and we'll make a video, and then we'll post it on the internet.' She tilted her head in a beseeching way, but the look on her face was implacable. 'Do you think you can help me with that?'

Silence fell as Angela waited for an answer. The jail cell became so quiet that Sonya could hear her pulse pounding in her ears. Her mouth was dry and her throat was sore and she felt like she was going to vomit. But she had to answer the question.

'What . . . what do you want me . . . to say in the video?'

Angela looked pleased. 'It's very simple. You'll go on camera and say you were abducted by a gang of right-wing gunmen, like the ones in Michigan who almost kidnapped their governor. You'll say the kidnappers plan to hold you hostage until the protesters in New York cancel their climate-change demonstrations and leave the city. Of course, the video will have the opposite effect on the protesters. They'll become enraged at the mistreatment of their beloved figurehead by thuggish climate-change deniers. They'll take out their anger on the police, the government, the businesses, the whole system. The resulting uproar will give us the cover we need to carry out our operation.'

There was another stretch of silence. Angela kept staring at her with that implacable expression, hard and determined and self-assured. She was probably waiting for Sonya to praise the cleverness of her plan, and that would perhaps be the safest way to respond. Except the plan wasn't clever. It was an utter disaster.

Sonya swallowed hard. She had to push down her fear and nausea. She needed to sound reasonable. 'What do you think will happen . . . after you've eliminated your targets?'

'I *know* what will happen. Thousands of chief executives and politicians will quit their jobs and go into hiding. The leaders who remain at the corporations and government bodies will finally get serious about slashing carbon emissions and slowing climate change. They'll do the right thing for future generations because they'll know that we'll kill them if they don't.'

'So, your organization will keep threatening leaders with assassination, indefinitely?' Sonya struggled to stay calm, to speak in a steady voice without any trace of incredulity. 'You think you can keep killing people for years and years, even though every police force in the country will be hunting for you?'

'Oh, yes.' Angela nodded. 'In fact, Prophecy will grow in numbers and power. We'll attract hundreds of dedicated recruits to conduct our missions. I see that very clearly in all my revelations.'

Sonya was at a loss. If she'd heard about Angela's plan in a different setting – if, say, she'd read about it in the newspaper – it would've been easy to laugh and dismiss it. But Sonya was at the woman's mercy, so she had to be tactful. 'Let me see if I understand what you're saying. You have visions of the future?'

'They're more than visions. They're detailed prophecies of the most likely futures branching ahead of us. I can see the good things that'll happen if we take bold steps, as well as the catastrophe of inaction.' Angela kept nodding, vigorously confirming her own statements. 'I can't explain why I have this ability. My friends in the neuroscience field were dumbfounded when I mentioned it. Some of my physicist friends say it might have something to do with quantum theory and the nature of consciousness, but I'm not sure about that. All I know for sure is that my prophecies are reliable. When it comes to predicting major events, I'm never wrong.'

Sonya nodded along with her, trying to be agreeable. 'OK, I respect that. You have faith in yourself. But you can see why other people might be skeptical, right?'

Angela frowned. She went still and narrowed her eyes. 'Yes, I see. You're saying *you're* skeptical.'

'I'm sorry, but I can't see the future, so I don't feel as confident about your odds of success. There's a good chance that your plan might just make the situation worse.' Sonya took a deep breath. 'For that reason, I'd rather not participate in your video.'

Angela said nothing for a good long while. Then, to Sonya's dismay, she shrugged. 'Well, it doesn't matter what you think. You're going to make the video whether you want to or not.'

Sonya should've been terrified. *Is she going to hold a gun to my head? Or torture me if I don't cooperate? Angela seems crazy enough to do it.* But for some reason Sonya wasn't frightened now. She'd pushed past her fear and realized that the only sensible option was defiance. She was incensed and disgusted and wanted nothing more to do with this visionary nutcase.

'Go fuck yourself. I'm not going to help you.'

Angela let out a sigh. She showed no anger, but she looked disappointed, shaking her head as she stared at Sonya. After a few seconds she stood up and reached into one of her jumpsuit's pockets. 'Well, I tried my best. Now you'll see why I abducted Ms Page along with you.'

She pulled something out of her pocket and flicked her wrist. A switchblade flashed under the jail cell's fluorescent lights.

Then she went to the corner of the cell, bent over Janet, and grabbed her by the hair.

TEN

Max leapt from his living-room couch as soon as he heard the intercom buzz. He sprinted past Agents Wilson and Martinez, who'd set up a miniature command post in his kitchen, and dashed out of his apartment, which was on the brownstone's second floor. His heart banging, he raced down the building's stairway toward the ground-floor vestibule, hoping against hope that Sonya and Janet stood on the other side of the brownstone's front door.

But it wasn't his daughter or his girlfriend. Standing on the stoop in the twilight was Nathan Carver, dressed in his usual old-guy-trying-to-look-cool outfit – a black hoodie, a backwards baseball cap. He carried a brown-paper bag from the Shake Shack on West 77th Street.

Max opened the door and attempted to smile. 'Hey.'

Nathan rushed forward and hugged him. 'I brought you some burgers. Oh my God, this is so horrible. How are you holding up?' He took a step back and gave Max a once-over. 'Shit, you look wiped out. Is that the T-shirt from the *West Side Story* number?'

Max looked down at his clothes. He'd taken off the stupid leather jacket when he got home an hour ago, but he hadn't changed out of the white T-shirt and tattered jeans. His fear had made him fuzzyheaded. He'd been in a daze ever since he left the Federal Building. 'Yeah, you're right. I'm a mess.'

'Is there any news?'

'Nothing positive since I called you.' Max had already telephoned everyone in the Doomsday troupe to tell them that Sonya and Janet were missing. 'A bunch of cops went to Central Park, asking everyone if they saw a pair of women matching their descriptions. One kid said he saw them getting into a black van, but he couldn't give the cops a license number.'

'Jesus. So it's definitely a kidnapping?'

'Looks like it.' Max shuddered, the truth kicking him in the gut again. He had to lean against the doorframe for balance.

Nathan bit his lip. ‘Come on, let’s go upstairs.’ He wrapped an arm around Max’s shoulders and gently turned him around. ‘We gotta eat these burgers before they get cold.’

Max let himself be nudged up the stairway. Wilson, the bigger of the two FBI agents, waited at the top of the steps, keeping watch. Nathan stared back at him, then twisted his lips into a goofy, theatrical grin. ‘Top of the evening, officer!’

Wilson blocked their path and pointed at Nathan. ‘I recognize you. I saw you in the park today, doing your song-and-dance routine.’

Nathan’s elastic face shifted to a look of mock horror. ‘Please! I’m not giving autographs now!’

Wilson pulled a notepad out of his blazer and leafed through its pages. ‘Your name is Carver, right? White male, forty-nine years old? Manager of information technology at Golden Key Advertising?’

‘Precisely.’ Nathan gave him a deep, formal bow. ‘I’m here to share a pleasant meal with my fellow thespian. May I pass?’

Wilson stayed where he was. ‘Let me ask you a question first, Carver. Are you active in any environmentalist groups? Besides the street-theater company, I mean?’

‘Ah, I see. You want to know if I’m a card-carrying member of the Climate Avengers. Isn’t that the name they’ve started using on CNN? To refer to the people who bumped off Tarkington and Humphrey?’

‘Just answer the question, please.’

‘I plead the Fifth, sir. Now I believe it’s your constitutional duty to get the fuck out of my face?’

Wilson frowned mightily, but after a moment he stepped aside and let them return to the apartment. Agent Martinez, standing in the apartment’s doorway, also gave them a hard look as they passed by. Nathan saluted him with the hand holding the Shake Shack bag, then led Max into the dining room.

They sat at the end of the dining-room table that was farthest away from the agents’ post in the kitchen. As Nathan noisily unwrapped the hamburgers, he leaned close to Max and whispered, ‘Why the hell are those G-men here?’

Max lowered his voice too. ‘In case I get a call from the

kidnappers. The agents said they need to be here to trace the location of the caller.'

Nathan raised one of his eyebrows and lowered the other. It was one of his comic expressions, a look denoting disbelief. 'They're bullshitting you, my man. They don't have to be in your apartment to monitor your phone line.'

'They don't?'

Nathan put one of the burgers in front of Max and picked up the other. 'No, that changed thirty years ago.' He bit into his burger and spoke with his mouth full. 'The phone companies redesigned their networks to make it easy for the government to trace and wiretap calls. The agents can listen in from their headquarters.'

Max thought it over. Nathan was an expert on all technical issues, thanks to his day job, so Max had no reason to doubt him. But he didn't want to start doubting the agents either, because he was counting on them to find Sonya and Janet. 'Well, they also said they'll give me instructions during the call. You know, they'll tell me how to respond to the kidnappers' demands.'

Nathan's eyebrows were still lopsided. 'That's also bullshit. They're here to keep an eye on you.' He lowered his voice again. 'You said the FBI treated you like a suspect, right? All those questions they asked about your emails?'

Max nodded. In his phone call with Nathan earlier that evening he'd described the scene in the interrogation room. 'Yeah, they were suspicious at first. Especially the commander, Agent Reyes. But by the end I convinced her I wasn't involved with the fanatics.'

'Are you sure about that? Maybe the agents are still suspicious. Maybe they're watching you because they think you'll lead them to the Climate Avengers. Believe me, that seems to be a lot more important to them than finding Sonya and Janet.'

Max stared at his untouched hamburger. He didn't want to admit it, but Nathan was right: the FBI wasn't making much progress on the kidnapping case. Their agents couldn't locate Jason Torricelli, the NYU fuckster who'd befriended Sonya; he'd disappeared along with his father, the garbage-hauling kingpin. Maybe the lack of progress was simply bad luck, but it was also clear that rescuing Sonya and Janet wasn't the FBI's number one priority. The government was a thousand times more concerned about protecting the three bastards at the top of Max's climate criminals list.

Nathan swiftly finished off his own burger, then leaned closer to Max. 'I'll tell you something else: it's not just the emails. The Feds have another reason for suspecting you.' He reached into the Shake Shack bag and pulled out a large order of fries. 'Ask yourself this: why did these Climate Avengers rely on *your* article when they were drawing up their hit list? There are a million other articles they could've used. Do you have any idea how many worst-polluter lists there are?'

Max looked askance. 'What are you talking about?'

'I looked it up on the web, right after I got off the phone with you. I googled "climate criminals" and scrolled through the search results.' He grabbed a fistful of French fries. 'All the results on the top pages were from the major websites, stories on CNN and the *New York Times* and *USA Today*. There was an article titled "Worst Climate Criminals" on *National Geographic*'s website, and just below it was a *ScienceDaily* story with the exact same headline. But *your* article, the one in the *Journal of Climatology*? It was way down in the search rankings, on the very bottom of page twenty-nine.'

'Well, that's not surprising.' Max felt himself getting defensive. 'Stories on the popular websites always show up higher in the rankings.'

'And get this: when I clicked on the *Climatology* link to read your story, I couldn't even access it. I got a message saying I had to pay four hundred dollars for a subscription.'

'That shouldn't be surprising either. Most of the serious science journals operate that way. And that's what started the whole email exchange in the first place, because the fanatics asked me to send them a free copy of my story.'

'But why did they go to all that trouble?' Nathan dropped his fries on the table and raised his hands in bewilderment. 'Why would terrorist lunatics spend so much time and effort on research? Why not just use the list of climate criminals that the *New York Times* published, or the one in *USA Today*?'

'Because my list is better!' Max's voice rose. 'I worked for months on that fucking story. I calculated every goddamn ton of carbon emissions that each of those bastards was responsible for.'

'OK, OK! Keep it down!' Looking worried, Nathan craned his neck and glanced at the entrance to the kitchen. Fortunately, neither of the FBI agents emerged. After several seconds, he turned back to Max and drew close. 'Listen, I know how smart you are, but the agents don't. To them, you're just a clown, and they can't understand why the terrorists contacted you. So they must assume you have another connection with the bad guys.'

Max pushed his hamburger across the table so he wouldn't have to keep staring at it. Although he appreciated Nathan's good intentions, his friend had only given him something else to worry about. In all likelihood, the FBI *was* surveilling him. Instead of searching for Sonya and Janet, the agents were probably scouring his apartment for clues, looking for 'another connection.' Meanwhile, his daughter was probably freaking out in some remote cabin or basement, maybe tied to a mattress, maybe pleading for her life. And his girlfriend, if she was in the same place as Sonya, was probably trying to calm her and praying for rescue.

Imagining it, even for just a second, was agony. Max lowered his head and rubbed his eyes, trying to stop himself from seeing it. *Fuck! I can't just sit here! I need to do something!*

Then the intercom buzzed again.

This time, Agent Martinez stayed with Max and Nathan in the apartment while Agent Wilson went down to the ground floor to see who the visitor was. Soon Max heard the sounds of a heated argument downstairs, dominated by a familiar Doomsday trouper's voice whose shrill decibels went right through the brownstone's walls. Then the apartment's door swung open and Adele barged inside, with Wilson in hot pursuit. The ex-ballerina was half the size of the federal agent, but it looked like she was ready to tear him apart. Her face blazed with fury, as pink as a Spaldeen, and her chest heaved inside her yoga top.

'Max! Are you all right?' She gave him a look that was half concern, half outrage. Then she pointed over her shoulder at Wilson. 'What kind of Nazi bullshit is this? Are the cops imprisoning you in your own apartment? Do they think they can dictate who has the right to visit you?'

While Adele shouted her rhetorical questions, Larry and Eileen followed her into the apartment, brushing past the FBI agent in the doorway. Larry caught up to Adele and stood silently beside her, which was his default position in their relationship. Eileen lagged behind and lingered near Wilson, looking him up and down before she sashayed into the dining room. She wore a red body-hugging dress that was a little risqué for this type of gathering.

Nathan stood up and wiped his hands on his pants. ‘Well, well. I’m glad you could all make it.’ He tapped Max’s shoulder to get his attention. ‘I thought you could use some company, so I invited everyone here. You don’t mind, do you?’

Max shook his head. He was touched by their concern. His eyes stung as he stared at all his friends gathered around the dining-room table, loyal and caring and eager to help. And at the same time he felt a jolt of hope, because he’d just realized how the Doomsday Company could help him. He had the beginnings of a plan.

But he didn’t want the FBI agents to hear it. Max rose from his chair. ‘Hey, guys? Can we move this party to the bedroom?’

Nathan grinned. ‘What exactly do you have in mind? We’re here for you, buddy, but there are limits, you know.’

Max grabbed Nathan’s arm and pulled him out of the dining room. ‘I just want to show you something.’ He jerked his head toward the kitchen, where the agents had returned to their post, although he wasn’t sure if his friends would get the hint. ‘It won’t take long.’

One by one, they filed into the bedroom, which wasn’t in the best shape for visitors. In the six weeks since Max and Janet had put their relationship on hold, he’d stopped making his bed and picking up his clothes. Nathan and Larry didn’t seem too disturbed by the mess, but Adele made a face as she entered the room and Eileen refused to take more than a couple of steps inside. She pointed at a pile of socks and underwear on the floor. ‘That’s a real turn-off, Max.’

Max kicked the pile under his bed, then stepped toward Eileen. ‘Sorry about this. I brought you in here because I’m worried about the agents listening in on us. And you can help me with that, actually.’ He sidled closer to her. ‘Could you go back to the kitchen and chat up those goons? I want to make sure they don’t press their ears to the wall. And while you’re at it, see if you can get some useful information from them. You know, the timing of their shifts, the names of the other agents on the case, that kind of thing.'

Eileen's eyes lit up. It was as if she'd just won an audition. 'I'm on it!' She tossed her platinum-blond hair behind her shoulder, already playing the role of the glamorous spy. Then she spun around and left the bedroom, and Max closed the door behind her.

He did some more last-minute tidying, clearing the tangled blankets off the bed so Nathan and Adele and Larry could sit down. Max stood opposite, bent over them, like a football coach huddling with his team.

'OK, here's the situation.' He lowered his voice. 'The FBI isn't doing enough to find Janet and Sonya. We'll have to force those bureaucratic assholes to give the kidnapping just as much attention as they're giving the Climate Avengers.'

Adele leaned forward, jumpy and zealous. She balanced on the edge of the bed, ready to leap into action. 'What do you have in mind? A protest at the FBI headquarters?' She turned to Larry. 'It's a good idea, don't you think? We can go to Central Park and talk to the kids who are camped out there. Once we spread the news about Sonya and Janet, they'll be royally pissed. They'll march downtown with us and raise fucking hell!'

Larry started to say something, most likely an expression of enthusiastic approval, but Nathan waved his hand to cut him off. 'Wait, let's think this through. The FBI hasn't even announced the news of the kidnappings yet.' He trained his eyes on Max. 'Did the agents tell you why they're keeping it quiet?'

Max nodded. 'They said they're not a hundred percent sure it's a kidnapping, since they haven't heard anything from the kidnappers yet. Which is bullshit, if you ask me.' As he talked, he grew more and more indignant. Some of Adele's outrage had flooded into him. 'Why would Sonya voluntarily go into hiding just a day before her big speech at the UN? And why would Janet go with her?'

'You're right, it makes no sense.' Nathan shook his head.

'But there's nothing stopping *us* from going to the news media, right?' Max was thinking out loud, looking at the strategy from all angles. 'Spreading the news of the kidnapping won't hurt

Sonya and Janet. If anything, it'll help. We want everyone to be on the lookout for them. So let's prepare a statement for the press.' He turned back to Adele. 'You seem to have some fervent opinions about the FBI, so you should write the first draft. Just make sure you stress the unfairness of it all, OK? You can say something like, "The FBI is throwing all its resources at the Climate Avengers, sending hundreds of agents to New York to keep the billionaire polluters safe and sound, and meanwhile they're doing virtually *nothing* for two ordinary women in extraordinary danger." And so on and so forth. Got it?'

'Fuck yeah!' Adele whipped out her phone and started pecking at its screen. 'I'll write it right now. It'll be ready in ten minutes.'

Max was pleased. He'd found a good use for Adele's never-ending indignation. Then he moved on to Nathan. 'I have a job for you too. Until the Feds get off their asses and start doing their detective work, we'll have to do it ourselves. Do you feel up to it?'

'Of course!' Nathan beamed. 'I was born to be a gumshoe! Do you have any idea how many times I've watched *The Maltese Falcon*?'

'This is more of a high-tech investigation. I need your computer expertise.' Max took out his iPhone and clicked on a Twitter link he'd saved. He turned the phone around and showed Nathan the web page, which displayed all the #SonyaMirsky tweets. 'Dozens of people on Twitter posted anonymous threats against my daughter. Is there any way you can dig up their internet records? I'm thinking that maybe one of those repulsive motherfuckers was involved in the kidnapping.'

'Absolutely.' Nathan's voice turned serious. 'I can figure out their IP addresses, or at least some of them. There's a standard procedure – you send a tweet that lures them to a site that grabs identifying data about their hardware.'

'And that reveals their names?'

'Not exactly. The personal information is hidden better. But I have my ways. I can track down those Twitter trolls. Then we can give their names to the FBI and make sure that the agents start knocking on their doors.'

'Thank you, Nathan. That would be a tremendous help.' Max swallowed hard, feeling an unexpected surge of emotion. Although he'd always admired his fellow Doomsday troupers for their onstage talents, until now he'd never realized how capable they were offstage as well. Max's friends were rising to the challenge, working together to help him. He was impressed and grateful.

Last but not least, he focused on Larry. 'OK, your turn. Your day job is at an investment firm, right? You analyze stocks for them?'

Larry squirmed, clearly uncomfortable. He didn't talk much about his job; when he did, Adele usually scowled and made a comment about the evils of capitalism. Now, though, Adele was busy composing their press release, her eyes glued to her phone's screen. Larry leaned toward Max. 'Yeah, that's my specialty. I make stock recommendations by examining the finances of each company. I go through their balance sheets, their quarterly reports. When I'm not singing or dancing, I'm a numbers guy, basically.'

'Perfect. Hold on a second.' Max stepped toward his bedroom closet and opened the door. 'I have some financial documents for you to analyze.'

Deep inside the closet, behind all the outdated suits and shirts hanging from the clothes rod, was a stack of cardboard boxes. Max kept talking as he wrestled one of the boxes out of the closet. 'I'm an old-fashioned journalist. I relied on paper records when I started working thirty years ago, and I haven't changed. I still write articles now and then, and when I'm done I store all my documents here.' With a great heave, he carried the box across the bedroom and dropped it in front of Larry. 'This contains all the records I dug up for the climate criminals story.'

Larry looked down at the box. 'I don't understand. How will this help us find Sonya and Janet?'

'Think about it. There must be a reason why the kidnapping happened at the same time as the Climate Avenger killings. And during my interrogation, the FBI agent said the two things might be connected. I told you about Jason Torricelli, right? The guy who hoodwinked Sonya? His father owns Torricelli Demolition, a garbage disposal company, and the Feds found a woman's body in one of the company's trucks. It was the masked woman who approached me at the Stygian Energy building and said her group had just poisoned Tarkington.'

Larry gave him a blank look. 'I still don't get it.'

'Look, I don't really understand it either, but the Climate Avengers are obviously using my article to pick their targets for assassination. And maybe there's a clue inside the research materials I collected for that story, something I missed. I found all kinds of financial records for the people on my climate criminals list, but some of the documents in that box were way too complicated for me. I bet you could analyze them a lot better.'

Larry still looked confused, but he opened the box anyway and started riffling through the papers. Nathan, though, seemed dissatisfied. He shook his head and frowned at Max. 'Sorry, but I don't buy your argument. Why would the climate terrorists kidnap activists like Sonya and Janet? It's much more likely that the kidnappers are right-wing reactionaries. You know, brain-dead yahoos trained by Fox News to hate immigrants, Democrats, and climate activists.'

'But what about the connection between the Climate Avengers and Torricelli Demolition? The masked woman's body in the garbage truck?'

Nathan let out a dismissive snort. 'That's not much of a connection. It's probably just a coincidence. I've seen the trucks from Torricelli Demolition, they're everywhere. If you have a body you need to dump, where else are you gonna put it?'

While Max considered this, Larry bent over and pulled a folder out of the cardboard box. 'You know, Max, I'd love to take a closer look at these documents. I once wrote a brokerage report on Jonathan Humphrey's company, Texxonoco, and it really turned my stomach. Humphrey was promoting all these university research projects, pretending he cared about the environment, but it was all just greenwashing. He told the press that the research was about cutting carbon emissions, but he was actually paying the scientists to figure out better ways to drill for natural gas.'

Max stared at the folder. He'd fixed on something Larry had said. 'Those research projects you're talking about? Was one of them at Columbia?'

Larry nodded. 'You know about it? It was a longtime project that started way back in the Eighties, I think. I don't know what it was called back then, but Humphrey gave it a new name, something that sounded more eco-friendly. Something with

"Green" in it.' Larry thought it over for a moment, looking up at the bedroom ceiling. Then he snapped his fingers. 'Yeah, it was "Nothing but Green."'

Max shivered. He'd seen that phrase today. It was in the email that the fanatics had sent him.

And he remembered it, just barely, from much farther back. Decades ago.

Nathan waved his hands at Max, trying to get his attention. 'Uh, Mirsky? You OK?' He stood up and stepped closer. 'Hey, snap out of it, buddy.'

But Max just stood there. *Nothing but green. Is that the connection?*

And he stayed in that trance until five seconds later, when Eileen burst into the bedroom. She headed straight for Max and clutched his arm. Her lovely face was wet with tears.

'Oh God.' With her other hand, she held up her phone. 'You need to see this.'

Nathan rushed to her side. 'What is it? What happened?'

She ignored him and stared at Max. 'The video from the kidnappers just went live. I saw the agents watching it on their laptop.' She raised her phone to eye level so he could view the screen. 'It's Sonya.'

ELEVEN

Aleida Reyes had seen plenty of shit storms in her career. When she was a Marine she'd served in Iraq and Afghanistan, and when she was a rookie agent at the Bureau's Los Angeles office she'd infiltrated the city's biker gangs. But in terms of sheer chaos, nothing could match the thunderous mob that swept into Lower Manhattan at midnight and surrounded the Federal Building.

From where she stood, just outside the building's entrance, Reyes saw a long line of cops in riot gear. They were arrayed along the security perimeter, which stretched down Broadway and curved around the block. The harsh beams of the building's floodlights reflected off the cops' helmets and illuminated the yellow strips on their body armor. The officers stood behind the barricades at the perimeter, staring straight ahead, preparing for the onslaught. The mob was still streaming downtown, thousands of protesters flooding the streets, most wearing bandannas or balaclavas to hide their faces. Although they were chanting and screaming and taunting the cops, no one had thrown any bottles yet or rushed the barricades. But Reyes knew that all hell would break loose in a few minutes, and she needed to get out of there before that happened.

Assistant Director Hastings, the man in charge of the New York field office, stood twenty feet away, conferring with the NYPD captains who'd been called in to defend the FBI headquarters. He had to shout at the cops so they could hear his orders over the crowd noise, and his beefy face reddened under the floodlights. Then the police captains dispersed, and Reyes approached her boss, who didn't hide his displeasure when he saw her. Hastings was difficult enough under ordinary circumstances, and Reyes girded herself for hostilities as she stopped in front of him.

'Sir! I need to leave the field office and go uptown.' She spoke so loudly it hurt her own ears. 'I just got an urgent call from one of the VIPs who requested our protection.'

Hastings scowled and stepped toward her. He was adept at the old-school Bureau technique of using his bulk as a tool of intimidation, and now he loomed over Reyes, whom he outweighed by at least a hundred pounds. 'You can't leave. All the cars have been requisitioned. Go back to your office and handle it over the phone.'

'I've already arranged my transportation, sir.' Reyes pointed north. 'I instructed Agent Wilson to drive down here and pick me up. He left Martinez behind at the Mirsky apartment to continue the surveillance of the suspects there.'

Hastings stepped closer. She smelled onions on his breath. 'Now that you mention it, I have some concerns about that part of your investigation. It certainly didn't help the situation when Mirsky and his friends shot their mouths off to the press. Your agents couldn't stop them from interfering?'

Reyes wasn't surprised by the criticism. Her boss had no compunctions about second-guessing his subordinates. 'Sir, once the kidnappers released the video, Mirsky was bound to react. At that point, the demonstrations became inevitable.'

'Demonstrations? Is that what you call this?' He jutted his double chin toward Broadway, where the protesters were edging closer to the cops. 'It's more like the Alamo.'

He paused, waiting for a reaction. Like many of the FBI's top brass, Hastings seemed to take a perverse pleasure in needling the people of color at the Bureau. The Alamo comment wasn't exactly racist, though he clearly hoped it would get a rise out of her. But Reyes said nothing. Her policy was to ignore the micro-aggressions and save her ammunition for the macro stuff. Besides, she was Dominican, not Mexican.

Hastings frowned. He seemed disappointed at his failure to provoke her. 'So what's the status of your case? Who are you looking at *besides* Mirsky?'

'First off, we have a description of the woman who disguised herself as a caterer to poison Jonathan Humphrey. We made a sketch of her and sent it to all our people. We're also investigating everyone connected to Torricelli Demolition, especially now that Jason Torricelli and his father have dropped out of sight.' Reyes tried to sound optimistic. Given the dearth of evidence, she was doing the best she could. 'And we're looking hard at everyone in Mirsky's theater group, the Doomsday Company. My working theory is that Mirsky was collaborating with the climate-movement radicals, but he got into a dispute with them, most likely over their violent tactics.'

'How does his daughter's kidnapping fit into your theory? In the video she says her kidnappers are against the climate protests.'

'Yeah, there are some conflicting stories in this case. We're still trying to figure it out.'

'You better make some progress quick, Reyes. Do you have any idea how many jerkoffs in Washington are breathing down my neck?'

'Believe me, sir, we're working on it. I'm hopeful that our surveillance of Mirsky and his friends will turn up something soon.'

Hastings furrowed his brow and gave her a skeptical look. After a moment, though, he turned his attention back to the crowd on the other side of the barricades. 'All right, carry on. Just don't make this fucking circus any worse, OK?'

'Yes, sir.' She nodded and walked away, keeping her face blank until she was thirty feet from the asshole. Then she leaned to the side and spat on the sidewalk, getting the shitty taste of deference out of her mouth.

Staying within the security perimeter, Reyes entered the government building on the other side of Duane Street and took the stairs down to the basement. She navigated the underground corridors until she reached the emergency exit, where she swung open the heavy door and emerged on Reade Street, a block south of the Federal Building. She was behind the bulk of the protesters now, and none of them paid any attention to her, since she didn't appear to be with the cops or the FBI. Just to be on the safe side, though, she turned up the collar of her blazer to make it look less cop-like, and then she headed for her rendezvous with Agent Wilson.

As she walked west on Reade, she scrutinized the activists rushing in the opposite direction, outraged and eager for battle. For the most part, they were ordinary young men and women, and on any other night they would've been sleeping or club-hopping or watching Netflix. But now they were waving pictures of Sonya Mirsky and holding signs that said 'HOW DARE YOU?'

and 'SAVE SONYA, SAVE THE EARTH.' Although Reyes couldn't fathom the logic of their protest – why were they aiming their rage at the FBI, which was trying to rescue Sonya? – she understood the emotion behind it. The protesters were rallying around a symbol, a focus for their despair and frustration: the tear-streaked face of the young woman they'd seen on their phones, pleading for her life in the kidnappers' video.

Reyes turned right on Church Street and speed-walked north. About a hundred yards ahead, an unmarked car idled near the street corner. It was a black Chevy Tahoe, and a careful observer could tell it was a law-enforcement vehicle; it had pushbars on the grille, a disk antenna on the roof, and black rims on the wheels. But that idiot Wilson had turned on the blue lights at the top of the windshield, making his identity crystal clear to the whole crowd. Some of the protesters yelled abuse at him as they marched past the SUV, and it was only a matter of time before they started throwing things.

Reyes dashed the last few yards and wrenched open the car's passenger door. 'Turn off the goddamn lights!' Glaring at Wilson, she closed the door behind her and strapped herself in. 'What are you waiting for? Get us out of here!'

'Yes, ma'am.' Wilson gave her his usual smirk, the one implying that it was the biggest joke in the world for him to be taking orders from her. Then he shifted the SUV into reverse and started performing a laborious three-point turn, because the idiot had parked in the wrong direction. He nearly hit a couple of guys in balaclavas as he backed up, and they responded by pounding the car's trunk. Another guy hurled a bottle that smashed against the grille, and a woman lobbed a water balloon that burst on the hood. Except, Reyes noticed, the fluid inside the balloon wasn't water. It looked like green paint.

Wilson leaned on the horn. 'FUCKERS! GET OUT OF THE WAY!' Then he shifted into drive and revved the engine. The protesters scattered, and the Tahoe barreled north on Church Street.

As they pulled away from the crowd, Reyes noticed that the woman who'd thrown the paint balloon was now speaking into a two-way radio. *Shit*, she thought. *These kids are well organized.*

Reyes turned back to Wilson and pointed at the green splotch on the car's hood. 'You need to avoid any groups of protesters. I think they marked us.'

Wilson chuckled. 'You're kidding, right? Those assholes? You really think they're smart enough to do that?'

'Go up the West Side Highway. Less chance of getting trapped there.'

'Yes, ma'am. I'll do my best to avoid trouble.' The smirk again. 'If you ask me, this whole mess was avoidable. We should've kept Mirsky in custody and arrested all his friends too. If they'd been in jail, they couldn't have released any statements to the news media, right?'

Reyes didn't bother to answer. She knew why an incompetent like Wilson had been assigned to her unit, because the same thing had happened to several of her female friends in the Bureau. Men in general didn't like working for women, and that was even more true of the men in the FBI. They resisted assignments to units with female commanders, which meant that most of Reyes's agents were low-performing jokers who had no choice in the matter.

As they sped up the West Side, Reyes turned on her phone and checked the Bureau's Hazard Mapping site, which received data from all the NYPD's traffic cameras. According to the maps, large crowds of demonstrators were moving south out of Central Park and swarming across Midtown. The biggest east–west streets – 34th, 42nd, 57th, etc. – were jammed, making it impossible to get to the East Side that way. But because Central Park was emptying, the transverse roads that crossed the park were clear.

Reyes pocketed her phone. 'Get off the highway at 79th. Then go to Fifth Avenue and 81st.'

Wilson didn't smirk this time, which was a relief. They traveled in merciful silence past Hudson Yards and Riverside Park. When they entered Central Park at 81st Street, Reyes saw no one on the tree-lined paths on either side of the transverse road. The half-million protesters had abandoned their tent cities on the park's lawns, and the noise of their drums and whistles and megaphones was just a distant rumble, far to the south.

Then, as the SUV approached an underpass near the Metropolitan Museum of Art, Reyes glimpsed some movement on the stone arch that curved over the transverse road. She looked up and saw a section of chain-link fencing topple from the archway.

'LOOK OUT!!'

Agent Wilson saw it too late. He swerved to the right, but the fence crashed down on the hood, and the SUV slammed into the concrete wall of the underpass.

Reyes felt her seatbelt tighten and heard the *bang* of the airbags inflating. She lurched to the right and her head thumped against the side-curtain airbag, which wasn't as hard as the dashboard or the window but wasn't exactly soft either. A bright orange light flashed behind her eyelids, followed an instant later by a stabbing pain that plunged deep into her skull.

She was out for two or three seconds, or maybe a little more. When she opened her eyes, woozy shadows swirled around her, which she soon recognized as the deflating airbags and the cracked windshield behind them. Then she looked to the left and saw Wilson clawing at the bags and reaching for the handle of the driver-side door. He got the door open, but before he could step outside there was a torrent of pelting noises, like a sudden hailstorm battering the SUV. Reyes looked over her shoulder and saw a dozen silhouettes in the roadway, skinny figures standing just outside the mouth of the underpass, all of them throwing rocks at the back of the car.

She blinked a couple of times, fast, to stop the swirling inside her head. *Jesus Christ. They're kids. Late teens or early twenties. Stupid fucking kids.*

After a moment the pelting stopped, as abruptly as it had started. The dozen ambushers, having made their point, turned tail and ran off, racing down the transverse road toward Central Park West.

Wilson stumbled out of the SUV. Swaying and glassy-eyed, he stared at the retreating protesters and yelled, 'FREEZE, MOTHERFUCKERS!' Then he reached inside his blazer and pulled out his nine-millimeter service pistol.

Reyes flung open her door. She scrambled around the front of the car, still dizzy, still nauseous, struggling like hell just to stay on her feet. She shouted, '*Stand down, Wilson!*' but the idiot didn't seem to hear her. He raised his pistol, using both hands to steady it, and tilted his head as he peered down the gunsights.

At the same time, Reyes came up behind him, lifted her right foot high, and aimed it at the back of his knee.

She'd learned this move twelve years ago, during her martial arts drills at the Academy, and it worked like a charm. Wilson screamed and went down. He dropped his gun as he fell flat on his chest.

Reyes picked up the pistol from the roadway. She removed its magazine, racked the slide, and ejected the bullet from the chamber. Then she looked down at Wilson in disgust. 'You're suspended, asshole. I'm keeping your weapon.'

'CHRIST! YOU BROKE MY FUCKING KNEE!'

'I did you a favor.' She opened the rear door of the SUV. 'If you'd shot one of those kids, you'd be going to jail. I wouldn't have had any qualms about testifying against you.'

She bent over Wilson and grabbed him under the armpits. Mostly using her leg muscles, she started dragging him toward the car's door.

'WHAT THE FUCK ARE YOU DOING NOW?'

'Shut the hell up. I'm taking you to the emergency room.'

With a fair amount of exertion, she managed to haul Wilson into the SUV's backseat. Then she yanked the section of chain-link off the car's hood and used her multi-tool to cut away the airbags so she could get into the driver's seat. The Chevy was still drivable – those Tahoes could take a lot of punishment – and five minutes later Reyes was outside New York Hospital, leaving Wilson in the care of the ER nurses.

After another five minutes she parked in front of the immense Fifth Avenue townhouse belonging to Charles Roche, the VIP who'd demanded a meeting with her. He was the seventy-five-year-old founder of Roche Industries, which supplied drilling equipment to nearly every fossil-fuel business in the country, and his estimated net worth was over sixty billion dollars. More relevant to Reyes, though, was the fact that he'd witnessed the murder of Jonathan Humphrey nine hours ago.

Also: he was number three on Max Mirsky's climate criminals list.

* * *

'Good evening, ma'am. Can I see your badge, please?'

The bodyguard was one of the biggest men Reyes had ever seen. He was at least six foot ten and built like a tank, so formidable that he dwarfed all the antique tables and chairs in the high-ceilinged foyer of Roche's mansion. He wore a skin-tight black T-shirt that advertised his bulging pectorals, and nestled against them was a Glock 20 in a leather shoulder holster. He had a thick black beard and shrapnel scars on his forearms, and in short he looked a lot like the Special Forces guys whom Reyes had met during her tour in Afghanistan. Roche Industries, she knew, had plenty of operations in the Middle East, and its security division was full of ex-SEALs and ex-Rangers.

But Reyes intended to give this bulldozer the benefit of the doubt. She took out her FBI badge and let him eyeball it. 'Sorry I'm late. I ran into some trouble on the way over here.' She pointed at the pair of bodyguards who'd accosted her in front of the mansion and accompanied her inside. 'You know, I already showed my badge to your friends here.'

'For obvious reasons, we're being very careful tonight.' The big guy held up a black device that resembled an iPhone with an oversized camera lens. 'I've been ordered to take extra precautions, and when it comes to identification, biometrics are better than badges, right? So let me check your peepers to see if they match our records.'

Reyes took a closer look at the device in his hand. It was a SEEK scanner, designed to recognize the unique patterns in the iris of the human eye. The FBI and the military had thousands of those scanners, and Reyes wasn't too surprised to see that high-end security guards had them too. What did shock her was the contents of the guard's database. 'Wait a second. How did you get the records of my iris scans? That information isn't supposed to leave the Bureau.'

'I'm afraid your question is above my pay grade, ma'am.' He stepped closer and positioned the scanner a few inches in front of her eyes. 'May I?'

Reyes made him wait a moment, then nodded. As he trained the scanner's infrared beams at her, she wondered what other classified data the FBI had shared with Roche Industries. She'd known that Charles Roche was well-connected politically – he gave tons of money to his Republican friends in Congress, and he'd toyed with the idea of running for office himself – but she hadn't realized that his influence extended so deeply into the federal agencies. Now she had yet another reason to hate this Climate Avengers investigation: if she fucked it up, her career would be over.

After a few seconds, the guard's scanner beeped and he looked at its screen. 'Hello, Special Agent Aleida Reyes, birthdate three-nineteen-eighty-two.' He held out his massive right hand. 'I'm Harlan Tate, vice president of corporate security at RI.'

Reyes made a note of his name. She planned to look into *his* records as soon as she got back to her office. 'Pleased to meet you, Harlan.' She grabbed the top half of his hand and gave it a perfunctory shake. 'Now can you take me to your boss?'

'One more thing.' He pointed at the left side of her blazer, underneath which was her own shoulder holster. 'You'll have to leave your service weapon with me while you're talking to Mr Roche. That's another precaution we're taking.'

She shook her head. 'Sorry, can't do that.'

'Agent Reyes, I'm sure you're aware of the extraordinary threat that—'

'Look, I was willing to entertain Mr Roche's request for an in-person meeting, but not if he's going to pull this shit.' She turned around and headed for the exit. 'If he still wants to talk, just tell him to call me on the phone.'

She was halfway to the townhouse's grand doors when Harlan called her back. 'OK, OK. You can keep your piece.'

Reyes looked over her shoulder at him. 'No more games? You're gonna stop wasting my time?'

With a grimace, Harlan strode across the foyer. 'Come on. He's waiting for you.'

She followed him down a marble-lined corridor to a well-hidden elevator. They stepped inside and Harlan punched an elaborate sequence of buttons on the panel. Reyes assumed they were going to ride up to a penthouse suite on top of the mansion, but the elevator jolted downward. 'He's got a panic room?' she asked. 'In the basement?'

'It's more like a panic floor. Three bedrooms, two offices, a kitchen, and a command center, all well below street level.' Like other elite bodyguards whom Reyes had observed, Harlan seemed to take great pride in his employer's resources. 'Also, a pair of thousand-gallon water tanks and a diesel generator for power. An entire platoon could hole up there for months.'

Reyes nodded, pretending to be impressed. 'That's good. And your boss plans to stay down there for the time being? Until we resolve the situation?'

Harlan hesitated before answering. 'It would be better if you posed that question directly to Mr Roche.' The elevator stopped descending, and the door opened. 'Right this way, please.'

They walked through what looked like the command center, a room full of desks and screens. Then they passed a wine cellar, a well-stocked pantry, and a chef's kitchen with spotlessly clean appliances. Finally, they came to an enormous carved-oak door, like something you might see in a medieval cathedral. Harlan knocked on it. 'Sir? Agent Reyes is here.' A buzzer sounded, and the bodyguard heaved the door open.

Reyes stepped into a large, dark office with Persian rugs on the floor and towering bookcases against the walls. The only light in the room came from a Tiffany lamp on a gorgeous antique desk beside one of the bookcases. An elderly man sat behind the desk, but the lamplight illuminated only the lower half of his face: bloodless lips, age lines around the mouth, and a thin, pale nose. Even though it was way past midnight, he still wore a suit and tie, as well as a tie clip that gleamed like a golden hyphen on his chest.

His lips moved. 'Please sit down, Agent. Harlan, you can stay in the room and observe.'

Reyes came forward and sat in a comfortable wingback chair in front of the desk. Harlan chose a spot in the corner of the office and folded his arms across his chest, keeping his eyes on Reyes. It was a little distracting, but she tried her best to ignore him and focus on his boss. 'Mr Roche, I want to—'

'What's the status of your investigation? Have you located the blonde bitch who murdered Jonathan?'

His voice was tense. There was anger in it, and some fear too. Reyes wished she could see Roche's eyes so she could get a better read on the guy, but the top half of his face was just a gray outline in the darkness. 'We're looking for her. We made a sketch of her likeness and put it in the hands of every cop in the city.'

'A sketch?' His chin jutted and his upper lip curled, exposing perfectly white teeth. 'What about surveillance photos? Surely you checked the security cameras at Texxonoco's headquarters?'

'The building's security system went down this afternoon, shortly before the board meeting started. We're assuming that the perpetrators hacked into it somehow.'

'So the bitch had help?'

The B-word grated in Reyes's ears, but she hid her irritation. 'Either she had help, or she's very capable. We interviewed all the other caterers who were in the building at the time, and none of them had any suspicions about the woman. She told them she was filling in for an employee who was sick, and she basically charmed the hell out of them.'

'Charmed, you say?' His lips quivered, glistening in the lamplight. 'Believe me, you wouldn't call her charming if you saw the face of my friend as he was dying. It was *horrible*. It was . . .' He reached for the silk handkerchief in his jacket and coughed into it. He was breathing fast now. 'No, you don't have any idea what it was like, because you didn't know the man. Jonathan was brilliant. Perhaps the finest young leader in Texxonoco's history. And he had so many years ahead of him, so many more things to . . .'

Roche's voice trailed off, and he dabbed his lips with the handkerchief. In truth, Reyes knew, Jonathan Humphrey hadn't been such a fine person. Her investigation of the victim's background had already turned up evidence of tax evasion, securities fraud, and the sexual harassment of half a dozen women who'd worked for him. But Roche's affection for Humphrey sounded genuine, so she gave the old man some time to collect himself.

After a few seconds he took a deep breath and put away his handkerchief. 'Just tell me one thing, Agent. What are your chances of finding the bitch?'

This time Reyes couldn't help but frown. 'It all depends where she is. She may have left the country by now. If that's the case, the odds of locating her aren't good. *But*,' – she held up a finger to emphasize the word – 'the group that claimed responsibility for the murders has vowed to keep killing its enemies. And I don't think these people are bluffing. They're going to strike again.'

Roche leaned forward, and the lamplight edged upward on his face, shining on his cheeks and the pouches below his eyes. 'Why do you think so?'

'You're on their hit list too, and the perp could've poisoned you today just as easily as she poisoned Humphrey. But she left you alone. Because this is a terrorist group, and these killings are part of a political strategy.'

He shook his head, clearly agitated. 'What? You're not making sense.'

'The climate radicals are trying to send a message to the chief executives of all the fossil-fuel companies. They're warning you that you're all targets. And their message will be even stronger if they manage to kill one of you *now*, after you've taken steps to defend yourselves. That would be the terrorists' way of showing how powerful and inescapable they are.'

'So you're saying I'm the blonde bitch's prime target now?' Weirdly, he didn't sound upset about this. On the contrary, his voice grew enthusiastic. 'She's gunning for me?'

'It's very possible.' She pointed at Harlan, who stood motionless and silent in the corner. 'That's why I'm glad you and your team have beefed up your security measures. And you'll have to keep your guard up until we take down these terrorists.'

'But at the same time, this gives us an opportunity, doesn't it?' Roche's pale, wet lips broke into a smile. 'While this bitch is stalking me, maybe we can trap her. The NYPD should flood this neighborhood with police officers tomorrow during my reception for the UN delegates.'

'Excuse me?' Reyes wasn't sure she'd heard him right. 'A reception?'

His illuminated chin moved up and down. 'Yes, here in my townhouse, starting at noon. I hold a lunch reception every year during General Assembly week, primarily for the foreign ministers of various nations in Europe and the Middle East. It gives them a chance to socialize with some of our country's business and political leaders. This year's guest list is particularly distinguished.'

She was dumbfounded. 'And you're planning to go ahead with this event? Even after what happened today?'

'Oh yes. I won't give in to terrorism. The radicals can't stop me from doing what's right for our country.'

'Are you sure that's wise?' Reyes glanced at Harlan, hoping he would speak up and agree with her. 'In light of the threats made against you, wouldn't it be safer to postpone this reception or find a different way to—'

'Why are you second-guessing me?' Roche raised his voice. 'Do you think I'm incapable of protecting myself?'

'No, but—'

'Harlan, I need your assistance. Please tell Agent Reyes about our security arrangements for tomorrow's reception.'

The bodyguard dutifully stepped forward, grinning as he faced her. 'I can assure you that everything is under control. Two hundred ninety-nine guests will be attending the event, and each has been thoroughly vetted by my team. We'll scan their biometrics before they enter the townhouse to ensure that no impostors slip inside. Each guest will also pass through a full-body scanner to check for weapons.'

Reyes shook her head. 'That's the least of your problems. Did you happen to look outside your mansion anytime this evening? The whole city is a mess, and it's going to get even worse tomorrow.'

'We've increased our staffing to meet the need. We'll have twenty-five armed guards deployed at the building's perimeter and access points. We'll also have undercover guards mingling with the guests in the main ballroom, the reception parlors, and the courtyard.'

'Wait a second, the courtyard? The guests will be roaming outside too?'

'The courtyard is fully enclosed by the townhouse, so it's a secure space. Plus, we'll have guards with sniper rifles on the balconies.'

Reyes raised her hands and clasped her forehead in disbelief. This sounded like a recipe for an unprecedented cluster-fuck. 'Look, none of that will do you any good if the protesters decide to storm your castle. The vast majority of them are just random innocent kids, but there seem to be a few bad actors in the mix.

If some of them are connected to the terrorists, they might lead the crowd to your mansion.'

Before Harlan could reply, his boss leaned across his desk, bringing his whole face into view for the first time. Under the lamplight, Roche's craggy brow was striped with shadow, and his bloodshot eyes blazed furiously. 'Controlling the masses is *your* job, Agent. You'll need to work with the police department to set up barricades on Fifth Avenue and the side streets. And make sure you instruct those officers to search the crowd for that bitch. She might come here to agitate and inflame the demonstrators, and that would give us a chance to take her out.'

Reyes leaned forward too. She wasn't about to take orders from this patrician piece of shit. 'Sorry, but you're not the only one in this city who needs protection. The Bureau and the police force are already stretched thin, and we don't have the resources to guarantee your safety if you go ahead with your plans. I'm strongly advising you to cancel your reception and leave New York immediately. Or shutter the doors and windows of this building and hide on your panic floor for the next few days.'

Patches of color spread across Roche's pale cheeks, like dead meat warming under the Tiffany lamp's glow. Clearly, he wasn't accustomed to opposition. 'Don't be stupid. I know your superior, Glen Hastings. He won't be happy if he finds out you're not cooperating with me.'

She'd had enough. She got to her feet and stepped away from Roche's desk, relieved to put some distance between herself and that cadaver. 'Go ahead and call him. I'll tell my boss the same thing I just told you.'

'Oh, I'll be sure to call him. And there's something else you should know.' He curled his lip and showed his teeth again. 'You have an additional reason to bolster the security of my event, because I just invited another VIP to the reception. Are you familiar with Senator Coal? That's not his real name, of course, but I've heard that's what they call him down in Washington.'

Reyes hadn't thought this cluster-fuck could get any worse. But she was wrong. 'You're talking about the senior senator from West Virginia? He'll be at your party?'

'Yes, indeed. Perhaps you'll perform your duties more diligently now, since the senator's safety will also be at stake.'

She winced. Senator Coal was also on the climate criminals list.

He was number two.

TWELVE

If his reasons hadn't been so urgent, Max would never have gone back to his old school. For more than thirty years he'd stayed away from Columbia University, steering clear of the campus during all his perambulations across the Upper West Side. He supposed it was a primitive instinct, inherited from cautious forefathers whose anxieties had kept them alive. Max avoided Columbia because that was where his life had fallen apart.

He got off the subway at the 116th Street stop and hurried through the forbidding gate of College Walk. The campus was almost empty, mostly because it was only eight a.m. and so many of Columbia's students had joined last night's protests, which had continued until dawn. Max and the other Doomsday troupers hadn't marched downtown with the thousands of activists; they'd stayed in Max's apartment so they could field all the interview requests from the media. But they'd watched the late-night demonstrations on TV, and Nathan seemed pleased that they'd drawn so much attention to the kidnapping and the FBI's inadequate response. Max, though, was uneasy. In the video released by the kidnappers, Sonya said she wouldn't be freed until all the climate activists left New York. So were the protests actually helping her and Janet?

Max didn't know. The uncertainty was excruciating.

He walked briskly, passing Pulitzer Hall. Columbia's stately, red-brick buildings still filled him with dread, although he couldn't blame the school for the breakdown he'd suffered there. In retrospect, it was inevitable. After all, his parents had abandoned him when he was only four years old, and a trauma like that is bound to have effects. His grandmother, his beloved Sadie, had taken him in and kept him happy and safe, but despite all her good intentions she'd just postponed the day of reckoning. Eventually he had to confront the fact that his parents never returned, not even for a visit. To have not one, but two parents with such appalling heartlessness was either a stroke of horrifically bad luck or a sign that Max wasn't worth returning to. He started to seriously consider this second possibility while he was at Columbia, and that was why he fell apart.

And there it was, straight ahead, the very spot where Max truly realized his worthlessness. It was on the steps in front of Low Library, right next to the Alma Mater statue, the bronze mother staring indifferently into space.

He rushed by it, turning left and striding fast on the brick walkway. Ten years after his breakdown, after hundreds of hours of therapy and after he married Cheryl, he'd vowed that he would become a good parent, if only to counterbalance the awful example that his own parents had set. So now he dashed past Low Library and headed for Pupin Hall, where he hoped to meet someone who could help him find his daughter.

The building's official name was the Pupin Physics Laboratory, and it was nearly a hundred years old. Max had taken a freshman physics class there, and he'd once sneaked into the building's basement to gawk at the abandoned cyclotron where the Manhattan Project scientists had done their first atom-splitting experiments. He'd heard about the cyclotron from a grad student named David Swift, one of the teaching assistants for his physics class. David was friendlier than most of the introverted physicists at Columbia, and he was very involved in campus activism. When Max mentioned his own interest in the environmental movement, David introduced him to one of the student groups that were pushing the university to take a stronger stand on that issue.

The group was called Nothing but Green.

Amazingly, David Swift still worked at Columbia. Max had found him in the school's online directory, listed as a Historian of Science and occupying an office on Pupin Hall's third floor. After Max had made this discovery last night, he sent an email to the listed address and left a voice message too, and when he didn't see any replies this morning he immediately got on the subway. If he had to, he would stand all day in front of David's office.

First, though, Max needed to get into Pupin Hall. Security was a lot tighter now than it had been in his undergrad days; you needed to wave a university ID card at a card reader to unlock the building's front door. He loitered near the entrance until a short, pimply student used his ID to get inside, and Max slipped in behind him before the door closed. The student was oblivious, but there was someone else in the building's lobby, a maintenance man in blue overalls, who stood on a ladder next to an enormous globe. The stairway was on the other side of the lobby, and Max kept his head down as he walked past the globe, which was at least eight feet in diameter, its North Pole almost touching the ceiling. But just before Max reached the safety of the stairs, the maintenance man pointed at him. 'Hey, *you*!'

Max stopped short. He turned around, his mind racing, trying to think of a convincing explanation for his trespass. 'Sorry, I left my wallet at home. I'm just—'

'Can you hand me that rack of bulbs?' Now the man pointed at a toolbox on the floor. On top of the box was a rectangular package containing dozens of tiny LED lights. 'I'd get it myself, but going up and down this ladder kills my knees.'

Relieved, Max picked up the package and handed it over. As he did so, he noticed that the maintenance man was an older guy with graying hair and tired eyes. Also, his overalls were in terrible shape, stained and frayed, and they had no 'Columbia Maintenance' markings.

'Thanks.' The man smiled at Max, then began taking the LEDs out of the package and inserting them into sockets on the huge globe. Its surface was studded with thousands of the tiny bulbs, covering every ocean and continent. 'I decided to polish up this display because of Climate Emergency Week. It's the least I can do for the cause, right?'

Max looked for the first time at the sign beside the globe. It said, 'HEATING THE EARTH: SURFACE TEMPERATURE PROJECTIONS FOR THE NEXT 100 YEARS.' He'd seen similar graphics on the web, but this was more impressive, a big, bold three-dimensional presentation of the data. 'Wow, I like it. There should be a globe like this at every gas station. Just to remind the drivers what they're doing to the planet.'

'Yeah, good idea. I just updated the display software to show the latest simulation developed by our department's climate modeling group. And no surprise, the new simulation predicts even higher temperature increases.' He squinted at one of the

LEDs before inserting it. 'I decided to replace the defective lights at the same time, so I found a ladder and put on some working clothes. But I'm getting too old for this shit.'

This wasn't a maintenance man, Max realized. He looked more carefully at the guy, who pursed his lips as he handled the LEDs. It was like staring at an age-progression image, a youthful face reworked and refashioned to show the merciless effects of the past three decades.

'Are you David Swift? Professor in the physics department?'

The man smiled again. 'Technically, that's my department, but I teach history of science. I also teach a course on climate change, hence this.' He gestured at the globe. 'And who are you?'

'My name is Max Mirsky. I'm . . .' He'd been anticipating this moment, but now he didn't know where to start. 'You probably don't remember me, but thirty-five years ago I was in a physics class where you were a teaching assistant.'

'Thirty-five years?' He inserted the last of the LEDs into the globe, then slowly climbed down the ladder. 'Most students come to see me because they want me to change their grades, but in your case it's a little late for that.'

'No, I'm here to pick your brain about something. There was a student organization you were involved with back then, a group of environmental activists. It was—'

'Wait a second.' David stopped smiling and looked Max in the eye. 'You're *the* Max Mirsky? Sonya's father?'

Max nodded. His daughter's kidnapping had made him famous. And the look that David gave him now – trying for sympathy but mostly horrified – made it impossible for Max to say another word. *He's looking at me that way because he assumes Sonya will die. He thinks there's no chance that the kidnappers will release her.*

David stepped closer and clasped his arm. 'Hey, are you OK? You want to sit down?'

Max shook his head but still couldn't speak.

'Come on, let's go someplace where we can talk.' David let go of him and pointed outside. 'We'll get some coffee, OK? I just need to take care of one thing first.'

He took a step backward and crouched near the bottom of the

huge globe. He reached for its South Pole and grabbed an electrical cord that extended downward from a hole in Antarctica. Then he plugged the cord into an outlet on the floor.

The thousands of LEDs on the globe came to life. At first, they shone cool blue on the planet's surface, but after a few seconds a good number of the lights shifted to yellow, especially in the Arctic Ocean. Then more lights turned yellow across Eurasia and North America, and the LEDs in the Arctic shaded to red. The crimson stain spread across every ocean and continent, and soon the model of the Earth was a giant blazing ball, flashing scarlet light across the lobby.

David came back to Max and led him out of the building.

They went to the café on the ground floor of Dodge Hall, which had outdoor seating in front of the building. David found a table far from the walkway, so they would have some privacy. The only disadvantage, from Max's point of view, was that they were too close to the Alma Mater statue, but he angled his chair so he wouldn't have to look at it.

David put a cappuccino on the table in front of Max. Then he took a sip of his own coffee and leaned back in his chair. 'You know, I sort of remember you now. You were a funny kid, the joker of freshman physics. But your grades weren't so great. You didn't major in physics, did you?'

Max had no interest in telling the whole disastrous story of his college days, so he kept his answer brief. 'I majored in English. Then I became a journalist.'

'And I remember something else.' David lifted his chin and looked up at the clouds, as if his distant memories were archived there. 'You used to hang out with an international student, a young woman from Barbados. She was in that physics class with you, right?'

Max nodded. That was Cheryl, his late wife. He didn't want to talk about her either, so he said nothing.

David took another sip of coffee. 'I remember her because she was so idealistic, so fiery. I saw her at all the protests on campus.' He stared at the clouds for a few more seconds, then turned back to Max. 'So, what can I do for you, Mr Mirsky? I've been following the news stories about your daughter's climate campaign ever since she started it, and I truly admire her courage. I'll do anything I can to help.'

Usually, Max loved to hear compliments about Sonya, but now it sounded strange. Maybe he was imagining it, but there seemed to be a valedictory tone in David's voice, a sense that he was praising something that was already lost. Max wanted to scream, *Sonya isn't lost!* but instead he leaned forward and firmly tapped the tabletop. 'OK, I assume you heard the statement I released last night? About how the FBI only cares about the billionaires and isn't doing shit for my daughter and my girlfriend?'

'I heard it, and I agree with you. I don't like what these Climate Avengers are doing, but they certainly showed where our government's priorities lie.'

'But just complaining about it won't help Sonya. If the FBI won't do the work, then I have to do it.' He thumped his chest for emphasis. 'And I'm not just a desperate father playing detective. There's a connection between me and at least one of the climate terrorists. They chose my criminals list for a reason, they made contact with me yesterday for a reason. If I can figure out what the reason is, maybe that'll help me identify the kidnappers.'

David raised his hand, stopping him. 'OK, I hear you, but I don't understand. From what I've seen on the news, the terrorists are radical left-wingers and the kidnappers are right-wing militants. So how can—'

'The truth is, we don't know who the kidnappers are. I watched Sonya in that video, I saw the look on her face, I felt the terror she was feeling. She was just repeating what the kidnappers wanted her to say. She didn't believe *any* of it.' Max clenched his hands. The image of Sonya was in his brain now, making him want to scream again. He had to close his eyes for a moment before he could continue. 'The FBI hasn't released this information yet, but the body of one of the terrorists was found in a garbage truck yesterday. And that truck belonged to the father of one of the people involved in the kidnapping. I don't believe that's a coincidence, no matter how many trucks that family owns.'

'So the terrorists and the kidnappers might be the same people?'

'I know, it sounds nuts. Why would the climate radicals do

this to a nineteen-year-old girl who's done so much for the movement? But they're killers, they're crazy people. They're beyond explanation.'

'And this connection between you and the radicals? Did you write about them? You said you're a journalist, right?'

'No, the connection is here. At Columbia.' Max turned his head and forced himself to look at the Alma Mater statue. 'Texxonoco Oil & Gas used to fund some of the researchers in Columbia's chemical engineering department. They were developing new chemical additives that improved the effectiveness of the fluids pumped into fracking wells.'

'Sure, I know about that. The students and the faculty association fought that project for forty years. We finally convinced Columbia five years ago to stop taking Texxonoco's money, but by that point the damage was done. The fracking wells were already everywhere.'

'And the project was called Nothing but Green?'

David frowned. 'Ironic, right? Texxonoco was making it sound like they were doing the world a great favor by pumping more natural gas out of the ground. We called it Nothing but Greenwashing.'

Max frowned too. Although he'd never written an article specifically about the Columbia research, he'd worked on plenty of stories about fracking. The fossil-fuel industry fell in love with the technology because the new additives made it easier for the high-pressure fluids to fracture underground strata and release the natural gas deposits. Starting in 2003, Texxonoco drilled thousands of fracking wells across the country, from North Dakota to Pennsylvania. Worse, they had the nerve to claim they were actually helping the environment, since natural gas burns cleaner than coal or oil, producing less atmosphere-warming carbon dioxide. What they didn't say was that each gas well leaked tons of methane into the air, and methane heats the atmosphere eighty times more efficiently than carbon dioxide does.

David put down his coffee cup and pushed it across the table. He seemed too disgusted to enjoy it now. 'And do you know what was the most devious thing of all? The name Nothing but Green wasn't even original. Texxonoco stole it from one of the student organizations that was *opposed* to the project. There was a group called Nothing but Green that was pretty active on campus in the Eighties. That was when you were an undergrad here, right?'

Max was glad that David had mentioned it first. Maybe that would make his theory a little more believable. 'Yeah, that's right. That was the group you told me about when I was a freshman. And you took me to one of their meetings.'

'Really?' David looked askance. 'I don't remember that.'

'Well, you left the meeting early.' This was going to be awkward, but Max plowed ahead. 'You seemed a little out of it that day.'

'You don't have to mince words. I was drunk.' David shrugged. 'I had a drinking problem back then. For a while I neglected everything in my life except the booze. It got so bad, I had to leave the grad program for a couple of years.' He pointed at Max. 'But let's get back to you. I still don't see your connection with the terrorists.'

'I saw that phrase again yesterday. Nothing but green. It was in one of the emails the radicals sent me.' Max had seen the words twice, actually – once on his phone before he deleted the email, and again on the FBI's transcript of the message. 'I didn't notice the phrase when I looked at the email, I was too worried about everything else that was going on. But last night someone reminded me about Texxonoco's fracking research, and I remembered that activist group at Columbia.'

'Yeah, OK, but—'

'Hold on, let me finish. A few months after I went to the group's meeting, I joined one of their protests against Texxonoco. It started out normal – we marched to Low Library with our signs and banners, and we chanted "Nothing but green" and our other slogans. But then it went crazy.' Max glanced again at the Alma Mater statue. Looking at it made him uneasy, but it also helped him remember. 'A tall girl showed up wearing a bird mask, a really creepy thing with a feathery headdress and a long yellow beak. Nobody knew who she was, but she took over the protest. She started shouting, "I would gladly die for the Earth!" and soon everyone was shouting it. Then she took out a switch-blade knife and made a long cut on her palm. She went over to that statue right there, climbed up the pedestal, and smeared her blood all over the sculpture.'

'Jesus.' Now David stared at the statue too.

'I was freaked out. The girl was waving the knife around, and I thought she was going to slit her own throat or maybe stab someone else, because now she was screaming, "I will gladly *kill* for the Earth!" So I went looking for help and found a campus security guard. We ran back to the statue, and the girl in the bird mask jumped down from the pedestal. She pointed her knife at me and yelled, "Traitor to the Earth! I won't forget this!" Then she raced off, fast as hell, and the guard couldn't catch her. Meanwhile, the other protesters started glaring at me, like they agreed with the crazy girl about my disloyalty.' Max shook his head. One of the people fuming at him had been Cheryl, but he saw no point in mentioning this. 'The thing is, I was caught up in my own problems at the time, so I pushed the episode out of my head. I never even tried to figure out who that girl was. But now that I'm thinking about it again, I see all the similarities. The terrorist who sent me the email said she was a student at Columbia. And she used that phrase "traitor to the Earth" as well as "nothing but green."'

Max was out of breath by the time he finished. He looked down at the table, feeling jittery and cold, even though it was a warm day and getting warmer. *No good deed goes unpunished, that's the moral here. Cheryl and I broke up after that protest, and I went into a tailspin so bad I had to leave Columbia and check into the Renaissance Mental Health Center. And it's not over yet, not even after all these years. Now Sonya and Janet are paying the price.*

When Max finally raised his head, David was scrutinizing him. The look on his face was a mix of sympathy and skepticism. 'Max, you seem really distraught. Do you have any friends you can be with right now?'

Max rolled his eyes, exasperated. 'You think I'm imagining all this?'

'No, not at all. You should give your information to the FBI. Maybe last night's protests will get them to take the kidnapping more seriously.'

'They won't listen to me. You don't believe me yourself, do you?'

David took a deep breath. 'I'm sorry, but criminal investigation isn't my field of expertise. In this case, I can't tell the difference between a clue and a coincidence. You'll just have to go with your gut feelings.'

'That's fine. You don't have to agree with me. I'm hoping for something else from you.' He leaned across the table. 'I didn't really know the students in Nothing but Green. I only went to a couple of their meetings before that protest, and I don't remember seeing any tall, crazy woman there. But I got the impression that you were the group's mentor, at least before you started having problems. Can you think of *anyone* who might've gone nuts like that?'

To Max's relief, David didn't dismiss the question. Instead, he looked up at the sky again, thinking. The cumulus clouds hung motionless above them, stalled on a vast bubble of unseasonably hot air. While Max shifted in his seat, waiting for David to answer, he realized that the grace period of good weather was over. It was going to be an intolerable day.

Then David shook his head. 'Sorry. I don't remember their names. I can barely recall their faces. Maybe if I hadn't been so wasted all the time . . .'

'Please, keep trying.' Max's stomach churned. He felt so desperate. 'Didn't anyone stand out?'

'There was that international student from Barbados. Do you still keep in touch with her? She might be able to remember those people better than I can.'

'She's dead.' Max *really* didn't want to elaborate on this, so he quickly changed the subject. 'What about in the years afterward? When you returned to the grad program, did you get involved again with the activists?'

'Not so much. There were different students on campus by then, different groups. I was pretty busy too, because I'd switched my grad studies from physics to history of science.' He tapped his index finger against his chin, still thinking. 'In the early 2000s I belonged to a group called Earth Wise, but I don't remember any unhinged women at those meetings. There was a male student who seemed pretty weird, but you're only looking for women, right?'

Max raised his arms in surrender. At this point he was grasping for anything. 'OK, tell me about this guy. What made him weird?'

'Well, he was a physics major, so he latched on to me once he heard about my background. He was extremely bright but obsessively single-minded, only interested in certain subjects. His favorite topic was weaponry – nuclear bombs, hypersonic missiles, anything high-tech and destructive. That was all he wanted to talk about.' David squinched his mouth in distaste. 'It made me uncomfortable. And confused. Why would any environmentalist be so interested in weapons of mass destruction? It was such a strange contradiction.'

Max felt a surge of adrenaline. He wasn't sure why this brief character sketch rang an alarm in his head; maybe it was only because David had given him absolutely nothing until now. But he didn't argue with his body's reaction. He was going with his gut feelings.

'Do you remember the student's name?'

David nodded. 'Yeah. Eventually he got his doctorate in physics, and then he went to work for a defense contractor. Boeing, I think. His name was Tom Stroman.'

THIRTEEN

Erin strutted into the gold-trimmed lobby of the Sky Tower on East 71st Street. It was a posh apartment building with a real stunner of a doorman, a regular Adonis. But there was also a concierge standing behind the reception desk, and Erin could tell right off that he was an effing twit. He wore an elegant suit, but his face looked like rare roast beef, and his smile was a line of gristle in the meat.

'Good morning! Welcome to the Sky Tower!' Even his voice was greasy. 'May I ask who you're here to see?'

'I'm Meg Taylor from Allure Hair Design.' Erin struck what she hoped was an alluring pose. She wore the uniform of the real Meg Taylor, whom Erin had ambushed an hour before, leaving her bound and gagged in her bedroom closet. She also carried Ms Taylor's case of wigs and hairsprays. 'I have a ten o'clock house call with Ms Darling in Apartment Twenty-nine W, please.'

The concierge reached for the phone on his desk, but he took his damn time, using the opportunity to leer at Erin's chest. 'Well, well. It's quite early in the day for Ms Darling. I assume you're readying her for some delightful lunch date?'

Erin nodded but said nothing. She was afraid that if she opened her mouth, she would tear three new arseholes into this gobshite. He obviously knew all about Carrie Darling's profession and mostly likely profited from it as well, taking hundred-dollar tips from the lecherous tycoons who were Carrie's regular clients. If there were any justice in the world, Erin would be slaughtering this eejit today instead of her assigned target. But who in God's name would ever pay for a job like that?

After a fucking eternity, he got Carrie on the line and allowed Erin to go upstairs. In the elevator, she closed her eyes and tried to cleanse her mind, washing away all extraneous thoughts. When she arrived at the twenty-ninth floor, she calmly strode down the hallway and rang the buzzer for Apartment 29W.

Carrie did a double take when she opened the door. She creased her beautiful forehead and arched her beautiful eyebrows, and her lips formed a beautiful oval below her absolutely beautiful nose. She wore fancy silk pajamas with a leopard-skin pattern. 'Uh, hello? Where's Meg? Who are—'

'Sorry, love. Meg called in sick.' Erin brushed past her into the apartment. 'Allure sent me here at the last minute, and I have another appointment at eleven, so there's no time to waste.'

She stepped into a living room decorated like Mata Hari's parlor, with a plush rug on the floor and a brothel lamp in the corner and an enormous gilt-framed mirror strategically placed on the wall opposite an overstuffed sofa. Erin bent over a glass-topped coffee table, opened Meg Taylor's case, and removed an item of her own that she'd packed beside the hairsprays. 'Let's get started, Ms Darling. Should we do your hair first or the nails?'

Carrie hesitated, then reluctantly stepped forward. 'Did Meg tell you what I wanted? I'm going to a reception at noon, so I'll need—'

'Don't worry. I've got everything covered.' Erin stepped behind her and reached for Carrie's beautiful auburn hair, as if she were about to start brushing out the tangles.

But instead, she pulled out a stretch of duct tape from the roll in her hand and clamped it firmly over Carrie's mouth. Then she grabbed Carrie's arms and bound them behind her back with another piece of tape. Last, she pushed the girl down to her knees on the rug and taped her ankles together. Erin had done this so many times, she'd become as proficient as a rodeo hand, trussing her victims in well under ten seconds.

Carrie looked up at her, wide-eyed, and moaned behind the tape. At the same time, a dark stain spread across the crotch of her silk pajamas. Meg Taylor the hair stylist had reacted the same way, and Erin felt a wee bit sorry for both of them. In the end, though, she didn't blame herself for their suffering as much as she blamed the capitalists they served. If there weren't so many damn billionaires throwing their money around, you wouldn't see so much high-class whoring, would you?

Erin patted Carrie's hair, which really did need some untangling. 'I'm not gonna hurt you, love. I'm only gonna borrow your appearance for a couple of hours. And that's more of a compliment than an insult, don't you think? Imitation is the sincerest form of flattery, so it is.'

She left Carrie kneeling on the rug and closed the living room's window shades. Next, she pushed the sofa closer to the big mirror on the wall but kept the coffee table between them, turning it into a dressing table. She picked up Carrie by the shoulders and lowered her wet bum onto one of the sofa cushions. Then Erin sat next to her and rummaged through Meg Taylor's case, looking for another item she'd packed inside it.

She found the iris scanner and turned it on. As she adjusted the device's settings, Carrie leaned away from her, shivering. Erin needed her to stay still for this procedure, so she clasped Carrie's shoulder and spoke in a hushed voice. 'Now, now. You think I'm here to punish you, but that's the furthest thing from my mind. I'm not gonna judge you for pleasuring those scumbags. It's society's fault, not yours.' After a few seconds, Carrie stopped shaking, and Erin aimed the iris scanner at her left eye. 'I mean, just look at your man Charles Roche, for example. Why does our capitalist system give so much fucking money to a donkey like him? He's only gonna spend it on hoors and parade them around at his parties. And no one can blame you for taking his cash, because it's easy work, right? Flirting with his rich friends and occasionally tickling his old shillelagh?'

Erin kept the device steady as it captured hundreds of images, recording the ring of intricate patterns in Carrie's beautiful blue eye. Then Erin moved on to her right eye's iris. Carrie was as still as death now, as quiet as a lamb. The same thing always happened with hostages – they got so frightened, they'd jump out the window if you told them to. 'But while I have your attention, I'll give you some advice: sometimes the richest man in the room isn't the steadiest employer. These billionaires are never satisfied, they always want *more*. They're constantly on the lookout for another sexy brasser to replace the one they have.'

Carrie remained motionless, so it was hard to say whether she took this advice to heart. *Oh well*, Erin thought. *At least I tried.*

The scanner beeped when it had collected enough images, and then Erin connected it by cable to a larger device, a black cube that she took out of Meg's case and set on the coffee table. The cube let out a low hum when Erin turned it on, starting its nineteen-minute cycle. Then she stood up and pointed a finger at Carrie.

'I've been real nice to you so far, yeah? And I'll keep on being nice as long as you don't move at all while I go to your bedroom. I need to take a gander at your wardrobe.'

Carrie nodded ever so slightly. Satisfied, Erin headed for the woman's walk-in closet.

The selection was just as large and varied as she'd expected. Fortunately, she and Carrie were about the same size, and in less than a minute she found a vampy black sheath dress that fit her perfectly. The dress's hem was high, just ten centimeters below her crotch, which was both provocative and functional – if necessary, she'd be able to throw a mean kick. She also chose a pair of matching stilettos that might prove handy in a fight, as well as a long silver necklace that seemed strong enough to be useful.

When Erin returned to the living room, Carrie did another double take and moaned again. Erin gave her a sympathetic look as she sat down next to her. 'Ah, don't fret. It's only one outfit, and you have so many. I'm sure you look better in it, but it's not so bad on me, eh?' She reached into Meg's case again and rummaged through a pile of wigs. 'All right, let's see. Which hair color matches yours?' She picked up a long auburn wig and held it next to Carrie's mane. 'This one's pretty close, yeah? And the length is right.'

Erin slipped the wig over her own dirty-blond mop and shook the reddish tresses from side to side. Then she put her hand on Carrie's back and pushed a bit, getting her to sit up straighter. 'Now, look right at the mirror. I'm gonna do my best to match your eyebrows.' She searched the contents of Meg's case one more time until she found the makeup kit. 'Lucky for me, the resemblance doesn't have to be perfect. Charles Roche will be the only one at the party who knows what you look like, and even he doesn't know you that well. Men are so fucking oblivious, right? They hardly look at your face anyway when you wear a dress like this one.'

Erin used a makeup brush to apply the auburn dye to her eyebrows. Once they looked sufficiently similar to Carrie's brows, she started working on her foundation, brushing on powder that mimicked the precise shade of Carrie's skin. As she remodeled her features, she kept her eyes on the mirror, glancing back and forth between Carrie's reflection and her own. The poor girl was shivering again. Erin tried to think of something that would calm her.

'You know, love, we have something in common besides our good looks. I know about performing services for men. I was never a hoor, but I served them in other ways.' She brushed foundation on her forehead, covering a few wrinkles there. 'I took orders from men. I marched in their militias. And get this: the commander of my paramilitary brigade was my da. He never had any sons, so he raised his daughter to be a soldier. How fucked up is that?'

Carrie kept shivering.

'I also know how hard it is to free yourself. I mean, I got away from them geographically, my da and his mates and their fucking lost cause. But how far did I really get? Like it or not, I'm still in the family business. I'm still stalking enemies and shooting them down.'

Now tears leaked from the corners of Carrie's eyes. Erin belatedly realized that talking about the Provos probably wasn't the smartest way to calm the woman. It was difficult to watch her crying, to see the collateral damage up close, and Erin felt a sudden urge to chuck this whole Charles Roche assignment. She wanted to peel the duct tape off Carrie and apologize, then leave the Sky Tower and take a taxi to JFK and hop on an airliner headed anywhere but Ireland. She'd saved enough money to start a new life, and she had some skills that could prove useful in a variety of professions. She could be a safari guide in Botswana, for example. Or a sheep rancher in the Australian Outback.

But no. She was as trapped as Carrie and everyone else. If there was even the slightest chance that she could save her father, how could she ignore it? How could she let him rot in prison if Angela was right and there was a golden future where he could walk free?

The black cube on the coffee table emitted a trio of high-pitched notes, a little tune to alert Erin that it had finished processing. She lifted the cube's lid, and inside the compartment were two contact lenses that the device had just tinted and imprinted. She held one of the lenses up to the light and inspected the blue ring printed on the tiny transparent cup, marked with Carrie's unique pattern of iris striations. Then she slipped the lens onto her left eye and put the other lens onto her right. She picked up the iris scanner again and held it in front of her face, and the device let out a confirmatory beep. According to the scanner's readings, she was Carrie Darling.

She did a quick search of the living room and found Carrie's little black handbag, which contained her driver's license and all the other old-fashioned proofs of identification. Erin added only two items of her own to the bag, a tube of lipstick and a burner phone that couldn't be traced to anyone. Nothing else on the coffee table – the extra wigs, the makeup kit, the iris scanner, the black cube – was needed anymore, so she swept all that crap back into Meg's case.

She looked in the mirror again, comparing her face to Carrie's one last time. They didn't exactly look like twins, but it was close enough. Then she grasped one of the poor girl's bound arms. 'OK, love, it's time for you to go into your closet. You're lucky it's a walk-in, you'll have plenty of room.'

Carrie trembled so hard, the sofa creaked.

'Come on now, it won't be so bad. You'll only have to stay in there for a few hours. And you've already peed yourself, so you don't have to worry about that.'

Erin tugged at her arm and Carrie slowly stood up. The girl was a bit shaky on her feet, but Erin managed to lead her out of the living room and into the closet. She kicked all the shoes into the corner so the girl would have some room to lie down, and she balled up a few scarves to make a soft pillow for her. She used another scarf to make a blindfold, tying it around Carrie's head and over her eyes. 'There you go. You can have a nice little nap now. When I'm done with my job, I'll make an anonymous call to that concierge downstairs and tell him you got locked inside your closet.'

Carrie lay on her side, resting her head on the scarf-pillow. Her tremors subsided somewhat, although her bound legs kept jerking back and forth on the floor. Erin empathized with the girl, she truly did, but nevertheless she had to deliver a firm message before they parted ways.

'One more thing, love. After they break you out of this closet, the cops and FBI agents are gonna ask you a fuckload of questions. But you're just going to tell them that the intruder put this blindfold on you as soon as you opened your door, and you didn't get even a glimpse of the bastard. All right? Can you do that?'

Carrie nodded rapidly on her pillow, but of course she would agree to anything right now. Erin needed to make the consequences of non-compliance very clear.

'We've only known each other for half an hour or so, but you're a smart girl, and I think you've seen that I'm awfully good at what I do. Which means that no matter where you go over the next few years, no matter which paths of life you choose to travel, I'll be able to track you down. And if I find out that you told the cops anything about me? Even something as trivial as my lovely accent? Then I won't be so nice the next time we meet. Understand?'

Now Carrie nodded so vigorously the bundled scarves under her head began to unravel. Smiling, Erin closed the closet's sliding door and wedged an umbrella in the doorsill so Carrie couldn't open it from inside. Then she used another scarf to wipe her fingerprints off the doorknob and everything else she'd touched since entering the apartment, including all the items in Meg's case. She still had plenty of time – it was only ten forty-five, and Charles Roche's limo driver wasn't due to pick her up until eleven thirty.

She was almost done with the cleanup when her burner phone rang. She took it out of Carrie's handbag. 'Yes?'

'It's me. There's been a change of plans.'

Erin frowned. The voice was Carl Hauser's. They'd been instructed not to communicate with each other today unless there was a dire emergency, so she braced for the worst. 'What is it?'

'We just found out that someone else is coming to the party, a last-minute invite. The number two guy on our list.'

Carl avoided mentioning any names – although they were using an encryption app, there was still a chance that the Feds could intercept and decrypt the call – but Erin knew exactly who he was referring to. 'So, what should I do? Go after number two instead of number three?'

'We want you to go after both. Two birds with one stone, so to speak.'

Erin hated the metaphor, which wasn't even close to being accurate. A stone was a simple object, easy to aim and throw. It wasn't anything like a swarm of a dozen self-navigating drones. 'It's possible to do that? Technically?'

'Our tech guy thinks so. He's adjusting the software right now. Half a dozen of the things will fly toward number two, and the other half-dozen will home in on number three.'

She didn't like it. Their margin of error would be cut in half. Plus, they were asking her to do twice as much work. 'What about my compensation? Is that going to be adjusted too?'

'You'll get double pay. You're posing as the party girl, right?'

'Yeah, that's one way to describe her.'

'Then you can come on to both guys. Just make sure you mark them by twelve thirty. That's still the go time.'

Then he hung up.

FOURTEEN

Agent Reyes's motto was 'Hope for the best, but prepare for the worst.' Her day was going pretty well so far, but she had a sneaking feeling that her luck wouldn't last.

By eleven thirty a.m., Reyes and her team had secured the streets around Charles Roche's mansion. She'd persuaded the NYPD to send two hundred cops to the perimeter of a no-go zone surrounding the Fifth Avenue townhouse. Better yet, those cops faced off against only a few dozen protesters on the other side of the barricades. After spending all night marching across Manhattan, the vast majority of the activists were currently asleep on the lawns and benches of Central Park. And though Reyes had been up all night too, now she was busy giving orders to the SWAT teams and K-9 squads on East 81st Street, where bomb-sniffing dogs circled the stretch limousines that were waiting to proceed to Roche's reception.

When she wasn't giving orders, she was scanning the streets, on the lookout for trouble. Among the smattering of protesters, Reyes noticed several holding two-way radios. They seemed to be monitoring the police activity and reporting their observations to someone. She sensed the presence of a small, secret group that was pursuing its own agenda under the cover of the mass demonstrations. They were the same people who'd ambushed her and Agent Wilson last night, and they might also be connected to the terrorists who were killing the climate criminals. Reyes would've loved to interrogate a few of the suspicious radiomen, but she hadn't seen them do anything illegal yet. Something was coming, though. She was sure of it.

The other problem was the weather. It was already eighty-five degrees, and the forecasters said it would hit the upper nineties this afternoon, which was fairly hellish for mid-September. And, as every cop knew, hot weather was a trigger for civil unrest. That was yet another reason to hate global warming.

She made her way back to the mansion's grand entryway,

where a dozen of Harlan Tate's men stood at attention on the marble portico. All twelve of the private bodyguards looked remarkably similar to Harlan, so much so that Reyes wondered whether he was hiring his cousins. Each man was as big as a linebacker, and each was decked out like a Special Forces soldier, in a black T-shirt and camouflage pants and wraparound sunglasses. Also, each man cradled an Uzi submachine gun, the ultimate crowd-control weapon.

Standing on the sidewalk nearby was Agent Martinez, who'd been promoted to Reyes's righthand man last night after Agent Wilson's suspension. She'd always preferred Martinez over Wilson, although he'd joined the Bureau only a year ago and still made some rookie mistakes. He was wiry and curly-haired and a quick thinker, and he didn't seem too broken up about Wilson's crash-and-burn. In his bland gray Bureau suit, Martinez didn't look nearly as intimidating as the twelve Rambos in front of the townhouse, but Reyes knew his record – he'd outscored all his classmates at the Academy in the marksmanship and martial arts drills. She wanted him by her side when she confronted Harlan, so she gave him a hand signal and he followed her through the mansion's carved doors.

The vast high-ceilinged foyer had been converted to a security checkpoint. More of Harlan's men stood on the sidelines, keeping watch, while other guards scrutinized the line of party guests. They patted down the early arrivals, checked their names against the guest list, used iris scanners to confirm their identity, and finally led them through the body scanner. Harlan himself towered over a table on the other side of the scanner, questioning the guests before allowing them to pass. It was a good setup, Reyes had to admit, and Harlan seemed to be a capable interrogator. She watched him quiz an elderly bearded man wearing a keffiyeh, greatly surprising the old sheikh by asking the questions in fluent Arabic.

Reyes waited until the two men exchanged salaams of farewell. Then she and Martinez headed for Harlan's table. Martinez took up position behind her, standing silent and watchful against the marble-lined wall, while Reyes sidled next to Harlan.

'Who's that guy you were just talking to?' she whispered.

'He's the Saudi oil minister. He and Mr Roche have been close friends for decades.' Harlan's voice had that annoying tone she'd noticed last night, the fawning pride in his employer's accomplishments. He surreptitiously pointed at a guest going through the body scanner, another elderly man in a white thobe and keffiyeh. 'And that's the prime minister of the United Arab Emirates. He and Mr Roche went falcon hunting in the Arabian desert last winter.'

Reyes let out an unimpressed grunt. She didn't give a fuck about the billionaire's hunting buddies. 'You see any problems yet? Any guests who seem off?'

Harlan shook his massive head. 'No, but we're just getting started. So far we've processed only fifty of the three hundred on our list.'

'All right. Let me know if you have even *minuscule* concerns about any of the guests, please. I can keep an eye on them during the lunch party.'

'That won't be necessary, Agent.' He frowned. 'My men can take care of security inside the mansion, and your people can run the show outside. That sounds like a fair division of labor, doesn't it?'

'Fuck no, it doesn't. In case you forgot, there's a United States senator coming to this shindig. You better fucking believe I'm gonna be watching him like a hawk.' She heard a commotion behind her, a chorus of excited voices, and she looked over her shoulder toward the mansion's doors. 'Speaking of which, there he is.'

Reyes had done some homework last night on the senior senator from West Virginia, who called himself the Mountaineer on his congressional website. His campaign ads showed him cruising down country roads on a motorcycle and crouching in coal mines with sooty guys in hard hats, but in real life he looked nothing like a mountaineer or a coal miner. He looked like an aging, shambling janitor dressed up in a fancy blue suit, with an American flag pin on his lapel. He had thin gray hair atop a block-like head, and his jowly face had a look of janitorial exasperation, as if he were thinking *Fuck, they want me to unclog their toilet AGAIN?* The senator was flanked by a pair of uniformed officers from the US Capitol Police, which was a poor substitute for Secret Service agents, in Reyes's opinion. If she wanted to guarantee his safety, she would have to stay close to his sorry shambling ass for the next two hours.

Roche's security guards scanned the irises of the senator and the Capitol Police officers, and then the three men filed through the body scanner. When they reached Harlan, he beamed like a six-year-old and stretched his monstrous hand toward the senator. 'Sir! Welcome to Mr Roche's home! I'm Harlan Tate, vice president of corporate security for Roche Industries, and I'm delighted to see you again!'

'Yes, I remember you, Harlan!' He grabbed two of Harlan's fingers and gave them a hearty shake. 'Say, where's your boss? How come he's not here to greet his guests?'

'Mr Roche is in his office upstairs, taking care of an important matter, but he'll be down momentarily. In the meantime, is there anything I can do for you, sir?'

'Well, as a matter of fact, there is.' The senator turned to Reyes and grinned. 'You can introduce me to this pretty young thing here.'

Reyes didn't wait for an introduction. 'Special Agent Aleida Reyes, sir. I'm in charge of the task force investigating the radicals who've infiltrated the climate protests.'

'My, my! That's a big job for a little lady like you.' Now he resembled a janitor making a hapless pass at one of his tenants. 'You know, I saw some of those protesters on my way over here, and when I waved to them from my car they started screaming and cussing. And do you know what they called me? Senator Fucking Coal. How do you like that?'

Reyes decided not to answer the question directly. 'Sir, I'd like to accompany you for the duration of this event, if you don't mind. The Bureau is very concerned about the threats that have been made against you, and—'

'Oh, I don't feel threatened, not at all.' He waved his hand in a dismissive way and simultaneously glanced around the room to see who was listening to him. 'In fact, I like that name, Senator Coal. I'm *proud* to represent the hard-working coal miners of West Virginia, and I'll do anything to defend them against the scurrilous lies of those lazy, good-for-nothing radicals out there.' He raised his voice and turned around, appealing to all the guards and party guests within earshot. 'So go ahead, call me Senator Coal! I won't mind at all!'

Several shouts of 'Senator Coal!' echoed across the room, including a very loud one from Harlan. Then one of the Arab sheikhs came over and clapped the senator on the back, and the two men stepped a few feet away to have a private conversation. Reyes kept one eye on them, ready to follow the senator into the ballroom when he was done talking to the sheikh. Meanwhile, the guards scanned the irises of three more guests, including a striking young woman in an outrageously short dress. She wore a heavy silver necklace that swayed between her breasts as she joked with the guards and tossed her auburn hair fetchingly.

Harlan stared at her too, then quickly turned away. Reyes poked him in the ribs to get his attention. 'Hey, who's the hottie? What country is she prime minister of?'

For once, the big bodyguard seemed reluctant to talk. He shrugged and examined some papers on the table. 'She's one of Mr Roche's friends.'

'You've seen her before?'

'Yeah, a few times. From a distance.'

Reyes was getting the picture. 'You're keeping your distance because you don't want to pry into your boss's private life?'

Harlan sighed. 'Look, Mr Roche is like any other man. He enjoys the company of young women.'

'But he's paying for this woman's company, right? And judging from the looks of her, I bet she doesn't come cheap. What's her name?'

'Uh, let me see.' He riffled through his papers, but he clearly knew damn well what her name was. It was the strangest thing – Harlan was embarrassed on his employer's behalf. 'It's, uh, Carrie Darling.'

'Seriously? That's her real name?' She looked again at the woman, who'd stepped into the body scanner and raised her hands over her head, swinging her hips with a little extra gusto. Under ordinary circumstances, Reyes wouldn't have given a shit about Roche's hooker, but she was on high alert now and fixating on anything that felt hinky. 'Do me a favor, Harlan. Get her handbag from the X-ray machine and bring it over here. And let me ask her a few questions, OK?'

With another sigh, he went to the X-ray machine. The woman blew a kiss at the guard who'd scanned her, then sauntered over to Agent Reyes, who stared hard at her for several seconds. In response, Ms Darling smiled and said, 'Oh my God, I love your hair! It's almost the same color as mine!'

Her voice was hard to place. It had a Southern California ring to it, although it was more like what you'd hear on a TV show about the place. Reyes kept staring at her until Harlan brought over the handbag, and then she pointed at the woman.

'Ma'am, I need to inspect the contents of this bag. Do I have your permission to do that?'

'Of course! It's a cute little thing, isn't it? And I got it on sale, too.'

Reyes opened the bag and looked inside: keys, credit cards, lipstick, a cheap cell phone, two twenty-dollar bills, and a package of chewing gum. She fished out a New York State driver's license and checked out the woman's photo, which didn't do her justice. Her legal name was indeed Carrie Darling and she had a Manhattan address.

'You live on East Seventy-first Street, ma'am?'

'Yeah, only ten blocks away. I could've walked here, but Chuckie insisted on sending a limo for me. Crazy, right?'

She was either very dumb, Reyes thought, or very good at playing dumb. Looking for clues, Reyes reached into the bag again and pulled out the tube of lipstick, which seemed to be an antique. It was made out of some heavy, gold-plated metal, and it had an unusual hourglass shape. Curious, she held it up to the light. 'Do you mind if I open this?'

'Go ahead! Isn't it adorable?' Darling leaned across the table, showing way too much cleavage. 'I found it on Etsy. It's vintage, like a hundred years old.'

Reyes uncapped the heavy tube. The lipstick inside was dark red and glittery, speckled with silver. It was ridiculously garish, in Reyes's opinion, but these days the young girls seemed to love that kind of stuff.

'I'm saving it for later,' Darling confided. 'I mean, these parties are so stuffy, and Chuckie would have a fit if I did anything too crazy in front of his friends. But he won't mind if I put it on after everyone else is gone.'

Reyes really didn't want to think about that. She put the lipstick tube and the driver's license back into the handbag and returned it to the woman. 'Thank you for your patience, ma'am.'

'No problem! It was nice meeting you!'

Darling pivoted on her stiletto heels, turning toward the ballroom. She didn't make it very far, though; one of the Capitol Police officers bumped into her, probably intentionally, and she got into a lively, laughing dialogue with the young man. Reyes felt a twinge of envy as she watched them; although she'd had a few boyfriends during her six years in the Marines and her twelve years at the Bureau, they were all *serious* relationships, fraught with tension and conflict. In her whole life, she'd never been so carefree and flirtatious, so playfully happy. And it was probably too late for her to feel that way now.

After another half-minute the sheikh ended his conversation with Senator Coal, and the two men walked down the grand hallway toward the ballroom. Darling and the two Capitol officers followed about ten feet behind, their laughter caroming off the marble walls.

Reyes tapped Harlan's arm. 'I'll check in with you on the radio. Stay on channel three.' Then she turned around and stepped toward Agent Martinez, who hadn't moved an inch in the past fifteen minutes. She drew close to him and whispered in his ear. 'Go upstairs to Roche's office and keep watch over the guy. I'll stay with the senator.'

Keeping her eyes on the Mountaineer, Reyes headed for the reception.

'I'll tell you one thing, I'm glad I'm in New York today and not West Virginia. I mean, I don't want to say anything bad about the senator's home state, but have you ever been there?'

Erin pretended to laugh at the stupid comment from the Capitol police officer, whose surname (according to the nametag on his uniform) was Abelson. In reality, though, she wasn't happy. The lady cop was following them, the one who'd inspected her handbag. *Shite! What does she want now?*

Senator Coal was a few meters ahead, saying howdy to everyone in the hallway. Officer Abelson kept his voice down so his boss wouldn't overhear his witticisms. 'I was in West Virginia with the senator last week, and it was a nightmare. You have to drink bottled water in some of those towns, because the coal mines messed up all the groundwater. But don't ever mention that to the Mountaineer! That man lives and breathes carbon.'

Erin laughed again, this time throwing her head back so she could peer at her pursuer. The first task was to determine what kind of cop she was. She wore one of those awful blue blazers that the NYPD detectives are so fond of, but she seemed too straitlaced and uptight to be a New York bobby. More likely she was federal. There was a bulge under the left side of her blazer, strongly indicating the presence of a shoulder holster, which held a Glock nine-millimeter if she was indeed FBI. The agent's gaze was mostly fixed on the senator but occasionally she looked to the left and right, scanning the hallway. She was probably there to provide an extra layer of protection for the bigwig. Which was a smart move, given the ineptitude of the two Capitol Police boyos.

But Erin was smart, too. She glanced at the beautiful Cartier watch she'd lifted from Carrie Darling's apartment: it was five past twelve. She had twenty-five minutes to mark her targets, and that was more than enough time.

Soon they reached the ballroom, which was nearly as big as a jet hangar. The floor and walls were finished with every conceivable type of marble – white, cream, rain-forest green – and crystal chandeliers the size of Volkswagens hung from the lofty ceiling. At one end of the room was the most impressive bar Erin had ever seen, stocked with enough wine and spirits to keep a whole football league drunk for a week, and at the other end was a thirty-piece orchestra playing saccharine show tunes. And directly opposite the ballroom's entrance was a long wall of French doors and high windows, all looking out on the immense inner courtyard where the luncheon tables were arrayed.

Dozens of white-jacketed waiters crisscrossed the room, bearing trays of hors d'oeuvres and champagne glasses. Erin grabbed a glass and took a sip, listening with one ear to Abelson's banter as she tracked the movements of the nosy federal in the blazer. The auburn-haired agent stepped a bit closer to the senator, who was surrounded by American capitalists and European diplomats eager to shake his hand, as well as several waiters proffering cocktails and foie gras. It was hard to get a clear view of him amid the crush, and the federal had to circle around to the other side of the well-dressed scrum.

Now the agent couldn't see her, and Erin jumped at the opportunity. She deposited her champagne glass on a passing waiter's tray, then opened her handbag and took out her antique lipstick tube. Holding both hands in front of her mouth, she pretended to touch up her lips, but instead she smeared a thick red streak on the palm of her left hand. She quickly closed her hand to hide the streak, which sparkled with silver dots. They looked like glitter but were actually radio-transceiving microchips.

Erin put the cap back on the heavy metal tube, which was solid enough to block any signals from reaching the microchips remaining inside it. Then she turned back to Officer Abelson. 'Sweetheart, could you introduce me to the senator? I know, he seems like a lunkhead, but my folks back home just love that man.'

Abelson gave her a big, dumb smile. 'It would be my pleasure!' He snaked his hand around her waist and they pushed into the scrum together, with Abelson repeatedly barking, 'Excuse me, sir!' in a very official tone until the capitalists and waiters made way for them.

In a few seconds she stood in front of Senator Coal, who immediately dropped the hand of the nondescript tycoon he'd been greeting. He looked as if he'd just struck it rich in one of his state's coal mines, or (more realistically) as if he'd just pocketed a hefty donation from one of the coal-mine executives. He cocked his blocky head and gave her a once-over, his mouth open wide and wetly lascivious.

'Whoa! And who might you be? You're a sight for sore eyes, honey. You're like a tall glass of water in this dry desert of old men!'

Erin put on a demure smile and a tentative manner. 'I'm, uh, a good friend of Chuckie Roche. My name is Carrie Darling.'

'Well, that's a darling name, Darling!' The senator looked around to see if any of his rich buddies would laugh at his pathetic joke, and of course they did. 'Where the hell is old Chuckie anyway? Is he gonna miss his own party?'

'Uh, I don't know. I haven't seen him either.'

'Maybe you should go upstairs and drag him down here. You have ways of persuading him, right? I bet he'd listen to *you*!'

The capitalists chuckled again. The senator clearly recognized that Carrie Darling was Roche's whore, and he was making jokes at her expense to amuse his idiot friends. Erin felt a wave of fury so strong, she almost slammed her fist into the Mountaineer's windpipe, killing the fucking bastard right then and there. But she controlled herself and shyly extended her right hand. 'Yes, I'll go look for him. It was nice to meet you, sir.'

As Erin had expected, Senator Coal spread his arms wide, going for a hug instead of a handshake. 'Bring it in, Darling! Any good friend of Chuckie's is a better friend of mine!'

Erin let it happen. She'd known from the start that she wouldn't have to throw herself at the senator; all she had to do was give the ugly wanker a chance to throw himself at her. He clamped his hands on her back and fingered her bra strap as he drew her in close. At the same time, she slipped her hands inside his jacket and clasped the sides of his barrel-like chest, wiping the lipstick and embedded microchips on the right side of his shirt, just below his armpit.

When Erin finally disentangled herself from the senator, his dipshit friends were beaming in vicarious delight. She wanted to murder them all, but she kept a smile on her face and slipped away, averting her eyes from Officer Abelson's disappointed expression. As she crossed the ballroom she noticed the auburn-haired FBI agent staring at her, and Erin felt a surge of alarm, wondering if the federal had seen what she'd done. For a moment Erin thought she might have to start running, but soon the agent went back to eyeballing Senator Coal, craning her neck to get a better view of him through the crowd.

No, she didn't see it. She has no fucking idea. One down, one to go.

Erin looked at her left hand to make sure there were no microchips still clinging to it. Then she checked her watch again: twelve fifteen p.m. Time to go upstairs and find Charles Roche.

At twelve twenty-seven Reyes got a radio call from Agent Martinez. She unhooked the two-way Motorola from her belt and held it next to her cheek. 'You got something to report, Martinez?'

'Roche is on the move.' The agent was breathing fast. 'He and two bodyguards just left his office in a hurry. I'm following them down the third-floor corridor right now.'

'Are they coming here? To the ballroom?'

'Negative. They're headed for the elevator on the west side of the townhouse.'

Reyes nodded. She'd expected this to happen. Until now Roche had shown nothing but arrogant defiance in response to the threats against his life, but his attitude had smacked of false bravado. He'd probably been a little scared all along – who wouldn't be? – and in the past few minutes his hidden fear had apparently grown into terror. Now that three hundred guests had entered his mansion, Charles Roche had decided to take the elevator down to his panic floor. And in Reyes's opinion, this was a wise move. It would've been even wiser to cancel the reception, as Reyes had advised him to do last night, but she was glad that Roche had finally come to his senses.

'All right, thanks for the update, Martinez. Alert me again when you reach the secure location.'

'Will do. Over and out.'

So, Reyes thought, that was one less thing to worry about. Now all she had to do was keep shadowing Senator Coal for another hour and a half. He and his crowd of sycophants had slowly drifted across the ballroom and stepped through the French doors to the townhouse's inner courtyard. They loitered in clusters near the luncheon tables, which were draped in gorgeous linens and set with priceless china and gleaming silverware, but no one sat down yet; there were too many murmured secrets to exchange – all that inside information about crude-oil futures and currency exchange rates and political coups being plotted in Sudan and Indonesia. The *sotto voce* conversations swirled around Reyes as she hovered in the background, and it occurred to her that some of these party guests were committing white-collar crimes that would cause a whole lot more devastation than anything the Climate Avengers could pull off. But she shouldn't think about that. It simply wasn't her concern. She had a job to do, simple and straightforward.

But as she'd noticed before, the weather was a problem. It was clearly a lot hotter this afternoon than any of the party planners had anticipated. The air conditioners in the ballroom were running full tilt, and a cool breeze blew through the open French doors to the courtyard, but those chilly gusts were no match for the blanket of baked air settling upon them. Reyes looked up at the rectangle of sky above her, bordered by the eaves of the mansion's inner walls, and it seemed to be bleached white, like over-washed jeans. The waiters frantically set up outdoor air conditioners all over the courtyard, running power cables through the townhouse's doorways and windows, enlarging this reception's carbon footprint to the size of a small city's, but it still wasn't enough to lower the ambient temperature. Some of the diplomats in the crowd loosened their ties, and most of the fat cats took off their jackets and draped them over their chairs.

Senator Coal also took off his jacket, exposing a white dress shirt distended by his beach-ball stomach. In his left hand he held his third rum-and-Coke – he seemed to down each drink in a single swallow – and his right hand slapped the back of a man whom Reyes believed was the chief executive of ExxonMobil. And as the Mountaineer raised that arm to give the executive's shoulder a manly squeeze, Reyes noticed a dark red stain just below the senator's armpit.

Holy shit. Is he bleeding?

Reyes lunged forward, pushing aside an African president in a dashiki. *Is it a gunshot wound? Or maybe someone stabbed him?* But the senator was guffawing at something the chief executive just said, so he clearly wasn't in pain. *What the hell? Did he cut himself while shaving his armpits?*

Then her two-way radio squawked again, another call from Martinez.

'Ma'am? We got a situation here.'

Without breaking stride, Reyes grabbed her Motorola. 'Talk quick. What is it?'

'It's that woman, Darling. She—'

A blast of static suddenly drowned out Martinez's voice, radio noise interfering with the channel three signal. At the same moment, Senator Coal turned his torso, and tiny glints of light reflected off the red stain on his shirt.

Oh fuck. The glitter. The lipstick.

A waiter stepped into her path, and she knocked over his tray of cocktails. She bounded the last few yards toward the senator, who spun toward her when he heard the glassware shatter, his jowls tensing. Then he lifted his double chin, because there was a high-pitched whine coming from above, getting louder by the second.

Reyes looked up, too. Silhouetted against the rectangle of bleached sky were six dark crosses, diving fast.

Erin was frantic. With just five minutes left until go time, the job had gone tits up.

She stood outside the locked door to Roche's office on the townhouse's third floor. Five minutes ago she'd knocked on the door and pleaded, in her best imitation of Carrie Darling, 'Chuckie, open up. It's me, Carrie.' A moment later, a gruff voice yelled, 'Go away!' She knocked again and got the same response. Then she shucked off her stilettos and banged them against the door so hard that both of the heels snapped off, but this time she got nothing but silence for her efforts.

It was goddamn bloody frustrating. This was the most complicated operation she'd ever undertaken, employing gear so high-tech it would make an Air Force general spurt in his pants, and the whole thing had been banjaxed by a fucking locked door.

Desperate, she looked up and down the hallway, searching for anything she could use to break into the office. This floor of the mansion was less crowded with antique furniture than the others, and there were no chairs or ottomans or end tables she could hurl at the office's door. A big wide porcelain vase, about the size of a fat child, stood by the wall just a few meters away, but when Erin ran over to see if it would make a suitable battering ram, she quickly realized it would shatter at the first blow.

Ah, Jesus! What a fucking fiasco!

Any second now, Carl Hauser would turn on the radio transmitter he'd positioned on Cedar Hill in Central Park, less than a quarter-mile away. The powerful signal would activate all the micro-transmitters that weren't still inside Erin's lipstick tube, and each silvery chip would start broadcasting a homing beacon. Then Carl would fire the dozen drones from the launch tube, and they'd zoom across Fifth Avenue, whizzing high above the heads of all the cops and agents and mercenaries guarding Roche's mansion. With any luck the drones would make a pincushion of Senator Coal, but they wouldn't come anywhere near Charles Roche unless Erin managed to mark the grizzled fuck in the next four minutes.

Then, like a miracle, the office door opened and a brute holding a machine gun stepped into the hallway. Erin instinctively ducked behind the huge vase as the bodyguard looked both ways, gazing down the length of the corridor. Then he gave the all-clear signal to the people behind him, and Charles Roche emerged from the office, flanked by another giant bodyguard and the youngish FBI agent she'd seen downstairs, the quiet junior partner of the auburn-haired hard-ass. The four men hurried down the hallway toward the mansion's west wing, which Erin had already surveyed while she was searching for Roche's office. There was an elevator at that end of the hallway and a bank of windows overlooking Fifth Avenue.

Erin gauged the speed of the men, the distance between her and them, and their general alertness. The FBI agent held a two-way radio to his right ear, and with his other hand he gripped Chuckie's right arm and pulled him along as fast as the old man could manage. The bodyguard to Roche's left kept his eyes on the Uzi-toting monster at the head of the formation, and neither he nor the agent took a moment to look behind them. All in all, their situational awareness was sorely lacking, and Erin was going to make them pay for it. She opened her lipstick tube, drew another streak on her left palm, and recapped it. Then she launched herself down the hallway, her stockinged feet silently padding the carpeted floor.

She caught up to the men just before they reached the end of the corridor. Erin tackled Roche from behind like a rugby player, wrapping her arms around his torso and pressing her palms against the front of his suit jacket. Roche yelped like an injured puppy as they hit the floor and rolled on the carpet, coming to rest just below the bank of windows.

The two bodyguards and the FBI agent instantly pointed their guns at her, but she lay beneath Roche and held him in place like a human shield. At the same time, she nuzzled her face against the side of Roche's head and wept hysterically. 'Oh Chuckie, don't run away from me! You know how much I love you!'

The three armed men looked down at her for a few seconds, and Erin could see each of them coming to the same conclusion: she's crackers, but not life-threatening. They lowered their weapons, breathing hard with relief, but Roche squirmed in her embrace and screamed at the trio of men standing around them. 'Help me, you imbeciles! Get her off me!'

The two bodyguards bent over and grabbed her. One of them broke her hold on Roche and turned her over onto her stomach, and the other wrenched her arms behind her back and pressed his knee down on her ass. Erin shook her head and yelled, 'No, I'm a guest, I'm Carrie Darling! Chuckie invited me!' but the goons on top of her didn't loosen their grip. Meanwhile, the FBI agent helped Roche to his feet, holding him steady until he stopped swaying. Erin tilted her head back, trying to catch the old man's eye. 'Please, Chuckie! Tell them who I am!'

Roche blinked a few times as he stared at her. One of the bodyguards was shoving her chin into the carpet, which was actually a good thing, since that would make it harder for Roche to tell the difference between her and his whore. But then she felt something scratchy against her left ear, and she realized that in the tussle her auburn wig had slid to the side.

Roche's rheumy eyes widened. 'Christ! You're not Carrie!' He reached down and snatched the wig off her head. The thing dangled from his hand as he stepped backward. 'Fucking hell! You're the blonde bitch!' Pointing at her, he turned to the FBI agent. 'That's the one, the assassin! Why are you just standing there? *Arrest her!*'

The agent held out his hands. 'Calm down, sir. Do you mean—'

'She's the bitch who poisoned Jonathan!' Roche took another step backward. Then he looked down at the front of his jacket and saw the smear of lipstick running from the lapel to the handkerchief pocket. The red color didn't show well against the suit's dark fabric, but the smear glittered with the light coming in through the windows. 'Holy God! Holy *fuck*! Look what she did to me!'

'Sir, please . . .'

Roche ignored the agent and wriggled out of the jacket, being careful not to touch the stained part. Then he threw it on the floor and backed up a couple of meters. *'That's poison, too! The bitch just tried to kill me!'*

The agent gave up on trying to calm the old geezer and pulled out his two-way radio again. 'Ma'am, we got a situation here.' As he waited for a response, he stepped toward the jacket splayed on the floor. He crouched beside it so he could get a closer look at the glittering lipstick smear. 'It's that woman, Darling. She—'

'*Agent!*' Erin's heart thudded. She'd just heard a high-pitched whine, coming from the other side of the windows. 'Get away from that—'

Then the windows shattered, spraying glass everywhere.

They were smarter than bullets or artillery shells. As Reyes sprinted toward Senator Coal, the fucking crosses actually detoured around her before smashing into the senator's chest.

All six of the projectiles hit his torso within half a second of one another, but each swooped in from a different angle. One came at him from the right, taking the most direct route to the lipstick smear below his armpit. Another struck the left side of his chest and plowed horizontally through his ribcage to reach the target. A third plunged into the crook between his neck and shoulder. As they pierced his skin, they shed the wings and propellers that had made them look like crosses, leaving only the pointed fuselages to drill holes into his lungs and heart. They didn't stop until they'd spent their momentum, either lodged deep inside the senator's body or dropping from crater-like exit wounds to clink against the flagstone floor of the courtyard.

The Mountaineer juddered with the impacts. He stared in confusion at Reyes as his heart stopped and the internal bleeding began. Then he collapsed against one of the luncheon tables, pulling the fancy tablecloth and china settings down with him.

Within seconds the courtyard was a screaming mob scene. All the party guests and waiters took one look at the mutilated corpse and fled. They stampeded toward the mansion's French doors and flailed at one another as they fought to re-enter the ballroom. Agent Reyes was the only one in the crowd who refused to abandon Senator Coal, even though there was nothing she could do for him. She bent over his slumped body, which lay facedown on the blood-soaked flagstones.

Fuck. They got him. Even after all our precautions, they still got him.

And what about Roche?

She tried to contact Agent Martinez on the two-way radio, but there was no answer.

Erin watched it happen; more collateral damage. But this time she saw it much too close.

And she couldn't blame the FBI agent, couldn't call him a bleeding eejit who'd blundered into his own demise. He did the smart thing, the thing he'd been trained to do. As soon as the third-floor windows shattered, he hit the deck and covered his head. Unfortunately, he sprawled right on top of Roche's jacket.

It happened so fast, she saw the six drones dive into the agent's prone body before she could close her eyes. Even worse was hearing the half-dozen thumps against the floor. The drones struck him with so much force, they tore right through his flesh as well as the layer of carpet and hammered the hardwood below.

But the worst part of all was seeing that bastard Roche several meters down the hallway, wheezing and gaping but completely unscathed. The old prick backed up a few steps, then turned around and ran off, screaming like a soprano.

No. No fucking way. You're gonna get what's coming, you gobshite.

Both of Roche's bodyguards had been hit by the flying glass shards, and in their shock and confusion they'd let go of Erin's arms and eased off her body. So it was a simple matter for her to turn right-side up and knee one of the big fuckers in the groin. Then she grabbed his Uzi and fired a burst into the other fucker's stomach. Last, she slammed the machine gun's barrel into the first guy's skull, and he went down like an oak. She didn't even bother to finish him off; he wasn't worth the bullets.

By this point, though, she heard the tromp of boots coming from the direction where Roche had disappeared. The prick's screams had drawn more guards to the third floor, and now they were racing toward the sound of the machine-gun burst. Erin absolutely hated to let Roche go, but for consolation she recalled her father's favorite nursery rhyme, a couplet he'd taught her when she was just four years old, after she got into a scrap with the wee lads at her day-care center: 'She who fights and runs away may live to fight another day.'

So she dashed in the opposite direction, heading for the side of the mansion facing East 81st Street. She knew there was a balcony on this façade of the townhouse, and although a sharpshooter was stationed there, he was smoking a cigarette instead of holding his sniper rifle. All she had to do was open the sliding glass door and act like a damsel in distress, hiding the Uzi behind her back until she got close enough to shoot off the sniper's kneecaps. Then she climbed over the balcony's stone ledge and scrambled down to the roof of the portico above the mansion's north entrance.

The situation on the streets surrounding the townhouse was a lot more chaotic than it had been an hour ago. Carl had told her that Prophecy's operatives would lead a huge march of protesters to the mansion by twelve thirty, and there they were now on Fifth Avenue and 81st Street, a crowd of thousands swarming around the block, holding signs that said 'SAVE SONYA, SAVE THE EARTH' and 'SQUASH THAT ROCHE.' The protesters had pushed right past the cops at the barricades, and the crowd's leading edge was less than a meter from the sidewalk, held back only by the presence of a dozen armed bodyguards on the steps below the portico. One of the guards, a big pale fellow with a black bandanna tied around his head, brandished an Uzi in his right hand and held a bullhorn in his left.

'*ATTENTION!*' The guy had a Russian accent, reinforcing Erin's suspicion that some of Roche's bodyguards were mercenaries. '*You are participating in an ILLEGAL PROTEST. We are authorized to SHOOT YOU if you come any closer!*'

The protesters were outraged, of course. They boomed their displeasure, screaming obscenities at the guards, and the front-line marchers defiantly moved nearer. In response, the Russian yelled, '*I WARNED YOU!!*' and fired his Uzi into the air.

Erin had seen enough. Leaning over the edge of the portico's roof, she shot a burst into the Russkie's back. The other guards panicked when he went down; they turned tail and retreated, rushing to get inside the mansion.

Now all the protesters looked up and stared at Erin, wondering whether she was enemy or friend. So she tossed her gun aside and raised a fist toward the sky.

'THE FUTURE IS OURS!' She was winging it, shouting the first clichés that came to mind. 'DOWN WITH THE OPPRESSORS! WE CAN'T EAT MONEY! THERE IS NO PLANET B!!'

As the protesters cheered and surged forward, Erin slid down one of the portico's columns and jumped to the sidewalk. Then she escaped into the crowd, threading and jostling through the shouting, sweaty multitudes, on her way to Cedar Hill and her rendezvous with Carl.

Reyes knelt beside Martinez's body.

Through the broken windows, she could hear the crowd roaring outside and the occasional crash of a bottle thrown against the townhouse, but none of the demonstrators had tried to storm the mansion's locked doors. Roche was safely lodged on his panic floor, and his party guests were cowering inside the ballroom, waiting for the protest to subside and the crowd to disperse, so they could safely leave the mansion in their armored limousines.

In the meantime, Reyes was going to stay with her partner. Considering how badly she'd failed him, it was the least she could do.

She tried to think good thoughts about honor and duty, about the worthiness of the sacrifice Martinez had made, but it was impossible. All she could think of was the lying mouth of that murderess, her long savage legs under that short black dress, her cute little handbag full of death. After a while she realized with some chagrin that Roche had been right about the assassin.

She was a bitch.

And Reyes was going to kill her.

FIFTEEN

Sonya woke to the sound of footsteps outside her jail cell. They were quiet steps, just a gentle tapping against linoleum tiles, but the sound was deafening compared with the absolute silence of a moment ago. It was enough to jolt Sonya from her uneasy sleep and make her sit up on the sad excuse for a bed that jutted like a shelf from the cinderblock wall.

The footsteps grew louder and then stopped. Judging from the sound, Sonya guessed at least two people stood on the other side of her cell's door. She wasn't bound or gagged anymore, so her first impulse was to jump out of bed and start screaming on the off chance that the visitors were cops or FBI agents searching the building for her. But so many bad things had happened in the past twenty-four hours that she no longer trusted her impulses. Worse, she couldn't turn to Janet for advice, because the kidnappers had separated them. Sonya felt like she wasn't quite human anymore, like she was turning into a creature of pure fear, wincing at the thought of more punishment. So she sat there, frozen, too scared to let out even a whimper, while her visitors unlocked the heavy door and slid it open.

One of them was Angela, and that was bad enough, but the other was a hulking bald guy with a big purple bruise on his face. The baldie wore scuffed boots and muddy jeans and a polo shirt with dark sweat stains around the armpits. He'd obviously had a very bad day, and his scowl was a silent warning: *don't make it any worse*. Angela looked unhappy too, her pale chin quivering, her deep-space eyes darting to and fro, as if some difficulty or setback had thrown her off balance. She stepped past the bald guy and stood in front of Sonya, her right hand deep inside the pocket of her jumpsuit, toying with the jingling items at the bottom of it.

'Good afternoon, Sonya. Did you get some rest?'

It was a strange question to ask, since Angela must've already known the answer. A security camera hung from the ceiling of the jail cell, and it had undoubtedly recorded all the hours Sonya had paced back and forth and pounded her fists against the door and finally collapsed on the hard bed. But instead of pointing this out, Sonya simply nodded and said nothing. Better to save her strength.

Angela jerked a thumb over her shoulder, aiming it at the bald guy, who stood motionless in the corner of the cell. 'This is Carl, my assistant. He's here just in case you decide to do something stupid. But I don't think that'll happen. You're an excellent student, and I think you've learned a few things from your experience yesterday.'

Sonya nodded again. She pictured the switchblade that Angela was jiggling inside her pocket, the same knife she'd held to Janet's throat while they recorded the video last night. Sonya had read from a script, crying in front of the camera, terrified that if she mispronounced even a single word the wild-haired fanatic would start cutting. Yes, it was a learning experience.

But despite the fear, Sonya managed to lift her head and look Angela in the eye. 'Where's Janet?'

Angela looked askance. She seemed amused. 'It's interesting that you're so concerned about your father's girlfriend. You must have a very good relationship with her. Did she comfort you after your mother died?'

Sonya's stomach twisted. *How does she know that?* But then she reminded herself that she'd talked about her mom's death in a few of the media interviews she'd done in advance of her UN speech. The reporters loved to ask the question, 'Who's your greatest inspiration?' and Sonya had told them the truth. Angela had clearly read the articles and was now fucking with her head.

'Please, just tell me where Janet is.'

Angela smiled and sat down beside her on the narrow bed. 'Don't worry. She's in a room exactly like this one. But don't bother trying to communicate with her by banging on the walls. She's in a different cellblock, on the other side of the building.'

The twisting in her stomach got worse, because Angela was sitting much too close. Sonya couldn't help but lean away from the woman, who smelled of sweat and something else, something coppery and sharp. But Angela didn't look offended. Her smile broadened.

'I'll tell you a secret, Sonya. I knew your mother. Cheryl and I were students at Columbia at the same time.'

Angela's voice turned low and confidential. *She's still playing games. She's using the facts from the news stories to fuck with me.* But Sonya had never mentioned her mother's name in any of the interviews she did, nor the fact that her mom had gone to Columbia. So maybe Angela was telling the truth? She looked like she was in her fifties, which was the right age.

'We weren't close, not at all. In fact, I don't think I ever said a word to Cheryl.' Angela gazed at the cell's blank wall, still smiling. 'But I admired her from afar. She saw the injustice of the world and tried to make it better. I was truly impressed by everything she accomplished after graduation, all the work she did for the mentally ill and the homeless.'

Sonya took a deep breath. She needed to get a grip on herself. It didn't matter whether Angela had actually known her mother or not. The important thing was to find her weak spots and outwit her. If Sonya wanted to get out of this place alive, she needed to calm her nerves and think clearly.

'Angela, why are you here now?' Sonya looked her in the eye again. 'Do you want me to make another video?'

'No, not yet. But soon.' She leaned back, trying to make herself comfortable on the very uncomfortable bed. 'I'm here because I want to pick your brain. I told you yesterday about my skills of prophecy, correct? How I can see the forking paths of the future?'

Sonya tried not to frown. She'd hoped for a different conversation topic. When you're talking with someone who has your life in her hands, the last thing you want to hear is more evidence of her insanity. 'Uh, yes, you mentioned that.'

'I'd like to give you a little more detail about those skills, so you'll understand what I can and can't see. As you can imagine, there are inevitable limits on the ability to predict future events.' Angela held up her hand and started ticking off points on her fingers. 'One, it's impossible to foresee *every* event that will occur on any given path. The human mind simply can't hold all that information. I've tried to focus on what I call "the global inflection points," the major events that will determine whether our civilization survives or falls to pieces.'

Sonya noticed that Angela's chin was starting to quiver again. Although her voice remained steady, something was clearly upsetting her.

'And two, an even bigger challenge is to distinguish the most likely paths among the nearly infinite number of possible futures. Sonya, have you enrolled in any physics classes at NYU? I know you're only a sophomore, but perhaps you've taken the introductory course?'

Sonya shook her head. Her dad had urged her to take physics, but she'd refused, partly because he'd recommended it too strongly.

'I'll give you the simple explanation, then. According to quantum theory, there are many paths branching from every interaction of particles, but only a few of those futures are likely. And the same is true for a very large system such as human civilization. It's analogous to the climate models that forecast the effects of global warming on various parts of the world. You can't predict the temperature at any location at any particular time, but you can say with fair certainty what the temperature averages will be if we don't stop carbon emissions. The point is, the minor deviations *don't matter*. I can't see every detail of the future in my prophecies, but when it comes to the major events I'm *never wrong*.'

Her voice rose, growing much too loud for the limited space of the jail cell. Sonya glanced at Carl the bald guy and saw him scowl again. It occurred to her that Angela was speaking to him as well, maybe trying to defend herself against some accusation or doubt. Yes, something had definitely gone wrong with their plans, and now Angela was struggling to contain the damage.

Sonya knew this piece of information could prove useful, so she filed it away in her head. She waited until she was sure that Angela had finished talking, and then she pointed at herself. 'Well, I don't have that kind of skill. I can't see visions of future paths, likely or unlikely. So why do you want to pick my brain?'

Angela smiled again. 'Because you're what I call "a worldline crux." You play a major role in *all* the possible futures.' She gave Sonya a look that would've been flattering if it hadn't been so disturbingly intense. 'Let's consider a hypothetical situation, all right? Let's assume I was never born. In this alternate reality,

Hollister Tarkington and Jonathan Humphrey would still be alive, still free to poison a dying biosphere. You would be there too, gaining more and more fame over the years as you demanded action from the world's leaders. And what, in your honest opinion, would be their most likely response? Would they shut down their coal mines and ban combustion engines? Or would they just keep making pledges and promises?'

Sonya gave her a defiant look. 'Of course I think we can win. I wouldn't fight if I thought it was hopeless.'

'Yes, I love your spirit! But how long would it take? How many years and decades would you have to keep fighting? Please, be honest now.'

'I have no idea. Maybe twenty years. Maybe my whole life.' Sonya paused to think it over. 'Honestly, I think the decision-makers will get more serious as the climate disasters get worse. Sooner or later we'll reach a tipping point. The costs of global warming will become unbearable – trillions of dollars, millions of lives. Then we'll see real action.'

'Exactly. I agree with you one hundred percent.' Angela had the audacity to give Sonya an approving pat on the back. 'But as you know, climate change will be more devastating for some countries than for others. In a few decades, rising sea levels will submerge the Marshall Islands. Heat waves will make parts of Asia and Africa uninhabitable. If drought and famine kill twenty million people in India, the Indian government will be ready to take serious action, but what about the rest of the world? The fuel guzzlers in America and Europe and China might keep burning carbon anyway.'

Sonya was getting annoyed. She'd heard all these depressing arguments before. 'I'm sorry, but where are you going with this?'

'Think about it. The most likely outcome is war. Specifically, terrorism, the war of the powerless against the powerful.' Angela shrugged, as if helpless against the inevitability of it. 'Before the end of this century, you'd see a surge of asymmetric conflict, fought mostly by small bands of zealots armed with drones and other inexpensive weapons. They'd blow up coal mines and sabotage drilling rigs. They'd vandalize diesel trucks, attach explosives to cruise ships, and shoot down airliners. And they'd assassinate the business and government leaders who oppose climate action. In other words, they'd do exactly what Prophecy is doing right now.'

'So you're saying you're just ahead of the curve? That's how you justify it?'

'Look at me.' Angela leaned forward until her face was just inches from Sonya's. Her expression was fierce and unsettling. 'Imagine yourself fifty or sixty years from now. You've spent your whole life protesting and organizing and advocating, but all your efforts have come to naught. The world is hotter and stormier, and unlivable in many places, and half of the planet's species are gone. At that point, wouldn't you do *anything* to save the rest? Wouldn't you make the same decision I did?'

Sonya didn't answer right away. Under different circumstances – if she were in an NYU classroom, for example, instead of a jail cell – she might've given Angela's question more careful consideration, because it was a good question. In a global emergency, shouldn't the usual laws of morality be suspended? Wouldn't a person on the brink of losing everything have a good excuse for breaking a few commandments? Especially if she'd already tried every peaceful means of saving the Earth?

Right now, though, it was a moot point for Sonya, because she wasn't about to have a philosophical debate with her kidnappers. But she wanted them to think she was taking the question seriously, so she put a thoughtful look on her face and lowered her head. She was going to use some of the acting skills her father had taught her.

She bit her upper lip until it really hurt. That was her technique for making the tears come to her eyes. Then she looked up at Angela. 'I suppose you're right. At that point I'd probably do anything. But we're not there yet.'

'Oh, you're wrong. We're at the point of no return right now.' Angela held out her hands and flourished them like a lecturer. 'If we keep spewing greenhouse gases into the air for the next ten years, the damage will be irreversible. The carbon dioxide will stay in the atmosphere and heat the planet for centuries. The only thing that can save us is an immediate shutdown of the fossil-fuel industry, completed within the next two years at most. Yes, it'll cause short-term disruptions to the economy, but that's better than a global catastrophe, right?'

Sonya nodded. It was easy to agree with Angela now, because everything she'd just said was absolutely correct.

'That's Prophecy's goal. That's our mission.' Angela clenched her hands. 'First, we'll eliminate the man at the top of our criminals list, just to prove that no one can escape us. Then we'll announce our demands. We'll vow to kill the leaders of all the fossil-fuel companies that fail to switch to renewable energy by the end of next year. We'll also execute any politicians who vote against climate legislation or obstruct the efforts to reach net-zero emissions.'

Sonya certainly didn't agree with this strategy, but she kept nodding anyway. She needed to show that her resistance was wavering, that she was coming over to Angela's side. She fashioned a new expression, trying to look sadly resigned. 'When will that happen? Your announcement?'

'Tomorrow night. And when we make our video, I want *you* to be in it.' She stretched her hand toward Sonya and clasped her shoulder. 'We're going to tell the world that Prophecy rescued you from the alt-right kidnappers, and in gratitude you've decided to join our organization. Your support will help us tremendously, Sonya, because of your natural appeal to young people. We need to get the next generation behind our hardline strategy to make it work over the long term.'

It was very difficult for Sonya to restrain herself. She wanted to tell Angela in no uncertain terms that her plan was nuts. But instead, she pretended to consider it. 'You're asking a lot from me, you know.'

'Yes, but—'

'I'd have to go on the run with you. I'd have to drop out of college and abandon all my friends and family.'

'Sonya, you just said you were willing to devote your whole life to this cause. So why not start now?'

'Even worse, I'd have to give up my principles. Basically, you're asking me to become a terrorist.'

'No, you'd be following the highest principle of all. What could be more important than saving human civilization? All our values, all our beliefs, they'll simply vanish into thin air if our species goes extinct.'

Angela stretched her hand out again, and this time she touched the back of Sonya's neck. It was a gentle touch, and Angela clearly meant it to be soothing, but Sonya wanted to scream. Accepting a caress from a murderer was challenging. Sonya sat there, very still, and swallowed hard.

'If I'm going to sacrifice so much for your cause, you'll need to sacrifice something for me.'

Angela withdrew her hand from Sonya's neck, thank God. 'Of course. I've given everything to Prophecy, all my father's dirty money, so our resources are considerable. What do you want?'

'Let Janet go. Once she's free, I'll become your most dedicated soldier.'

From the corner of the jail cell, Carl cleared his throat, loudly and deliberately. Sonya glanced at the bald guy, who looked more unhappy than ever. Angela glanced at him too, then gave Sonya a wary smile. 'Carl doesn't believe you. He's probably wondering if you'll actually cooperate with us after I release your father's girlfriend. Once she's gone, I'll lose my leverage over you.'

'If we're going to work together, we have to learn to trust each other.' Sonya extended her right hand. 'And besides, Janet doesn't deserve this. She's an activist, one of the good guys. She's doing her part for the cause, performing with my dad in the Doomsday Company.'

Angela didn't take Sonya's hand. In fact, she frowned at it. 'Your father disappointed me. I met him at Columbia too, at a protest. He's weak and afraid.'

'Look, we can have a long conversation sometime about all my dad's flaws. But don't punish Janet for it.' Sonya kept her hand out, waiting.

Carl cleared his throat again, and now Angela frowned at him, clearly peeved. Then she grasped Sonya's hand and shook it. 'OK, we'll release her. I'm learning to trust you.'

'Thank you.' Sonya grinned for the handshake, although she felt pretty fucking conflicted. In particular, she worried that Angela wouldn't keep her word. 'So, when will you let Janet go?'

'As soon as possible. We have to move our operations out of this facility tonight, so I suppose we could release her at the same time.'

'Wait, who's moving?' Sonya tried to sound casual, but of course she was thinking about opportunities for escape.

'We need to be in Manhattan, close to Madison Square Garden. That's where our final target will be tomorrow.' Angela turned back to Carl. 'Is Erin going to meet Stroman again this afternoon? To pick up the new equipment?'

Carl nodded. He seemed reluctant to say anything in front of Sonya. He certainly hadn't learned to trust her yet.

Sonya decided to fill the silence. 'When you say *final* target, are you talking about the number one guy on the criminals list?'

Angela gave her a hard look. 'How familiar are you with the list your father published in his obscure journal?'

Her tone was harsh and alarming. *Shit, is she suspicious? Does she see through my act?* But Sonya tamped down her panic and smiled, trying again for casual and innocent, hoping to hide any hint that she was gathering intel. 'God, I know all about that damn list. Almost every day last winter, Dad called to tell me about all the statistics he'd found. Megatons of methane here, gigatons of carbon dioxide there. I'd say, "Dad, can you wrap it up? I have a class in ten minutes." It was endless.'

'Yes, I know the type. He can't see the forest for the trees. His list of climate criminals was well-researched, but I knew I couldn't rely on it entirely.' Angela grimaced. She seemed to have some weird animus against Sonya's father. 'Did he also talk about how he selected the number one climate criminal?'

'Oh yeah, that was his favorite topic. He said, "Sonya, if you want to know which corporation is responsible for the most carbon emissions over the past fifty years, there's really no contest. It's Saudi Arabia's state-owned oil company, and the man in control of that enterprise is the crown prince of Saudi Arabia. Which makes him the worst climate criminal in the world."'

Angela shook her head. Her grimace intensified and became a look of contempt. 'I'm sorry, but I disagree with that conclusion. I disagree with it so strongly that I've chosen a different target for tomorrow's operation.'

'Really?' Sonya was surprised, although she shouldn't have been. There was no law forcing Angela to follow her father's list. 'Who will you—'

'The worst criminal is an American. He's the man who halted all our progress on reducing emissions. He canceled the plans to clean up the nation's power plants and improve its gas-mileage standards. Worst of all, he destroyed America's credibility when it comes to climate action. Other nations are now less willing to make commitments, because he reneged on ours.'

'I don't—'

'You know him. Everyone knows him. Half the country loves him and half detests him. And he's holding a rally at Madison Square Garden tomorrow.'

'Holy shit. Are you serious?'

'Yes. Our next target is the former president of the United States.'

SIXTEEN

Max Mirsky had many complaints about journalism – the low pay, the long hours, the frustration that comes from endlessly writing about the same types of disasters – but during his career as an investigative reporter he'd learned one very useful skill: how to find people. Which is what brought him to Port Morris, an industrial sliver of the Bronx between the Bruckner Expressway and the East River.

It was a broiling afternoon, nearly a hundred degrees Fahrenheit at three p.m. Port Morris was especially hellish because it was full of warehouses and workshops and had no shade trees whatsoever. The air was heavy with diesel fumes from all the trucks rumbling down the streets, and a sour winey odor drifted from the oil tanks that stood like humongous paint cans along the river. At each street corner Max had to step over pools of fetid water, stinking in the heat and coated with swirls of iridescent chemicals. *God, every puddle here is a Superfund site.* No one else was outside except a few listless sanitation workers. Several tanker trucks idled near the fuel-oil terminal, spewing more exhaust as they waited to load up, but all the drivers stayed inside their air-conditioned rigs. As Max walked past, he saw them smoking cigarettes behind their steering wheels, despite the 'DANGER NO SMOKING' signs everywhere.

He was looking for the building occupied by Microwave Technologies Inc. That was the name of the company registered to Thomas Stroman in New York State's business-incorporation records, which Max had searched online after his meeting with David Swift. The records didn't include a telephone number for the company, and its mailing address was listed only as 'Locust Avenue, Bronx' with no accompanying street number, but Locust Avenue was just nine blocks long, and Max had assumed he'd easily find the company's building by starting at the north end of the street and checking each doorway as he headed south. Unfortunately, those nine blocks were lined with two-story windowless buildings with no numbers or signs above their dented steel doors.

Although there was plenty of graffiti on the buildings, Max got the impression that the businesses inside were still operating. Above each unmarked door was at least one security camera, and he could hear the HVAC units roaring on the rooftops. But after walking the length of Locust Avenue three damn times, he still had no clue where Microwave Technologies was. He felt the panicky tightening in his chest again, that sense of utter helplessness. *Oh Sonya, hang on. I'm doing everything I can to find you.* He fumbled for his iPhone, taking it out of his pocket to check whether Stroman's business was pinpointed on Apple Maps (it wasn't).

That was when he saw the news alert about the senator's assassination. Max's eyes stung from the sweat streaming down his forehead, and his vision blurred.

Fuck. They got number two.

According to the news story, an FBI agent had also been killed, but Charles Roche was unhurt. *What the hell happened? Did the fanatics skip over him for some reason?* The story had few details about the assassination – it didn't mention whether the senator had been poisoned, like Tarkington and Humphrey, or murdered in some other way – and there was no information at all about the perpetrators, except that they hadn't been apprehended yet. *Why are the Feds being so cagey? Why don't they ask the public to help them find the assassins?* The news made Max even more skeptical that the FBI could rescue Sonya and Janet. If the federal agents couldn't stop the crazies from killing a US senator, what good were they?

He wiped the sweat from his brow and lingered in the rectangular shadow of a truck parked near the tank farm. Although Max was a marathoner and in terrific shape for his age, this weather could wear anyone down. Gazing south, he saw the Triborough Bridge and the Manhattan skyline, and beyond them a dark blanket of clouds along the horizon. A second news alert on his phone warned that a tropical storm had unexpectedly veered from the mid-Atlantic toward the New York area. It was creeping north, the alert said, and its winds were gaining speed, mostly because of the ocean's unusual warmth. Cooked by the gases rising from Port Morris and a million other places, the Atlantic had spawned yet another hurricane, which was expected to make landfall either late tonight or early tomorrow.

In the meantime, Max braced himself for a fourth inspection of the industrial buildings on Locust Avenue. But as he stepped out of the truck's shadow, he spotted a young woman on the other side of the street, about a block away. She was the first woman he'd seen in almost an hour – all the truck drivers and sanitation workers he'd observed in Port Morris were men – and she was also quite attractive, a lithe blonde in denim shorts and dark sunglasses and a crop top, striding fast and purposefully down the hot sidewalk.

Max ducked behind the truck's cab and spied on her, this lovely visitor to an unlovely neighborhood, as out of place as Grace Kelly in a low-budget horror film. She came to a squat gray building splattered with graffiti, stopped at its unmarked door, and tilted her head back to peer at the security camera above it. At the same time, she banged her fist against the door, three loud slams that echoed down the street. A few seconds later, the door buzzed open, and the mysterious blonde disappeared inside.

Damn. Was that important or just random?

As Max leaned against the truck, he considered the possibilities. Maybe the woman really was a low-budget film actress. A windowless building with thick concrete walls was a perfect place for a movie studio, since it was already soundproofed. It certainly wasn't a glamorous location, but maybe this studio specialized in less sophisticated films. Porn, to be exact. Wouldn't an adult-film production company want to base its operations at an anonymous, low-rent site like this one?

Peering over the truck's hood, Max scrutinized the two-story structure. He pored over every square foot of its façade, from the piss stains at the base of the wall to the concertina wire that edged the rooftop, but he found no further evidence for his porn-studio theory. He did see something new, though, a subtle detail that had escaped his notice before. At the far end of the building, just a few inches above the sidewalk and partly hidden by a drainpipe, was a small black plaque affixed to the concrete, an inconspicuous identifier for anyone in the know. Three white squiggles were etched into the plaque, stacked in curvy layers: the international symbol for microwaves.

Max's vision blurred again. He felt lightheaded, dizzy with fear and hope. Now that he'd found Stroman's hideout, he had to consider his next steps, which had been completely hypothetical until now.

First, he took out his wallet and found the business card that Agent Aleida Reyes had given him. Max had his doubts about the FBI's competence, but where else could he turn? When he dialed Reyes's number, though, he got a busy signal, despite trying three times. Probably the FBI's phone lines were flooded with calls after the assassination. Even if he got through, he wasn't sure Reyes would take him seriously; the connection between Stroman and the Climate Avengers was tenuous at best, based at it was on Max's memories of a protest at Columbia long ago and David Swift's recollection of an oddball physicist. And in the unlikely event that Reyes took an interest, could she or her partners get here in time? Max had no idea who was inside the Microwave Technologies building, but he had the feeling they wouldn't stay there for long.

The next person he dialed was Nathan Carver. The call went to voicemail, but at least Max knew his friend wouldn't dismiss him as a crackpot. He tried to keep his voice steady as he left his message.

'Nathan, it's Max. Remember the guy I told you about this morning? Tom Stroman, the weirdo physics student that the Columbia professor knew? I think I found his company. I'm on Locust Avenue in the Bronx and I'm gonna check out the gray building on the corner of One-thirty-fourth Street. If you don't hear from me again in ten minutes, call nine-one-one and tell them you saw flames on that building's roof. This whole area is soaked in petroleum, so the firefighters will probably show up quick and maybe rescue me. Thanks, buddy.'

Then Max hid his iPhone and wallet under a pile of cardboard trash on the sidewalk. He was going to knock on the building's door and pretend to be a passerby who desperately needed to take a shit. It wasn't the greatest cover story in the world, but it was the best he could think of right now. With any luck, the person answering the door would be Stroman, and he would let

Max inside to use the bathroom. Then Max would check out the place and start a conversation with the guy, on the lookout for anything incriminating, any real evidence that might get the FBI's attention. And if, in the worst-case scenario, Stroman got suspicious and rifled through Max's pockets, he would find nothing connecting him to Sonya or Janet.

Max's polo shirt was heavy with sweat. He took a deep breath and crossed the street, quick-stepping like a man in dire need of relief. When he reached the gray building's door, he knocked on it hard and looked up at the surveillance camera. 'Uh, excuse me? Can I come in and use your bathroom? I'm sorry about this, but it's an emergency.'

He stood there, squirming at the doorstep, waiting for someone to buzz him in. If he looked as frantic as he felt, surely someone would take pity on him, but nothing happened for several seconds. The sun beat down on his head through the oily haze, scalding his ears and the back of his neck. The waiting and the silence were annoying the hell out of him, and every part of his anatomy was dripping.

Then, just as he was about to knock again, the steel door opened wide, revealing the blonde in denim shorts. She smiled and put a hand on her hip, angling her body for his benefit. 'Hello, love. So, you need to use the jacks, yeah?'

Max hadn't expected the Irish accent. Was she Stroman's girlfriend? Or maybe one of the radicals? Whatever her affiliation, she seemed unusually friendly, and that alone made Max wary. 'Yeah, if that means "toilet," that's what I need.'

'Well, come right in then, you poor suffering creature.'

She took a step back and held the door open for him. If anything, her smile was even bigger now, openly flirtatious, as if she thought his impending bowel movement was the hottest thing she'd ever heard of. Max hesitated, suddenly afraid.

Something's wrong. This is happening too easily. No one in New York lets you use their bathroom without an argument first.

'Hey, you know what? I don't have to go anymore. The urge just went away. But thanks for—'

'Oh, don't be scarlet, love.' She lunged at him, quick as a jungle cat, and grabbed his wrist. 'After you've finished doing your business, we can have a little chat.'

Max dug his heels into the sidewalk, but the blonde yanked him through the doorway. Then she rammed his head against the door, and everything went black.

Nathan had taken a day off from his job at Golden Key Advertising so he could do some internet sleuthing for Max. One by one, he was identifying the assholes who'd posted anonymous online threats against Sonya, and he was examining their activity on other websites, especially the dark-web sites where so much criminal commerce took place. He got so immersed in the hunt for electronic clues that he didn't see the voice message from Max until five minutes after it came in. Nathan immediately called him back, but there was no answer, and five minutes later Max failed to make the promised second call at the ten-minute mark.

Although Nathan was bonkers with worry by this point, he faithfully followed his friend's instructions and called 911. He told the dispatcher about the fire at Locust Avenue and 134th Street, and then he paced across his apartment for the next thirty minutes, waiting to get either a call from Max or an update from the commander of the fire station in the South Bronx. Nathan finally got through to someone in the ladder company that responded to his 911 report, but the news wasn't good: the firefighter said they found no blaze at the Locust Avenue address, and furthermore, the building appeared to be locked up and empty.

Max, my man, I think you did something stupid. How the hell am I supposed to get you out of this mess? Nathan grabbed the keys to his Prius and ran out of the apartment.

Max dreamed he was sailing on the Aegean Sea, tied to the mast of an Ancient Greek trireme. His tormentor was a woman with flaming yellow hair, a minor goddess who'd pulled his ship into an undersea cave that smelled powerfully of petroleum. It was quiet and blessedly cool down there, and Max was so tired. He wanted to stay still and keep dreaming this dream forever, but the goddess raised her trident and poked him in the ribs.

He opened his eyes and the room spun around him. It was a windowless basement with a workbench on one side and racks of electronic equipment on the other. He sat in a metal folding chair, his hands bound behind his back with some kind of wire and his ankles tied to the chair legs. His forehead ached from the blow against the steel door, and he could feel the dried blood on his cheeks and eyelids. But the worst part by far was seeing the face of the blonde Irishwoman, who smiled again as she stood over him and prodded his chest with a long whip antenna.

'Wakey, wakey, shake and bakey!' She brandished the antenna like Zorro, tracing a big Z on his polo shirt with its bulbous tip. 'You've been napping for a good long while, boyo, almost an hour. You missed all the excitement when the fire brigade came by.'

Shivering, Max stared at her. He was so frightened and confused, it took him a few seconds to realize what she was talking about.

'Spare me the innocent look, you naughty fellow.' She angled the antenna's tip upward and tapped it against the tip of Max's nose. 'You called the fire department before you knocked on our door, yes? Betting they would save your arse when they arrived?'

There was no point in denying it. Max nodded, squinting, trying to focus on this woman and stop the room from spinning. Although the antenna wasn't sharp, he didn't like the way she was swinging it around.

'Ah, I thought as much.' She paced in front of his chair, slapping the antenna against her palm like a schoolmarm with a ruler. 'It was a terrible plan, because you didn't think ahead. All we had to do was lock the place up tight and drag your unconscious arse down to the cellar. The firefighters weren't going to break into the building if there was no sign of a fire.' She stopped pacing and pointed the antenna at him. 'I can't really fault you, though. You're an amateur, and you made an amateur's mistake. I don't think very highly of the police in this country, but even the stupidest of the lot would've called for backup.'

Again, Max saw no reason to argue with her. In fact, he decided right then and there to tell her everything. He was no hero, not even close. His best strategy – his only strategy – was to throw himself on her mercy.

'You're right. I'm not a cop.' He swallowed hard, pushing down a tide of nausea. 'I'm a father.'

All at once, she stopped smiling. Max had assumed that telling the truth would mollify the woman, but she didn't look pleased. She narrowed her eyes. 'Yes, I figured that out while you were dozing. You didn't bring any identification with you, but you couldn't hide your pitiful face.'

Max was confused again. 'You know who I am?'

She nodded. 'Unlike you, Max, I'm a professional. Which means I do background research. If you google Sonya Mirsky, your picture shows up too.'

Hearing his daughter's name seemed to pull a switch inside him. It shut down the current of fear in his veins and ignited a spark of hope. 'Where's Sonya? Is she all right?'

She shrugged. 'How should I know? Wasn't she kidnapped by a bunch of fascists? Instead of asking me, you should be talking to the Proud Boys. Or maybe your friendly neighborhood QAnon shaman.'

She was lying. Max was sure of it. 'No, there's a connection between you and the kidnapping. Someone else in your organization, the old woman with the long ponytail, she wound up in a garbage truck belonging to Torricelli Demolition. Which is owned by the father of one of the kidnappers.'

'Christ, listen to you! You're the worst kind of amateur, the kind that likes to theorize.'

'Please. I'm begging you.' Max's torso wasn't tied to the chair, so he was able to lean forward and catch her eye. 'I just want to know if my daughter is OK.'

The Irishwoman grunted, sounding quite annoyed. 'I told you, you're talking to the wrong person. I wasn't involved in that job. Kidnapping teenagers isn't my cup of tea.' She shook her head. 'But there's no reason for anyone to hurt her. She's probably safer where she is than on the streets right now. I was out there today and believe me, it was madness.'

'So you know where Sonya is?' Max rose from the folding chair. Although the wire around his ankles tied them firmly to the chair's front legs, he managed to shuffle forward a bit, dragging the back legs across the basement's floor. 'Just take me to her, all right? You can lock me up in the same place where she is. I won't care at all, as long as I'm with her.'

She grimaced and tossed the antenna aside. 'Jesus, you're a

cheeky one. Sit your fucking arse down.' She grabbed his shoulder and pushed him back into the chair. The elbows of his bound arms, wrenched behind his ribs, crashed painfully against the chair's metal back. 'You're in no position to give orders, boyo. Understand?'

Max nodded. This Irishwoman was terrifying when she got angry. Her face reddened and her eyes blazed as she leaned over him, and she seemed capable of almost anything.

'I'm the one asking the questions now.' She tapped her index finger against her chest. 'And the first question is, how did you find old Tommy boy? He's the secretive type, so he is.' She glanced at a door on the left side of the room, which had a big 'DO NOT ENTER' sign. 'And yet you waltzed right into his hidden lair. Who told you about it?'

Max put a cooperative smile on his face. 'It was easy, actually. Thomas Stroman's name and business address are in New York State's corporation records. I can give you the web address of the archive if you're interested.'

'Ah, grand. But what gave you the idea that Stroman was involved in any nefarious activities?'

'We both went to Columbia, and we were both involved in climate action groups. And I remembered that he had an obsessive interest in weapons, especially high-tech weapons. I knew that wasn't a strong enough connection to get the FBI interested, so I decided to investigate him myself. Because I'm desperate. Your friends kidnapped my girlfriend, you know, as well as my daughter.'

Max was lying a bit, omitting any mention of David Swift, and for a moment he worried that the Irishwoman would detect the deception. But her only response was another glance at the DO NOT ENTER door. 'Obsessive, that's a good word for him. I think old Tommy is "on the spectrum," as they say.' Then she turned back to Max and frowned. 'For an amateur, it looks like you made an accurate guess, Mr Mirsky. But in terms of your personal welfare, it certainly wasn't a lucky guess. What the fuck am I gonna do with you now, eh?'

Before Max could answer, a loud *click* came from the room's left side, the sound of a deadbolt sliding out of its socket. A second later, the DO NOT ENTER door opened and a pale, skinny man in jeans and a grungy T-shirt appeared in the doorway. He carried a gray metal box in his hands, about the size and shape of a shoebox. As the door closed behind him, he raised the box to eye level, displaying it proudly. 'I've finished the adjustments. The device is now fully functional.'

The Irishwoman gave him a smile, clearly forced. 'That's brilliant, love. You're a fierce mechanic, so you are. If this thing works as well as the drones did, I'll be a happy lass.'

'You should also know that I listened to the last few sentences of your conversation with Mirsky. For your information, I'm not autistic in any way. My cognitive processes are completely normal.'

His monotone voice seemed to undercut this statement, but the Irishwoman just kept smiling. 'Oh, I was only codding you, Tommy. You're as normal as they come.'

'Good. I'm glad we're in agreement on that. And regarding the Mirsky problem, there's an obvious solution.'

'Ah sure, that's marvelous. What do you have in mind?'

Stroman lowered the metal box and pointed at Max. 'You should kill him. We don't have to worry about disposing of his body, because I'm abandoning this workshop and going on the run after the grand finale tomorrow. I'll be long gone by the time his corpse starts to stink.'

Max laughed. This reaction was surprising as hell, even to himself, because Stroman had just proposed murdering him, and that was no laughing matter. But the way Stroman had said it, without a trace of emotion, was so damn ridiculous that Max didn't know what else to do.

He stopped laughing, though, as soon as he saw the Irishwoman's face. She obviously didn't think the idea was ridiculous. She furrowed her brow and pursed her lips.

Max let out a peremptory '*Wait!*' He rose halfway out of the chair. 'Couldn't you take me now to where Sonya and Janet are? I mean, you have them safely hidden away somewhere, right? So why can't you just take me there?'

She shook her head. 'They're way across town. The cops are inspecting the traffic on all the bridges, so I can't cart you around in somebody's trunk, can I?'

'I'll cooperate! I'll sit in the backseat and if the cops stop the car I swear I won't say a word—'

'Oi! Shut your gob!' She bent over him and yelled into his face. *'I'm trying to think, for fuck's sake!'*

Max sank down into the chair, shaking. The situation didn't seem funny anymore, not in the slightest. He'd never experienced this kind of terror, knowing he could die within the next few seconds. It was like standing on a knife-edge ridge in the Rockies, with a sheer drop on either side, thousands of feet down. A strong wind blows you sideways and there's nothing to hold on to and you flail your arms, trying like hell to keep your balance. Max felt that vertigo now, death on either side of him, and he didn't like it, not one fucking bit.

And if I die, what will happen to Sonya?

Finally, the Irishwoman turned back to Stroman. 'Here's what we'll do with this eejit. We'll tie him up nice and tight and lock him in that closet over there. The cops might raid this place after I finish tomorrow's job, but you said you'll be on the run by then, right? And I'll be out of the country too, so it won't matter if this donkey tells them everything he knows.'

Stroman stepped forward, his face blank, his box cradled under one arm. 'Your plan is suboptimal. What if he breaks free somehow? Or what if someone rescues him before our mission is complete? There's a chance he told a friend where he was planning to go today. When this friend realizes that Mirsky is missing, he might lead the authorities here, and then Mirsky will inform them of our identities.'

The Irishwoman shrugged. 'You're right, it's a risk, but it's acceptable. The police and the FBI already know what I look like, so Mirsky's information won't help them. I'm gonna scoot out of here as soon as you hand me that box, and you should leg it too, in case the cops come snooping around tonight. Just find yourself another hidey-hole and you'll be right as rain.'

'But why take any risk at all? Do you have qualms about killing him?' Stroman edged closer to her. 'That would be a surprising attitude for someone in your line of work. How many targets have you eliminated over the course of your career?'

Max held his breath as he stared at them. He wanted to shout something in his own defense, but he sensed that anything he said would only count against him, so he clamped his mouth shut. His only hope was that the Irishwoman would win the argument. He tried to focus on her alone, averting his wet eyes from the man who wanted him dead and sending a silent plea to the blonde tormentor. *Please. Don't listen to him. Don't kill me.*

After a moment she scowled, giving Max a look of raw fury. He cringed in his chair, its metal hard and cold against his bound arms. But then she turned aside and trained her rage on Stroman, jabbing a finger into his scrawny chest.

'Jesus, Mary, and Joseph! Are you questioning my professionalism?'

Stroman took a step backward, his eyes widening. 'No, but—'

'A professional doesn't slaughter folks willy-nilly, understand? And I've seen enough collateral damage today, watching your drones tear the shite out of that federal agent.'

'My drones performed flawlessly. It wasn't my fault that—'

'Just shut it! This man isn't my target, and he has a daughter. That probably means nothing to a schizoid like you, but I have my standards.' With her cat-like quickness, she reached for Stroman's box and wrenched it out of his hands. 'Now I'm running off to finish the job, and I'm leaving you in charge of Max the eejit. Just throw him in the closet and lock the door, get it? And you better not disobey me and kill him anyway, Tommy boy. If you do, I'll hunt you down, and you won't like the consequences.'

She loomed over Stroman, her teeth bared. He nodded, acquiescent, retreating until his back hit the wall. 'Yes . . . yes, of course.' His bony chest heaved inside his T-shirt, and his Adam's apple bobbed in his throat. 'That won't be a problem. And, uh, good luck with your—'

'Fuck off. I don't need your luck.'

She glanced once more at Max, giving him the same ferocious look she'd just given Stroman. Then, holding the metal box like a football, she turned toward the stairway and hurried out of the basement, climbing the steps two at a time.

A few seconds later, a door slammed upstairs. The room became very quiet, and when Max took a deep breath it seemed to scrape against the silence. He sat there, motionless, while Stroman stepped away from the wall and came toward him. *He's going to throw me into the closet now. Or drag me in there, more likely.*

But instead, Stroman punched Max in the face.

The first blow broke Max's nose. The second smashed his front teeth in. With the third blow, Stroman aimed at the same spot on Max's forehead that the Irishwoman had pummeled. When the punch landed, Max went under again.

This time he was unconscious for only a few minutes. He opened his eyes to see Stroman carrying a gray metal box that looked identical to the one he'd given the blonde. With bloody hands he mounted the box on a tripod and then raised it to the height of Max's eyebrows. Then he removed the metal plate at the box's front end, exposing an antenna with flaring waveguides that made it look like the mouth of a horn.

Max bit his torn lip, fighting to stay conscious. 'What . . . what are you . . .?'

'This is the prototype microwave transmitter.' Stroman didn't look at him. He seemed to be fiddling with the controls at the back of the device. 'It's essentially the same as the transmitter I gave to Erin.'

Erin? Max was so woozy, he had only the faintest grip on reality. *Was that her name? The Irishwoman?*

'She said . . . she said . . .'

'I heard what she said. And I plan to follow her orders. I don't intend to kill you.' Stroman flicked a switch on the device and it started to hum. 'But she didn't say I couldn't hurt you, did she?'

'Hurt me . . . no, you can't . . .' Max shook his head. It felt like his brain was sloshing around inside his skull.

'And she said nothing at all about irradiating your cortex. So I have to assume it's all right to use you as a test subject.'

'No . . . no . . .'

He swiveled the transmitter on its tripod until the horn-type antenna pointed directly at Max's head. 'Please try to stay still. This will be interesting.'

SEVENTEEN

'Yes, sir, I'll do that. Thank you very much.'

Those were the last words of the debrief that Agent Reyes gave to her superiors regarding the attacks at the Roche mansion. Specifically, that was her mortified response to the final comment from her boss, Assistant Director Hastings, who said, 'There'll be a full investigation of what went wrong today, Reyes, and believe me, you'll have to answer a lot more questions. In the meantime, I'm removing you from the command of the task force. Go to Special Agent Ballard and get another assignment.'

Reyes kept a blank look on her face as she went to Ballard's desk at the field office, and she didn't complain when Ballard assigned her to oversee the vehicle checkpoint that the Bureau had set up on the Triborough Bridge. But once she got inside her unmarked Tahoe, she pounded the steering wheel and yelled at the windshield loud enough to make it shudder. Cursing and seething, she pulled out of the Federal Building's garage and headed for the FDR Drive.

She understood why Hastings had ordered a reorganization. The Bureau's mission had changed after the senator's killing, since there were fewer targets to protect now. The two men remaining on Max Mirsky's climate criminals list had basically made themselves untouchable; Roche was burrowed underground on the panic floor of his townhouse, and the crown prince of Saudi Arabia had left New York in his private jet, rushing back to the security of his palace in Riyadh. The Capitol police were guarding everyone in Congress, doubling up the protection for all the climate-change deniers, and the president was staying within the confines of the White House, surrounded by his usual Secret Service army.

With all those precautions now in place, the Bureau could devote more resources to tracking down the Climate Avengers. The pressure to solve the case was growing more intense by the hour as the TV networks endlessly rehashed Senator Coal's assassination. The pundits were mourning him as 'America's salt-of-the-earth senator' and 'West Virginia's guardian angel.' He also got some posthumous love from the former president, who'd had the Secret Service code name 'Mogul' when he'd been in the White House but was more often referred to by law enforcement as 'Pumpkin Head' or 'The Cheeto.' The ex-president had detested the FBI during his four-year term, and now he told Fox News that the senator had been murdered by 'a deep-state conspiracy against Christian conservatives who won't buckle under the woke socialists and climate loonies.' The Bureau needed to prove him wrong very soon, before he convinced half the country that the Feds themselves had launched the killer drones.

The need for speed was what made Reyes so goddamn angry about her reassignment. She knew more about this investigation than anyone else, and yet she'd been kicked off the case. Yes, an unprecedented cluster-fuck had happened on her watch, but she'd begged Roche to cancel the reception. Didn't that count for anything? Should she be blamed for a fiasco that became inevitable when that asshole billionaire insisted on throwing his party?

The worst part was, she couldn't do anything for Martinez. She'd made a solemn vow to hunt down the bitch who'd killed him, but instead Reyes was going to the Triborough Bridge to babysit the cops and Homeland Security officers who were questioning the commuters and opening their car trunks, searching for an assassin who'd probably fled Manhattan hours ago. It was way beyond frustrating. Just thinking about it made her go speed-of-sound ballistic.

She directed her fury at the Tahoe, propelling the car onto the FDR Drive at eighty miles per hour and swerving around the civilian vehicles. But there was a traffic jam near the 23rd Street exit, of course, and it was slow going even with her lights and siren on. As she blared her horn at the cars in the passing lane, a call came in on her two-way radio from Agent Feeney, another member of the task force she'd formerly commanded. She snatched the radio from her belt and glared at it.

'Feeney, didn't you hear the news? You have a new boss, Special Agent Yarrow.'

'Uh, yes, ma'am, I'd heard that.' Feeney's voice was a slow drawl. He was nearing retirement age and not too energetic. 'I just wanted to inform you about—'

'You need to talk to Yarrow. I'm off the case.'

'Ma'am, I'm having some trouble getting Yarrow on the horn, and this is an urgent matter. I've lost sight of the subject I was assigned to follow, Mr Max Mirsky.'

Reyes sighed. Although this wasn't her investigation anymore, she couldn't help but get aggravated about it. 'How did you lose him?'

'Well, I followed him to the Columbia campus this morning and then back to his apartment, but around noon there was all that commotion on the East Side and I got called away to help with—'

'Come on, Feeney, spit it out.'

'Ma'am, when I returned to his apartment building at three o'clock, nobody answered the doorbell. I assumed he went out for lunch or something, but it's been an hour and a half since then and he hasn't come back.'

Reyes tightened her grip on the radio while she steered one-handed down the highway. 'Listen carefully, OK? Call Yarrow again and ask for phone trace approval. If Mirsky didn't power down his phone, the trace will tell you his location.'

'But, ma'am, like I said, I can't get Yarrow on the—'

'Goddamn it, he's at the field office! Go the fuck down there if you have to!'

'Uh, roger that, ma'am.' His drawl was sheepish now and barely audible. 'Over and out.'

The traffic thinned as Reyes passed 61st Street, and soon she could see the Triborough up ahead. Then she got another radio call, this time from NYPD Lieutenant Ed Svoboda, who was in charge of the cops at the bridge.

'Agent Reyes? What's your ETA?'

'I'll be there in five minutes. Too much goddamn traffic.'

'Someone's asking for you here. Asking really insistently.'

'Someone from the Bureau?'

'No, not even close. You gotta see this to believe it.'

Nathan Carver hated social media. He would've greatly preferred a world without Facebook, Instagram, Twitter, and TikTok.

Because he spent his workdays wrestling with hardware and software, in his spare time he wanted nothing to do with the internet; he wanted human interaction on the streets of New York. So he'd become a connoisseur of the city's hidden corners, a doyen of its niches and byways.

But when he hopped into his Prius to save his best friend Max, he didn't know where to go. Should he drive directly to Locust Avenue in the Bronx? Or should he head first for the nearest precinct station and round up a posse? Uncertain, he stayed in his parking spot on East 95th Street and turned on the car radio, which screeched with warnings of rush-hour traffic and security checkpoints on all the major roads. According to the 1010 WINS traffic report ('You give us twenty-two minutes, we'll give you the world'), the cops were stopping every car on the Triborough, Queensboro, and George Washington bridges, as well as the Lincoln, Holland, and Midtown tunnels. Nobody seemed to know what the police were looking for, but it probably had something to do with the Climate Avengers, who were doing their damnedest to ruin a good cause.

At the end of the traffic report, the radio announcer added that the checkpoints were manned by 'hundreds of officers from the NYPD, the MTA, the TSA, and the FBI.' That last acronym reminded Nathan of his conversation yesterday with Max, who'd mentioned an interrogator from the FBI, a woman named Reyes. Would she be helpful if Nathan contacted her now? If he told Agent Reyes about his fears for Max's safety, would she do her job and try to rescue him? And how should Nathan get in touch with her?

He did the sensible thing first and called the FBI's general number in Washington, but he got an automated response and couldn't reach an operator. Then he tried the number of the FBI's office in New York, but the same thing happened.

Fuck it, he thought. *Time to get creative.*

He opened his car's glove compartment and removed the notepad he kept there for recording his inspirations. He conceived a plan in three minutes, jotting down the steps with quick pen strokes. Then he tossed the notepad on the passenger seat and started the Prius's engine.

As Nathan drove up First Avenue, he telephoned Larry, Adele, and Eileen, all the available members of the Doomsday Company.

He assigned them their various roles, deploying them along the fringes of Manhattan like a director blocking his actors across the stage. In the absence of Max and Janet, it was Nathan's duty to become the troupe's director, choreographer, and composer, so he instructed Larry to go to the GW Bridge, Adele to the Queensboro, and Eileen to the Lincoln Tunnel. Nathan himself drove to the Triborough, which was just five minutes away.

The Triborough's toll plaza didn't have tollbooths anymore – they'd been demolished when cashless tolling became the norm – but because the highway widened to eighteen lanes there, it was the perfect spot for a checkpoint. The cops formed a line across the lanes, inspecting all the cars and trucks leaving Manhattan. Behind the leading edge of vehicles was a traffic jam of historic proportions, creeping and beeping. But Nathan managed to avoid the worst of the snarl by veering into the breakdown lane on the highway's shoulder. Instead of lining up for a turn at the checkpoint, he parked his Prius on the shoulder and turned off the engine. Then he grabbed his notepad again and stepped out of the car.

It was astoundingly hot outside, but Nathan didn't mind. He scribbled some notes on his pad while a sweating cop lumbered over to his Prius. The cop's uniform was soaked from the shoulders down, and a bead of perspiration hung from the tip of his nose. 'Hey, buddy. You can't park there.'

Nathan put an abject expression on his face. 'I'm so sorry about this, officer, but my car broke down. Despite my best efforts, it just won't start.'

'Oh man. That's shitty luck for you.' The cop scratched his slick neck and pointed at the mass of idling cars on the plaza. 'It's gonna take hours to get a tow truck through this mess.'

'That's all right. I truly appreciate your assistance, sir.' Nathan stepped closer to him. 'And there's something else you can help me with. I've heard that FBI agents are also working at this checkpoint, and I'm trying to locate a female agent named Reyes. Have you seen her this afternoon?'

The cop squinted at him. 'What?'

'It's an urgent matter, actually. I believe a friend of mine is in grave danger, and I've already called the fire department to the address, but—'

'Look, I don't know what you're talking about. Just get back in your car and wait for the tow truck, OK?'

Nathan nodded. He'd more or less expected this. 'Officer, would it be all right if I waited *on top* of my car?' He climbed onto his Prius's sloping hood. 'I have a problem with claustrophobia, you see.'

The cop stared at him for a second, then shrugged. It was too hot to argue. 'Whatever floats your boat.' He turned around and headed back to the checkpoint, plodding bowlegged like a Wild West gunslinger.

Nathan scrawled a few more hasty sentences on his pad, thinking about gunslingers and cowpokes and square dances. Which, in turn, led him to think of the title song of *Oklahoma!* That was his second-favorite song in his third-favorite musical.

Yes, that would be a good melody for this message. The song's meter will fit the words once I make a few adjustments.

He clambered over the Prius's hood and windshield and stood on top of the car's roof. Then he faced the traffic jam and began to sing.

It was even weirder than Reyes had imagined. Just twenty feet away from where she'd stopped her Tahoe, a tall, gangly, middle-aged man was belting out a show tune on top of his Prius.

Reyes knew the song – she'd seen a revival of *Oklahoma!* on Broadway just a few months before. And to tell the truth, this guy's version of the tune was almost as good as the one she'd seen onstage. His voice boomed over the Triborough toll plaza, loud enough that the commuters could hear him from inside their air-conditioned cars. Despite the heat, several drivers rolled down their windows to hear him better, and Reyes did the same.

But the weirdest thing of all was how the guy had changed the song's lyrics. His version of the tune was about *her*.

Aaaaaaaaaaagent Reyes,
I need to speak with you immediately!
I'm a friend of Mirsky,
Remember him, Max Mirsky?
Now his life's in danger so extreme!

Aaaaaaaaaaagent Reyes,
Max disappeared today while surveilling
A physicist who's linked
To the Climate Avengers (we think)
He could be the key to the whole thing!

His real name is Thomas Stroman (Thomas! Stroman!)
He's done defense work for the Pentagon (Penta! Gon!)
And when I searrrrrrrched
The dark web to view his new worrrrrrrrk
I saw some really bad shit
He's building weapons for bad guys!
Go and get him, NYPD and FBI!
If you don't hurry, Max will die!

By the time the singer got to the second verse, Reyes recognized him. He was one of Mirsky's fellow actors in the Doomsday Company; she'd seen him in the security-camera footage of their *Oliver!* parody, which they'd performed on West 57th Street just before Hollister Tarkington's demise. She even remembered the actor's name – Nathan Carver – from the surveillance reports that Agents Wilson and Martinez had written. According to the reports, Carver was jocular, disrespectful, and most likely too undisciplined to be involved in any terrorist group. If he'd approached Reyes in a more conventional manner – say, by coming to her office – she probably would've shown him the door. But his crazy song had grabbed her attention.

After listening to the chorus, Reyes took out her phone and logged on to the Bureau's counterintelligence archive. This was a quick-reference website that listed all the defense contractors who'd been given top-secret security clearances, which made them high-value targets for Chinese and Russian spy agencies. Thomas Stroman was indeed on this list. And when Reyes clicked on his name, she saw a summary of the projects he'd worked on: 'Consulting on asymmetric warfare tactics; development of portable microwave-pulse weapons; technical refinement of low-cost drone swarms.'

Aaaaaaaaaaagent Reyes,
You need to go to Locust Avenue
It's in Port Morris
That's part of the Bronx
One-thirty-fourth Street and Locust Avenue!

Aaaaaaaaaaagent Reyes,
It's a gray building on the street corner
Go there right away
Please do not delay
Because that's where Max and Stroman are!

Reyes shifted her Tahoe into drive and sped past the Prius, using the breakdown lane to go around the traffic jam. She flashed her FBI badge at the cops working the checkpoint, then accelerated toward the Triborough's Bronx-bound lanes. Port Morris was just to the north, the very next exit.

She got the radio call from Agent Feeney as she careened down the Bruckner Expressway. 'Ma'am? I have a fix on Mirsky's phone, and I'm heading there now. He's at—'

'Locust Avenue and One-thirty-fourth Street, right? In the Bronx?'

'Whoa, how did you—'

'I'll meet you there.'

EIGHTEEN

It was an intolerable noise, a loud, screeching whine, grating and metallic. It was like the shriek of a key-cutting machine as the rotating steel blade bites into the brass key.

Except Max didn't hear this noise with his ears. The whine blared inside his brain without touching his eardrums. It seemed to come from within him, from the very center of his skull, a frantic alarm that was triggered in his cortex when Stroman aimed the microwave transmitter at him.

Max was already sick with pain from the beating Stroman had given him, but the noise was a new kind of agony. It felt like some horrible parasite had wormed into his head and was thrashing inside him, turning his brain cells to jelly. He convulsed in the metal folding chair, twisting and squirming. The noise quieted when he bent all the way forward, because he'd moved his head below the microwave beam that was streaming from the transmitter. But then Stroman adjusted the angle of the device, tilting it downward on the tripod until the beam pointed at him again, and the noise and pain returned full force.

Stroman stood behind the tripod with his head bent at the same angle as the transmitter. He furrowed his brow, focused and intent, observing Max carefully. His gaze was parallel to the microwave beam.

'Talk to me, Mr Mirsky.' His tone was clinical, emotionless. 'What are you experiencing right now?'

Max couldn't speak. He could barely hear Stroman above the shrieking inside his head.

'Is it a high-pitched buzzing? That's a common reaction.' Stroman nodded, confirming his own guess. 'The technical term for it is the microwave auditory effect. The US military has known about it for decades. It's excruciating, yes? And yet I don't hear it at all, because I'm not standing within the microwave beam.'

Stroman's voice only made the agony worse. He seemed to

sense that his explanation was aggravating Max's pain, and this encouraged him to keep talking.

'You see, when the microwaves come to you from a distance, they can heat the fluids in your head only slightly, just a fraction of a degree. But you can make the effect much bigger by pulsing the beam in the right way, turning it on and off, on and off, hundreds of times per second. That creates a pressure wave inside your brain that impacts the cochlea in your inner ear. Hence you get the sensation of noise even when there's no sound in the room.'

Max arched his back and half-rose from the chair, lifting himself out of the beam's path. The noise in his skull quieted again, but only until Stroman readjusted the transmitter, tilting it up to track the position of his head.

'For fifty years the military tried to build a weapon that used this effect. They worked on MEDUSA, a device intended for crowd control, dispersing rioters by making them dizzy. Some researchers even tried to develop "Voice of God" weapons that could put the sounds of words inside people's heads. It didn't work, of course.' Stroman smiled, clearly amused. 'Then came the Havana syndrome, when American diplomats in Cuba got mysterious migraines and fits. The Russians were testing their own microwave weapons, you see. That was when the Pentagon asked for my help.'

Max started to scream. It was the only way to drown out the inner whine, which was like a drill running through all his brain lobes. His screaming seemed to agitate Stroman, who winced and pointed at him.

'*No, you're going to hear this!*' He raised his voice to the same volume as Max's. '*I succeeded where the others failed!*' He reached for the back of the transmitter and turned a knob. '*Look what it can do!*'

The noise ceased, but what replaced it was worse. Something exploded in Max's mind, scattering bits of it everywhere. He stopped screaming and slumped back in his chair, limp and numb. His vision turned fuzzy, and he felt a sensation that was more horribly intense than any pain or panic he'd ever endured. It squeezed him from all sides, crushing the breath out of him. His heart pounded and his stomach burned. He felt a sudden warmth in his crotch as he pissed himself.

Stroman seemed to leer at him, but Max couldn't tell whether this was really happening or whether he was imagining it. The boundary between his consciousness and the rest of the world was dissolving.

'The crucial breakthrough was customizing the weapon. To maximize the effect of the microwaves, you have to match the beam pulses to the dimensions of the target's skull. While you were unconscious, I took some crude measurements of your cranium and adjusted this transmitter accordingly. I was able to make more precise adjustments to the device I gave Erin, because we obtained access to her target's classified medical records. He's a bit taller than you, and his skull is somewhat bigger than yours.'

Max was losing his mind, literally. He couldn't remember where he was. Or the name of the man who was torturing him. He was lost in a whirlwind of unbearable pain, and he just wanted it to end.

'Right now the beam is at a low-power setting. At this level, the microwaves can trigger confusion and seizures, but at higher settings they can cause permanent brain damage and death. In your case, I think the best choice would be brain damage. You won't be able to tell the authorities anything useful if you're in a coma, correct?'

Everything was going. The whirlwind flung his thoughts in all directions, and his memories faded to invisibility. He couldn't remember where he was born, where he grew up, who he married. Where was he headed all those years, why did he fight so hard? He couldn't remember why it had all seemed so important.

But even as everything receded, one stubborn image clung to the inner walls of his skull, a stubborn image of a stubborn girl with dark skin and hair in cornrows. She was the core of his consciousness, the thing he held most precious, and he kept his hold on her while everything else was torn away from him.

Sonya! No! I won't leave you!

It was the only thought left in his head, but it was fucking powerful, and it gave him the strength for one last desperate act. He leaned back in his chair until the fingers of his bound hands touched the back of the folding seat. He gripped the crimped edge of this seat with all his remaining energy, grasping it as fiercely as he gripped the image of Sonya in his mind. Then he rose from the chair and spun it around by pivoting on one of his bound feet. He turned his back on the torturer and lifted the chair behind him so that its metallic back blocked the path of the beam.

In some deep part of his brain, Max must've remembered a bit of physics he'd learned in college: metallic surfaces reflect microwaves. So when the beam hit the chair's metal back, it bounced off the thing and struck the head of the man behind the tripod.

His name is Stroman, Max thought. His memories became accessible again as soon as the microwaves started frying someone else's brain.

Stroman clutched the sides of his head and whimpered. The shock was apparently so great that he reflexively staggered backward instead of doing the sensible thing and stepping out of the beam's path. And that was a lucky break for Max, because it allowed him to press his attack. Edging backward, he positioned the chair so that it was just inches from the transmitter's horn antenna. Microwaves reflected off the chair's metal in an intense spray that showered Stroman, turning his whimpers into screams. Then he crumpled to the floor, and Max decided that enough was enough. He took one more step backward and smashed the chair into the transmitter, which fell off its tripod and shattered.

His next move was obvious: get the hell out of there. Although his hands were still bound behind his back and his ankles still tied to the chair legs, he could waddle across the basement, dragging the chair noisily behind him. He headed for the stairway that went up to the ground floor and threw himself down on the steps. He couldn't walk upright on the stairway – with his leg movements so restricted, he'd probably lose his balance and fall backward – but he could clamber up the stairs, pushing the balls of his feet against each step and sliding his torso up the incline. At the same time, he started shouting at the top of his lungs.

'*Help! Police! HELP!*'

He was halfway up the stairs when he looked behind him and saw Stroman rise from the basement floor. The torturer shook his head and swayed on his feet for a moment, then lurched toward the stairway. Along the way, he grabbed something from his workbench, a miniature drone with a long slender spike attached to its nose. Clutched in his right hand, it looked like an ice pick, and he raised it above his head when he reached the steps.

Max's only weapon was the chair tied to his legs. Arching his back and looking over his shoulder, he swung the thing behind him, side to side, like a stegosaurus swinging its spiked tail to ward off a tyrannosaur. But Stroman, springing up the stairs, batted the chair away with his left hand and brought the spike down with his right.

It plunged into Max's arm, just below the shoulder, and he let out a howl. He screamed not so much from the pain now but from his despair, the certainty of failure. He'd tried so hard to find his daughter, but it all ended here. *I'm sorry, Sonya. I couldn't do it. I won't make it.*

Stroman's face was blank. He wrenched the spike out of Max's arm, which spurted blood on the torturer's shirt. Crouched on the steps, Stroman raised his right hand again, this time aiming for Max's chest.

Then something hit Stroman's forehead. The blow was so sudden and forceful, it sheared off the top of his skull. He tumbled backward down the stairs while the gunshot echoed against the basement walls.

Max had just enough time to see Agent Reyes at the top of the stairway, holding her gun with both hands. Delirious, he thought of *West Side Story* and managed to give her a weak smile.

Maria!

Then he lost consciousness once more.

NINETEEN

Angela Nova had detested her father while he was alive, and she hated him even more after he died, but she had to admit that he'd been a clever businessman. On the rare occasions when Sam Novacek hadn't been belittling or berating his daughter, he'd given her some useful advice, including this little gem: 'Whatever you do, always have an exit strategy.'

She remembered those words as she hurried out of the Arthur Kill Correctional Facility with Carl Hauser and Sonya Mirsky. The abandoned prison on Staten Island had turned out to be a good headquarters for Prophecy, but perhaps its greatest advantage was its proximity to the Arthur Kill, the gray waterway that ran between the island and New Jersey. Tied to a dock on that waterway was Angela's exit strategy, a Thunder Cat speedboat she'd inherited from her father. While the setting sun glared over the tank farms on the Jersey side of the river, she marched down the dock's rickety length toward the sleek red boat with its 450-horsepower engines. Carl and Sonya followed close behind, with the former keeping a tight grip on the latter's arm to make sure she didn't bolt.

Angela had once loathed this speedboat almost as much as she'd hated its owner. Its engines spewed an extraordinary amount of carbon into the air, equivalent to the exhaust of a couple of semi-trailer trucks. It could reach speeds as high as 130 miles per hour, and Sam Novacek had loved to drive it full throttle across New York Harbor, swamping any sailboats or kayaks in his wake. In her former life, Angela had been a marine zoologist, and it had been particularly painful to see her father zooming past the harbor's dying saltwater marshes. His company, Novacek Construction, had paved over acres of wetlands in New York and New Jersey – a desecration that Angela would *never* forgive – and his speedboat antics added insult to injury. It was a deliberate assault against something she loved.

Now, though, she saw the Thunder Cat as a necessary evil.

With the New York police inspecting all the traffic on the bridges and tunnels, the only way for her to traverse the city safely was to ply its bays and tidal straits. Novacek Construction, now controlled by Angela, had exclusive access to a pier on Manhattan's West Side, which was typically used for unloading bulky construction materials such as the steel beams for skyscrapers. That pier was Angela's destination, and if a harbor patrol boat tried to intercept her en route – which was highly unlikely, given the NYPD's lack of initiative and imagination – she would simply outrun it. She was using her father's hellish tools for a holy cause.

Carl and Sonya boarded the speedboat first and settled into the two seats at the back. Angela started up the obscenely powerful Mercury engines, then cast off the docking lines and got behind the boat's wheel. Steering north, she cruised up the Arthur Kill.

It was a ravaged, contaminated waterway, its banks littered with oil tanks, gas tanks, power plants, and rail yards, not to mention the immense Fresh Kills Landfill, which used to be the world's biggest garbage dump. At the center of this toxic landscape was the Staten Island boat graveyard, a dumping ground for wrecked tugboats and barges that sat in the mud at all angles, their rusty hulls poking out of the shallow brackish water. Angela stared at the wrecks – glittering in the twilight – as the speedboat cruised past. *It's just like my visions. If we do nothing, the whole world will look like this.*

Her visions had been especially troubling over the past few hours. Prior to this afternoon, she'd foreseen everything so clearly: the poisoning of Tarkington and Humphrey, the skewering of Charles Roche and the abysmal senator. But when her operation failed to kill Roche, she couldn't help but second-guess herself. Had she misinterpreted what she'd seen? Had she missed one of the forking paths of history, a hidden branch that snaked between the alternate realities she'd glimpsed? She still believed she could predict all the major events of the future, but what was the line between major and minor? If she eliminated four of her five targets but Roche survived, could she still scare the plutocrats into abandoning fossil fuels? Would her efforts put the world on the right path, or would they fall short?

Angela felt as if she teetered on a precipice, where the tiniest step would mean the difference between salvation and disaster. As she made small corrections to the Thunder Cat's course, trying to keep the speedboat within the Arthur Kill's shipping channel, the scenery around her seemed to waver and fluctuate, shifting back and forth between two vastly different visions. In one of the future landscapes, all the tank farms and power plants were gone, and in their place were gorgeously revived marshes on both sides of the tidal strait. The sawgrass was alive with herons and hawks and a couple of plucky zoologists observing the wildlife from their kayaks. Beyond the marshes were rows of wind turbines on the distant ridges, and cities shining with millions of solar panels, everything sustainable and carbon-free. It was a vision too beautiful for words, a living embodiment of Nothing but Green.

But in the other vision, the air was steamy and the landscape was flooded. The Atlantic Ocean had risen by dozens of feet, and seawater had swept across coastal New York and New Jersey. The wrecks in the boat graveyard were completely submerged, and filthy waves lapped against the ruptured oil tanks and warehouses. Worst of all, there wasn't an animal or person in sight. The acidification of the oceans and the collapse of the biosphere had led to global devastation of farms and fisheries, and now everyone was dead, even the plutocrats.

Angela clutched the speedboat's steering wheel as tightly as she could, trying to hold on to the present reality – the mountain of landfill to her right, the Goethals Bridge up ahead – while the competing visions of the future flashed inside her head. Then she felt a tap on her left shoulder. Sonya had leaned forward in her seat and managed to get Angela's attention, despite Carl's restraining grip on her arm.

'Are you going to free Janet now?' The nineteen-year-old had to shout to be heard over the noise of the Mercury engines. 'Can you radio your people still at the prison?'

Angela shook her head. 'We have to maintain radio silence. The federal agents have excellent signals-intelligence capabilities, so we can't risk any wireless communications right now.'

'But you said you'd free her as soon as we left the prison! You said—'

'Just wait until we reach our base in Manhattan. We have the facilities there for sending encrypted messages. As soon as we get there, I'll contact the prison and give the order to release your friend.'

Angela looked over her shoulder to gauge Sonya's reaction. The girl frowned, clearly unconvinced. 'I won't help you till I see proof that Janet's free. That means seeing a news report about it on TV or the web.'

'Yes, you'll see it on the news. By midnight tonight, at the latest.'

In truth, Angela had no intention of releasing Janet Page. Max Mirsky's girlfriend knew too much, and she might disrupt tomorrow's operation by giving the authorities a vital clue about Prophecy or its leader. At the same time, though, Angela needed Sonya's cooperation, because in all her visions she saw the heroic girl standing beside her, allied to Angela's cause whether they succeeded or failed. So, for the short term, the optimal strategy was to string Sonya along, promising to satisfy the girl's conditions but delaying their fulfillment for as long as possible. Tomorrow night, after the final target was dead, Angela would tell the girl the truth; until then, she would keep Sonya close by.

The girl kept frowning. Sonya wasn't stupid and obviously suspected she was being lied to, and it looked like she was about to say something else. But Angela faced forward and gunned the speedboat's engines, drowning out any further objections.

In a few minutes the sun sank below the New Jersey wastelands, and the Thunder Cat hurtled beneath the Goethals Bridge. Angela steered the boat east, toward the Kill Van Kull, and soon they reached the heart of New York Harbor. To the south, the Verrazzano-Narrows Bridge stretched its lights across the horizon, which was darker than usual for this hour because of the tropical storm offshore. The meteorologists had given the storm a pretty name – Yolanda – but it was going to be nasty. The horrors of global warming seemed to be pursuing Angela, threatening to stop her before she could slay the beast.

To the north, though, the view was more promising. The Manhattan skyscrapers gleamed like beacons. They lit Angela's path. They showed her the way.

* * *

By nine p.m., Angela had dropped off Sonya at Prophecy's forward operating base, a hidden warren of rooms in the basement of the Moynihan Train Hall. Novacek Construction was a subcontractor in the ongoing renovation of the building, which was on West 33rd Street next to Madison Square Garden, and a dozen bodyguards hired by Carl were keeping the basement rooms secure from now until tomorrow afternoon. Those guards took custody of Sonya and locked her inside a room that wasn't much different from the cell she'd occupied at the Arthur Kill prison. Then Carl got into the driver's seat of a black limousine and chauffeured Angela to Rockefeller Center.

On the ten-minute drive to West 50th Street, Angela changed into some newly bought clothes that were in boxes on the limo's backseat. She peeled off her olive-green jumpsuit, which smelled pretty rank after two days of wear, and slipped into a blue silk evening gown she'd ordered from Saks Fifth Avenue (its price, according to the receipt, was four thousand dollars). She'd never seen the dress before, much less tried it on, but it fit her well enough, as did the matching high-heel shoes (fifteen hundred dollars from Bergdorf Goodman). By the time Carl pulled up to the marquee at 30 Rockefeller Plaza and she stepped out of the limo, she was no longer Angela Nova. She'd reluctantly returned to her old identity and her legal name: Annie Novacek, Sam's prodigal daughter, a quiet zoologist who'd spurned her father and his business until she'd inherited it.

Wobbling a bit on the heels, she strode into the building's Art Deco lobby and approached a tuxedo-clad attendant standing by the elevator banks. He checked her name against the guest list on his iPad, then invited her to take the elevator up to the Rainbow Room.

After ascending to the sixty-fifth floor, the first thing Angela saw was a huge sign at the ballroom's entrance, proclaiming 'SAVE AMERICA AGAIN!!' in red-white-and-blue letters. That was the name of the former president's political action committee, which had already raised five hundred million dollars to return the arrogant fascist to the White House. His fundraising efforts had been so successful that he'd stopped attending his own parties; even though he was miles away at the moment, probably watching television at his mansion in New Jersey, hundreds of capitalists had flocked to this ten-thousand-dollar-a-head affair just for a glimpse of his advisers and spokespeople. Angela recognized several of the tycoons gathered on the ballroom's lacquered floor, but she was interested in only one of them, a short, obese kingpin in a voluminous gray suit. She headed straight for him, interrupting an intense conversation he was having with the chief executive of Home Depot.

'Hello, Wellington. Good to see you.'

She extended her right hand, hoping to avoid any contact more intimate than a handshake, but Wellington spread his arms wide and went in for a hug. 'Annie! Well, bust my buttons!' He pressed his doughy gut against her. 'I haven't seen you in ages!'

He had an avid grin on his rotund face, which was just as soft and jiggly as his stomach. Wellington Cannon and Sam Novacek had been best friends and business partners for forty years; they'd made wildly profitable investments in Manhattan real estate, and Wellington had used his share of the proceeds to start a media company called the True America Network. This venture was a great success too, becoming the preeminent purveyor of right-wing news and opinions, including tirades so imbued with white supremacy that even Fox News would've been afraid to broadcast them. The former president adored True America, and Wellington returned the love by shaking down his wealthy friends for campaign contributions. In secret, Wellington and his friends surely despised the fascist clown, but they were in awe of his ability to arouse red-state voters and convince working-class people to side with the billionaires.

Angela was deep in enemy territory but, thanks to her father, she knew how to navigate this sordid stratum of society. She smiled demurely at Wellington and his companion, pretending to be a fellow magnate and Republican, a middle-aged heiress who shared their biases and obsessions. 'Yes, it's been way too long. How are you, Welly?'

'Fine and dandy, thank you kindly. Oh Lord, where are my manners?' He belatedly glanced at the Home Depot CEO standing beside him. 'Bob, let me introduce you to the daughter of our dear departed friend Sam Novacek. She spent thirty years toiling as a zoologist, of all things, before taking the helm of Novacek Construction.'

The CEO shook her hand, stiff and polite, but he obviously wasn't interested in participating in this reunion, so he excused himself and went to the open bar for another drink. As soon as the man departed, Wellington stopped grinning. He squinted at Angela and leaned in close. 'You know, I didn't see you at Sam's funeral. Were you mourning in private, perhaps?'

She had to be careful now. Wellington knew how much she'd hated her father, so naturally he was suspicious of her. She needed to put him at ease. 'It was a rough time for all of us. But I've gained some perspective over the past year, and now I'm ready to move forward.'

'And do you expect me to forgive you? For how you treated your father?'

'No, I don't expect—'

'You're right, who needs forgiveness? You have the billion-dollar company that Sam left in your hands. What else could you possibly need?'

'Please, let's not fight. I want to remember the good and forget the bad.'

She smiled again as she spouted this pablum, which had to qualify as one of the biggest lies she'd ever told. But in this case, the lie was better than the truth, because it convinced Wellington to stop attacking her. He took a deep breath and closed his mouth.

For several seconds they just stared at each other while the party swirled around them. Then, in search of a new conversation topic, Angela gestured at the crowd of fat cats scattered across the ballroom. 'This shindig feels like a pre-game tailgate, doesn't it? You're warming up for the big event at Madison Square Garden tomorrow?'

Her comment wasn't really meant to be funny, but Wellington chuckled. His anger had clearly ebbed. 'Ah, that's a good analogy. Our political superstar certainly loves to play games in front of a large crowd.'

'How much campaign cash do you think you'll raise for him tonight? Ten million? Twenty?'

Wellington shrugged his massive shoulders. 'Hard to say. Thanks to the assassinations, the stock market is plunging, and nobody is generous during a bear market.'

'Yes, that was a tragedy. But at least your friend Chuck Roche came out of it safe and sound.'

'He's not my friend anymore.' Wellington grimaced. 'Your father was close with Chuck – they used to go hunting together and I would join them sometimes – but that's all in the past.' He edged closer to her and lowered his voice. 'Roche was getting a little too involved in Republican politics, you see. He started making noises about running in the presidential primaries, and that pissed off you-know-who.'

Angela nodded. She'd heard rumors about this. 'I can see why that would annoy your superstar. In a head-to-head contest, Roche would be more popular with the blue-blood crowd. And he could stay in the race till the bitter end because he has ungodly amounts of money.'

'Yeah, Chuck's a *real* billionaire, not a wannabe. But can you imagine that crusty old fart on the campaign trail? Trying to win over the unwashed masses while twirling his onyx cane?' Wellington chuckled again. 'No, the Pumpkin Head is the safer bet, the bigger vote-getter. And if he hates Roche, the True America Network has to hate Roche too, because our network always agrees with the Pumpkin Head. Which explains all the snarky comments about Chuck that you may have heard recently from our analysts and commentators.'

Angela's strategy was working. Wellington had shifted to a confidential, just-between-us tone. Now she would try to take it a step further. 'You have a devious mind, Mr Cannon. I think that's what my father always liked about you.' She bent over the plump politico and brought her lips close to his ear. He smelled like a public toilet, but she tamped down her nausea. 'Remember the Christmas party at Dad's offices in 1989? I made the mistake of stopping by with my college friends, and we spotted you in the conference room, in a very compromising position. With two young ladies who definitely weren't Novacek Construction employees.'

Wellington's torso jiggled in amusement. 'Sure, I remember it well. Carl Hauser supplied the libidinous entertainment that night. Does he still work for your company?'

Angela nodded. 'We can't let Carl retire, he's too valuable. He has contacts all over the city – the mayor's office, the Department of Buildings, the steelworkers' union, you name it.'

'What about the sex workers' union? I'd be interested in tapping into his contacts there.'

It was a joke, but it also wasn't a joke. Wellington's lips were moist, and his eyes darted. Angela almost had him. She just had to act coy for a little longer. 'Oh, please. Aren't you too old for those kinds of games?'

'Hey, I'm a sexy seventy-two-year-old. And there's a lot of me to love.' He slapped the sides of his stomach. 'Don't I deserve a little reward at the end of the day? For all the hard work I do at True America? For the good of my country?'

Angela rolled her eyes, pretending to be merely exasperated with him when in fact she was thoroughly disgusted. She pointed at him. 'Are you serious, Welly? You really want me to ask Carl to find a working girl for you? Tonight?'

'I'm as serious as a heart attack. Which is exactly what might happen to me if Carl finds the right kind of girl.'

Angela let out a sigh of surrender. 'All right, I'll call him. I can't believe I'm doing this for you.' She removed an iPhone from her handbag and stepped away, heading for the bar. 'I'm gonna need a drink to get through this. You want me to bring you something? You still drink Kahlúa and cream?'

'That would be wonderful, darling.'

As she crossed the ballroom, she held the iPhone to her ear, but she didn't actually call Carl. She didn't have to; he already knew what he needed to do. When she reached the bar, she ordered a glass of water for herself and the Kahlúa and cream, into which she sprinkled several grams of sedative. Then she brought the cocktail to Wellington and spent the next fifteen minutes standing beside him while he chatted with the chief executive of Revlon.

Finally, she glanced at her phone and whispered in Wellington's ear, telling him that his call girl was waiting downstairs. Angela led him to the elevator, keeping a firm grip on his arm because he seemed a bit dizzy from the excitement and the sedative. She escorted him to West 50th Street, where the black limousine was idling by the curb with Carl Hauser still at the wheel. The limo's rear door was already open, allowing Wellington to get a good look at Erin O'Malley, who sprawled rather seductively on the backseat, wearing nothing but denim shorts and a crop top.

'Hello there, Welly. Care to go for a ride?'

The fat capitalist could barely walk by this point, but through the sheer force of lust he managed to stumble into the limo. Erin helped him lie down on the backseat while Angela joined Carl in the front of the car. Just before Wellington slipped into unconsciousness, he stared blankly into space and slurred a question.

'Hey . . . baby . . . how much . . . is this gonna . . . cost?'

Erin shook her head. 'You don't want to know, love.'

TWENTY

The first thing Max learned about Heaven was that – contrary to everything he'd ever heard about the place – it was neither serene nor blissful. Instead, it was full of pain: deep aches, excruciating twinges, and profound disorientation.

On the plus side, though, all of Max's friends were there. Nathan loomed over him, as gawky and goofy as ever, his rubbery face threatening to break into a grin. Eileen was there too, her arm wrapped around Nathan's waist, her hourglass torso leaning against his side. She and Nathan appeared to be a couple in Heaven, a status they'd never achieved on Earth. Larry and Adele were a heavenly couple too, standing on the other side of Max's bed, and their relationship seemed unchanged; Adele said something strident, and Larry nodded vigorously in assent. And standing next to them was Agent Reyes, with the radio clipped to her belt and the telltale bulge under her blazer where her gun was.

Whoa, that's weird. Why is an FBI agent carrying a gun in Heaven?

And where's Janet? Where's Sonya?

Oh shit. This isn't Heaven.

It's a hospital.

I'm still alive.

As Max opened his eyes wider, his friends got excited. Nathan bent over the hospital bed, smiling like a proud father, and Eileen began to cry. Adele started cooing to him in a baby voice ('Max, you're awake! Look, he's awake!') while Larry backed her up in a similar tone ('Hey, buddy, how ya doin'? Oh man, you had us worried!') But Agent Reyes had no visible reaction. Clearly, she was biding her time, patiently waiting for her chance to ask Max some questions.

The pain in his head sharpened as he grew more alert. He raised a hand to his face and gently touched the bandages on his dented forehead and broken nose. He ran the tip of his tongue along a smooth metal strip that stabilized his loosened front teeth. But the worst moment came when he shifted his weight on the mattress and felt the bone-deep agony in his bandaged left arm. He let out a groan, and Nathan patted his shoulder.

'Better not move around too much, my man. You were out cold all night and for most of the morning. The doctors said you'll be fine, but you gotta take it easy.'

Max nodded very slowly, taking care not to jar his aching head. Then he reached for Nathan's hand and squeezed it. 'Thank you.' It came out as a whisper. 'You saved my life, right? You called the FBI?'

'It was more of a team effort.' Nathan gestured at all the members of the Doomsday Company. 'We didn't know exactly where the FBI agents were, so we split up and went to all the checkpoints. And we used the magic of musical theater to get their attention. I performed "Oklahoma" at the Triborough, and Eileen sang a new version of "Some Enchanted Evening" at the Lincoln Tunnel.'

Eileen wiped her eyes and nodded. 'I changed the title to "Some Endangered Mirsky."'

'And I did a number from *The Music Man* at the Queensboro.' Adele pointed at herself, then started to sing. '"You got trouble in Port Morris, folks, trouble with a capital T, and that stands for Tom Stroman!"'

Larry looked down at the floor. 'I tried to do a *Sound of Music* number at the GW, but it was a flop. The best line I could come up with was "How do you solve a problem like Max Mirsky?"'

'And let's not forget the real star of the show.' Nathan pointed at Reyes. 'This valiant federal agent heard our musical message and raced to the rescue.'

Max focused on her. Reyes said nothing and didn't crack a smile. Her grim expression scared the shit out of him. He lifted his head off his pillow. 'What's going on, Agent? Did something happen to Sonya? Or Janet?'

Reyes shook her head. 'Nothing happened. We still don't know where they are.'

'OK, I can help. I have some new information. I don't know where they are, but now I know for sure that the climate nuts kidnapped them. It wasn't the right-wingers, that was all just bullshit.'

'Hold on, Mr Mirsky.' Reyes turned to Nathan and the others. 'I'd like to talk with Max in private. Could you all wait in the hallway for a few minutes?'

Without any protest, the Doomsday Company filed out of the room. Their brisk obedience wasn't surprising; thanks to Reyes, their estimation of the FBI and its competence had apparently improved. The agent closed the door behind them and approached Max's bedside. She removed a pen and notepad from one of her blazer's pockets.

'Are you feeling well enough to answer some questions, Mr Mirsky?'

He wasn't, not really, but he nodded anyway. 'Go ahead.'

'What was your relationship with Thomas Stroman? How did you know him?'

Her voice was harsh, almost prosecutorial. Which made sense, Max thought. He was a victim, yes, but from the FBI's point of view, he was also a suspect. Reyes probably assumed he'd been collaborating with Stroman. That was the most logical explanation for why she'd found them together in Port Morris.

'Can I ask *you* a question first? Stroman's dead, right?'

'Why do you want to know?'

'Well, the fucker almost killed me, so I have no affection for the guy, but if he managed to survive that gunshot, maybe he could tell us where Sonya and—'

'He's dead. I would've preferred it if he'd survived, but I had to make a quick decision.'

Max remembered the gunfire on the basement stairway, Stroman's head jolting backward, the bloody spike still in his fist. It was a quick decision but a good one, Max thought. If Reyes had hesitated, *he* would've been the dead guy.

The agent frowned. 'Can we get back to my first question now? How did you know Thomas Stroman?'

'I didn't know him. Yesterday was the first time I ever saw the guy, and that was one time too many.'

'Then how did you wind up at his place of business?'

Max's head throbbed. This was going to take a while. 'It was a hunch. Remember the emails I got from the terrorists? They used the phrase "Nothing but green," and that was the name of a climate action group I belonged to when I was at Columbia. So I did some poking around at the college yesterday and learned the name of a sketchy physicist who once belonged to a very similar group. That was Stroman.'

Reyes scribbled a few notes on her pad, but she still seemed skeptical. 'When were you at Columbia? Over thirty years ago?'

'I know, it was a leap, a crazy guess. But I was on the right track, wasn't I? When you searched Stroman's workshop, did you find any evidence connecting him to the murders?'

Max had little hope that she would answer this question, but Reyes surprised him by nodding. 'Oh yeah, that *pendejo* was part of it. The spike he used to stab your arm? It matched the drones that killed the senator. And Agent Martinez, my partner.'

The change in her tone was even more surprising. A few seconds ago she'd been a calm, careful investigator, but now she sounded seriously angry. And though her transformation was a bit frightening, it made Max like her more. He admired Reyes for showing some emotion. He wanted her to be just as furious as he was at the fuckers who'd kidnapped his daughter.

Max sat up in the hospital bed, wincing but determined. 'And what about the microwave transmitter? I smashed the hell out of that thing, but your forensics people must've examined the debris, right?'

'A transmitter? That's what it is? We couldn't make heads or tails of it.'

'That's the weapon they're gonna use on their next target. Stroman was testing it on me, using the microwaves to mess with my brain. And before the Irishwoman left the building, he gave her a device just like it.'

'Hold on. You saw someone else there?'

'Yeah, she had an Irish accent. She was young, good-looking, blonde. She was the one who admitted that they'd kidnapped Sonya and Janet.'

The expression on Reyes's face turned murderous. She reached into the inside pocket of her blazer and pulled out a photograph. 'This picture was taken by one of the security cameras at the Roche mansion. Is this the same woman you saw?'

Max nodded. The photo showed her in a short black dress and an auburn wig, but it was definitely the Irishwoman. 'Yeah, that's her. She plays rough, that one. She knocked me out before I could even shake hands with her. And when I came to, she interrogated me.'

'Did she say anything about the people she's working for? Who they are, where they're located? Or anything about her next target?'

He closed his eyes and tried to remember. 'No, she didn't say anything specific. I asked her where Sonya and Janet were, and she said they were "across town," I think. But she didn't mention any names, nothing like that.' Then a memory came back to him, and he opened his eyes with a start. 'But Stroman mentioned *her* name. He said it was Erin. And he said something about their target too, how he'd seen this guy's medical records and used the measurements of his skull to calibrate the settings on the microwave weapon. Strange, right?'

Agent Reyes wrote all this down in her notepad. 'Anything else?'

'Yeah, he said this guy's records were *classified*. Like in a top-secret report or something. Which would make sense, I guess, if they're targeting the number one guy on my list. I mean, the medical records of the Saudi crown prince might be in a CIA report, right?' Max thought it over. 'But no, that doesn't make sense, because Stroman also said their next target was taller than me. And I know that the crown prince is only six feet tall, and I'm six foot two.'

Reyes stopped writing. She lowered her notepad and bit her lip, as if a crucial thought had just occurred to her. 'And Charles Roche is five foot nine, at the most. So maybe they've stopped relying on your list. They could be using different criteria to pick their targets now, because they want to make it harder for us to guess the next one.'

'We can narrow it down, though. I mean, who else has medical records that are classified? The president, I suppose. But he's also six foot even, right?'

'The *current* president is.'

The agent turned away from Max and stared into space for a few seconds. She returned her pen and pad to the pocket of her blazer, and the thoughtful expression on her face gradually changed to a look of utter certainty.

Without another word, Reyes rushed out of the hospital room.

When Max's friends returned to the room, he asked them if anyone had located his iPhone. Nathan showed him a transparent plastic bag containing his belongings.

'The Feds found your phone and wallet where you hid them.' Nathan pointed at the phone inside the bag. 'I'm sure they searched those items quite thoroughly, so now the FBI knows all about your Natalie Wood fetish.'

Adele pointed at the bag too. 'And I put some new clothes in there for you, one of Larry's shirts and a pair of his khakis. Your old clothes were a bit, uh, soiled.'

Max felt a surge of gratitude toward his friends, but it was accompanied by a pang of guilt, because now he would have to lie to them. 'You guys are the greatest, seriously. But the thing is, I can barely keep my eyes open. Can you all come back here this afternoon, maybe? I think I need a few more hours of rest.'

The Doomsday Company let out a chorus of apologies. One by one, they tendered heartfelt goodbyes and promised to return this afternoon with various goodies. Larry said he'd bring over a pepperoni slice from the pizzeria down the street. Eileen offered to share some of her cannabis gummies.

Max waited until they'd all left the room, and then he turned on his phone. The time, he noticed, was eleven forty-two a.m.

He went first to the *New York Times* website. The lead story was about the assassination of the West Virginia senator, and it had some new details. The fact that it was a drone attack had become public knowledge last night, triggering widespread panic. Politicians and chief executives across the country were seeking shelter in basements and cellars. Airlines had grounded their jets, and people were avoiding road trips too, since everyone could picture all too well a swarm of spiked drones crashing through a cockpit window or an SUV windshield. Carbon emissions around the world had plunged, just as they did after 9/11, but the *New York Times* said the long-term effects were impossible to predict. The White House was urging the public to stay calm, and the National Guard was manning checkpoints on the highways, aiding the law-enforcement teams who were pursuing the terrorists.

Max scrolled through all the related articles until he found one about all the parades, carnivals, baseball games, and church picnics that had already been canceled because of Killer Drone Hysteria, as the *Times* was calling it. Most indoor events, though, were proceeding as scheduled, since they were presumably less vulnerable to an aerial assault. In particular, the article mentioned that the former president was going ahead with his rally this afternoon at Madison Square Garden, despite the terrorist threat and the ominous approach of Hurricane Yolanda. One of his spokesmen, a shameless flack named Hal Patterson, said his boss was 'totally unafraid of those cowardly climate terrorists and ready to tear them apart with his bare hands.'

Max knew Patterson. The guy had once been a reputable journalist for *Newsweek*, and Max had become friendly with him because they'd occasionally attended the same press conferences, but after *Newsweek* imploded a decade ago Patterson switched to a more lucrative career in the public-relations industry. He'd had great success managing the reputations of some shady characters in the cryptocurrency business, and a year ago he became the leader of the former president's billion-dollar disinformation campaign. Max still had Patterson's cell-phone number, and he dialed it from his hospital bed.

'Hey, Hal? It's Max Mirsky. Remember me?'

There was a long pause. 'Mirsky? Editor of the *Journal of Incredibly Obscure Climatological Studies*?'

This had been a running joke between the two men ten years ago. Hal Patterson had found it very amusing that Max's readership barely cracked a thousand subscribers.

'Yeah, that's me, still toiling in obscurity. As opposed to you, my friend. You've really hit the big time, huh?'

'What can I say? Shit floats to the top. So, what's up? What's happening with you, old buddy?'

Patterson seemed unaware of Max's situation. Although Sonya's kidnapping had been widely reported, Hal clearly hadn't realized the connection between her and Max. Patterson was an absurdly self-centered person – much like his new employer –

and people like that tend to be oblivious to anything that doesn't directly concern them.

'Hal, I was wondering if you could get me press credentials for the big rally today at the Garden. I just got an assignment to cover the speech, a last-minute freelance gig from the *Wall Street Journal*.'

'*The* Journal? Sounds like you're moving up in the world too. And lucky for you, it's the one national newspaper that our campaign doesn't despise.' He laughed at this statement, even though it wasn't funny. 'OK, Max, the credentials will be waiting for you at the Thirty-third Street entrance. Just get there early, at least an hour before the speech. The goddamn security folks are making us jump through a million extra hoops today.'

Max thanked him and said goodbye. Then, very gingerly, he began to take off the thin blue hospital robe emblazoned with the words 'NEW YORK PRESBYTERIAN.' Tilting his head in any direction was painful, and raising his wounded arm was unbearably worse, but somehow he managed to strip off the robe and put on the clean clothes that Adele and Larry had loaned him. He stepped into his shoes, put his phone and wallet into the pockets of Larry's pants, and shuffled toward the door, cursing and grimacing.

It was a stupid decision, but he couldn't stop himself. Although he no longer thought of Agent Reyes as his enemy, he still didn't trust her. The agent's top priority wasn't rescuing Sonya and Janet; it was preventing another assassination. If she spotted Erin the Irishwoman in Madison Square Garden, her go-to move would probably be the same one she'd used on Stroman: a bullet to the head. But Max needed to keep the Irishwoman alive, at least long enough for her to tell him where his daughter and girlfriend were.

He shuffled out of the hospital, slow and steady, then hailed a taxi on East 68th Street. The sky was packed with low, gray clouds, careening in a vast, vaporous spiral. The first raindrops from Hurricane Yolanda started to fall.

TWENTY-ONE

Erin didn't mind dressing up as a man. In fact, she enjoyed it. During her late teens and early twenties, when she'd been a soldier in her father's paramilitary brigade, she'd trained with plenty of buff young Belfast men and dressed like them too, making herself just as hard and stunning as they were. So putting on this disguise now had a sexy, nostalgic appeal.

Plus, her body was suited for it: small tits, flat ass, lanky arms and legs. She wore baggy jeans and a bulky sweatshirt to hide any hint of her figure, and she tucked her hair under a close-cropped brown wig. She also wore a glue-on beard-and-mustache combo that made her look like Bradley Cooper in her favorite movie, *American Sniper*. She held her True America Network credentials in one hand and her Digisuper video-camera lens in the other, and she stood in line with a dozen scraggly television cameramen at Madison Square Garden's press entrance on West 33rd Street.

At least thirty cops and private guards manned this security gate, operating the X-ray machine and the body scanner and patting down the journalists, but Erin could tell they were mostly useless gobshites. There were only two people she had to worry about, a short guy in a fancy pinstripe suit and a tall guy in a much plainer gray suit. The shorty seemed to be in charge of the operation, and he yelled a lot at the guards and cops, constantly urging them to pick up the pace. In contrast, the tall guy just stood in the corner, barely moving but watching *everything*. A coiled wire snaked up from the collar of his jacket and curled around his right ear. He was Secret Service, and those fuckers were no joke.

When she reached the X-ray machine she put her sneakers, belt, and burner phone into a plastic bin on the conveyor belt, and in the next bin she gently rested the boxy Digisuper lens, which was the size of a carry-on suitcase and weighed more than twenty kilograms. Nobody had any reason to wonder why she was treating the lens with such care; it was a premium piece of optics used only by professional TV cameramen and priced at over a hundred thousand dollars. And this particular lens was even more valuable, because Erin had custom-retrofitted it, removing most of its optical and electronic innards and replacing them with the microwave device that Stroman had given her.

She went through the body scanner and presented her True America credentials to one of the security guards, who skimmed her forged information while another guard gave her a careless pat-down. Everything was going fine until she noticed that her TV camera lens had yet to emerge from the X-ray machine. The operator behind the machine called over another technician to study the scans, and after staring at the screen for half a minute the technician called out to the short guy in the pinstripe suit. 'Uh, Mr Patterson? Could you come over here and take a look at this?'

The guy hurried toward them, looking annoyed. 'What's the holdup?'

Instead of responding to him, the technician stared at Erin. 'Sir? Is the Digisuper lens yours?'

Erin stepped toward him, trying her best to look casually masculine. 'Yeah, it's the latest model.' She brought her voice down to its lowest, gruffest register. 'You're being careful with it, right?'

'It looks weird. I've never—'

'I told you, it's brand new. Comes with all the bells and whistles.'

From the corner of her eye, Erin saw the Secret Service agent step away from his corner. He'd sensed something amiss, and now he was heading toward them.

Shite. Time to make a call.

She reached for her burner phone, which had already come through the X-ray machine along with her shoes and belt. Still trying to look unconcerned, she dialed Angela's number. 'Here, let me call my boss. He can explain it to you.' At the same time, she flashed her credentials at the man named Patterson. 'I'm with True America.'

That got Patterson's attention. He looked at Erin with a mix of curiosity and wariness. 'I don't think we've met before. You are . . .?'

'Eric Luce. I just started working at the network.' With the hand that wasn't holding the burner phone, she grabbed Patterson's hand and shook it strenuously. 'But you know my boss, right? Wellington Cannon?'

'Oh yes! Of course!' Patterson smiled, but his eyes were full of trepidation. 'Wellington is one of the few good guys in the media business. A patriot and a true friend to us.'

By this point, Angela had answered Erin's call, although she didn't say a word on the phone line. As they'd previously arranged, Angela was at Prophecy's operating base, in a sub-basement room a block away from the Garden, presumably holding a gun to Wellington Cannon's head. A moment later, Wellington came on the line, his voice a little shaky but not alarmingly so. 'Uh, yes? How can I help you?'

'Boss, Mr Patterson has a question about the new camera lens. I'll put him on.' She offered the phone to the short guy. 'Mr Cannon wants to speak with you.'

Patterson took the phone and put a gracious grin on his face. 'Wellington! How are you doing today, old friend?'

He retreated to the far end of the room and lowered his voice as he conversed with True America's chief executive. The Secret Service agent looked on, ready to intervene if necessary, and the journalists in line behind Erin started to grumble about the delay. Finally, Patterson ended the call and returned to the X-ray machine, glaring at the technician. Wellington must've really given him an earful.

'Let the thing go through. It's just a new model with some extra parts.'

The technician seemed hesitant. 'But it looks so—'

'What's the fucking problem?' Patterson's face reddened. 'It doesn't have any bullets in it, does it? Or any trace of explosives?'

'No, but—'

'Then it's safe! Jesus, you people are driving me crazy!'

The technician restarted the conveyor belt, and Erin picked up her device from the bin. She waved goodbye at Patterson, then headed for the TV journalists' section on the arena's second floor.

Max asked his taxi driver to stop at a Duane Reade drugstore on 34th Street so he could buy a bottle of ibuprofen. He swallowed five of the pills, then shambled over to Madison Square Garden, getting thoroughly soaked by the strengthening storm. The winds howled across Midtown, and sheets of rain pelted the bumper-to-bumper cars and trucks whose drivers had decided too late to get out of the city.

By the time he reached the Garden's press entrance, there was a line of angry journalists extending out the door and down the block. Max asked an irate *New York Post* reporter what was going on, and the reporter's first response was, 'Shit, what happened to your face? Did you get mugged?' Max shook his head and asked his question again, and this time the reporter pointed at the security guards up ahead and said it was taking them forever to scan everyone and check their press credentials. But after a couple of minutes the line started moving again, and Max eventually passed through the body scanner and picked up the credentials that were waiting for him there.

Just past the security gate he caught a glimpse of his friend Hal Patterson, who was quick-stepping toward one of the stairways going down to the Garden's field level. Max wondered why Hal was in such a rush, and for a moment he considered following the guy, but there was no way he could keep up with him. Max's head ached and his left arm throbbed.

God, I can't do this. I should've stayed in the hospital. What the hell am I doing here?

Still, Max kept going. As he trudged down the concourses that looped around the arena, he scanned the crowds of rallygoers who were flooding into the Garden, loud men wearing red-white-and-blue T-shirts and smiling women with big hair and oversized campaign buttons. He suspected that most of them came from New Jersey and Long Island and upstate New York, since New York City itself didn't have so many Republicans. Max paid special attention to the younger women in the crowd, some of whom wore bright red bikini tops that had the word 'SAVE' over one breast and 'AMERICA' over the other. He stared so intently at the women that they averted their eyes, probably repelled by the sight of his bruised face and bandaged head.

But Max didn't care. He was looking for the Irishwoman.

* * *

According to the Bureau's handbook, one of the most important duties of an FBI agent is to alert her superiors if she believes there is 'a high probability of imminent terrorist activities.' Although Agent Reyes was in hot water with her boss – she'd infuriated Assistant Director Hastings by continuing to work on the Climate Avengers case – she informed him of her latest interview with Mirsky and her suspicions about the next attack. She requested an emergency meeting with the security detail protecting the former president, and Hastings ordered her to come to the temporary command post that the Secret Service had set up for the rally in Madison Square Garden.

The post was in an office near the entrance to the Garden's field level, just a short walk from the stage where the Pumpkin Head was scheduled to appear. Three Secret Service agents sat behind desks, each gazing at a laptop that showed surveillance-camera video from various sections of the Garden. Standing beside them was their commander, Special Agent Garner, a big, blustery man with a checkered reputation; according to the rumors Reyes had heard, he'd partied too heartily during the current president's last European trip, so the Secret Service had transferred him to the less prestigious squad that safeguarded former presidents. Assistant Director Hastings stood to Garner's left, and behind them was a short guy in a pinstripe suit who looked kind of weaselly.

And standing at the very center of the room was the Pumpkin Head himself, with his arms folded across his hefty torso and a petulant scowl on his orange face. As soon as Reyes came inside, he unfolded his arms and pointed a stubby finger at her.

'Who's this?' He turned his head and aimed his scowl at Hastings. 'Is this the agent you told me about?'

Hastings nodded. Like most of the FBI top brass, he'd disliked the former president ever since his catastrophic first term, but because there was a very good chance that the Pumpkin Head would return to the White House, Hastings was polite and cooperative in the man's presence. 'Yes, this is Special Agent Aleida Reyes. She called this meeting to discuss the new information regarding threats to your safety.'

'You're talking about the climate nuts? The socialists trying to take away our cars and toilets?' He kept pointing at her, thrusting his finger as if he were pressing an invisible button. 'Those tree-huggers are crazy. They're trying to destroy our economy.'

Reyes stepped forward, unintimidated. She was going to stick to the facts. 'Sir, our investigation has focused on the small cell of radicals hiding within the climate movement, the terrorists responsible for murdering—'

'Yeah, I'm not scared of them. They're not strong, they're weak. They're a bunch of cowards, if you want to know the truth.'

'Well, sir, we're making progress in locating them. Yesterday we raided a workshop in the Bronx that we believe was producing weapons for the terrorists. We've definitively linked the machinery we found there to the autonomous drones that killed Agent Martinez and Senator—'

'Drones? Why do I have to worry about drones? In case you didn't notice, this is an *indoor* arena. And besides, the Secret Service has everything under control.' He turned to Agent Garner. 'Tell her how well protected I am. The Secret Service is giving me even better security than what they're giving that sleepy old man in the White House. And that's only fair, because the old man didn't really win the election anyway.'

Garner paused, clearly wondering what to take seriously and what to ignore. 'Uh, yes, the Secret Service is doing its job. We've taken every precaution against a possible drone attack. We've boarded up all the windows on the building's periphery, and once the rally begins we'll seal off the arena from the concourses around it.'

Reyes kept her eyes on the former president. 'We have evidence from a witness who says the terrorists will use a new kind of weapon in their next attack, possibly a directed-energy weapon. He's also given me information that suggests the target of this attack will be you, sir.'

'Yeah, I know about your witness. Your boss already told me about this guy Mirsky. He's a liberal goofball, right?'

Hastings averted his eyes from Reyes. He must've shared some of her new information with the Pumpkin Head before she arrived, probably delivering it with a healthy dose of skepticism. Hastings was more of a politician than an investigator, which meant he usually told people what they wanted to hear. Now he gave the former president an apologetic look. 'Sir, I don't think Max Mirsky is a reliable witness, but out of an abundance of caution I agreed to let Agent Reyes come here and tell you—'

'You're wasting my time, that's what you're doing.' He turned back to Reyes and pointed his finger at her again. 'You don't like me, I know that. Because you're part of the deep state, and the deep state hates me. But when I get elected again, all that's gonna change. This time I'll get rid of *everyone* who won't do their jobs right.'

Agent Reyes bit her tongue to stop herself from responding. She'd never seen a grown man act this way. He was so childishly arrogant, there was no point in trying to talk to him like an adult. The only workable strategy was to use short sentences and say simple things in a slow, firm voice, as if she were speaking to a stubborn four-year-old.

'OK, sir, forget all that. Let's talk about the hurricane instead. You've seen the television reports about Yolanda?' She knew the answer was yes, because he was famous for his nonstop TV viewing. 'This storm poses an immediate danger to everyone in New York who isn't on high ground. For your own safety and for the safety of your supporters, you need to cancel this rally and—'

'Where are you getting this bullshit?' He stepped forward until he loomed over her, glowering. 'From the fake news? It's just a little rain, for Christ's sake.'

'I saw it with my own eyes. I was outside just two minutes ago and—'

'And I say it's bullshit. I got a weather report right here, and it says the storm won't come anywhere near New York.' He reached into his jacket, creasing his long red tie, and pulled out a colored printout that looked like a weather map of the area. 'See that? The hurricane's heading out to sea.'

Reyes stared at the map, which showed Yolanda's spiral arms stretching toward New York Harbor. Someone had used a black Sharpie to draw an arrow to the right of the storm, pointing toward the Atlantic Ocean. 'Sir, did you draw that arrow yourself?'

Reddening, he stepped backward and glared at Hastings.

'Didn't you tell me that this agent disobeyed your orders? Didn't she keep working on the investigation after you ordered her not to?'

Hastings frowned. Clearly, he didn't enjoy betraying his colleagues, but he would do it if necessary. 'Yes, sir, that's true. And Agent Reyes failed to notify me before leading the raid in the Bronx yesterday.'

'Then why haven't you fired her yet? Why is this lousy agent still working for you?'

Reyes could see where this was going. She shook her head and gave her boss a pleading look. 'Sir, I'm close to solving the case. I checked Interpol's records and identified an Irish mercenary named Erin O'Malley. I think she's the one who—'

'You're suspended until further notice, Reyes.' Hastings came toward her and held out his hand. 'Turn in your gun and badge, please.'

In disbelief, she removed the pistol from her shoulder holster and handed it to him. It was even harder to turn in her badge, but she did it. The former president grinned as he watched the handover. Then he pointed at the three Secret Service agents sitting at their desks. 'Hey, morons! Get off your asses and throw this nasty woman out of the building. And make sure she doesn't get back in.'

Five minutes later, Reyes stood in the howling rain outside Madison Square Garden. In a daze, she wandered into the shelter of Penn Station, where thousands of commuters packed the corridors and waiting areas, looking up at digital screens displaying all the cancellations on Amtrak, New Jersey Transit, and the Long Island Rail Road. Then she made a decision and took out her phone.

She dialed a number she'd memorized fifteen years ago, when she was a twenty-five-year-old Marine serving in Afghanistan. She'd met some genuine badasses during her tour there, some wild-eyed warriors who didn't give a fuck about discipline but were insanely, intractably, unswervingly loyal. She'd kept in touch with them over the years, so she knew they were still in the service and now stationed at Joint Base McGuire–Dix–Lakehurst, about sixty miles away in New Jersey.

And they owed her a favor.

TWENTY-TWO

Sonya Mirsky had a lot of time to think. And she used it to come up with a plan.

She'd started strategizing soon after the speedboat ride to Manhattan. She was seriously pissed, mostly because Angela had broken her promise to free Janet, but also because Carl had locked Sonya in an empty room in the basement of the Moynihan Train Hall. Later that night Carl briefly interrupted her ruminations by throwing an obese, smelly, unconscious man into the room with her; when this man finally awoke the next morning, he grumpily disclosed that he owned the True America Network. But through it all, Sonya kept thinking and plotting, and she made her final preparations after Carl and Angela dragged Wellington Cannon out of the room at noontime, saying he was needed for a quick phone call. When they returned with the fat-ass ten minutes later, Sonya was ready to execute her scheme.

She got to her feet as soon as they opened the door. As Carl shoved Wellington into the room, Sonya put on an indignant expression and strode toward Angela. 'What is this? You expect me to keep sharing a room with this alt-right stooge? With this broadcaster of disinformation and QAnon garbage?'

Angela let out a sigh. She'd changed into a new jumpsuit, Sonya noticed; this one was forest-green instead of olive-green, but it was just as ugly, and it seemed to have equally deep pockets. 'I apologize, Sonya, but this is the only suitable place for you and Wellington.'

'I thought I was important to you. Didn't you say that I was a "worldline crux"? And that my future path was going to align with yours, no matter what?'

Angela smiled, clearly pleased that Sonya had remembered. 'Yes, that's all true.'

'Then why are you treating me the same shitty way you treat this fascist?'

Wellington looked up from the corner of the room where Carl had dumped him. His hands were bound behind his back and his suit pants were soiled. 'Please. I'm not a fascist. I'll do anything you say, but please don't—'

'Shut up, asswipe.' Carl glared at him and raised his fist, and Wellington shut his mouth quick. Then Carl marched back to the doorway and waited there for Angela. He seemed impatient to leave.

But Sonya couldn't let them go just yet. She stepped closer to Angela and lowered her voice. 'I hate that True America pig. He's a propagandist. His network has turned so many people into climate-change deniers.' Sonya bit her upper lip, using her tried-and-true method to make herself cry. 'And I'm one of their favorite targets. Do you know what the idiots on True America said when I was invited to speak at the UN? They called me a "libtard in diapers." And "a whining schoolgirl with her panties in a twist." They broadcasted an interview with a coal miner who said I should be spanked with a pickax.'

Angela glanced at Wellington with sudden fury in her eyes. Her right hand delved into the pocket of her jumpsuit and toyed with the jingling objects at the bottom of it. Then she took a deep breath and turned back to Sonya. 'You're right, he's despicable. But he's also useful right now.'

'How? What's he doing for us?'

'We have an operative at the rally in Madison Square Garden.' Angela lowered her voice too and edged closer. 'Her cover is that she's a cameraman for the True America Network. But other people from the network are also in the arena, reporters and producers and anchormen, and they might start to question her. If they do, she'll need to get Wellington on the phone to back her up. He already helped her get through the security gate.'

Sonya shook her head, pretending not to understand. Her tears were flowing freely now. 'I don't care! I hate all those fascist assholes!'

'Yes, you have every right to hate them.'

'They're abusive! And they're liars! I fucking *hate* them!' She choked out a sob and buried her face in her hands.

She wasn't sure if her ploy would work. Angela was one of the least empathetic people she'd ever met. But a moment later

Sonya felt the woman embrace her. Angela pulled her in close, her hands gently clasping Sonya's shoulders.

Which meant that Angela's right hand was no longer in the pocket of her jumpsuit. Sonya removed her own hands from her face and lowered them to Angela's waist, as if she were about to return the hug. But instead, she thrust her left hand into Angela's pocket and pulled out the switchblade.

Sonya opened the knife and backed up fast, retreating to the corner where Wellington sprawled. She knew she couldn't threaten Angela with the switchblade; that woman was too strong and wily, and Carl was just a few feet behind her. But Wellington's hands were tied behind his back, and Sonya could easily kneel beside him and hold the knife to his throat.

'*Don't move!*' Sonya grasped a thick gray hank of Wellington's hair and pulled back his head, but she kept her eyes on Carl and Angela. 'If you take one fucking step, I'll cut this pig's head off!'

Carl lunged forward anyway, but Angela grabbed his arm and held him back. Wellington whimpered pitifully, and when Sonya glanced down she saw a trickle of blood running down his neck. Angela's knife was sharper than she'd thought. Sonya eased up on the pressure, but kept the blade near Wellington's jugular.

'Don't test me. I hate this fucker so much, slicing his throat would be a *pleasure*.' Sonya was appalled by what she was saying, and yet it came to her so easily. *That's what happens when your back is against the wall.* 'Now you're gonna listen to me, OK? You're gonna listen very carefully.'

Without letting go of Carl, Angela raised her free hand, with the palm facing outward, like a cop stopping traffic. 'Sonya, please, you don't know what—'

'*Shut up!* I'm the boss now. You're gonna give me what I want, or else you can say goodbye to Mr True America.'

'What do you—'

'Take out your phone and call whoever's in charge of your prison in Staten Island. You're gonna tell them to release Janet.'

Janet Page was sick to death of listening to Jason Torricelli. Being kidnapped was bad enough, but being forced to endure the rambling monologues of a spoiled-brat NYU sophomore with a serious cocaine problem? That was pure torture.

'Look, you don't know my dad, so you have no fucking idea. He's a total douchebag.' Jason leaned forward on the cot in Janet's jail cell and tilted his nose over a business card on which he'd sprinkled a liberal amount of coke. 'But he's got his hooks in me, you know? He won't give me a fucking penny unless I toe the line. Which explains how I got into this whole mess.'

He noisily snorted the coke, then tilted his head back and closed his eyes. He'd already offered Janet 'a toot' and she'd curtly declined. Jason was willing to share his Bolivian marching powder with her, but he wouldn't loosen the wires that bound her hands behind her back. He was a truly screwed-up kid.

After a few seconds he opened his red eyes and tapped the business card he'd just hoovered clean. It said 'Torricelli Demolition Inc., Waste Removal and Incineration,' and it had a Staten Island address. 'This is where the cash comes from.' Jason tapped the card harder, smacking it with conviction. 'It's a fucking empire of garbage. The incinerator is a few miles from here, down Arthur Kill Road. Huge building with giant smokestacks. And it stinks like hell.' He let out a druggy laugh. 'Before Mom ran off with her hair stylist, we lived in a house that was downwind from the incinerator. Dad had the bucks to move to a better neighborhood, but he insisted on staying in that shit-hole. He used to say, "Stop complaining, that's the smell of money."'

Jason reached into his pocket, pulled out a glass vial, and poured some more powder on the business card. The kid's problem was obvious: his father was an asshole, and he was desperate for a mommy figure who could replace the woman who'd bugged out on him. Janet had already offered him some motherly wisdom, telling Jason that the first step to really improving his life would be to untie her hands and let her out of this goddamn jail. But the moron just shrugged off her advice.

'You know what's the worst part of this deal? Working with that dipshit Carl Hauser.' Jason lowered his voice and looked over his shoulder, even though Janet was pretty sure the abandoned prison was empty except for the two of them. 'Carl's a pimp from way back. He used to get hookers for Angela's dad and his pals. Torricelli Demolition was partners with Novacek

Construction on lots of projects, so Carl started getting whores for my dad too, and one of those girls took some bedroom photos. You know, pictures of some really sick things. And ever since then, Carl's been holding that shit over Dad's head and bossing us around. Right now he's using our garbage trucks to move his stuff across the city, taking most of it to the docks by our incinerator. That's where he's gonna stage his big fucking escape act.'

Once again Janet considered trying to reason with this imbecile. She could tell him that it was never too late to do the right thing. And that the prosecutors would probably take pity on him because of his dysfunctional upbringing and his abysmally low IQ. Or she could take advantage of her Doomsday Company skills and sing a song to him about life choices. That was what Max or Nathan would probably do. The chances of success were minuscule, but maybe it was worth a try?

But before Janet could start crooning, Jason's iPhone buzzed. He was so startled he spilled the coke off his business card. He yelled, 'Fuck!' and then fumbled for his phone, finally digging it out of his pocket.

'Hello . . . yeah, this is . . . yeah, I'm with her right now, I've been watching her the whole fucking . . . wait, what are you . . . what do you want me to . . . shit, are you serious? How do I . . . but what will happen when . . . all right, all right! Stop shouting at . . . yeah, OK, I'll do it right now.'

Jason looked dazed. He lowered the phone and shook his head, rapidly and hard, probably trying to clear some space in his drug-addled brain. Then he stood up and stepped behind Janet and started undoing the wires around her wrists.

'It's your lucky day, lady. You're getting early release.'

Sonya kept the knife at Wellington's throat until she got confirmation that Janet was out of the prison. She didn't take anyone's word for it; she ordered Angela to toss her iPhone across the room so she could speak to Janet herself. (Jason Torricelli had been instructed to give his phone to his former prisoner when he released her.)

Holding Angela's phone to her ear, Sonya heard the keening of fierce winds, high-pitched and incredibly loud. The storm she'd seen in the distance yesterday had obviously walloped

Staten Island. She pressed the phone harder against her ear and listened intently for Janet's voice.

'Sonya? I'm . . .' – the roaring wind drowned her out – '. . . as fast as I can, heading away from the prison, but I'm not . . . all the roads are flooded and I can't . . . Jesus, I've never seen such a . . .'

'Listen to me, Janet!' Sonya practically screamed into the phone. 'You know what to do, right?'

'I already tried to . . . but when I dialed nine-one-one, all I got was . . . I mean, it's a fucking natural disaster here and all the cell-phone towers are probably . . .'

Then the line went dead. It wasn't the best news in the world, but it would have to do.

Sonya closed the switchblade and let go of Wellington, who crumpled into a fetal heap, shaking uncontrollably. Then she placed the knife and phone on the floor and slid them back to Angela. Carl was already charging toward her, but Sonya didn't try to defend herself. She'd done everything she could.

'Go ahead, kill me.' She stared defiantly at the bald bastard, who was less than ten feet away and closing in fast. 'I don't give a shit.'

TWENTY-THREE

Erin couldn't believe she'd found such an excellent sniper's nest, right in the middle of Madison Square Garden. From where she stood, she had a perfect view of the stage that had been set up on the arena's floor, about ten meters below her and thirty meters ahead. She felt as if she'd just won the Assassination Sweepstakes.

She stepped down to the front row of Section 224, on the lip of the cantilevered tier that overlooked the stage. Seven television cameras were positioned along the edge of the balcony, each installed on a swiveling pedestal, and behind six of those cameras were six overweight, bearded, slovenly men, all wearing baseball caps. Television production was obviously a very sexist profession. Although Erin was only pretending to work in this field, she was still outraged. If she hadn't disguised herself as a man, she would've stuck out like a sore femme. Was there some union rule demanding that every camera operator have a willy?

Each cameraman sat on a movable chair that slid along curved rails on the floor, allowing him to stay directly behind his camera as he pivoted it to the left and right. Erin supposed this was useful for televising the arena's basketball games. Because the players moved so quickly from one end of the court to the other, the cameras needed to pivot quickly too. But it also reminded her of the swiveling anti-aircraft guns in World War II movies. As the cameramen peered at their viewfinder screens and gripped the camera handles to adjust tilt and focus and range, they looked as dogged as Air Force gunners who carefully tracked their targets before shooting them out of the sky.

The camera belonging to the True America Network was at the left end of the row. Erin approached it with a serious, weary expression, imitating the faces of the cameramen from the other networks. Following the instructions Tom Stroman had given her, she removed the bulky, boxy telephoto lens from the camera and replaced it with the Digisuper lens she'd brought with her, the one with the microwave transmitter hidden inside. Then she attached the appropriate power cables and tested the transmitter, which was operating just fine according to the display on her screen. The device used more electricity than a television camera, but it was unlikely that anyone would notice the extra current.

Once the mechanism was ready, she settled back in her movable chair and observed the mob in the arena. Thousands of people were coming down the aisles and trying to find their seats. It was a colorfully dressed crowd, loud and cheerful. Women yelled greetings at each other across the rows and sections and tiers, and men shouted enthusiastic profanities that were intended, Erin supposed, to cement their ideological solidarity. She didn't really understand American politics – it was too much like a game or a professional sport. These right-wing Republicans had come to Madison Square Garden to cheer on their team, their champion, their Most Valuable Player. The fact that the opposing team was nowhere in sight didn't seem to bother them. They clearly preferred a one-sided contest, a game they always won.

After a few minutes the arena's overhead lights dimmed and a fervent voice boomed out of the massive loudspeakers: 'Ladies and gentlemen, welcome to the Save America Again rally! Please rise for our glorious national anthem.'

The crowd jumped to its feet and applauded. Even the cameramen stood up, grunting and groaning, and Erin rose from her chair too, trying to blend in. The anthem blared across the Garden while columns of uniformed soldiers and police officers marched across the arena's floor, where the best seats were, and ascended the stairways on both sides of the stage. A dozen of the soldiers and cops carried American flags onstage, and blinding images of the flag were displayed on the immense video screen behind the podium.

It was one of the most distressing sound-and-light shows Erin had ever seen. In terms of ridiculous jingoism, it rivaled the spectacles in North Korea, but seeing it in New York was much less amusing. Erin, after all, was from Northern Ireland, so she knew how civil wars could spring from this bullshit.

After the anthem, everyone had to stay on their feet for the Opening Prayer, which was delivered by a handsome evangelist in an elegant suit. This preacher went way over his allotted time, shaking his fist and pounding his Bible and railing against socialist conspiracies, while many of his listeners raised their hands over their heads and swayed to the rhythm of his insane sermonizing. Then there was an introductory speech given by one of the ex-president's biggest supporters, the pudgy governor of Mississippi. Erin followed the lead of the other cameramen and pointed her device at the governor, pretending to film him. She didn't turn on the microwave transmitter yet, although she was sorely tempted as his speech went on and on, mostly describing how much he adored the strong, courageous leader who'd been wrongfully ousted from the White House by the fishiest presidential election in American history.

Jesus, Mary, and Joseph! I should zap him just to shut his effing gob.

Finally, the wee wanker finished his speech, and deafening applause rose from every section of Madison Square Garden as the former president joined him onstage. Towering over the governor, he wrapped the little imp in a bearhug, and the wanker's eyes bulged with fear as the famously hefty mogul squeezed him. Then, after releasing the governor and nudging him offstage, the ex-president turned his beaming orange face toward his enraptured audience. The screen behind him showed his visage monstrously enlarged, magnifying every pore in his forehead, every moist bloodless curve of his smarmy lips.

Erin waited until he took position behind the stage's lectern, his jowls just above the microphone. Then she aimed the transmitter at his head and turned it on.

For Max, posing as a journalist at the rally turned out to be a mixed blessing. The press badge around his neck aided his search for the Irishwoman, since it allowed him to move freely from one section of the Garden to another without being hassled by the security guards. But the badge also drew some hostile attention from the rallygoers, many of whom were vocal critics of the working press. 'Fake news!' and 'Lamestream media!' were the most common insults. He also heard several comments about his bruised face, most of them expressing approval of the beating he'd suffered. Ironically, though, his injuries probably saved him from further physical abuse. One of the hecklers in Section 211 put it succinctly: 'Leave that guy alone. It looks like someone already taught him a lesson.'

Max's strategy was to walk down each aisle to the front row, then turn around and survey all the women in each section. But it was a rowdy, restless crowd, and even during the national anthem they couldn't stand still. They ran up and down the aisles, bustling past one another and eyeing the unoccupied seats, everyone striving to get the best view of the stage. During the Opening Prayer hundreds of people did a kind of religious dance, rocking from side to side and waving their arms over their heads, and that made it difficult for Max to see the people behind them. And they kept milling around and switching seats during the Mississippi governor's speech, since it was just a pallid warm-up act. Clearly, the rallygoers wouldn't sit still and pay attention until the main attraction came onstage.

It was also difficult for Max to study each face long enough and carefully enough to be certain that he wasn't staring at the Irishwoman. He couldn't limit his search to the blondes in the crowd, because Erin was obviously adept at disguising herself; she'd worn a wig in the photo that Agent Reyes had shown him, which meant he had to examine all the brunettes and redheads in the Garden as well. He couldn't ignore the older women either, because Erin could've caked some heavy makeup on her face and put on one of those big silver helmet-like wigs that seemed very popular among the middle-aged women in this crowd.

Max started to despair as he made his way around the arena. At the rate he was going, he wouldn't find Erin in time. And what would happen after she executed the ex-president? In all likelihood, she'd either escape from Madison Square Garden or be shot to death while trying to flee. Either way, Max wouldn't get a chance to interrogate her. He'd lose his last, best hope of finding Sonya and Janet.

Distraught, he stopped to catch his breath in the aisle between Sections 214 and 215. Just then, he saw Hal Patterson, his contact in the former president's press office. Hal raced up the aisle and grasped Max's arms. 'Mirsky! Who did that to you? Which section were they in?'

Hal winced as he stared at the damage to Max's face. He'd obviously assumed that some of the hooligans in the crowd had roughed him up, which wasn't an unreasonable assumption.

Max shook his head. 'Don't worry. I got hurt yesterday.'

'Yesterday?' Hal looked confused.

'Yeah, it was a dumb accident. You can relax, OK?'

Hal let out a long breath. 'Jesus, that's a relief. I can't stand this part of the job. How can I get reporters to cover the campaign if they're in mortal danger at the rallies? It's a big fucking problem.'

'Listen, Hal, I'd love to talk, but I have to go to—'

'You got the credentials I left for you? Sorry about the wait at the security line, it was a nightmare. We had a problem with this TV guy who brought in a newfangled camera lens, and it held everything up.' Hal pointed at the stage, where the governor of Mississippi was wrapping up his speech. 'Hey, you want a chance to interview that dope? After the rally we're going to—'

'Wait a second.' Max felt dizzy. His whole body trembled in alarm. 'What did you say about a camera lens?'

Hal shrugged. 'It's not important. It made the security guys nervous because it looked strange on the X-ray screens, but it turned out to be nothing.'

'Whose camera was it?' Max couldn't believe how stupid he'd been. *How could I have missed it?* 'Which television channel?'

'Max, are you all right? You look kind of—'

'Damn it, just tell me where that camera is!'

Hal took a step back. 'Uh, shit, it belonged to some new guy with True America.' He gestured at the opposite side of the arena. 'He should be with the other TV cameramen, at the front of Section Two-twenty-four. Hey, where are you—?'

Max bounded past him and rushed toward the row of cameras.

Erin noticed the exact moment when the microwave beam started scrambling the ex-president's brain.

It happened just after he gripped the microphone on the lectern to adjust its tilt. He flashed a toothy smile at the cheering crowd and said, 'Wow, thank you very much everybody,' and his audience roared in response. After a few seconds he leaned toward the microphone again to repeat his insincere thank you, but this time he only got as far as 'Thank you very—' before his eyes widened and his orange brow furrowed.

He turned his head to the left and right, obviously looking for the source of the screeching alarm that the microwaves had set off inside his skull. The crowd kept cheering, even louder than before, and a naïve observer might've assumed that the former president was simply scanning the arena to marvel at his supporters, or that perhaps he was searching for a VIP or special guest in one of the front rows. No one but Erin knew what was really going on, and she relished the look of bewilderment on the eejit's face.

Ah sure, it's confusing, isn't it? You can't figure out where the noise is coming from. But this is nothing, boyo, this is just a taste. The transmitter is on its lowest setting.

To his credit, the gobshite attempted to soldier through it. He shook his head, trying to get the screeching to stop. He stuck a stubby finger in his right ear and twisted it madly. He kept the smile on his face, pulling back his bloodless lips, but now his grin looked pained and skeletal. As he bent over the lectern, he struck the microphone with his chin, and the amplified bump echoed against the Garden's concave ceiling.

'And a very . . . a very special hello . . . to all my friends in . . . all my friends . . .'

He probably couldn't hear himself talk, so it was no wonder he was having trouble getting the words out. But the crowd still hadn't realized that something was wrong. They just kept cheering.

Erin turned up the transmitter's power. In her mind's eye, she could see the invisible beam lancing across the arena and smashing into the head of the man onstage.

He staggered at the moment of impact and clutched the sides of the lectern to stop himself from collapsing. Shuddering, he stretched his chin toward the microphone, but he didn't cry out for help. Instead, he kept trying to smile, but now his jaw quivered and his lips flapped and a string of drool spilled from the corner of his mouth.

'All my . . . all my . . . special . . . speciallllllllll . . .'

The cheering ebbed, but no one in the crowd screamed in horror or rushed toward the stage. The former president had suffered bouts of dizziness and confusion in previous appearances, sometimes stumbling down ramps or slurring his words or struggling to lift a glass of water, and afterwards he'd always denied that there was any problem. And his supporters had always believed his lies, so now they couldn't accept that something was truly wrong with him. Their collective denial muffled the arena as everyone waited for him to shake off this spell and continue his speech.

Sorry, love. You can't shake it off this time.

Erin ratcheted the transmitter's power to its highest level. Instantly, the ex-president arched his back and lost his grip on the lectern. He fell backwards, and his heavy torso hit the podium with a thud that could be heard in every corner of the arena. He lay face-up on the stage, his eyes closed, his face slack. Erin adjusted the angle of the transmitter to keep the pulsing microwaves focused on his head, so they could deliver their final blows to his cerebrum.

The cops and Secret Service agents raced across the stage and converged on the body lying next to the lectern. Erin watched them with great interest; because the microwave beam had been adjusted to match the ex-president's skull, she wasn't sure how much it would affect people with smaller or larger heads. As it turned out, the effect was noticeable. One of the cops knelt beside the body to check its pulse, and as soon as the cop's head moved into the path of the beam he clamped his hands over his ears and fell to the side. A Secret Service agent took the cop's place, and within seconds he also staggered away. Erin wondered when they would finally realize what was happening, but she didn't plan to stick around long enough to find out. She rose from her movable chair and turned away from the stage and gazed at the shocked people standing behind her in Section 224. She was plotting her escape route.

Then she saw Max Mirsky. The battered eejit was racing down the aisle, pointing at her and shouting.

She was disguised as a man, but Max recognized her. For as long as he would live, he'd never forget the face of the Irishwoman, no matter how much fake hair she put on her chin and cheeks.

'That's the one!' he yelled at the stunned Republicans, all

standing in the section's rows and anxiously peering over one another's heads. 'See that cameraman over there? He's the one who did it! He shot an energy beam at the stage!'

In any other setting, this would've sounded insane. But a large number of the former president's fans were conspiracy theorists who firmly believed in space aliens and satanic cults and government plots employing all kinds of electromagnetic radiation. In their state of shock, they were also inclined to believe Max's absurd claim, which happened (weirdly enough) to be true.

'I'll prove it! He's wearing a disguise!' Still pointing at Erin, Max leapt down to the section's second row, just behind the TV cameramen. 'Grab that guy and pull hard on his beard! It'll come right off, because he's actually *a woman*!'

This statement struck a chord with the crowd too, since right-wingers are so suspicious of anything that smacks of gender fluidity. Half a dozen men in the second row charged toward Erin, clambering over the waist-high glass barrier that separated the spectators from the TV cameramen. Max rushed toward the barrier too, wondering if he could climb over it without pulling the stitches in his wounded arm. He was worried that the Republicans would beat Erin to death before he could ask her where Sonya and Janet were.

But Erin didn't seem worried. She frowned at Max, creasing her forehead. Then she calmly detached the bulky lens from her television camera and pointed it at the men scrambling toward her.

Oh shit. Max dove for the floor. *I should've seen this coming.*

Luckily for Erin, the microwave transmitter was equipped with a battery that enabled portable operation for up to ten minutes. She put the device on a low-power setting – there was no need for overkill – and swept it from left to right, panning across the heads of the ugly gobshites straddling the barrier.

They tipped over and fell on their arses, clonking against the cameramen from the other networks. Then she aimed the beam at a second wave of would-be heroes in Section 224. She wanted to zap Mirsky too, just for the sake of revenge, but that irritating eejit had ducked out of sight, so she focused on clearing a path for her escape. Carrying the transmitter under her arm like a rugby ball, she hurtled over the glass barrier and dashed up the aisle, firing microwaves at anyone who got in her way.

She followed the same strategy on the concourse at the edge of the arena, and on the escalators leading down to the ground floor. Security guards were racing to lock down Madison Square Garden, but Erin scattered them like duckpins. With a banshee scream, she ripped off her male wig and her fake beard and barged out of the building through an emergency exit.

Rain was bucketing down on West 33rd Street, so she turned off the transmitter and tucked it under her sweatshirt. She had to keep both hands under the heavy device, which made her look like a grotesquely pregnant woman caressing her belly, but no one else was there to see it. Floodwaters were already coursing down the empty street and lapping over the curbs, and the winds were flinging random bits of garbage over the waterlogged cars. It was a nasty storm, a real lasher, but Erin lowered her head and started jogging west toward the Hudson River.

Her job was done. Now it was time to collect her payment.

Max followed her out of Madison Square Garden. It was like driving behind an ambulance in heavy traffic – the cops and security guards tumbled to the side when Erin pointed the transmitter at them, and before they could recover their senses Max raced down the path she'd cleared.

By the time he got outside, she was several hundred feet ahead of him, and he could just barely see her in the rain-drenched distance, running west on 33rd Street. Max set off in the same direction, fighting the wet gales and splashing across the canal that used to be Eighth Avenue. He slogged and waded as fast as he could, but he couldn't keep up. Soon Erin was almost past the colonnaded Moynihan Train Hall, which stretched all the way to Ninth Avenue. At times the sheets of rain veiled her from Max's sight, and all he could see was the thick gray storm that was battering Manhattan.

Then the rain let up and the mist lifted for a few seconds and Max saw something amazing. Three figures had appeared to the left of Erin, and they seemed to be running beside her on the sidewalk. Two of the figures were just as tall as Erin, but the one in the middle was shorter. And though Max's eyesight was totally unreliable at such a distance, he could've sworn that the shorter figure's skin was dark.

'*Sonya!*' He screamed, he howled, he keened like the wind. '*SONYA!*'

TWENTY-FOUR

Agent Reyes had turned in her gun and badge, but her boss hadn't asked for her radio, which was still clipped to her belt. After she was expelled from Madison Square Garden, she spent almost an hour hunkered down in Penn Station, waiting for a phone call, and to pass the time she listened to the frantic communications on her radio's police and Coast Guard channels. As a result, she got a pretty good sense of how Hurricane Yolanda was fucking with New York.

In some ways it was a virtual repeat of 2012's Superstorm Sandy. Yolanda flooded the same low-lying coastal areas that Sandy did: the Rockaways in Queens, Coney Island in Brooklyn, New Dorp Beach in Staten Island. But Yolanda's winds were stronger than Sandy's, and its storm surge was higher. A monstrous swell of seawater from the Atlantic rushed into New York Harbor and slammed against the southern tip of Manhattan, inundating the Financial District. The surge swept across Chinatown and Chelsea too, and the floodwaters poured into all the subway tunnels. The power was out in Lower Manhattan, and according to the radio reports it would soon be out in Midtown as well.

But Reyes didn't need the radio to tell her how bad the hurricane was, because the storm eventually burst into Penn Station. The floodwaters sluiced uptown from Chelsea and funneled into Penn's entrances, cascading down stairways and escalators and terrifying the thousands of commuters who'd been stranded in the station's hallways when the trains stopped running. They raced for higher ground, forcing their way into the office buildings of Penn Plaza, where they huddled near the windows on the upper floors and watched the city drown.

There weren't enough police officers to maintain order in the station, and the NYPD couldn't bring in reinforcements because the streets were impassable. At one point Reyes tried to help the cops control the crowd, but they were suspicious – she had no badge, no authority – so they told her to back off. Frustrated, she pulled out her phone, intending to dial the memorized number again and leave another urgent voice message. But before she could touch the screen, the phone buzzed in her hand. The person she was trying to reach had finally called her back.

'Yo, Reyes? This is Mad Dog. I'm on my way.'

'What? Where are—'

'Can't talk now. Gotta . . .' A metallic thump and the whine of a powertrain drowned him out. 'Just meet me at West Thirtieth and the river. I'll be there in ten.'

Then the line went dead.

Reyes shoved the phone into her pocket and started running. She barreled out of Penn Station and turned right on 31st Street, sprinting west.

The sight of his daughter, even though it was a distant glimpse, transformed Max entirely. All his aches and pains vanished, just like they did in the final mile of every marathon he'd ever run, and he was charged with desperate energy. He sped down the sidewalk, taking long strides and lifting his feet high above the filthy, frothing waters. He stopped screaming her name but fixed his eyes on her.

Soon he realized he was catching up. Sonya was less than five hundred feet ahead, crossing Ninth Avenue with Erin and the two others, a tall woman in a jumpsuit and a burly bald man. Now that Max was closer, he saw that Sonya's hands were tied behind her back; the bald guy was gripping her arm and dragging her across the flooded street. Max grimaced and ran faster, but by the time he reached the avenue several cars had floated into the intersection, blocking his path. He had to wade around the stalled vehicles, and for a terrible half-minute he lost sight of his daughter. But after he crossed the canal he redoubled his pace, and at Tenth Avenue he saw the four of them up ahead, jogging past Hudson Yards. They ran south until they reached 30th Street, then turned west toward the river. Max dashed after them, struggling again to catch up.

Then, above the noise of the wind and the floodwaters, he heard someone running behind him. 'Mirsky? What the fuck?'

Without breaking stride, he glanced over his shoulder. It was

Agent Reyes. She'd appeared once again in his moment of need. Her clothes were soaked and her hair was dripping, but her face glistened with fervor. She caught up to Max, her feet splashing beside his, and pointed at the four runners a hundred yards ahead.

'Jesus, is that who I think it is?'

Max nodded. He was out of breath and his lungs were burning, but he tried to answer. 'It's Erin . . . and she's with . . . Sonya . . . don't know . . . the other two.'

'Fucking hell!'

Reyes leapt forward, and Max strained to keep up with her. They descended toward sea level as they neared the Hudson River, and the floodwaters rose from their shins to their thighs. Up ahead, the Climate Avengers were fording the West Side Highway, which had turned into a raging watercourse packed with bobbing vehicles. Max's heart throbbed in his throat as he watched them wade across the channel, Erin and the bald goon pulling Sonya along. Then the four of them scuttled onto a ridge of higher ground, the raised embankment at the river's edge, and turned south again, heading for a gray industrial pier half submerged by the Hudson's waves.

'Come on, Mirsky!' Reyes roared like a drill sergeant. 'Move your ass!'

Instead of wading across the highway, she dove right into the dirty floodwaters and started swimming across the lanes. Max did the same, breast-stroking so he could keep his head above the muck. But as he swam past the highway median, he saw something huge and dark floating toward him. It was a double-decker intercity Megabus, toppled over on its side and drifting north in the flooded southbound lanes.

Max yelped and switched to a freestyle stroke. He windmilled his arms and didn't even pause to breathe. His muscles cramped and he saw white flashes behind his eyelids. He'd reached his limit. He wasn't going to make it.

Then Reyes grabbed his arm. Grunting and cursing, she pulled him out of the water and onto the embankment. He lay on the wet concrete slab, coughing the foul fluids out of his throat, while the Megabus glided past.

After several seconds he sat up and saw Reyes running alongside the river. She headed for the gray pier, but she was too far behind. The Climate Avengers were already at the far end of the pier, next to a steel cradle that held a sleek red boat above the Hudson. The big bald guy shoved Sonya into the speedboat, aided by Erin and the woman in the jumpsuit. Max heard the groan of the cradle's motor as it lowered the boat and its four passengers into the roiling river. Then the twin outboard engines started with a roar and propelled the craft away from the pier. The speedboat accelerated downriver, its nose tipped up, jumping from wavetop to wavetop.

Max rose shakily to his feet. He wiped the saltwater from his eyes, but the scene in front of him remained the same, crushing and hopeless. Soon the boat shrank to a red dot on the gray horizon. Then it disappeared behind the mist.

No! SONYA!!

But after a moment he heard yet another sound, a loud whomping that seemed to come from above. He turned to the right and for the first time he noticed a one-story prefab building at the river's edge. The sign above the building's door said 'West 30th Street VIP Heliport.'

Then a black helicopter emerged from the mist above the Hudson. The winds buffeted it from all sides, but the aircraft steadily approached the heliport and slowly descended to an elevated platform a few feet above the floodwaters.

Reyes ran back to him and grabbed his arm again. '*Let's go!*' She pulled him toward the helicopter. '*It's Mad Dog!*'

Aleida Reyes – formerly US Marine Captain Reyes – settled into the co-pilot's seat of the EH-60 Black Hawk while Max strapped himself into one of the passenger seats in back. This was one of the stealth choppers used by the Navy SEALs, but its flight controls weren't so different from those on an ordinary Black Hawk or on the Venom helicopters she used to fly. With an exuberance she hadn't felt in years, Reyes put on a helmet and a radio headset, then turned to the aging, bearded SEAL in the pilot's seat.

Mad Dog throttled up the rotors and lifted off from the heliport. Once they were airborne, he jerked his thumb at Max. 'Who the hell is that guy?'

'It's a long story. If I'd left him behind, he would've probably drowned.' Reyes stretched her arm toward the cockpit window, pointing south. 'The target is a red speedboat moving—'

'Yeah, I spotted that little dinghy when I was flying in.' Mad Dog gave her a gappy smile. He had terrible teeth. 'It's a Thunder Cat, a real sweet ride. I saw one at a boat show once. But today's not the best day for boating, is it?'

As if to confirm his comment, a sudden gust hit the Black Hawk and nearly knocked it into the river, but Mad Dog calmly righted the chopper and pointed it south. Reyes should've been terrified, but instead she smiled back at Mad Dog. She'd *missed* this. 'You found a sweet ride too, it looks like. Who'd you steal this chopper from?'

'No theft was necessary.' He shook his head. 'I was at Dix–Lakehurst when I checked my phone and heard your voicemail, and I knew this EH-60 was just sitting in one of the hangars. So I told my CO I needed some adverse-weather flight training, and he signed off on it.' He chuckled as he put the chopper into a steep climb, fighting a vicious downdraft. 'Of course, he probably thinks I'm on the edge of the storm and not at the center. But this baby doesn't show up on radar screens, so he'll never know the truth, right?'

'What about Phantom? And Rat Face? Are they coming too?'

Mad Dog shrugged. 'They were off base when I got your message, and I didn't want to wait around for them. It sounded like you needed help in a hurry.'

'Yeah, that's true, but I might also need more firepower.' Reyes pointed ahead at the wide bay where the Hudson converged with the East River. The Thunder Cat was just barely visible on the choppy gray water, trailing a wake between Governors Island and the Statue of Liberty. 'Those wackos have access to some nasty hardware. You saw the news about the drones that killed my partner?'

'Hey, don't sweat it. Before I left Dix, I sent a red alert to Phantom and Rat. And unlike my CO, they can track my location. They'll show up, I bet.'

Reyes had her doubts about this. For any active-duty US serviceman, going 'off base' usually meant getting shit-faced. But she wasn't going to let her disappointment show. *Never look a gift horse in the mouth, much less a gift Black Hawk.*

She smiled again at Mad Dog. 'Thanks for coming, Dog. It's a damn nice gesture, and pretty unexpected given the fact that you're a fucking Navy squid.'

'And for a stupid fucking jarhead, you're not so bad yourself. I'll never forget the aerial show you put on in Nimruz. That was some mighty fine flying.'

Mad Dog was referring to their first encounter in Afghanistan, when Reyes had flown to the rescue of his SEAL team after their helicopter conked out in Taliban territory. Using her chopper's Gatling gun and a few Hydra rockets, she'd mowed down the mujahideen who'd surrounded Mad Dog and his buddies, earning the SEALs' lifelong respect and the right to call on them for emergency assistance. She'd never imagined she'd actually exercise this right, but now that the Bureau had taken her gun away, what else could she fucking do?

Speaking of guns, Reyes needed to ask about their available armaments. 'I don't suppose you have any rockets or missiles on this crate?'

'No, ma'am. And no bullets for the Gatling. Officially, this is a flight-training exercise, not live-fire, so I couldn't requisition any large-caliber ammo.' Mad Dog winked at her. 'But I smuggled an M16 aboard, plus a service pistol and a flare gun. They're in the buoyancy bag behind your seat.'

Reyes nodded. She focused on the red speedboat, which had turned west and entered the channel between Staten Island and New Jersey. Mad Dog had closed the distance between the Black Hawk and the Thunder Cat, and now they flew just a hundred yards behind the boat and a hundred feet above it. If the day had been calm, Reyes could've pointed an M16 out of the chopper's side door and chanced a shot at Erin O'Malley, but that was out of the question now. The boat was tossing around in the storm surge, and the helicopter was rocking with the winds, and any bullet aimed at Erin was just as likely to hit Mirsky's daughter.

No, they had to wait until the speedboat docked and its passengers disembarked. Then Reyes could rappel out of the Black Hawk and hunt the bitch down.

Soon they passed under the Bayonne and Goethals bridges, Mad Dog flying low to avoid the strongest gusts. The channel below them was relatively narrow and much calmer than the open harbor, since the bulk of Staten Island was sheltering them now from the full force of the hurricane. The Thunder Cat sped past oil tanks and power plants on the Jersey side of the channel and a rail yard on the Staten Island side, and up ahead was the mountainous Fresh Kills Landfill and the smokestacks of a garbage incinerator. Reyes was wondering where the hell the speedboat was going when Mirsky suddenly stuck his head into the cockpit, leaning forward between the pilot and co-pilot seats. He'd put on a helmet and headset, which looked ridiculous on him.

'Shit!' Mirsky pointed at the cockpit window. 'What the hell are you doing?'

Mad Dog turned toward him, visibly pissed. 'No, what the hell are *you* doing? Get back in your fucking seat!'

'You're following too close! You gotta steer away from—'

'You see that open door, moron? If you don't strap yourself in *this second*, you're gonna fall right out of the cabin!'

Reyes noticed that Mirsky was pointing directly at the Thunder Cat, which was now less than two hundred feet ahead. And when she stared at the boat, she saw Erin O'Malley kneeling backward on one of the rear seats. Erin reached for something tucked under her sweatshirt, and after a moment she pulled out a bulky device that looked like an oversized video camera. Then she pointed it at the Black Hawk.

Reyes lunged for the co-pilot controls. 'Fuck, he's right! We gotta—'

She felt an electric shock inside her skull, a banging, clanging detonation. It burst between her ears and paralyzed her arms, which hung motionless and rigid in front of her. She couldn't turn her head either, but out of the corner of her eye she saw that Mad Dog had gone into a seizure too. His right hand locked around the cyclic stick, and his left clenched the collective.

Then the Black Hawk lurched and started to fall.

The helicopter had been drawing closer for the past five minutes, but Erin waited until it came within fifty meters of the boat's stern. The lashing rain had let up for a moment, which was a lucky thing, since Stroman had told her that raindrops absorbed microwaves. She pulled out the transmitter from under her sweatshirt and switched it to its highest power setting. She also turned the knob that adjusted the beam width, enlarging it to cover the entire cockpit of the Black Hawk.

The blast of radiation was silent, but its effect was immediate. The chopper skewed to the left and its nose jerked downward. One of its passengers fell out the side door and plunged into the Arthur Kill. The Black Hawk whirled and tumbled for another few seconds, its rotors breaking loose as they struck the water. Then it dove into the channel with a humongous splash.

Grinning, she lowered the transmitter, which had used up the last bits of its battery power. She turned around and faced the other occupants of the Thunder Cat – a horrified Sonya, a triumphant Angela, and a grimly determined Carl at the speed-boat's wheel. Quite proud of herself, Erin gave a little bow.

'Nice one, eh? I fucking banjaxed them.'

TWENTY-FIVE

New York Presbyterian was so crowded, Nathan could barely navigate the hospital's corridors. Hundreds of patients from Bellevue Hospital and NYU Langone had been transferred to Presbyterian because it sat on higher ground and hadn't lost its power yet. Nathan threaded his way past dozens of gurneys and wheelchairs to reach the seventh-floor nurses' station.

The nurses were insanely busy, answering phones and stabbing at keyboards and racing off to various code-blue crises. It took all of Nathan's acting skills to snare the attention of the nurse who'd been assigned to care for Max. He spread his arms wide and beamed at her.

'Nurse Kelly! So good to see you again! Could you please tell me where Max Mirsky is? I just went to the room where I visited him this morning but—'

'Your friend Mirsky ran out on us.' The nurse's voice was icy. 'He up and left without waiting for a discharge.'

Nathan cocked his head, perturbed. 'Really? That doesn't sound like—'

'It annoyed the hell out of me, but you know what? He did us a favor.' She grabbed a clipboard and started to walk away. 'Right now we need every bed we can get.'

Nathan took out his iPhone and called Max's number, but it went to voicemail. He stood there for a while, flummoxed, pondering the possible explanations for Max's disappearance. He was so deep in thought, he didn't notice Larry and Adele in the corridor until they called out his name.

Like most of the hospital visitors, his fellow Doomsday troupers were drenched from the storm. Adele scowled. 'Guess what? Max flew the coop. His nurse just told us he left the hospital without telling anyone.'

Nathan nodded. 'Yes, she told me the same.'

'That's weird, don't you think? After we spent all that time worrying about him? Why would he do something like that without telling us?'

Nathan didn't answer. Although he had his suspicions, he decided not to share them with Adele, who got upset so easily. In the ensuing silence, Larry held up a wet cardboard box from Little Italy Pizzeria. 'I brought him a pepperoni slice too. You want it, Nathan? Since Max isn't here?'

'That's very kind of you, but no.'

'Well, I shouldn't let it go to waste.' Larry opened the box and took out the slice.

Adele gave him a look. 'Ick, that's disgusting. I'm going to the cafeteria to get a yogurt. I told Eileen I'd meet her there.' She marched off, waving goodbye with the back of her hand.

'It's a shame.' Larry tossed the box into a nearby trash bin and folded his slice in half. 'I had some news for Max too. But it'll have to wait, I guess.'

'News?' Nathan was curious. 'Are you and Adele tying the knot, perchance?'

'No, no, nothing like that.' Larry covered his embarrassment by biting into his slice. He chewed noisily, and a drop of grease slid down his chin. 'It has to do with the assignment Max gave me. You know, when we were at his apartment a couple of nights ago.'

This was embarrassing, but Nathan couldn't recall the details of that conversation. 'Uh, yes, I think he gave you a box of documents?'

Larry nodded. 'Those were the financial statements of the climate criminals on Max's list. He asked me to see if there was anything unusual in those records, anything related to the murders or the kidnapping. And just an hour ago I found something, a financial connection.'

Now Nathan started to remember. 'What was it?'

'Remember Torricelli Demolition? The garbage company that Max mentioned? A sizable sum of money, two million dollars, was transferred earlier this year to Torricelli Demolition in return for "unspecified services."' He took another bite of pizza. 'The record of the transaction was buried pretty deep in a three-hundred-page appendix filed with the Securities and Exchange Commission. But Max told me to look at everything carefully, so I did.'

Although Nathan knew little about financial statements and appendices, he sensed that Larry was onto something. He felt a tingle in his gut, simultaneously exhilarating and terrifying. 'This is hard evidence?'

Larry handed his pizza slice to Nathan and wiped his hands on his pants. Then he reached into his back pocket and pulled out a folded sheet of paper. 'I made a copy of the relevant page in the appendix. Take a look.' He unfolded the paper and held it up for Nathan to see.

And there it was. Hard evidence in turgid prose written by some accountant.

Nathan reached for his iPhone and tried calling Max again.

Come on, Mirsky! Answer your damn phone!

TWENTY-SIX

Angela hadn't foreseen the helicopter, but she knew all along that nothing could stop her. So she wasn't surprised at all when Erin knocked it out of the sky.

'Carl! Turn the boat around!' Angela pointed at the crash site. The chopper had plummeted into a shallow part of the Arthur Kill, near the Staten Island side, and part of its mangled nose protruded above the swirling water. 'I want to see if anyone survived.'

She thought Carl might object – although the storm wasn't as fierce here, the choppy waves made navigation difficult – but he obediently steered toward the smashed Black Hawk. Erin craned her neck, clearly eager for a closer look. Sonya shuddered and looked away, but that was all she could do, because she was bound and gagged. Angela had learned not to underestimate that girl.

As they neared the wreckage, they saw that the cockpit window was gone, and so was the head of the craft's pilot. A twisted blade of the main rotor had sliced through the fuselage and decapitated him. But the co-pilot was alive. She squirmed in her seat, half-conscious, her legs bleeding and probably broken. Her left cheek was bleeding too, and her helmet had been knocked sideways, exposing her wet, tangled auburn hair.

Erin stood up suddenly and pointed at the survivor. 'Holy Mother! I know her! She's the G-woman from Roche's party, the FBI agent! I told you all about her, remember?'

Angela nodded grimly. This wasn't good news. A government agent had managed to track them down. And this agent must've shared some of her information with her colleagues, which meant that reinforcements might be coming soon. But what exactly did the agent know? And how much had she shared? Angela needed to find out.

'Erin, I need your assistance again. Could you—'

'Want me to go get her?' Erin's voice was unusually

enthusiastic. 'Extract her from that junkpile and bring her over here?'

'Yes, I'd like to ask her a few questions, if she can stay alive long enough to answer them.'

Erin pulled her sweatshirt over her head. 'I'm game, love. I wouldn't mind asking her a few questions of my own.' She stepped out of her sneakers and jeans. 'That woman gave me a hell of a time yesterday, and I don't forget that sort of thing.'

In just her bra and panties, Erin dove off the Thunder Cat. With a few quick strokes she reached the downed helicopter, and then she clambered into the cockpit and unstrapped the agent from her seat. She pulled the half-conscious woman out of the wreckage and swam back to the speedboat with one arm wrapped around her. Carl helped lift the agent into the boat, and Angela made room for her on the seat next to Sonya. Then Erin heaved herself aboard and put her clothes back on.

Angela scanned the waterway but saw no sign of the passenger who'd fallen out of the helicopter before it crashed. But it wasn't important – she couldn't imagine anyone surviving that fall, and the tidal currents were probably carrying the body out to sea. She turned to Carl and ordered him to resume their journey.

Their destination was Fresh Kills. The former garbage dump was slated to become a park in a few years, but until then it was a deserted site next to an industrial-size waste incinerator. The mound of landfill loomed two hundred feet above the Arthur Kill, making it an ideal place for a rendezvous during widespread flooding. But the main attraction, at least for Angela, were the tugboats and garbage scows docked in a nearby channel. Those seaworthy vessels were already loaded with everything she needed to continue Prophecy's crusade. One scow held tons of foodstuffs and enormous tanks of freshwater. Another carried weapons and computers and solar panels. Still another barge held satellite dishes and hundreds of gold bars in orderly stacks.

Carl maneuvered the speedboat into this channel. Several men stood near the docks, at the foot of the grass-covered mountain of landfill, and several more were stationed near the garbage incinerator, a mammoth building with towering smoke-stacks a quarter-mile away. As the Thunder Cat eased into its slip, Angela noticed that the men wore camouflage pants and balaclavas, and each carried a submachine gun. She hadn't recruited them herself; Carl had been in charge of hiring these mercenaries, who would protect Prophecy during the next phase of its campaign. As soon as Hurricane Yolanda passed, these men would help Angela launch her little fleet of barges and secretly move her operation to international waters. And then, according to her visions, Prophecy would spread worldwide. Environmental activists would praise her bold strategy and millions of people would join her cause. The plutocrats would surrender, and the fossil-fuel patriarchy would be overthrown. *Nothing but green!*

After tying up the speedboat, Carl and Erin carried the FBI agent to shore and laid her down on the muddy grass. Angela gripped one of Sonya's bound arms and escorted her to a lean-to that the mercenaries had built, an open-air shed made of scrap-metal sheets that plinked and pattered in the rain. Gently but firmly, she pressed down Sonya's shoulders, forcing her to kneel in the relatively dry dirt under the lean-to. In the following weeks and months, Angela planned to forge a partnership with this stubborn young firebrand, but right now the girl needed to keep still and follow orders.

Meanwhile, Erin bent over the agent, who lay face-up in the mud. The Irishwoman snapped her fingers right over the agent's nose, but there was no response. Frowning, Erin stepped away from her and approached the lean-to.

'Excuse me, Angela? I changed my mind about interrogating that one.' Erin pointed over her shoulder at the supine agent. 'She won't wake up anytime soon. If ever.'

'Well, why don't you wait here with us, then?' Angela gestured at the shed. 'It won't be long before the storm moves inland. In two or three hours we can board one of the tugboats and set off.'

'So, that's how you plan to escape?'

'It'll look just like an ordinary shipment of waste. No authorities will inspect barges that they assume are filled with garbage. In fact, they'll be happy to see the refuse leave the country.'

'Ah grand. But you can't go until you pay me.' Her eyes narrowed and her voice hardened. 'I warned you that my wages would go up if there were complications, and this job got pretty fucking complicated. According to my calculations, you owe me seven hundred and fifty thousand dollars. For your sake, I hope the money is nearby, in hundred-dollar bills.'

Angela put on a disarming smile, an expression designed to appeal and persuade. Erin had proved her worth, and it would be a shame to lose her. 'Are you sure I can't convince you to come with us? I can—'

'The answer is no. Give me my money, please, before I get ticked off.'

Angela recalled all too well what had happened the last time Erin got angry at her. She turned to Carl, who stood over the FBI agent, looking down at her. 'It's time to settle our debts, Carl. Can you take Erin to our storehouse next to the incinerator?'

Carl shook his head. 'I need to stay with you. Just in case this agent wakes up. Or the teenager makes trouble again.' He pointed at a nearby pair of gun-toting mercenaries, whose faces were masked except for their eyes. 'Those guys can take her there.'

Erin was clearly displeased. She scowled at the two armed men, then glared at Angela. 'No, those two can pick up the cash at the storehouse and bring it here.'

Before Angela could say a word, Carl angrily cleared his throat. 'All right, have it your way! Christ, what a bitch!'

He stepped over the agent and stomped toward the mercenaries. Halfway there, he turned toward Erin, looking as if he was going to insult her again, stretching his arm to point at her.

But he wasn't pointing. There was a pistol in his hand. Angela didn't notice it until after he fired and Erin fell backwards into the mud.

Carl stepped toward where she lay. He kept his gun trained on Erin, who opened her eyes wide and clamped a hand over the spurting wound in her stomach. He stopped about ten feet away from her, maintaining a wary distance, and grinned from ear to ear.

'That's your payment. Happy now?'

Janet was soaked all the way down to her bones.

Her dress, that ridiculous orange thing she'd put on for the Doomsday skit, was tattered and saturated after two hours in the storm, and her sneakers squelched with every step. Even her skin and muscles felt waterlogged, her pale damp flesh weighing her down. She shivered violently as she trudged along the highway, fighting the winds and the rain and a growing desire to just lie down in the floodwaters and let them carry her away.

She believed she was walking north on the Staten Island Expressway, although she couldn't be sure because the hurricane's gusts had knocked down most of the exit signs. She'd gotten disoriented after she bolted from the prison; just a minute after her release, she'd heard someone running after her, most likely that imbecile Jason Torricelli. The knife-wielding lunatic named Angela had probably ordered him to drag her back to her jail cell, but there was no way that Janet was going back there. Seeing no other option, she ran into a local park full of marshy, muddy woodlands and zigzagged between the trees until the imbecile gave up on her.

When she finally emerged from the woods, she found herself on this highway, which was empty except for a few abandoned cars and a sheet of brown water that was several feet deep at the road's lowest sections. She tried calling 911 on Torricelli's phone again, but now she couldn't even get a signal. So she started walking. On both sides of the road she saw nothing but roofless houses and downed trees, but she felt certain that sooner or later she'd run into a police officer. The only people she encountered, though, were bedraggled wanderers who seemed just as lost and desperate as she was.

At some point she passed a flooded golf course, and then a flooded warehouse surrounded by semi-trailer trucks lying on their sides. Then the highway curved west and ran close to the choppy waterway between Staten Island and New Jersey, which was chock-full of bobbing debris. Some of the floating garbage had piled up against a concrete building that used to be a shopping center and was now an atoll of trash. Bits and pieces of obliterated homes and vehicles were scattered across the area, along with thousands of plastic bottles and miscellaneous containers.

And there was a man lying facedown on the immense bed of garbage.

Janet turned away. She didn't want to see it. She knew the storm had probably killed hundreds of people today, but she had no desire to stare at any of the corpses.

Something made her turn back to him, though. The corpse had shifted his leg. She stepped a bit closer and saw him open and close his hands. A moment later, he lifted his head off the ground and stared right at her, blinking rapidly.

'Janet? What are you doing here?'

She sprinted toward Max.

TWENTY-SEVEN

The bleeding was bad enough, but it wasn't the worst part. Erin couldn't feel her legs. The bullet had drilled into her belly and blasted through her spine.

Carl stood a few meters away, gloating. Erin was fucking furious at him, sure, but she was even angrier at herself. She'd forgotten how much that bald eejit wanted to punish her. He'd craved revenge ever since she kicked him in the bollocks and slammed her forearm into his ugly face. And the punishment was just beginning, because the stupid scut wasn't going to do the humane thing and finish her off with a bullet to the head. No, he wanted her to suffer.

He grinned like a toad. 'What happened, little lassie? What are you doing down there in the mud, with a hole in your gut?'

The full enormity of the pain was kicking in, but Erin didn't wince. She put a snarl on her face and refused to say a word.

'*Carl!*' Angela charged out of the lean-to, gaping and wide-eyed. 'Have you lost your mind? What the *fuck* did you do?'

He shrugged. 'What's the problem? She served her purpose. We don't need her anymore, so I'm getting rid of her. The way she's bleeding out, she'll be dead in five minutes.'

'No, no, *no*! Erin is our *ally*!' Angela strode toward him, shaking her head. She pointed her left hand at Carl and stuck her right hand deep into the pocket of her jumpsuit. 'She can't die, because she's going to be a heroine of our cause! In future years she'll become the leader of our global militia and—'

'Stop right there, Angela.' Carl swung around and pointed his gun at her. 'And take your fucking hand out of your pocket.'

Angela stopped. Her face at that moment was the very picture of outrage: lips pulled back, eyes narrowed, eyebrows lowered, nose scrunched. Her reaction was so extreme, so wildly infuriated, that it seemed deadly funny to Erin. She would've laughed if she hadn't been in so much effing pain.

Very slowly, Angela removed her right hand from her pocket,

but she kept pointing at Carl with her left. 'This is wrong. This is *disgraceful*. This atrocity didn't appear in *any* of my visions.' She shook her head. 'Lower the gun, Carl. You're defying the inevitable path of the universe.'

Now Carl laughed, letting out a single sharp bark, which was nothing like the manic chortle Erin wanted to make. Instead of lowering his gun, he aimed it directly at Angela's brow. 'You're a real doozy, Annie. You know what your father used to say about you? I heard Sam say it a hundred times. "Something's wrong with that girl." And sure as shit, he was right.'

Angela appeared to be choking with rage, to the point where she couldn't even speak. Although Erin was feeling nauseous – one of the symptoms of blood loss, as any soldier knew – she managed to raise her head so she could take in the scene. One of the masked mercenaries had come forward to point his Uzi at Angela, and the other aimed his weapon at Sonya, who knelt under the lean-to. Carl took a step toward them, clearly enjoying himself.

'There's a reason you didn't see this coming, Annie. I hate to break it to you, but your visions of the future aren't real. They're just fucked-up pictures from your busted brain.' He waggled his pistol, gesturing at her head. 'Sam should've put you in a mental hospital, but he was too soft, too sentimental. I couldn't even talk him into changing his will. So instead of going to the loony bin, you became the richest nutcase in America.'

Angela said nothing, but Erin could tell she was plotting something. Her eyes darted back and forth between Carl and the mercenaries. The woman just didn't know when to give up, and the sight of her desperate, ridiculous scheming was too much for Erin. The laughter she'd been holding back came pouring out, along with a fresh stream of blood from her belly.

Carl scowled. 'What are *you* laughing at? Annie had you fooled. You totally fell for her bullshit.' He shook his head in disgust. 'Like her visions about your terrorist dad coming out of prison? And the trick she played on you with the stock market? Remember how she predicted the closing share price of Texxonoco on the same day you bumped off Humphrey and Tarkington?'

Erin didn't remember. She could barely stay conscious, so

how the hell could she remember anything? And what was the fucking point? So she just kept laughing.

'You think it's *funny*?' Carl spat the word at her. 'Annie knew she was tricking you. And I helped her do it. She said, "I need your help, Carl, because I can only see the major events, but I need to predict a minor event to convince Erin to keep working for us." I thought about it for a while, and then I came up with the stock-price trick.'

Angela finally found her voice. She swallowed hard and hissed through clenched teeth. 'It *wasn't* a trick! And my visions *are* real!'

Carl let out another mirthful bark. He kept his gun trained on Angela but stared at Erin. 'Before you kick the bucket, lassie, I'll tell you how the trick worked. If you know something about the stock market and you have enough money, you can manipulate the share prices.'

'It's not a trick if you're convincing someone of a greater truth!' Angela pointed at herself with both hands, jabbing her index fingers against her chest. 'And I *can* see the major events of the future!'

Carl ignored her and focused on Erin. 'Now, I don't have the billions of dollars you'd need to pull off that kind of market manipulation, but by that point I'd made contact with someone who did. Someone who'd been friends with Sam and who was just as pissed off as I was to see Sam's crazy daughter ruining Novacek Construction. We worked together and came up with a plan that would benefit both of us.'

Erin's vision was blurring now, and she lost the thread of the conversation. Carl said some more things she didn't understand, and Angela hissed at him again. It was all so stupid anyway, such a fucking waste of time. It wasn't worth her attention anymore. She stopped laughing and closed her eyes. She just wanted to forget all this shite.

But before she could slip into blissful blackness, someone kicked her hard in the stomach, and the pain was so great that it woke her up one last time. Erin opened her eyes and saw another man looking down at her, not Carl, not a mercenary. It was an older man with silver hair, twirling a black cane like a carnival barker.

Charles Roche. That gobshite. That lecherous fucking prick!

And that was the last thing she ever saw.

Max came from a long line of skeptical Jews. For generations they'd dutifully followed the religion's rituals while privately scoffing at all notions of divine authority. Until today – until this very moment – Max had wholeheartedly embraced his family's tradition of disbelief. But the miracle of his survival after the helicopter crash dealt a severe blow to this mindset. And seeing Janet on the very same trash-strewn promontory where he'd washed up after his near-drowning? It was enough to make any atheist start to wonder.

Janet crouched beside him, squatting between a rusty gas can and a mud-caked tire. 'Oh my God! Are you hurt?'

Max sat up and flexed his limbs. He must've blacked out after the long, exhausting swim to this trash heap. The bandages on his head had slipped off and his legs were stiff, but nothing was broken, and there were no new gashes in his flesh. Which was another miracle. 'I'm OK. What about you?' He gave her a quick once-over. 'Is that the Graziella costume? From the *West Side Story* sketch?'

She frowned. 'Yeah, I've been wearing it for three days now. Luckily, the storm gave it a thorough washing.'

God, he loved this woman. He wrapped his arms around her and hugged the damp, shivery body inside the torn dress. She hugged him back, clasping his ribcage and crying.

After a minute or so he gently pulled back and stared at her. 'What happened? Where were you?'

Janet pointed toward the southern end of the trash-gorged Arthur Kill. 'They took Sonya and me to an empty prison down there. That asshole Jason put us in a cell, and a crazy woman in a jumpsuit came in to see us, a real sicko named Angela. Then they separated us, and I didn't know where Sonya went. But just two hours ago she got me out of the prison. I don't know how Sonya did it, but—'

'Wait, a jumpsuit? I think I saw this Angela.'

'She's in charge of the terrorists. Where did you see her?'

'In Manhattan. She was with Sonya, running toward the river. They got in a speedboat and we followed them in a helicopter.

Then the helicopter started spinning and going down and I fell out the door and dropped—'

'Jesus Christ! Are you fucking kidding me?'

Max stopped himself. They would have plenty of time later to go over all the hair-raising details. Right now they needed to find Sonya. 'How far is that prison from here?'

Janet furrowed her brow, looking south again. 'Oh God, I don't know. I was running for a while, then walking in a daze. Maybe four or five miles?'

Max looked south too. It was getting toward evening, five or six o'clock, but the lingering storm made the landscape unnaturally dark. He glimpsed the giant mound of the Fresh Kills Landfill, which looked like it was only a mile away, but he couldn't see anything beyond it. 'We have to go that way.' He pointed at the mound and rose to his feet. 'The speedboat was heading south. Angela was probably taking Sonya back to the prison.'

'No, wait!' Janet stood up. 'You see those smokestacks next to the big hill?'

'Yeah, I think that's a—'

'It's a garbage incinerator owned by Torricelli Demolition. That dumbass Jason told me about it. He said Angela and her people were moving stuff there, to get ready for their "big fucking escape act." Those were his exact words.'

Max hugged her again. She was amazing. 'All right, that's where we'll go.'

He kept one arm around Janet's waist and took the first step in that direction. Instantly, though, he felt something tugging at his left leg. Looking down, he saw a rope looped around his ankle and suddenly remembered the Navy bag. Right after the helicopter crash, just seconds after he plunged into the Arthur Kill and came bobbing back to the surface, he'd spotted a large blue bag tossing in the waves, kept afloat by buoyant spheres labeled 'US NAVY.' He'd assumed it was a survival kit that had fallen out of the chopper with him, a bag possibly containing rations and water-purification tablets, so he'd grabbed its rope before swimming to shore.

Now he knelt beside the bag and unzipped it. 'You hungry, Jan? I bet there's some food in here and . . .'

Max went quiet when he saw what was inside. The bag did indeed contain several military rations, each brown packet labeled 'Meal, Ready-to-Eat.' But it also held three bulkier items wrapped in water-tight plastic.

A flare gun. A pistol. And an M16.

TWENTY-EIGHT

'Hello, Annie. Such a pleasure to see you again.'

Angela screamed. Not because he was Charles Roche, but because he was her blind spot. He was the singularity that had warped all the branches of reality, the black hole that had engulfed all her visions of the future. He'd emerged from the direction of the incinerator, flanked by a dozen of his Uzi-toting demons, mangling all the cosmic worldlines in his path. He had to be stopped, he had to be *annihilated.*

So Angela reached for her switchblade and charged at him.

She didn't get far. One of the mercenaries grabbed her from behind and put her in a headlock, while another seized the wrist of her right arm and squeezed it until she dropped her knife. Ten more men in balaclavas stood beside Roche, who ordered them to point their machine guns at Sonya even though she was bound and gagged, and at the FBI agent who lay comatose in the mud. The armed men shouted in Russian at one another, and they seemed to regard Roche as their commander, not Carl. Which made sense, Angela thought, because Carl was a mere tool, a minor cog in the cosmic machine. Roche was her real enemy, the Destroyer of Worlds.

He grinned, watching her struggle in the mercenaries' grip. Then he looked down at Erin, who'd stopped breathing and now lay still in a wide puddle of blood. 'Here's the bitch who almost murdered me yesterday. She nearly sank our whole venture.' Roche kicked her in the side, quick and vicious. Then he glanced at Carl, who'd put his pistol back in the shoulder holster under his jacket. 'It's a good thing you shot her, Carl. You know what they say about the Wild Irish.'

Angela glared at the old man. 'She was supposed to kill you, she was *destined* to kill you. I knew something was wrong when it didn't happen.'

'Ah, Annie.' Roche shook his head and sighed. 'The wrongness started long before that. When you were born, perhaps. Or a few months ago, when you put me on your hit list. I was quite hurt when Carl informed me that I was slated for execution. Maybe you hated me because I'd been good friends with your father? He was a rough-edged man, but he certainly knew how to have a good time.'

'You're on the list because you're a *destroyer*!' Angela writhed and squirmed, but the mercenaries just tightened their hold on her. 'You build the infernal tools, the drilling equipment, the refineries. The Earth itself *hates* you!'

'At first, I planned to have you committed.' Roche paced closer to her, poking the bottom end of his cane in the mud. 'But then I noticed whose name was at the top of your list and I saw an opportunity. I'm interested in expanding my horizons, you see, and the former president stood in my way. So, in order to clear my path to greater power, I decided to secretly facilitate your conspiracy, using Carl as my clandestine go-between.'

Angela stopped squirming. She stood there, paralyzed, aghast. 'My God! You're a worldline crux! You're in every possible future, bending them all toward catastrophe!'

'Worldline crux? That's an interesting phrase.' He cocked his head, clearly amused. 'In truth, though, I see myself as a statesman. Or at least a much better leader than the Pumpkin Head ever was. He was too mercurial, too unreliable for the business community.' Roche looked over his shoulder at Erin's corpse. 'And now, thanks to the Irish bitch, he's on his way to Arlington Cemetery, where I will deliver a beautifully moving eulogy at his funeral. And then, after a respectful amount of time has passed, I'll announce my campaign for the White House.'

'*No!* The universe won't *allow* it!' Angela bellowed at the darkening sky, appealing to the quantum fields that govern reality. 'The cosmos will find a way to stop you! Through the police, the FBI!'

'I don't think so. Carl and I did some careful arranging.' Roche nodded at the bald traitor. 'He fed me the details of your assassination plans, allowing me to play the role of Horrified Witness at Jonathan Humphrey's poisoning. And Carl warned me, of course, about the infiltration of my mansion, so I took steps to avoid running into the Irish bitch.' He grimaced. 'She found me anyway and smeared my best suit with her microchips. But I knew enough to fling the jacket aside.'

'*Fiend! Lucifer! Your fall is coming! You'll be found out!*'

'I don't think so. Why would anyone suspect me of involvement in those murders if I was an intended victim of your assassin? That makes no sense. Especially when all the evidence points to *you*.' He took another step toward her and sneered. 'And you won't be around to confuse the investigators with your insane accusations, because in a few minutes you'll be dead.'

'*My death won't change a thing!*' Angela screamed in the devil's face, loud enough to jar the axis of Creation. She would die, yes, but she would be resurrected as a raging wind that would steer history. '*You'll die too!*'

Roche chuckled. 'Yes, that'll happen eventually. But until then, I'm going to do whatever the hell I want.' He turned to Carl again. 'Let's tie up the loose ends, shall we? I recognize this federal agent lying here, she's the Dominican dyke who came to my mansion. Should we try to wake her up and interrogate her?'

Carl stared at the agent and shook his head. 'Nah, it's not worth it. She and her dead flyboy friend were chasing Annie, not you. We should cut the agent's throat instead of shooting her, so it'll look like Annie did it. That's her favorite method.'

'Yes, good idea.' Roche nodded, then cast a lascivious glance at Sonya. 'And I suppose we'll have to do the same to the Mirsky girl. It's a shame, she's such a pretty young minx.'

'And one more thing, Mr Roche?' Carl's expression was disgustingly obsequious. 'You're gonna let me have some of those gold bars that Annie loaded into that garbage barge, right? Because I'm gonna be on the lam for a while, and I'll need some—'

'Yes, yes, you'll get your filthy lucre. Including your share of the two million dollars I transferred to your asinine partner Torricelli.' Roche sounded annoyed now. He seemed already bored by the details of his planned cover-up and impatient to move on to other things. 'Now, pick up that knife from the ground and get to work. Or get one of the Russians to do it, they love that brutal sort of—'

A flash interrupted him. Angela looked up and saw a new red star blazing in the nearly black sky. *A supernova? A cosmic eruption? An undeniable sign of the universe's fury at Charles*

Roche? But no, the star was drifting downward, and soon it became apparent that it hung only a few hundred feet above their heads. A moment later, there was another red burst in the sky, accompanied by a popping sound that seemed to come from behind the smokestacks.

Carl pointed in that direction. 'Someone's shooting flares! From the top of the mound, behind the incinerator!'

Roche glowered in the crimson light. '*What are you waiting for?*' he roared at his mercenaries. '*Go get them!*'

Max fired the flare gun. It was the obvious choice. Neither he nor Janet had any experience with firearms, so they had no hope of picking off all the armed men they saw below them at the foot of the Fresh Kills mound.

But maybe they could distract the bastards and lead them away from Sonya. Just before firing the second flare, Max caught a glimpse of his daughter, kneeling under the metal roof of a lean-to shed, a quarter-mile away.

Oh God! I'll be there soon, Sonya!

Then he and Janet started running. They set off in different directions to confuse and separate their pursuers. Janet sprinted down the eastern slope of the giant mound, barreling toward the Staten Island Expressway. She was an excellent runner and not weighed down at all, since she'd refused to carry either the pistol or the rifle. With any luck, she'd outpace the armed men behind her.

Max headed south. While his enemies raced counterclockwise around the base of Fresh Kills, he sped counterclockwise around the mound's crest. That way, he would stay out of their view while he circled toward their starting point.

It was risky, but he had no choice. He tucked the pistol into the back of his pants, slung the M16 over his shoulder, and ran like hell.

TWENTY-NINE

Reyes wavered on the edge of consciousness.

The Black Hawk crash had seriously injured her, concussing her head and breaking both her ankles and snapping at least three of her ribs. Fighting so much pain and trauma, the higher parts of her brain had mostly shut down, and her grip on reality was exceedingly weak. She couldn't even call it a grip, actually. It was more like a fingerhold.

But she held on to it. She squeezed her eyes shut and bit her tongue hard, battling her body's strong impulse to pass out.

She focused on sounds to stay awake, on the sloshing of the floodwaters and the moaning of the winds and the urgent voices of the people standing around her. She couldn't always understand what they were saying, so she clung to the words themselves, those strangely intense chirps bouncing back and forth as she lay in the cold mud. She imagined them arranged in strings that laced over her body, sinuous sentences that tethered her to the world.

Then she heard a gunshot, and it smacked her out of her half-sleep. She opened her eyes just a crack and saw a bald man standing nearby with a pistol in his hand and the Irishwoman down on the ground. A moment later he pointed his gun at another woman, who yelled at him and called him Carl. Her name was Annie, and something was wrong with her. It was all very confusing, and Reyes almost gave up and blacked out. But then she heard a new voice, repellently familiar, and her mind snapped to attention.

Charles Fucking Roche. I knew he was up to something.

Reyes grew more and more alert. She listened to Roche argue with Annie, and although Reyes didn't fully comprehend the nature of their argument, the old man made it clear that he intended to kill the crazy woman, along with Max Mirsky's daughter and Reyes herself. This sharpened her mind even further.

Then a light shone down on her, dazzling enough to brighten her closed eyelids, and Roche shouted, '*What are you waiting for?*' Reyes opened her eyes just wide enough to see a pack of armed men running off toward a rescue flare. But four guards remained behind, two of them flanking Roche and two restraining Annie. Carl was there too, looking uneasy now. He bent over and picked up something from the mud.

A knife. A switchblade.

'What's the problem, Carl?' Roche's voice was thick with contempt. 'Feeling squeamish? Would you prefer to let one of the Russians—'

'Fuck no. I got this.'

Reyes heard Carl's shoes squishing the mud by her head. He crouched beside her, breathing hard. She slitted her eyes and noticed with relief that he was averting his own eyes from her face as he prepared to slaughter her. The switchblade trembled in his hand, but he slowly lowered it toward her throat. His ugly jacket flopped open as he bent down, and the stink of his sweat washed over her.

Closer. A little closer . . .

Her right hand shot toward him, striking like a rattlesnake. In one swift motion, she reached into Carl's jacket, pulled his gun out of its shoulder holster, and jammed the muzzle under his chin. Carl was just starting to realize his mistake when she fired.

But Reyes didn't stop there. She'd memorized the positions of the armed men standing nearby, and she fired at them in quick succession, ignoring the pains in her chest as she twisted in the mud next to Carl's limp body. All her marksmanship training came back to her – the Marine Corps boot camp at Parris, the Bureau drills at Quantico – and her eyes and hands automatically latched to their targets. First, she picked off the two men next to Annie, who wisely flung herself to the ground, and then she swung the pistol toward Roche's pair of bodyguards. She shot one of them in the head before he could level his Uzi at her. She got the other one in the back as he turned to run away.

Then she gave herself a second to breathe, thinking she had time to regroup and reorient because neither Roche nor Annie was armed. But in that moment her vision blurred and everything whirled around her. By the time she shook the dizziness out of her head, Annie was nowhere in sight and Roche had sprinted toward the scrap-metal lean-to where Sonya was. The bastard ducked behind the bound-and-gagged girl, making it impossible for Reyes to get a clear shot.

At the same time, he pulled his cane apart, separating its shaft from its handle. Jutting downward from the handle was a long silver blade that had been hidden inside the shaft. With one hand Roche gripped the back of Sonya's neck, and with the other he held the blade to her throat.

'*Drop the gun! Throw it far away!*' His voice was loud and firm, and the blade in his hand didn't tremble a bit. '*Do it NOW, or she dies!*'

Reyes took another breath and remembered her hostage-rescue training. *An agent never disarms herself. Try to keep him talking.*

'Killing her would be a dumb move, Roche. Once she's dead, there's nothing to stop me from blasting you.'

He laughed. The old guy seemed surprisingly unfazed. 'Ah, *señorita*, you're so transparent. You're trying to start hostage negotiations, correct? But that only makes sense if time is on your side and backup is coming. And in this case, *I'm* the one with the reinforcements.'

Then he screamed something in Russian, so loud it made Sonya cringe. He screamed it again, even louder, and Reyes thought she heard shouting in the distance.

Shit. His goons are coming back.

Roche's face was hidden behind Sonya's, but Reyes could've sworn he was smiling. 'Now, let me amend my warning to you. If you don't throw your gun away, my guards will kill you instantly. But if you do, I might be able to persuade them to take you prisoner. You have to decide quickly, though, because they'll be here soon.'

Reyes fought off another dizzy spell. She tried to recall more of her training, all the options and contingencies, but she couldn't think straight. Her vision blurred again, and when it cleared she saw the first of Roche's guards returning, running down the slope of the landfill mound and approaching the lean-to from behind. She shifted her aim, wondering how close to let him come before she fired.

But why is this guy alone? The guards were in a pack before. And when they ran off, they went in the direction opposite to where this guy is coming from.

Confused, she held her fire. Her vision blurred for a third time, and she let out a scream to stop herself from blacking out. Roche was yelling something about a FINAL WARNING, and Sonya was shrieking too, and the whole world was tilting and quaking. But then Reyes saw something that brought everything back into focus. The guy she'd assumed was one of Roche's guards was actually someone she recognized – a dirty, disheveled, desperate man with a rifle slung over his shoulder and a pistol in his hand. The yelling and shrieking drowned out his footsteps as he raced to the open left side of the lean-to, from which point he could take a shot at Roche without hitting Sonya.

Max Mirsky didn't hesitate. From just three feet away, he fired the pistol at Roche's head.

THIRTY

Max was so focused on Roche, so intent on completely eliminating the threat, that for a moment he forgot all about his daughter. He kept his eyes and his pistol trained on Roche's slumped corpse, watching for any sudden movements aside from the blood fountaining out of the man's skull. He was ready to shoot the son-of-a-bitch again if he showed even the slightest hint of life.

Max didn't come out of this murderous trance until Sonya threw herself at him, pressing her wet face against his shirtfront. At that point he finally noticed how hard she was shaking and how loud she was sobbing behind her gag. He tucked his pistol back into his pants so he could wrap his arms around her and untie the knotted rag covering her mouth. She kept on crying after Max removed the gag and while he unwound the baling wire that bound her wrists. She couldn't speak yet, she couldn't say a word, but that was all right, Max thought, that was OK. Right now she just needed to cry.

But someone else was speaking. Shouting at him, actually. He looked past Sonya and saw Agent Reyes crawling through the mud near several other corpses, about twenty feet in front of the lean-to. At first Max was delighted to see her alive, but his spirits sank when he saw the panicked look on her face.

'Mirsky! Get behind the shed!' She carried her own pistol, which she pointed over her shoulder. 'Those Russians are coming back any second!'

Max pulled Sonya behind the lean-to, which had a couple of scrap-metal sheets at its back. They dove to the ground behind this flimsy barrier, Max keeping an arm around his daughter as they lay on their stomachs. Reyes clambered toward them, wincing and cursing, using her elbows to drag herself forward. Her breath was raspy and her feet were bare and her ankles were grotesquely swollen, but she managed to slide her body next to his and reach for the M16 slung over his shoulder.

'I'm taking this rifle. Unless you're an expert marksman.'

'No, no, I'm not—'

'Just stay low. You're not gonna use that pistol again unless they come a lot closer.' She removed the rifle's magazine and checked the bullets inside. Then she reattached it, chambered the first round, and stuck the rifle's barrel through a gap between the metal sheets. 'The mercenaries will be coming from over there, the garbage incinerator.'

'Should we tell them Roche is dead? Maybe they won't kill us if they see—'

'Believe me, they don't like witnesses. Roche probably brought them into the country illegally, and now that he's gone they'll want to slip away unnoticed.'

'But what if—'

'*Shhh!*' Reyes pointed at the incinerator, which was just barely visible through the gap. In the silence, Max heard boots stomping the mud, a lot of them. And when he squinted into the darkness, he glimpsed several hulking silhouettes, maybe two hundred yards away.

Reyes peered through the M16's gunsights. 'That's close enough.'

She fired the rifle, and in the distance someone screamed. The silhouettes hunkered to the ground and shouted in Russian, undoubtedly cursing. Then they returned fire.

Their bullets pounded the lean-to. The noise was horrendous, like a million hammers coming down all at once on the metal sheets, which banged and juddered above them. Max flattened himself and pressed down on Sonya, burrowing as deeply as he could into the mud. But Reyes kept her head up and fired again. She squinted at her gunsights and took a deep breath before pulling the trigger. Then she did it again, careful and deliberate.

After half a minute, there was a pause in the barrage. Reyes shook her head fiercely, then turned to Max. 'I think I got . . . a couple of them. But there's still . . . at least half a dozen left. Those fucking Uzis . . .'

She blinked several times and her head drooped. Max became alarmed. '*Reyes?* Are you all right?'

'Fuck no, I'm not all right!' She glared at him. 'The Russians . . . are trying to outflank us . . . you'll have to . . .'

Then she let go of the rifle and her forehead hit the mud. At the same moment, another volley of bullets hammered the lean-to.

Shit, shit, SHIT!

Max picked up the M16 and tried to take aim, but the gun shook in his hands. He saw the silhouettes again, and now they seemed closer and scattered across a wide area. Reyes was right, they were going to outflank him. Some of them crept up the mound of landfill to his right, and the others slinked along the edge of the waterway to the left. Max fired several times at the gunmen on the slope, and the silhouettes ducked for a moment, but then they scrambled forward. In a few seconds they would move past the lean-to and have a clear shot at him and Sonya.

Max jumped to his feet. He couldn't save himself, but maybe he could draw their gunfire away from his daughter. He tossed his rifle aside and yelled, 'HOLD YOUR FIRE! I SURRENDER!' Then he raised his arms above his head and stepped away from the lean-to. He closed his eyes, steeling himself for death.

But instead of gunshots, he heard muffled pops.

The noises came from way off to his left, near the dock that extended into the waterway. When he opened his eyes and looked in that direction, he saw that the Russians who'd been skulking along the water's edge were now facedown on the ground. Then he heard more muffled pops, and the silhouettes on the mound dropped to the wet grass, one by one.

It was over in seconds. Max kept his hands in the air as two figures standing in waist-high water waded to shore. They wore wetsuits and carried long rifles with elaborate scopes and silencers. As they stepped over the corpses at the water's edge, they lifted their night-vision goggles to their foreheads.

Max raised his hands as high as he could. 'DON'T SHOOT! I SURRENDER! MY DAUGHTER'S BEHIND THE SHED, AND SHE SURRENDERS TOO!'

They didn't shoot. They barely looked at Max, who stepped protectively in front of Sonya. Instead, they headed straight for Reyes. One of the snipers knelt beside the agent, and flipped her over. 'Yo, Reyes? You awake?'

He shook her shoulder, and she opened her eyes. 'Phantom?'

'Yeah, and I got Rat Face with me.'

'Listen, I got some bad news about Mad—'

'We know already. We found his chopper.' Phantom gestured at the corpses strewn nearby. 'These are the shitbirds who offed him?'

She nodded, then closed her eyes again.

The other sniper leaned toward Roche's corpse and spat on it. 'Fucking Russians. They want a war? We'll give them a fucking war.'

Then both soldiers heard something and pointed their rifles to the left. Someone was staggering toward them, a tall, wild-eyed woman in a mud-spattered jumpsuit. There was blood on her too, splattered on her face and neck. In her right hand she held a grimy switchblade knife, but she seemed too dazed to do anything with it. She halted, swaying, when she saw the soldiers.

'Sonya?' She gazed blankly into space. 'Where are you, Sonya?'

Phantom edged toward her, holding his rifle at the ready. 'Please drop the knife, ma'am.' His voice was surprisingly quiet and polite. 'You don't have to—'

'I'm Angela Nova! I want to see Sonya!'

Sonya grabbed her father's arm and pulled herself to her feet. Max tried to hold her back, but she stepped within sight of Angela and narrowed her eyes. 'What the fuck do you want now?'

Angela raised her hands as if surrendering, but she didn't drop her knife. 'You were right. I made a mistake.'

'A *mistake*?' Sonya cocked her head in furious disbelief, an expression Max had seen on his daughter many times before. She gestured at all the bodies on the ground. 'That's what you call this?'

Angela nodded. 'Yes. My strategy was flawed. I should've followed yours.'

Then she slashed the knife across her own throat.

The two Navy SEALs secured the area and radioed for help. Rat Face headed east, following Max's directions, and found Janet hiding near the Staten Island Expressway. He also killed two more Russian mercenaries who'd gotten lost in the marshes.

By the time the SEAL returned with Janet, a Navy Medevac helicopter was landing between the dock and the landfill mound.

Phantom ran to the chopper, pulled a stretcher out of the side door, and hustled it over to where Reyes lay. Max and Sonya and Janet helped him place the agent on the stretcher and carry her toward the helicopter. Then they all boarded the chopper except for Rat Face, who was going to tag the corpses and preserve the crime scene until the investigators arrived.

It was the second helicopter ride of Max's life, and he didn't like it any more than the first. The hurricane had moved inland by then, making the journey a lot smoother, but Max still made sure that he and his daughter and girlfriend were securely strapped to their seats. The stretcher was tied down too, less than a yard from them. Although Phantom had given Reyes some heavy-duty painkillers, she seemed agitated as hell, breathing fast and rolling her head from side to side.

Max, Janet, and Sonya watched the agent with concern, but it was Sonya who stretched her arm toward Reyes and grasped her limp hand. The agent opened her eyes and studied the girl for several seconds. Something passed between them that seemed to calm and fortify Reyes. Then she turned to Max.

'Listen carefully.' The agent had to shout to be heard over the noise of the rotors. 'When you talk to the investigators, tell them *everything*. Don't leave anything out, understand?'

Max nodded. Reyes stared at him a while longer, apparently for emphasis, then turned back to Sonya. 'And you too. Tell them how you resisted the killers and helped us track them down. You see why it's important, right?'

'Yes.' Now Sonya clasped the agent's hand between both of hers. 'Everyone should know the whole truth. The people who stopped the terrorists were climate activists themselves.'

'Exactly.' Reyes gave Max a sidelong smile, then closed her eyes. 'You got a smart girl there, Mirsky. Maybe there's some hope for us after all.'

EPILOGUE

In Max's opinion, the best outdoor stage in Manhattan wasn't actually a stage. It was the plaza in Washington Square Park between the high-spouting fountain and the Washington Arch, just south of the southern end of Fifth Avenue.

The Doomsday Theater Company was scheduled to perform there at noon as part of the Broadway Climate Action Festival, which had taken over the park and the nearby streets. This event wasn't nearly as big as the city-spanning Climate Emergency Week two months ago, but Max estimated that twenty thousand people had come to Washington Square for the rousing speeches and performances. It was a miniature rebellion, fervent but peaceful, against the purveyors and enablers of global warming.

Max and his fellow troupers waited in the arch's shadow for their turn onstage. At the microphone, the director of the Sierra Club delivered a lengthy speech introducing the Doomsday Company to the crowd. It was rather boring and completely unnecessary, since the news media had already disseminated the troupe's story far and wide, broadcasting breathless descriptions of the Doomsdayers' battle against the Climate Avengers. But the crowd seemed to enjoy hearing the story again, and they applauded heartily as the Sierra guy talked about climate criminals and assassinations and the moral superiority of nonviolent protest.

Antsy, Max turned this way and that. It was an unseasonably warm November day, and he was sweltering in a long, tie-dyed robe that billowed around his arms and flowed down to his ankles. To his left, Janet wore a similar robe, making them look like the priest and priestess of a psychedelic cult. Nathan, Eileen, Adele, and Larry were costumed in a variety of hippie outfits – neon tank tops and headbands, dangling beads and daisy chains, flaring bell-bottoms and peasant blouses. And Sonya wore silver knee-high boots, a leather miniskirt, and a rainbow-colored crop top. She was showing way too much skin, but Max knew how she'd react if he said anything, so he kept his mouth shut.

He focused instead on the crowd, which seemed to occupy every corner of the park. They stood on the park benches and the lip of the fountain. They milled on the lawns and pathways, and they even packed the playgrounds and dog runs. It was an impressive turnout, and Max supposed that the Doomsday Company's notoriety had something to do with it. His stomach twisted as he surveyed all their expectant faces; although he was glad that the climate movement was gaining new followers, it was appalling that so many people had to die first. He thought of Angela and Erin and Stroman and Roche, and all their victims, both the guilty and the innocent. *What a waste. What a tide of blood.*

Then Max glanced to his right and saw an auburn-haired woman in sunglasses and a plain gray suit. He got the feeling that Agent Reyes had been surveilling him for some time, maybe the whole morning. She smiled and stepped toward him, clearly amused.

'Hello there, Mirsky.' Reyes kept her voice low, in deference to the long-winded Sierra Club guy. 'Love your costume.'

Max smiled back at her. 'Yours is nice too. You look just like an FBI agent.'

She shrugged. 'Yeah, that's why I decided to stick with the Bureau. It's the most fashion-forward federal agency.' Then she looked past Max and waved at Janet. 'Good to see you too, Ms Page.'

Janet stepped in front of Max and hugged Reyes. 'Oh my God, you look great!' She held the agent at arm's length and looked her over. 'How's the physical therapy going? You're walking OK?'

'I'm jogging now. And doing jumping jacks.'

'That's wonderful!'

Max's girlfriend had struck up an unlikely friendship with Reyes. Janet had visited her every day while the agent was recovering at Lakehurst Naval Health Clinic. The ostensible reason for the visits was to discuss public-relations strategy – how Max and Janet and Sonya should talk to the press, how they should steer the story away from sensationalism and toward something constructive. In reality, though, Janet visited Reyes because she was grateful. She gave the agent all the credit for their survival, and Max was inclined to agree with her.

And Janet found a way to express her gratitude. The whole

country was outraged by the assassination of the former president, but there were no villains left alive to blame and punish. Roche and Angela and Erin were dead, along with their armed minions, so the public had no targets for its fury except the bungling officials assigned to the Climate Avengers case. But Janet made it clear in all her media interviews that Reyes was an exception, the only competent professional among the law-enforcement dolts. As a result, Reyes kept her job. (Her boss, though, was fired.)

After Agent Reyes was back in charge of the investigation, she hunted down the few surviving malefactors. She led the team that arrested Jason Torricelli and his father, tracking them down with the help of the financial documents that Larry had analyzed so well. And Reyes wrung a confession and a guilty plea out of Harlan Tate, the head of security for Roche Industries, who'd hired the Russian mercenaries for his boss. Tate provided reams of testimony, not only about Roche's involvement in the assassinations but also about the billionaire's predatory sex life. In response, Congress passed a special law that dismantled Roche's company and confiscated his sixty-billion-dollar fortune, earmarking the funds to renewable energy subsidies. And when it became public knowledge that Max Mirsky had been Roche's executioner, he got five million new followers on Twitter.

Now Max got Reyes's attention by pointing at the engagement ring on Janet's left hand. 'Agent, did you notice this new development in our case?'

Reyes nodded. 'Congratulations. And didn't some of your friends also get—'

'They're jealous copycats.' Janet bent her head toward the agent and whispered fiercely. 'Once Adele found out that Max had popped the question, she forced Larry to propose to her. Then Nathan bought a ring for Eileen. The nerve, right? But that's what actors do, they always try to steal the spotlight.'

Max chuckled. Janet's irritation about this seemed hilarious to him. 'Well, I think our connubial bliss is already improving our performances. I mean, look at the size of this audience.'

Janet frowned. 'Bliss has nothing to do with it. We're symbols now.'

'Symbols? What does that—'

'Max, you shot a billionaire at point-blank range because he was threatening to kill your daughter. If that's not a perfect metaphor for the climate crisis, I don't know what—'

'Uh, excuse me?' Agent Reyes pointed at the cleared space in front of the Washington Arch, where the Sierra Club director had just finished his introductory speech. 'I'm no expert on theater, but I think you're on.'

She was right. The crowd was cheering, awaiting the entrance of the Doomsday Company. Max and Janet instantly tabled their argument and exchanged glances with Sonya and the others. Then they all stepped forward as one.

The giant loudspeakers behind them started playing a song from *Hair*, which was another of Max's favorite musicals. He loved its songs about drug trips and sex acts and crazy Sixties' spirituality. The musical was profane and provocative and pretty ridiculous in certain parts, but in essence it was hopeful, and that made it suitable for Max's purposes.

Sonya was the lead singer for this number, so she formed the apex of the company's triangle. Max and Janet swayed directly behind her, while Nathan, Eileen, Adele, and Larry gyrated in the back row. They were a many-colored tribe of climate-action idealists, a debauched, Dionysian band of dreamers. Sonya raised her microphone and began singing the song Max had written, set to the tune of 'Aquarius':

When the Earth is badly heating up
And common sense aligns with hope
Then we'll choose new forms of energy
And we'll give up that carbon crap!

This is the dawning of the Age of the Carbon Bust!
The Age of the Carbon Bust!
The Carrrbonnn Bussst!

Max and Janet joined in at the song's chorus, raising their arms toward the sky in ecstatic supplication. Larry grabbed Adele by the waist and held her high in the air, while Nathan did a slinky dance with Eileen. (Nathan had claimed his dance moves were based on a Hindu ritual, but Max was pretty sure he was bullshitting about that.) Then the troupers formed a conga line and snaked in front of the arch as they sang the song's bridge:

Solar cells and conservation,
Wind turbines and geothermal power,
No more burning coal or oil
Nor ripping forests from the soil,
Make the planet safe for people
And reserve more space for animals,
The Carbon Bust!
The Carrrbonnn Bussst!

Then the Doomsday Company transitioned to the second song in their *Hair* medley, the soulful 'Let the Sunshine In.' Max hadn't bothered to change the lyrics of this song; they were perfect as they were. He and Janet and Adele repeatedly chanted the song's title, while Sonya stepped forward to the front row of the audience and sang the counterpoint lyrics, urging the crowd to open their hearts and sing along. She flung her head back as she sashayed across the plaza, singing more beautifully than Max had ever heard her sing. Soon the crowd joined in, and their twenty thousand voices boomed over Washington Square, echoing against the arch and all the buildings around the park.

Max was exhilarated. It was a moment of epiphany. He felt like he'd just glimpsed the secret, the solution.

Yes, that's it. That's the answer.

Open up your heart!

AUTHOR'S NOTE
The Real Climate Criminals

In my novel *The Doomsday Show*, the top-five list of climate criminals includes three leaders of fossil-fuel corporations and two American politicians who resist and reverse efforts to curb global warming. In real life, however, it's more difficult to pinpoint the worst climate villains. We all exacerbate the problem of climate change every time we drive a gas-guzzling car or turn on a gas-powered leaf blower or do any of the million ordinary things that spew excessive carbon into the atmosphere (wasting food, flying on jets, setting the thermostat too high in winter or too low in summer, and so on).

But we can at least identify the companies that have added the most carbon dioxide to the atmosphere from the combustion of the oil, coal, and natural gas they extract (and the most methane leaking from their gas wells and other operations). The Climate Accountability Institute has compiled a list of the top twenty polluters based on their total production of fossil fuels from 1965 to 2018. According to the latest update of the list (released in December 2020), the biggest offender is Saudi Aramco, the oil and gas company based in Saudi Arabia and largely controlled by Saudi Crown Prince Mohammed bin Salman; over half a century, its operations led to the discharge of about sixty billion tons of carbon dioxide and methane into the atmosphere.

The next-largest polluters, in order, are Gazprom of Russia, Chevron and ExxonMobil of the US, and the National Iranian Oil Company. The full list is below (see https://climateaccountability.org/pdf/CAI%20PressRelease%20Dec20.pdf). When considered together, the top twenty companies are responsible for 35 percent of all fossil-fuel emissions worldwide since 1965.

Unlike some of the characters in *The Doomsday Show*, I don't advocate murdering the leaders of these corporations. But the climate crisis has worsened to the point where we need to consider all nonviolent acts of protest, including boycotting, shunning, shaming, and mocking anyone associated with the top polluters. If we don't get serious about vilifying them – and if we don't pass laws discouraging the further use of fossil fuels – they'll just proceed with the wanton destruction of our biosphere. Then we'll be left with a ruined planet and nobody to blame but ourselves.

Top Twenty Climate Criminals
(based on carbon dioxide and methane emissions from coal, oil, and natural gas produced)

1. Saudi Aramco, Saudi Arabia
2. Gazprom, Russia
3. Chevron, US
4. ExxonMobil, US
5. National Iranian Oil Company, Iran
6. BP, UK
7. Shell, UK
8. Coal India, India
9. Pemex, Mexico
10. PetroChina/China National Petroleum
11. Petróleos de Venezuela (PDVSA)
12. Peabody Energy, US
13. ConocoPhillips, US
14. Abu Dhabi National Oil Company, United Arab Emirates
15. Kuwait Petroleum, Kuwait
16. Iraq National Oil Company, Iraq
17. TotalEnergies SE, France
18. Sonatrach, Algeria
19. BHP, Australia
20. Petrobras, Brazil